Finding You Corin and Gina

And All It Took Was One Drop of Blood

Wendy Rasphoumy

Wendy Rasphoumy

PublishAmerica
Baltimore

First printing

ISBN: 978-1-60749-864-3 (softcover)
ISBN: 978-1-4489-9824-1 (hardcover)
PUBLISHED BY PUBLISHAMERICA, LLLP
www.publishamerica.com
Baltimore

Printed in the United States of America

This book is dedicated to my husband, Phaphone,
for your love, support, and friendship.
And also to my three beautiful children, Mary, Matthew, and Molly,
for giving me their unconditional love.

Acknowledgments

To my daughter Mary,
who encouraged and motivated me to share my story.
Exceptional thanks goes to my fellow nursing colleagues at the CRC
and to my supportive friends, who lent me their opinions and support.
Special loving note goes out to the Bui family.

Chapter One

There is only one word that best describes my life—"tragic". Up until I was 10, everything was normal and happy. Then people I loved or loved me started dying around me. Of course, I did not have anything to do with their deaths but according to the obituaries, I was the *surviving family member.*

It all started with the death of my father eight years ago. Frances Reynolds, Frank to his friends, was a big, burly man. The size of him was daunting. He looked like a frightening giant but his heart was pure and loving. He was Irish through and through, from the light reddish hair to the fair skin and blue eyes. He managed an oil rig team. He had a booming loud voice that was alarming to his employees but he was always soft and gentle with his family. He went to sleep one night and never woke up. We later found out he had a congenital heart defect—a *"ticking time bomb"* as the doctor described it. It broke my mother's heart. He was only 44 years old. I can remember his funeral so many people were there. They all said the same things. I guess death makes people say the same thing to save them from saying the wrong thing.

My mother, Mary Reynolds, discovered she had breast cancer exactly one year after my father died. I can remember the day she found the lump in her left breast. She was trying on bras and was adjusting her breast. The doctors told her it was small and surgery would be the first course of treatment. She was a beautiful woman. She had strawberry blond hair and light blue eyes. Her skin was fair with some freckling on her arms and face. She was strong and stubborn. After surgery she told me things were going to be fine and that I had nothing to worry about. We moved from Bismarck to Crew, Indiana to be closer to my father's brother, Josh Reynolds. A few months after we settled in Crew, she found another lump but this one was under her armpit. The doctors told her the cancer had come back and it was now in her lymphatic system. She had to undergo chemotherapy. One day, she collapsed in the kitchen floor while I was at school and laid there for hours. She battled cancer for two years but as stubborn as she was, she could not beat it. When it spread to her brain, she was no longer my mother. She died just before my 14th birthday.

At 14 years old, I went to live with my Uncle Josh Reynolds. He was a professional race car driver. Uncle Josh was a proud handsome man. He was 43 years old. His features were very similar to my dad but he was muscular and lean. He was confident and always walked with a proud arrogant sway. He had many girlfriends but he was always careful who he brought home because of me. He never married anyone of his girlfriends. He told me he was looking for someone who looked and acted like me, and so far *none of them came close*. The women he was seen with were always exceptionally beautiful with blond hair and super model type bodies envied by millions. I never worried that he would be swept off his feet by any of them. I just brushed them off. *Personally I think he liked being a bachelor.*

Our personalities were very similar, which made our relationship remarkable. He wasn't exactly a parent, and I wasn't a typical erratic teenager. Though it was hard for me losing both parents, I knew it was harder on him to raise a teenager. Life with him was very easy. Because he was a professional car driver, people at school thought he was so cool, which made things easier for me. He had started out as a mechanic for NASCAR and eventually started racing when he was 24 years old. I was very proud of him. We were both very private people.

In many ways he was the biggest influence in my life. He was there when I started my teenager years. He was there when I needed to talk about sex, my menstrual period, and even love. Most importantly, he was the person who taught me to drive. I spent so much time watching him at the racetrack that I started driving earlier than any other teenager—illegally of course. I was only allowed to drive on his property. Lucky for me, he had 150 acres of terrain. There I could race around heavily wooded areas and country grounds without any fear of killing anyone or getting caught. We had a common love for speed. While his love was for race cars, mine was for motorcycles. Not just any motorcycles but, *Ducati* motorcycles.

On my 18th birthday, he gave me a used Ducati Monster S4R Testastretta. He considered it to be my "liberation" gift. It was silver with red and black trim. With a 998cc V-Twin 130Hp, I drove it wildly. He knew that I would drive this way because he never taught me how to drive slowly. A lot of what he taught me was more like defensive driving than normal driving. Giving me this type of bike was a confirmation of the type of driving he had taught me. A Ducati is one of those bikes you would have to drive fast in order to appreciate its torque and power. Driving something this beautiful slowly was considered to be criminal in my eyes. At 80mph, the atmosphere around you disappears, and you are in a tunnel of your own world. Time ceases to exist and no one can enter your space. This was *my* happy place.

The other significant thing that happened to me upon my 18th birthday was the reading of my late parents' will. Up until now it wasn't necessary to deal with their estate. Uncle Josh took care of all my needs. Mr. Thomas Gaffney, my parents' attorney, made sure things were in order. This was the last thing that I had to deal with. Being their only child, I was left with all their worldly possessions and a key to a safe deposit box.

"What is this key for?" I questioned.

"Gena, it is a safety deposit key from Wellington Bank. We don't honestly know what is in the safety deposit box but we can make arrangements for you to go and take a look. Would you like to do that now?" He asked.

"Sure," I hesitated. I wasn't that interested. I assumed it was something my mother left for me, like maybe her personal jewelry or something like that. But Uncle Josh reminded me it would be good for closure—*lets' get it done and over with*. The safety deposit number was 628, which I assumed represented my birth date. As I waited for the bank teller to find the key to match mine, I suddenly felt a rush of excitement. *Maybe it was video recording of them telling me what they wanted from me, giving me some direction or guidance. I was eighteen and about to enter my senior year but I had no idea what I wanted or needed.*

"Place your key here, Ms. Randolph" the teller instructed.

After both keys turned, she pulled the long metal box from the wall and placed it on the table in the private showing room.

"Take as much time as you need to, just call me when your done" she informed.

"Thanks" I said silently. When the teller was gone from the room, I lifted the lid from the safety deposit box. Inside, I found another box. It was some sort of jewelry box a rather large jewelry box. Slightly disappointed, I removed the jeweled box from the safety deposit box. I did not want jewelry. Secretly, I wanted something touched or made by them a personal letter or something like that addressed to me. The jewelry box was a simple silver box with a single dark blue gemstone at each corner. In the middle of the lid was a clear square space, roughly the size of a postage stamp. I inspected the box closely and could not find a key hole or lift handle. I checked the safety deposit box to see if there were instructions or another key, but I found nothing. I could hear something inside the box when I shook it, but there was no way in. *Great, now I have a fancy jewelry box that I can't open.* Disappointed, I took the jewelry box and left the bank. On the ride home, I raised the box up toward the sun for a closer inspection. Against the sun, the box was exquisitely beautiful. The four blue gems at each corner of the lid were round and the size of my thumbprint. There was no engraving or intricate detailing in the metal.

"What's inside?" Uncle Josh asked just to make conversation.

"I don't know I can't open it." I informed him.

"Was there no key for it?"

"I don't see a keyhole, but there wasn't a key with it." I replied flatly.

"What's wrong, are you disappointed?"

"Well, it really doesn't matter I just thought maybe she left me some sort of personal letter or video to tell me what they wanted from me, you know, like when someone knows they're dying, so they leave some sort of personal memoir or guide" I said sadly.

"Hey, kiddo, I think they just wanted you to be happy." With a slightly devilish look, he finished, "If you want, I can pry open that box for you but I might end up destroying it" he responded.

I chuckled. "No, that's okay. I'll figure out how to open this thing eventually" I said.

We rode the rest of the way home in silence. I liked that about Uncle Josh, he never pry. He always allowed people to think and sort things out for themselves then when they were ready to talk he listens. That's why we were so compatible. When we got home, I immediately went to my room with my jewelry box. I left the jewelry box on my desk after I took one last good look at it. *Yep, definitely no keyhole*

The phone ranged jolting me from my chair. I answered the phone on the third ring.

"Hello"

"Hey Gena, how did it go?"

"Hi Peter, it was ok. I got a box" I said flatly.

"A box? What kind of box?" he questioned.

"I think it's a jewelry box" I said

"Well what's in it? Can I come over?" he asked.

He didn't really sound interested in the contents of the box, but he wanted to come over so I offered "Sure, do you want me to pick you up?"

"No, I can use my mom's car. Be there in a bit" he responded.

I have been dating Peter since April. We were good friends through out our junior year but as the friendship grew so did the relationship. Over the summer our relationship evolved into something more serious and loving. I still see him more as a friend than a boyfriend but maybe this was the natural order of love. He was very easy to like and eventually love. Everyone thought we were so well suited for each other. We never fought; we knew each other's likes and dislikes. Peter was the high school football player and I was his happy, sweet girlfriend. All of his friends were my friends. He was much more socialable than I was. We looked good together. He was 6'3 with short blond hair, with dark blue eyes; his body was lean but strong, muscular. I was 5'7 with long wavy brown hair, rather small in the breast area but since everything else was small it really didn't make such a horrible figure. As his eyes were blue, mine were brown matching my hair. My looks were simple, no real beautiful traits but to my uncle and Peter, I was beautiful. Of course they're biased. I thought my nose and lips were too small. It seemed like everyone around me had blue or green eyes but I had plain brown eyes. I've always had some complaints about myself but Peter's only complaint about me was that he did not like the way I drove. He didn't like my defiance to the speed limit.

The loud rumbling of the SUV up the driveway could be heard from my bedroom. Peter's mother was a tiny woman but she liked big cars—*it makes me feel safe she would often say* or maybe it was because Uncle Josh's house was so rural that you can hear anything coming. You can hear Peter coming into the house and talking football with Uncle Josh. After they got the basic questions and answers over with, he raced up the stairs.

"Knock, Knock, can I come in?" he said cheerfully.

He peaked around the door and winked at me. You can see why he is so easy to love. He just has this charm about him. He was also very patient with me. Many times I could see he wanted more from me but because we were friends, he never pressured me to do anything I didn't want to do. He entered the room and crossed over to my bed. He sat on the floor next to my bed. I sat up and slid down next to him on the floor.

"Hey, you look cheerful, how did your day go?" I asked.

"Busy but manageable. Are you okay, you sounded so sad on the phone?" he questioned

"Yeah, it's just old stuff coming back up. I'm alright. Sorry I couldn't make it back earlier. Do you want to see what I got?" But of course I was talking about the motorcycle; he however was looking at the jewelry box.

He grinned at me. "Wow this is really pretty, what's inside?" he wondered.

Rather annoyed I responded "I don't really know, I can't open it, there's no key or keyhole. There must be some sort of secret button or whatever, I just haven't bothered" I said nonchalantly.

"Well that's weird, the lawyer people didn't tell you how to open it?" he questioned.

"No, they didn't even know about. It was kept in a safety deposit box and the key was left to me, now do you want to see my real birthday present?" I said excitedly.

"I saw it outside; I really don't like the idea that you have something that can go up to 120mph. What was your uncle thinking? Has he ever seen you drive?" he said jokingly.

"He is a professional race car driver you know, I don't think he can really teach me how to drive slowly. Oh and by the way, I do have a license to drive it, someone signed off on that" I asserted.

"Yeah, but you were driving on your best behavior, we both know that is not how you normally drive" he corrected me.

"Oh you're just jealous because I was taught by one of the best race car driver and you were taught by your grandmother" I said jokingly.

I was really referring to his mother and he knew that. She drove like a grandmother. She sat so close to the steering wheel that there was no room for the air bag to deploy. She made driving look like some sort of painful exercise. It is just painful to watch the difference between Uncle Josh's driving posture and Peter's mom. Peter wasn't that far off. I silently smiled at the thought.

"Hey, before I forget, I have to tell you I won't be here this week. My mom wants me to go to Gainesville, Florida to see this knee specialist. Just the usual stuff nothing too big" he stated.

I looked up at him, surprised. "Why do you have to go all the way to Gainesville, Florida to have your knee checked? Can't you see someone here?" I worried.

"Well, if I want any kind of career in football, my knees have to be seen by someone who specializes in football players' knees not just any regular Ortho. I'll be gone for just one week. Now, listen I have a present for you too but it doesn't compare next to your *Ducati* so do you want to see it?" he said excitedly.

"You know you didn't have to get me anything," embarrassed by the frown from his face I quickly stated "but since you did, yes I want to see it" I said happily.

"Ok, so give me your hand" he commanded.

As I complied he placed a small white box in my hand. I hesitated for a minute thinking about all the boxes I'd gotten today. Slowly I lifted the top cover of the box and inside there was a key ring that had the red shield symbol of the *Ducati* motorcycle company.

"It's beautiful, thanks Peter" I whispered. I gave him a warm hug and held him there. He pulled back and gazed down at me. His dark blue eyes moved over my face then to my lips. He slowly placed his lips over mine. His kiss started off gentle and soft. He placed his hand in the back of my neck and pulled me tighter against his lips. The pressure of his lips increased steadily. He became hungrier and more impatient. He leaned forward pushing me back onto the floor. His hands came over my waist, pinning me down. As his lips slid down to my neck, I could feel his hands moving under my shirt. When his hand touched my breast I became tensed and rigid. The moment he felt me tensed underneath him, he abruptly pulled his hand back and sat upright.

"Sorry, I got a little carried away" he whispered as he tried to control his breathing.

I waited for him to collect himself before I moved away. We were both panting from what just happened. He placed his hands over his face and through his hair. I can tell he was fighting his frustrations. He sat there quietly. It was an uncomfortable silence. I wish I could feel strongly for him like he does for me but it wasn't there. I was dragging him around because of my indecisiveness. I wanted so badly to give him all of me but I knew he wasn't the one I wanted to be my first. I loved him but not enough to make love to him. It was such a guilty feeling of despair.

"Peter, I'm sorry. I'm just not ready for that. It's not you it's me. Please just try to understand" I pleaded.

I waited for him to respond but he just sat there. I can tell he felt bad for his actions but he was probably frustrated too. Above all else we were good friends, and this just felt so awkward. We wanted things to happen slowly and cautiously. We were afraid that if things went sour we would lose much more. We were both aware of the same fear.

"I'm sorry for pressuring you. It's just you're driving me crazy. Don't you want me at all? Because I want you so badly, it hurts for me to even think about it. I think of you constantly. I dream of you when I'm not thinking about you. It's like you want me but then when things start to get more serious you panic. Don't you want to be with me?" he pleaded.

"Peter you're everything that a girl could ever want, it is just I am not ready. Please understand" I begged.

I waited for him to say something but he just stared at the ceiling. Gently he stood up pulling me along with him. He wrapped his arms around my waist and whispered into my ears "Happy Birthday, Gena" Without letting me go he continued "Okay, I have to get home to pack but I'll see you when I get back. Do me a favor, drive carefully when I'm away" He softly placed his hands around me face and touched his lips to mine. "I going to miss you a lot" he said gently.

"Okay, will you call me when you get there?" I asked. I kept him in my embrace while I looked into his eyes. His eyes did not meet mine. Instead he hugged me tighter. I couldn't pinpoint the difference in his actions tonight but something was not right. He was saying that he'll be back but it seems like he was also saying final goodbyes. I was going to have to make a decision about our relationship when he gets back. I don't know what I was waiting for. What if he was the one for me and I'm just too stupid to see it. If I keep making him wait will he eventually just give up and I lose a great guy. *Frustrating*

When he left, I turned my attention back to the jewelry box. I looked at it more closely this time. The clear space in the middle of the lid looked like some sort of fingerprint pad, so curiously I placed my index finger over the clear space, secretly hoping that the box would somehow scan the fingerprint and "click" it would automatically open. But nothing happened. Disappointed and frustrated, I left the box there on the desk.

How ironic that I am standing over another box now.

This was the fourth funeral I've attended in my 18 years of life. If there was a curse upon people, I was it. Just weeks ago I was beginning to wonder about whether my life was just bad luck or that I was a curse. Now, this pretty much confirms that I am a curse. I stand here in front of the casket, uncomprehending what has happened in the past twenty days that has me in this unspeakable nightmare. *Can some one please wake me up?* I can't seem to grasp at reality anymore. *Is this real or am I just having a bad nightmare?*

Peter left for Gainesville, Florida on June 29 with his mother and never returned to Crew, Indiana. He did not call me when he got there like he was supposed to. I knew something was wrong when his father kept saying *"I'll let Peter explain when he comes home."* For two days, I selfishly thought that he had met someone in Florida and was stalling me. I was angry by his betrayal. For a time, I felt regret for what happened between us the last time he was with me. I thought for sure he was tired of waiting for me. Never in a million years did I think he was dying.

He wasn't in Florida to have his knees checked. He was getting experimental treatment for his type of Leukemia. During one of the treatments, he developed some sort of adverse reaction to the drug and his body's immune system shut down completely. He was immediately placed on High Risk Neutropenic Isolation; which basically meant that he could not be exposed to any kind of germs or bacteria because his body could not defend itself. He was not allowed any visitors, not even family. By the time I was told of his predicament, I was already too angry and hurt to grasp the full extend of his disease. When I realized that he was in serious trouble, I tried hopelessly to talk to him. The guilt I felt would haunt me, and I think he knew that, yet he left me out in the dark anyway. He wanted it that way. He did not want me to know what was happening to him or see him in his sick state. Any communication with Peter was through third parties. On July 9th, I received a note from Peter written on a prescription note paper:

"I am so sorry. I have always loved you."

The note was supposed to give me some sort of release from the punishment he was inflicting on me. I read those words over and over. Sometimes I read them as forgiving and sometimes they were punishing. I begged to see him. I pleaded with his parents but they were unyielding. They said he refused. He denied me access to him. He banned me from being near him or to see him or hold him. He refused to talk to me; he wouldn't let me respond to his note. I was so angry. I never got to respond to his note with my own words. He would not allow the nurses to take my calls or any notes. I wrote so many letters but they were returned to me unopened. He was punishing me. He wanted the last words. All that didn't matter now. He died nine days later on July 18th, all alone. When he died, no one was allowed near him. His mother was allowed to talk to him but through plastic mask, gloves, and gowns. He was gone. I had to accept defeat. At the end he had won. His funeral was attended by so many people. A lot of his friends were crying. I watched everyone around me crying and comforting one another. I sat there cold, not knowing how to act. Uncle Josh was holding me but I could not feel his arms. I was numb. It was so sudden. The pain was there. The loss was there but I could not cry. I watched his parents sobbing profusely but I just sat there across from his casket in total dismay.

How did this happen?

What went wrong?

Modern medicine doesn't allow something like this to happen. People don't die this quickly. My mother had cancer and she battled for 3 years before she died. I was numb. I walked around not feeling anything. Uncle Josh was there for me but it was not the same. Some of our friends came over but I did not want to talk to them. I sent everyone away. Every one of them reminded me of him. I lay in bed all night long waiting for Peter to call me and tell me of his busy day. It felt like any minute he would call and say *"What's up babe. Miss me?"* but that call never came. He was gone. I never cried for Peter. He did not want me at the end. His rejection of me was seen more as a punishment than protection. Uncle Josh told me he did it to protect me. He did not want me holding on to false hope. He did not want me to grieve him. He did not want me to have memories of him sick and dying, only good ones. He knew if I was there I would remember him sick not healthy so selfishly he denied me the memory. But Peter was wrong. The fact that he rejected my love for him at the end was far worst than any of his attempts at protecting me. I was his friend before I was his girlfriend. *Would that have made a difference?* The irony was that I would've given anything to have that last night back. I would have given him my love to change the outcome. *Did he know then that he was not coming back? Was that his way of testing me? Was that his last attempt at finding love with me?* These questions would go unanswered for the rest of my life.

Uncle Josh was really good at trying to keep me from going into despair. He took me with him to the races just so he could keep an eye on me. He tried to comfort me with stories of his losses but it wasn't even comparable because I didn't know those people. He even let me drink some wine one night. Everywhere he had to go, I was dragged along. He was winning in the ratings but he could not celebrate around me. I knew this was hard on him. He thought he could protect me from another loss. Many times he would remind me that the losses were just a part of life and I could not blame myself. He spent more time with me than with his cheerful road crew. He made sure there was always someone with me. He did not want to leave me alone while he was racing. I was babysat by his rode crew. I was not suicidal or catatonic but I was not myself. He felt guilty for not being able to stay home with me to help me go though the loss. Many times he would catch me staring out in the open and he would pull me back with some ridiculous assignment. He even banned me from my bike until he thought I wasn't going to do something stupid. I spent a lot of time thinking about what Peter wanted from me and why I could not give it to him. It didn't help that there was a lot of people named Peter, so when I hear it being called I would turn to look for him.

On August 4th, we arrived home from one of the longest road trips. I was happy to be back in my own room again. The answering machine was full of people calling to check up on me. I erased them all without listening to them. I wanted to suffer alone. I have never been one of those *group discussion* types of people. I hated to be around people trying to solve other people's problems. I had to do this on my own. I loved Peter but he was gone. No amount of wishing could get him back. *Acceptance, this was the first step in the healing process*

His mother had dropped off things that he asked her to give to me. At first I wasn't sure if I wanted those things but then I realized that it was a part of my life like Peter was and in order to heal, I had to accept them.

"Hey, these are for you. Do you want them now?" Uncle Josh asked.

He wasn't sure it was a good idea for me to be rummaging through Peter's things. I took it from him and placed it on my bed. I can see in the box that there was my yearbook from last year. Peter had asked to sign my yearbook. When I got it back he had written:

Gena,

I think we have something here. Do you want to give it a try?

Peter

He wrote those words knowing he was risking our friendship but he was ready and I stupidly was not. I remembered being scared and excited about venturing into a relationship with him. Our *first real* date was awkward because we tried to be nonchalant about the change. Holding hands were awkward. Our first kiss was nerve racking but nice. It was a milestone for us. Now this was the end. No more milestones. It was unfair that he died and I get to live and wonder what would've become of us.

"Don't get unpacked kiddo, we have to be in Indianapolis in the morning for the Allstate 400." Uncle Josh yelled coming upstairs.

"Come on Uncle Josh, can I just please stay home for this one. Just pick me up when you come back through. I am fine really." I begged. "Listen, I have to deal with this on my own. I'm just going to pack his things and put everything away. This will be my way of finding closure with Peter." I explained as I met him halfway down the stairs.

"I just don't know how to help you Gena. Seeing you so sad, you have had a lot of pain in your short life. I am just waiting for you to snap and go crazy. When you do I just want to be here to help you get through it." He gently placed his arms around my shoulders leading me downstairs.

"Thanks Uncle Josh but I will be fine. I have a lot of things to pack away and get ready for school. Please I will be fine. I still have you, right?" I confirmed.

"Okay kiddo, but listen I know how hard it is to be a teenager. The world doesn't seem so precious after so many losses but please if you start to sink, STOP AND THINK." He stated like it was some sort of commercial jingle. He thought I was suicidal.

"Uncle Josh, I don't have the courage to do myself in." I replied.

Standing there in the kitchen he scribbled the same jingle on a piece of paper and taped it on the refrigerator door.

BEFORE YOU SINK, STOP AND THINK.

"Well I still want you to watch me race on TV. It is going to be on at 4pm on Channel 9. Don't forget okay." He was still making sure I stay mentally connected. I think he thinks that if I was watching him I would less likely do something dangerous.

"I wouldn't miss your big race Uncle Josh. Drive carefully and be safe. Good Luck." I gave him a quick hug and kiss.

Regretfully, that was the last thing I said to him.

Here I am standing in front of his casket adorned with tons of red, blue and white flowers. *Uncle Josh's funeral*

It is even harder to think those words than to say them. After 16 years of being a professional race car driver, he was killed on track during a pit stop. He was on his 20th lap when his tires started wearing down, which is normal. He pulled in for a quick change but then his car tires ignited into balls of flames. The whole car was engulfed in seconds. His road crew worked as hard as they could but they could not get him out in time before he suffocated from smoke inhalation. It all happened on television. I watched it over and over again. Even before the NASCAR officials confirmed the story I already knew he was gone. I watched as the camera span across the fans. The looks on their faces were of disbelief and angst. Some were even crying.

My heart closed inward to protect me from the pain that was coming. My mind shut down to those around me. I didn't talk to anyone. I didn't want anyone near me. I did not want anyone to look at me. I did not want to hear anyone saying:

"I am so sorry for your lost."

"He was a great man."

No one here can possibly know or understand what it's like to lose two people you love over a span of 18 days. They have no idea of the pain I carried around. I felt alone and guilty. I was the sole survivor of a humongous catastrophe. The guilt turned into anger. I was angry for being left behind. *Why did I have to be the survivor, why couldn't I be the victim?* There was no one left but me. I had no one else to lose. This house became too big for me. My room was too small to stay in. I slept in his room. I missed my uncle. I missed his face. I missed his goofy smirks. The Reynolds family was all but wiped out.

After the funeral, I spent my daylight hours riding my *Ducati* recklessly everywhere. I could not go fast enough to escape the pain. I could not find my *happy place.* Many times it would have been easier to close my eyes while driving and just let whatever happens, happens. I thought about it many times while driving but each time, I thought about what he wrote on the paper in the kitchen.

BEFORE YOU SINK, STOP AND THINK.

Even in his death he was with me. The lost of my uncle was worse than losing Peter. I had spent the last 4 years with my uncle. He was my family and friend. He taught me everything I know. He was the last of my family. I had no one else left. The thought of the loneliness was unbearable. At night, I would curl up in his bed and let the despair take over. I would lay in silence looking up at the ceiling. I could not cry. It was like I had run out of tears. It was a weird kind of mourning. I didn't think it was normal but as much as I wanted to cry I could not.

Three days after Uncle Josh's funeral, a wave of uncontrollable emotions raged through my body and unleashed all the despair and loneliness that no single human being could endure all at once. It happened when I was trying to find Uncle Josh's car keys. I unconsciously called out to him to ask him where it was. When I caught myself talking to myself the loneliness slapped me in the face. *I finally cried.* I cried for hours. I could not stop crying. Breathing became hard to do. My brain could not stop the pain from tearing at my heart. I was dizzy. My dead legs would not help me. There I lay on my uncle's bed. I had nowhere to go. I didn't have anyone to turn to. I did not want to sleep in my bed because Peter's things were still on my bed. Some friends came over, each one took turns bringing food or comforting me but my mood and coldness eventually scared them away. I did not want anyone near me. I knew I did not have the courage to hurt myself. Evidently, I was too good of a driver to wreck the *Ducati*. After I had a good cry, my senses became clearer. I knew what I had to do but it was still too hard to move. My movement was slow and clumsy.

There on my desk I saw the jewelry box again. All this time it had been sitting there. I had no interest in opening it. What is the difference now…my mother's things, my father's things, Uncle Josh's, Peter's… I don't have enough strength to keep on packing dead people's things. So I left everything. I didn't want to be the one who packs people's memories away. I slowly made myself move to the kitchen. I can't remember when I last ate. I don't even know if there was any food in the refrigerator. There I saw my uncle's written sign.

BEFORE YOU SINK, STOP AND THINK

Somehow he was with me. "Thanks Uncle Josh" I whispered. I took the paper and traced his handwriting with my finger. I'd never really appreciated him until he was gone. He took me in when I had no one else. My thoughts were disrupted when the phone was on its third ring; I finally realized it was the phone.

"Hello"

"Hello, Ms Reynolds, this is Mr. Gaffney, your uncle's attorney. I am really sorry to bother you with this right now but I need to come by to settle your uncle's will before Friday. After Friday, I will be retiring and since your family was very near and dear to me I would like to complete this transaction myself. Can we meet tomorrow?" he requested.

"What day is it?" I had lost all track of time.

"It's Wednesday, I would like to see you tomorrow. It's a Thursday." He reconfirmed.

"Sure, Mr. Gaffney, when is the best time for you, I'm not going anywhere." I answered blandly.

"Well I can see you anytime after ten, is 11:00am good for you?" he asked

"That is fine, I'll be here." I replied dryly.

"Okay than I will see at 11am. Take care." he replied.

He said *take care*. What an odd man. I went back upstairs to my room. I went to my desk. Staring blankly at the jewelry box on my desk, I got angry. *Why can't I open this stupid damn thing?* Maybe I *will* pry open the edges, who really cares if I damage the box. I am the only Reynolds left anyway. Who makes such a stupid box with no key or keyhole? Maybe it was defected. *Why would my mom leave me a defected box?* I looked over the box again. I felt all around the box for any secret button or latch. *Nothing, how irritating!* I quickly ran downstairs into the kitchen to grab a knife. Upon coming back upstairs I grabbed my uncle's note off the counter. This was my motivational jingle. I remember once he wanted to pry it open for me. *Here's to you Uncle Josh.* Stupidly, I rushed back up the stairs with the knife in my hand.

I held the box firmly with one hand and twisted the knife in between the edges of the box. I was careful not to stab myself because I did not want to have to explain to people what I was doing. They may not believe me anyway. Next thing you know I may be committed for a suicide attempt. I tried slamming the box against the table but that did more damage to the table than the box. Frustrated I turned the box against the knife but because the metal was smooth the knife skidded upward and the tip pierced my index finger. Blood dripped everywhere. It looked like a massacred on my desk. *How much blood can I lose?*

"Damn it, now I have blood all over the damn thing."

I looked around for something to stop the bleeding but before I could turn away from my desk, drops of blood dripped from my finger down my hand and on to the clear space in the middle of the jewelry box. It seemed like everything happened in slow motion. I watched in disbelief as the clear space absorbed my blood like it was a sponge and not glass. Then suddenly I heard four distinct "clicks".

The jewelry box was opened by my blood.

Chapter Two

I sat at my desk astonished by what I just witnessed. I looked at the box. Where did this box come from? Was this really meant for me? This was not something my parents could have made for me. This box was a very advance piece of equipment. Most secure boxes use intricate numbers or combinations or fingerprint scanning but blood? I have never heard of such. Who would want a jewelry box with a blood scanner? Could this have belonged to my parents? Definitely not, the most advance piece of equipment my parents own was their cell phone and even that they had a hard time with.

My hands were shaking when I finally got up the nerve to lift the lid. Inside the box were a small CD and a key. *So, they made me a video.* They must have had help because I don't remember them being capable of recording themselves on CD. *This was so needed right now.* I was so excited I forgot about my bleeding finger. I grabbed the CD and got blood all over it. Perturbed, I ran into the bathroom and cleaned off my finger and the CD. I wrapped my finger in a face towel. I used tissues to wipe down the CD. It was too precious for me to damage.

I rushed the CD over to the DVD player and impatiently waited for the picture to come up.

After what seemed like minutes, my parents' image came up on the screen. They were both very young. They look like they were in their early thirties when they made this video. They were staring at the camera man. My mother was fidgeting. My father was sitting beside her supporting her shoulders. They looked like they were nervous.

"Gena, darling, if you are watching this video, this means that we were not able to celebrate your 18th birthday with you. We made this video to tell you that we love you and wish you a happy and fulfilling life." She stopped and hesitated continuing. Then after some coaxing from my father she started again. "We also wanted to tell you that we are not your biological parents." I could tell she struggled with those words. "You were brought to us by a woman named Alexandria Burren. She instructed us to care for you until she returned to claim you. At the time we were living in Dawson City in the Yukons. We got a call from her one year later asking us to keep you. Her only request was that we keep this a secret from you until you were eighteen. She instructed us to make this video and store it and the key in the jewelry box. If you're watching this video, you are aware of how special that jewelry box is. Through out the years we were able to gather some information about Alexandria Burren. She is originally from Inuvik, Canada. She has a large family that's still there. We were never able to verify this information since this town is very hard to get to. The jewelry box and the key inside were the two things she left with you. We don't know anything about the key. No matter what, we will always see you as our own. We love you dearly. Goodbye."

With that the video went blank. I replayed the video many times. I didn't know what to think. *Were they forced to lie on video?* This can't be true, so many emotions rushed through my body, and I didn't know how to react. I didn't know whether to cry or laugh. With everything that has happened to me, was this some sort of tipping point to see if I would snap. After watching the video for the eighth time, I begin to absorb the words. I looked at my parents. They were Irish descend. They both had straight red hair, blue eyes, and light fair skin. I looked at myself in the mirror. I had none of their features. I had long wavy brown hair and brown eyes. How did I get brown eyes if they didn't have brown eyes? I jumped up and grabbed a picture of Uncle Josh from my desk. I had none of his features either. *How come I didn't notice this before?* Everyone I thought was family was really not my family. I'm not even a Reynolds. So is my name *Gena Burren*?

I quickly went to my laptop and googled.

"***Alexandria Burren"***

But I didn't get any information. I then typed in

"***Burren in Inuvik, Canada"***

Every bit of information I found under that listing was about business deals. Then I typed in

"***Inuvik, Canada***"

Every bit of information I found about this town sounded like a nightmare. Who would live there? No wonder she left.

"Population of 3500" There were more people at Crew High School.

"The Sun does not rise at all for one long winter month" Who the hell can live without the Sun? What do they do when there is no Sun? Does that mean no school? Is that considered a day off from work?

"*Varying temperatures between 90 degrees to minus 60 degrees*" With temperatures like that no wonder we have global warming.

So my mother gave me away. She didn't want me. Maybe I was not planned, and she was not married. How can I look for her if she didn't want me in the first place? She gave me away to strangers? What kind of trouble was she in that she was so desperate? Not being wanted by my own mother hurt me more than I can care to admit. I didn't know what to do with this information. What did my parents wanted me to do with this? Why even bother to tell me that I was adopted when *my own mother* didn't want me? I don't need to find her. I don't even need her. I've been fine without her. I am eighteen years old now. I don't need a legal guardian. I don't need a parent who didn't bother to come back for me. What about my father? Did he know about me? Who gets crap like this thrown at them all at one time? I lay my head down on the cold hard wooden floor. What more can I handle? How much more heartbreak can I endure before I lose it? Darkness was coming and I laid there and let it take me.

I startled awake when I heard the door bell. I had fallen asleep on the floor in my room. *What time is it?* The sound of the door bell startled me again. *Crap Mr. Gaffney.*

"I'm coming Mr. Gaffney, just give me a minute." I yelled down the stairs. I quickly gather my hair up in a ponytail and brushed my teeth. I did not want him to take one look at how crazy I looked and declare me insane and lock me up. After a quick check, I ran downstairs and stopped just before the door to catch my breath. I quickly opened the door.

"I am so sorry; I fell asleep on the floor… I mean the futon." I lied but than I realize this was not the Mr. Gaffney. "I am sorry you're not Mr. Gaffney. Can I help you?" I stuttered.

Standing at my door was a man as big as my door. He was probably too big to come thru the door. He had jet black curly hair. His skin was rather tanned for anyone living in Indiana. I can almost bet he is *NOT* from Indiana. He looked like he was from some island like Hawaii. Yes, he looked Samoan. He was dressed in a black suit like a limousine driver. I looked at him studying his face.

"Excuse me but I am looking Ms. Gena Reynolds." He asked curtly in a growling voice.

I was little afraid to confirm myself, but after a few seconds I replied "I am Gena Reynolds. Can I help you?"

He turned to look back at the black limousine parked in my driveway and nodded. I followed his eyes to the black limousine but could not see thru the dark tinted glass. Who was in there? What did the nod mean? Was I a target for kidnapping? I became tense and panicky. With my luck, I would be killed and no one would even know. When was this nightmare life going to end? God, haven't I had enough testing? I looked around the driveway to see if there was anyone around to witness my death.

Oh great, I just opened my door to this gigantic man who is about to rob and kill me right here in front of my house.

This is going to really look good on the evening news.

"LOCAL GIRL INVITES DEATH IN AFTER BURYING HER BOYFRIEND AND UNCLE ALL IN ONE MONTH."

This is really not my year. "I am sorry but I am expecting a group of *LAWYERS* in a few minutes, so if you don't mind I have to close the door." I threatened.

The word *lawyers* should scare any normal human being away.

"I have a package for you." he said. He handed me a large manila envelope. But I did not take it. I was afraid it was some sort of trick.

"What is this?" I asked.

He turned to look at the person in the limousine.

"Ms. Reynolds this is very important. Please take it." He said as he grabbed my hand and placed the envelope in my palm. He abruptly turned and left. I closed the door quickly. After making sure I locked it securely, I ran to the front window and watched him enter the limousine and drive off. I tried to look inside the limousine but I could not make out the person inside.

What the hell was all that about? That was definitely not the Fed Ex man.

I did't know whether to feel relieved that I wasn't just killed or thankful that he was just the delivery guy. What was I thinking? After all those Girl Scout training and "Stranger Danger" teaching, I go and open the door to possibly the biggest killer *EVER*.

The door bell startled me back to reality. *Oh great now he is back to kill me.*

"Who is it?" I asked

"Ms. Reynolds, it's Mr. Gaffney, we have a reading at 11am today." he answered.

I was so relieved. I opened the door immediately. "Oh yes, Good morning Mr. Gaffney, please do come in." I graciously welcomed him. He was my protector whether he liked it or not. Before I closed the door I scanned around the front yard for the black limousine. It was gone.

We both walked to the dining room table and sat down.

"Mr. Gaffney, can I get you something to drink?" I asked. I don't know why I bother to ask him, there was nothing I could have offered him but tap water.

"Oh no, thank you. If you don't mind I would like to get started." He quickly replied.

"Okay, I am ready when you are." I stated.

"Well Ms. Reynolds, being the sole surviving member of the late Mr. Joshua Reynolds, you stand to inherit everything he owns. He left you with everything including his four race cars, this Indiana estate, his ranch in California, the profit stocks from NASCAR ownership, the Reynolds family trust fund and of course anything within his property. The gross estimate for his entire estate is 150 million dollars. How would like to handle this inheritance." He finished.

I sat there for a few minutes and didn't really know how to respond. I thought about the CD upstairs. Should I tell him that I was really not a Reynolds?

"Mr. Gaffney, is there no one else in my family that I could share this money with?" I asked.

Looking confused he replied "Ms. Reynolds, your uncle named you the sole heir to his estate, so it really doesn't matter if there are ten cousins out there. He named you. Not anyone else. Now you have to decide what you want to do with this money and that is entirely up to you, but he wanted you to have it all." He stated firmly.

This was typical Uncle Josh. He loved me. I was the only thing his brother left behind. He promised my mother that he was going to take care of me. I guess I just never really appreciated him. The material things didn't matter to me. I have everything I've ever wanted or needed, he made sure of that. I have his memories. I really didn't need his money. Throughout the years I have amass quite a bit of money due to always being the "sole survivor". *This was a pretty bad way of amassing wealth.*

"Can you just liquidate everything and put it into the Reynolds Family Trust Fund?" I asked

"If that is what you wish, you don't want to keep anything?" he asked.

"No, I have everything I need right now. If I run across anymore Reynolds, how would I go about including them in the trust fund?" I asked.

"Well, if you choose to share the trust fund all you have to do is have an attorney add them in the trust, but are you sure you want to do that? You're very young. One day you will have a family of your own. You should transfer this wealth to your children and grandchildren." He told me.

I don't know what my life is going to be like in the next hour, how could I be thinking of children and grandchildren. The man is clinically unstable, he definitely needs to retire.

"Thank you for your time, Mr. Gaffney. I will keep in touch with your office if I need anything further." I replied.

I don't deserve all this money. There has got to be more Reynolds out there that deserves some of this money. I wasn't even a Reynolds.

My real last name was Burren.

After Mr. Gaffney left I turned my attention to the manila envelope on the coffee table. I went over to pick it up from the table. It was definitely heavy. I spilled the contents from the envelope onto the coffee table. There were two plane tickets and a passport. I picked up the passport and open it up. It was *my* passport. How was this possible? I don't even remember taking my passport out of my room. I looked at the plane tickets. The first ticket was from Indianapolis to Edmonton, Canada. The second ticket was from Edmonton, Canada to Inuvik, Canada. Paranoid, I looked around.

What is going on? Is someone watching me? How did this person know about Inuvik?

I raced up the stairs and into my bedroom. I went over to my desk and yanked my desk drawer open, *my* p*assport* was not there.

Someone broke into my house to steal my passport than had it delivered back to me.

Okay calm down, I have to think. I have to set everything in order:

My *real* mother gives me away to total strangers.

Total strangers turn out to be great parents

Father dies

Mother dies

Boyfriend dies

Loving uncle dies.

Real mother lives in some scary town in the northernmost part of Canada.

Creepy delivery man delivers my passport and fares to Inuvik.

Well that just about sums up my life. It wouldn't be so bad to accept but it was almost unreal. Someone was planning something for me. I was been set up and the destination was Inuvik. Someone wanted me to see her? Do I want to see her? Maybe I should confront her and ask her why. Does she have kids now? Does she have another family? Maybe she doesn't want them to know that she had another child.

Who sent me these things?

Did she send me these things?

Was that her in the limousine? That can't be her. If that was her why didn't she just come out to see me?

Someone wanted me to come to Inuvik.

Maybe she was someone important and I was part of a plot to embarrass her. What other reasons could it be? *I have definitely been reading too many suspense novels.*

Whoever this person was, they wanted me in Inuvik for a reason. Maybe *to surprise her!*

I refused to be used that way but I wanted to see her too. I want to see my real mother but I will not surprise her on the street, not that way.

I will find her. If she wants to see me then we will make our own arrangements to see each other. I want to let her know that I am well and doing just fine without her. I want to show her that I was not someone that would be embarrassing to her. I was well versed, smart, cultured. I was not ugly or deformed. Maybe I'll show off my achievements. Let her know that I have a GPA of 4.0, read music fluently, play the piano gracefully all the things that would make a mother proud. Would she even care? I did't know but I would never know unless I see her. What's the point of attaining all those things if you don't have anyone to share it with?

I will find her and ask her to come to me. She owes me that much. She owes me an explanation. I don't want an apology because she gave me to some wonderful people. I will never regret that. I was part of a wonderful loving family, something she obviously could not give me. I will tell her about my adoptive parents and my loving uncle. Whatever the situation was for her, she made the right decision in giving me a better life. I will thank her for that.

I quickly located a Private Investigator from Dawson City in the Yukons by Internet search. I did not even bother looking for one in Inuvik. With a raging population of 3500, I doubted they ever needed the services of a private investigator. I scribbled the name and phone number on a piece of paper.

I dialed the number that was provided. My heart was racing—this was insane. But my curiosity was getting the best of me. It was too late to stop now. I wanted to know. I had to know. Knowing that she lives in Inuvik would haunt me for the rest of my life.

"Hello, Yukon Investigative Services, may I help you?" the nasally voice asked.

"Um, I want to find someone in Inuvik. Do you guys do that?" I asked carefully.

"Ah well, that is what we do. Do you have anything we can go by to find this person?" she asked.

"I have a name, Alexandria Burren." I said cautiously.

"Well that's great, I just need to get some information from you and go over our billing and payment process, okay?" she responded.

"Sure, when can you get me this information and also I want this done discreetly. Okay?" I requested.

"Absolutely, we can do that. You don't have to provide us with your name but we'll require that you pay up front by wire transfer. No credit cards or checks and regarding the time, well your in luck, my husband is in Inuvik right now, so we should be able to get you some information by Monday. Does that sound good to you?" she informed me.

"Oh that's great. Um on the discreet thing I meant that I want you to find her discreetly, I don't care if you have my information." I replied.

"Oh, I understand, okay, let's gets started."

I provided her with all the information she needed. I only had less than three weeks of summer left before my senior year starts. I wasn't sure what I would do with the information but if I had to go see her, like if she was not able to travel or something like that than, I would definitely need to do it before school starts.

Satisfied with what I did, all I can do now is wait. I picked up the plane tickets and threw them into the trash. Whoever sent them was using me to hurt her. I was not going to be used as a pawn in some game. There is no scandal for someone giving someone else a better life than what they could provide. I definitely got the better end of the deal. I live here in Indiana, she lives in Inuvik.

I scrambled up from the floor and lurched towards the bathroom. I glowered at the image in the mirror. I've definitely let myself go. My hair was all mangle in a deform attempt of a ponytail. My face was pale and the dark circles under my eyes made me look like a corpse. A shower was definitely needed. I swiftly undressed and got into the shower. I stood and let the hot water massage my entire body. Getting dressed I noticed my jeans were loose and my clothes didn't fit so nicely anymore. I've got to eat.

I went downstairs and fried some eggs. I needed some proteins. I hurried through my dinner, not tasting it. I tried to watch TV but sitting there on Uncle Josh's couch started to bring me down. It was too early to go to bed.

I made my way upstairs to finish packing Peter's things. After I boxed and taped everything, I moved it into the corner in my room. I haven't decided what to do with his things yet but I was definitely not ready to make a decision right now. What does someone do with all this stuff? People die everyday, they don't store dead people's things forever. When is the appropriate time to destroy it?

Right now, I needed to get to my *happy place*. I shoved my feet into my riding boots and dashed down the stairs. I exited from the back door. *My bike the only constant thing in my life.*

I rode around for hours. Killing time. At the speed I was doing the wind tore at the skin on my skull. The adrenaline coursed through my body. The trees disappearing around me, the blurring of everything, the timeless tunnel was forming. I was there. After weeks of being sad, I finally found my happy place. I know now that I would be okay. My life would continue. I was a survivor.

I got back to the house after 11pm and went straight to my room. I needed to sleep. Doing nothing was not appealing. I lay on my bed looking up at the ceiling. I tried to think of things I would say to her. I would not ask her why she gave me away. I think I can imagine what the reasons were. Who is my father? Does he know about me? Some time during the night the questions became dreams.

I spent the next three days packing a lot of Uncle Josh's most valuable things. He had trophies, metals and plaques from all his wins. It just seems like a waste with all these accomplishments. What's the point of achieving so much when you're going to die anyway? Sunday was particularly hard because I was going through his clothes and family memoirs. He had a lot of pictures of me growing up. To him, I was his only child. I cried myself to sleep that night.

I woke with a start—*was that the phone ringing?* I jumped over to the phone on my desk.

"Hello, hello!" I yelled.

"Oh! Hi, Ms. Reynolds. This is Faye Stewart from Yukon Investigative Services; we have some news for you regarding your interest. If you have a fax number I can fax you all the information we have on her." she added.

"Yes, it is the same number as my home number. Thanks." I replied.

I hung up the phone and waited. Looking at the fax machine I noticed it was 10:30 am. Well, I can't say I didn't get enough sleep. When the fax machine beeped, I devoted my attention to the three sheets of paper in the paper tray. *That's it.* Everything about her life was summed up in three sheets of paper. I quickly scanned the information.

The first sheet was her birth certificate. *Alexandria Malayna Burren.* What a beautiful name. Her birthdate was June 15. She was born in Inuvik, Canada. She would be 38 years old now. Her parents' names were William and Beatrice Burren. That would be my grandparents. I've never had grandparents before. I wondered if they were still alive. They should be in their sixties or seventies.

The next sheet was another official document. It was a Certificate of Death. She died on June 28. Twenty years later. She died due to "*complication during childbirth*". Tears welled up in my eyes. I didn't even know her and she was dead. That makes five people I know that is dead. That was a blow to all my plans. She died birthing me, how could that be?

This can't be the same person. I looked at the third page and it was a picture of her tombstone. The tombstone had her name beautifully scripted on the top and the dates of her life etched below it. Below the dates was her picture. I looked at the picture closely. This was my mother. I can see all my features in her but she was beautiful. She was only 20 years old when she birthed me and died. She had beautiful long brown hair. Her eyes were blue, so that means my father must have had brown eyes. Her features were regal. Etched below the dates were

"Most loving daughter, we will miss you our sweetest angel."

The words took my breath away and caused an ache in my heart. These were some beautifully chosen words. I blinked to let the tears fall. This was not what I imagined; finding her dead. My plans to find her were too late. She left behind parents that maybe dead too. The overwhelming loneliness started to creep up. I was surrounded by people dying. When was it going to my turn?

Feeling disappointed and dejected I went back to packing Uncle Josh's things. As I went to find a marker to write on the boxes; I noticed that the plane tickets I threw in the trash was on my desk table, neatly stacked next to the jewelry box. Did I do that last night? I could have sworn I threw them in the trash. Maybe I wanted to but didn't. I must be losing it. I stood there thinking about the events that led to me getting those tickets. Someone knows I am here.

Something wasn't right. If she died during childbirth, how could she have traveled to Dawson City to give me a way? Unless it wasn't her that gave me away, maybe I was stolen by some crazy woman who took me to Dawson City and gave me away? Somewhere in Inuvik, someone knows what happened to me. I had grandparents that didn't even know of my existence.

Now I really have to go to Inuvik. I sat there staring at the tickets. Maybe this was meant to be.

I dialed the number for Yukon Investigative Service again.

"Hello, Yukon Investigative Services may I help you?" she answered

"Um, Mrs. Stewart this is Gena Reynolds again, I wanted to know if you have any information on her parents. William and Beatrice Burren?" I asked carefully.

"Ah well, we can get that for you. It will cost you a little bit more." she informed.

"Yes please, just charge it to the same credit card." I said.

"Well, just wait by the fax machine for the next hour, I should get something thru to you soon." she responded.

"Okay, thanks again." I replied. She probably had that information right there and was waiting for me to call back to okay a new charge. So much for human kindness

As I waited, I googled their names. I didn't get much, just clips here and there from the Inuvik Chronicles regarding his business transactions. He owned the largest oil distributor in Inuvik, Canada. At least they were still alive.

I went downstairs to find something to eat. I found cereal but no milk. I guess I will have eggs again. Protein is good.

I waited impatiently, but before I was about to recall her, the phone rang.

I waited for the fax to finish. One page for $250.00. It's criminal.

When the fax came through, it was a handwritten note:

William and Beatrice Burren

1790 Discus Manor

Inuvik, Canada XOE OTO

867-773-2867

William Burren CEO Burren Oil Distributor.

Parents to Rolfe 44yrs, Idelle 42yrs,and the late Alexandria.

There weren't just grandparents; I had an aunt and uncle too. There is a whole family in Inuvik that I don't know and they don't know about me. I thought about the situation for a few minutes. Was I ready to open this book? What would this do to the memory of her? Maybe I should leave this alone. If they knew she was pregnant, they would have looked for me. Why didn't they look for me? I didn't have anything to gain from this.

I kept the information on my desk. Right now, I had to finish packing Uncle Josh's things. Once in a while I would glance at the information on my desk but I would chicken out. By Friday, I had everything packed. I went over to my desk to call the storage facility, looking down I saw the Burrens' information.

I picked up the phone and dialed the number. My fingers move robotically. I wasn't sure what I was going to say or ask but if I didn't do this now I would lose the nerve all together. Just get it over with—*closure I reminded myself.* On the fourth ring a female voice answered

"Hello, Burren Residence." she answered.

"Excuse me; I am calling for Mr.William Burren." I stuttered.

"May I ask whose calling?" she requested.

"My name is Gena Reynolds." I provided.

"Please wait Ms. Reynolds." she politely replied.

I sat there quietly waiting for someone to return to the phone. My heart was pounding against my chest. My breathing was fast but steady. My hands started shaking. Maybe I should just hang up. I'll do this when I'm ready.

"Hello." his voice was cautious.

"Hello, Mr. Burren—um, my name is Gena Reynolds. I don't really know how to tell you this but, um, recent events in my life, um, have led me to believe that I am your granddaughter." I said it slowly and deliberately. I didn't know if I could repeat it. I sounded like I had some sort of learning disability but it's too late now. I've already said it. This was definitely a way to give the man a heart attack.

I waited for what seemed like minutes and I did not hear anything. "Hello." I asked. *Great now I've just shock this poor old man to death. Just add him to my list.*

"Alexandria?" he whispered.

Surprised at him calling me by my mother's name I responded. "No sir, my name is Gena Reynolds, I believe, I mean I was told Alexandria was my mother." I stuttered.

"My God, your voice…" his voice was cut off abruptly so I thought my connection was lost but than I heard him stutter and what sounded like he was crying. Immediately a soft female voice spoke "Hello, who is this," she demanded.

"Hello, my name is Gena Reynolds, did something happen to Mr. Burren? Is he okay? I am really sorry to shock him like this. Please tell me he's okay. I did not mean to upset him." I pleaded.

"No, he's fine. Please hold on…" *Rolfe, Rolfe pick up the phone she yelled.* I can hear her calling for someone else and than I heard the background noise from another line.

"Hello, who is this?" he demanded. His voice was deeper and sterner.

What is with this family? Irritated I repeated "Hello, my name is Gena Reynolds, I called to talk to Mr. William Burren but someone just took the phone away from him. Is everything okay? I was talking to him about my mother, Alexandria." I explained carefully.

I was disrupted by the same female voice coming on "Do you hear her voice. She sounds just like her." she said calmly.

"Idelle, please. Ms Reynolds how did you come to the conclusion that Alexandria Burren was your mother?" he questioned.

"Well I was given this jewelry box when my parents died, and in that box was a confession made that I was not their biological daughter. They gave me the name Alexandria Burren and from there I obtained this phone number." I replied calmly.

"What did the jewelry box look like?" he asked.

I was kind of shocked at the question. I just told him I was a long lost family member and he is inquiring about a box? What does the box have to do with anything? It's just a box.

"Did you hear what I just said?" I asked annoyed.

"Yes, Ms. Reynolds. I want to know what the jewelry box look like." He demanded.

"Well it is rectangular shaped. The metal I believe is silver. It has a blue stone to each corner." I described.

"Did you hear that?" the woman name Idelle said.

"How did you open it?" he asked.

"Um, this may sound crazy but I'm not really sure but I think I opened it by accidently getting blood on the clear part of the lid. I know how absurd that sounds but that is the only explanation I can give you right now." I sounded so crazy these people may have me arrested.

"Gena, we would like to meet you, where do you live?" he calmly stated.

Shocked by his quick reply, I stuttered "Um well, can I speak to my grandfather first? Who are you?"

"My name is Rolfe Burren; I am Alexandria's oldest brother. I am your uncle." He hesitated.

"Is Mr. William Burren alright?" I repeated.

"He is a little overwhelmed right now, but he will be fine. We want to meet you." He replied.

"I live in Indiana; if it is alright I can come to Inuvik." I asked cautiously. If these people were crazy I didn't want to bring them to my house.

"Gena, how old are you? Can you travel by yourself?" he asked.

"I am 18. I can travel by myself. I've done it before." I claimed.

"You said that your parents are dead, who is taking care of you right now?" he asked.

"Well that's another thing. My parents died many years ago and I've been with my uncle up until last week. He just passed away." I admitted.

"So, Gena, you're there all alone?" he asked.

"Yes, but I'm okay." I said confidently.

"Yes, I don't doubt that you are doing well. We are so glad that you found us. I will send someone to escort you to Inuvik. Tell me your address so we can make the arrangements." he declared.

"Really sir, I can travel by myself. I have your address I can come to Inuvik." I replied.

"Gena, I am sure you are capable of doing many things but the trip to Inuvik is quite treacherous. We would feel much better if someone we trust traveled with you. Please do not take any offense. It would make everyone here feel less worry." he firmly stated.

"Okay, um I live in Crew, Indiana in the United States. My address is 28 Hachette Road." I said. It felt uncomfortable telling strangers where you live. My "stranger danger" lessons have really been thrown out of the window now.

"Okay, what is your phone number? I will call you back with the details." he asked.

"My home number is 317-571-2387 and my cell number is 317-570-2589." I provided.

"Okay, Gena, I will call you back in a few minutes. Don't go anywhere?" he instructed.

"Okay, can I ask you one last thing; do you know who my father is?" I inquired

"Gena, why don't we get you home first then we'll work on that." he stated.

"Okay. So I'll wait for your call then. Goodbye." I whispered. He said *home*. I hope he didn't think I was going to live in Inuvik. This is my home.

It was probably less than ten minutes before the phone rang again. I picked it up quickly.

"Gena, this is Alain Burren. I have made arrangements to have you escorted to Inuvik. Do you have a pen? I need you to write this down." he stated. I scrambled around the room to look for a pen.

"Okay, I'm ready." I said.

"Mr. Bradley Teague will pick you up on August 26 at 8am. That's a Thursday. He will escort you to Inuvik. Just pack your most personal needs. Everything else will be provided for you. Do you understand? Oh, Gena! I am so happy that you contacted us. I can not wait to see you." he stated.

"Well, I'm a little overwhelmed myself. I wished I'd known about you guys sooner. I'm quite excited and anxious at the same time. There are so many things I want to ask about my parents." I explained.

"My goodness, your voice sounds just like her. If I weren't told about you I would bet my life that you were Alexandria. Your grandmother is in frenzy right now. She would talk to you but she can't stop from crying."—*Aunt Beatrice please just keep it together she'll be here soon. I can heard him coaxing her.*

"Okay, well I have to start packing. I can't wait to meet everyone. See you soon."

When I got off the phone, I felt nauseous. Something happened to me 18 years ago, my mother died birthing me and her family knew she was pregnant but never went looking for me. I was happy that they wanted to see me but I was uneasy about why I was never looked for.

The leading up to the trip was more of getting a lot of Uncle Josh's things in the right places. I donated a lot of his home furnishings. I gave his race cars to charity. Mr. Gaffney's assistance helped me put Uncle Josh's Indiana home and California home on the market. I didn't want to stay in his house. There were still a lot of things to do. They would have to wait until I got back. By Wednesday, the house looked empty except for the storage boxes stacked up in the rooms. I will take care of those things when I get back. I wasn't really sure what I wanted to do with the personal things.

I rushed up to my bedroom to pack. It was well after 4pm before I was finally ready. I carefully wrapped the jewelry box in some of my clothing and placed it in the middle of one of my luggage. I wanted to ride my bike one more time but it started to rain really hard so I just store the bike into the garage. I will have to deal with a lot of things when I get home. I have to sort out my living arrangements. I need to find myself an apartment. I'll just think about that when I get home. I went inside and cleaned out the refrigerator. I took out all the trash.

I tried to go to bed early but the excitement would not allow me to rest. I checked my alarm clock to make sure it was set. I realize for the first time in days I wasn't thinking about the recent events in my life. The timing of this was really uncanny. I decided since I could not sleep I will start a list of things I wanted to ask.

Things to ask:

What was my mother like?

Do I look a lot like her?

Did she want me?

Who is my father?

Why do you live in Inuvik?

Who is this woman who took me away?

What is the deal with the jewelry box?

What the key belong to?

Does anyone know who sent me the plane tickets and the mystery limo person?

I thought of the last question. Obviously my new family did not send it. No one knew I lived here except maybe the woman who gave me away. Only she knew who she gave me to. This has got to be it.

The woman who stole me from my dying mother is the mystery limousine person.

Chapter Three

I woke up many times during the night. Finally at 5am I gave up on sleeping. *I'll just sleep on the plane.* I lugged both of my lug gages down to the living room. I folded my list and stuffed it into my jeans. I looked around to make sure things were unplugged and turned off. I was acting like I was going on a vacation.

As the morning progressed, I got more and more restless. Anxiety mixed with excitement was quite uncomfortable for me. I rearranged the storage boxes. I pulled all the linens. I did anything but look at the clock. It seemed like time didn't progress.

Finally, I heard a car come up the driveway. I ran to the door and opened it. I watched as a black sedan pull up the driveway and an older man came out from around the car and up to greet me.

"Good morning Ms. Reynolds, my name is Bradley Teague. Your family sent me to escort you to Inuvik." He said. He was built and strong for a man of his grandfatherly age. I wouldn't really know. I've never had a grandfather or a grandmother but I can't be that far off. Both my parents lost their parents way before I was born. The only grandparents I have are the ones I'm about to meet. *How ironic.* I lose everyone here just to gain new family somewhere else.

"Good morning to you Mr. Teague, thank you for coming for me." I replied

"Ms Reynold, where are the rest of your lug gages?" he asked.

"Well, I packed lightly. This is a quick trip for me. I only have these two bags. Oh and please call me Gena." I replied.

"And, you can call me Bradley." He quickly took the bags from me and walked me to the car.

I started to get in the front seat but he stopped me.

"No. Gena, you sit back here." he instructed. As he held the back door open.

"Oh, thank you." I said quietly.

As the car backed away from the driveway, I was a little overcome with emotions and could feel the tears welling up. I blinked twice and held my eyes closed until I got control of myself. I was leaving home to go to some cold isolated town in the northernmost part of Canada. But in this town there was a family I never knew I had. As much as I hated to admit it; I missed not having a family. Just knowing there was family out there was good enough for me. I don't plan on living with them. But it was a comfort to know that they were out there.

"We are right on time, Gena. We should be at the terminal in half and hour." he said. I know he saw me crying but he didn't say a word. I was thankful for that.

"Bradley, what airline are we flying with today?" I asked.

"Sorry, Gena, we're not flying with any commercial airline. Mr. Burren has a private jet for you. It is faster and more comfortable." He stated.

"Oh wow, I've never been on a private jet before. So how long will it take to get to Inuvik in a private jet? What time will we get there?" I asked

"Well usually it would take 6 hours but today we'll stop in the Quebec

Territory to pick up Mr. Randall. We should be in Inuvik by 3pm today." He stated.

We arrived at the airport on time. I didn't have to do anything. Bradley escorted me to the jet. From the outside it looks like any other commercial jet but there were no logo. The inside of the plane looked more like someone's luxury apartment. Instead of rolls of seats, there were huge leather sofas and recliners. There was a kitchen with a bar and as far as I can see, it looked like there was bedroom at the end of the plane. Wow, what kind of family do I have? Maybe they were very influential and I was a kidnap attempt that went awry.

"Good morning, Ms. Reynolds, my name is Margaret. I will be your Flight Attendant today. Please have a seat anywhere. If there is anything I can do to make you more comfortable, please let me know." She smiled.

"Thank you, no I'm fine. Please call me Gena."

I made my way to last recliner. I peaked through the curtain and saw that it wasn't a bedroom but more like a conference room. This was like a flying executive office. This must be my grandfather's office jet.

After a few minutes I saw Bradley give instructions to the pilot regarding the Quebec Territory stop. After he was done talking to the pilot, he made his way towards me.

"Gena, these seats can swivel all the way around and they can recline back if you need to rest your eyes. If you need more privacy, I can pull the curtain around this area. I will be right over there if you need anything."

"Thank you, Bradley." I replied.

As soon as the jet took off my eyes got heavy and I was out. Last thing I remember was hearing the curtains pulled around me.

I was startled awake when the plane landed in Quebec Territory. I peaked out the window and noticed the sun was still very bright. I attempt to straighten out my hair but that was pointless. I kept the curtain pulled. I could hear the plane door opening. There were people moving around.

Oddly, my head started pounding. My stomach churned. A wave of nausea swept through me. Luckily I haven't eaten anything. Flying and lack of sleep was the worst combination.

I peaked from behind the curtain and asked "Excuse me Margaret, can I get some aspirin?"

"Oh, yes. I'm sorry. Did the landing wake you? Are you okay? You look pale? When was the last time you ate something? Let me get you something right now." She pestered.

"I'm not hungry, I don't think I should eat right now anyway, just some aspirin, please. My head is pounding." I begged.

Few seconds later she came back with some aspirin and a cool pack. "Here place this over your head; it will help with the pain. Do you normally get sick when flying?" she asked.

"No, I've never gotten sick flying before. I think I didn't get enough sleep last night. Maybe I'm a little dehydrated. Can I just have some ginger ale?" I replied.

As she pulled the curtain back, I saw the new passenger enter the cabin. He stood at the doorway for awhile talking on the cell phone. I could not stop myself from staring at him. He was like no one I have ever seen before. I could hear from the exchange between him and Bradley that this was Mr. Randall. I didn't get his first name. He stood there talking to Bradley like they were best friends. He had to duck to get thru the doorway. As he moved inside the plane, he greeted everyone like they were his college buddies. Because of his size, he looked to be in his twenties but when you look at his face he looked much younger. He had beautiful features over his nose and cheek bone. His eyes were turquoise blue. His dark brown hair was cut short and tidy. His chest was strong and broad making his blue shirt looked taut. The rest of his body was lean and muscular. As he walked towards the back of the plane, he stopped to ask Margaret for some water. For a brief second, he scanned over the entire cabin as if he was looking for something. He slowly walked towards me but I could not pull my eyes away, than his eyes caught mine. He stared back just as rudely as I was staring at him. The depths of his eyes hypnotized me. It seemed like time stood still as he moved toward my chair. He smiled directly at me.

Embarrassed by my manners, I pulled the curtain closed. "Idiot" I murmured. That was a bit scary but exciting; I could feel my heart beating irregularly. Wow, I wasn't aware of how strange that brief moment in time was. *Calm yourself down* I thought to myself. This headache was really causing me to do stupid things. I placed the ice pack over my eyes and lay back down. I hope we get to Inuvik soon. *God, that didn't even sound right, now I want to go to Inuvik.*

Wow, my head was pounding. The throbbing ache that came from around my temple to the area above my eyebrows was killing me. I could hear exchanges of conversation between him and everyone else but I didn't bother to open my eyes. I don't think my head has ever hurt this much before. *Great just my luck*, I'll develop some sort of brain tumor before I make it to Inuvik. I tried to zone him out. His voice was nice and pleasant but everything was causing my head to hurt. He voice was very welcoming and charming but at this moment it was not appreciated. Suddenly Margaret pulled back the curtain.

"Gena, we don't have any ginger ale but I can make you some chamomile tea, would that help?" she suggested.

"Gena, I didn't know you were awake. Do you have a headache? You haven't eaten all day, Maybe you should eat. I think you should eat before you take any medication." Bradley demanded. He and Margaret were both standing over me. Behind them I could see that he was looking at me. His blue eyes were incredible, mesmerizing. If my head wasn't pounding I would've love to just stare back, but the pounding was making it very hard for me to focus.

Embarrassed by all the attention I tried explained. "No, I just have a little headache; I really don't want to eat. Please can I just have some water?" I begged.

"Here take mine." He stood up and reached around Margaret to hand me the water, making me more aware of his presence.

"Thanks, I owe you one." I smiled.

"I think you just paid me back with your smile." he answered. "Hi, I'm Corin Randall." He stared right at me. He extended his hand out toward me.

I was mesmerized by how gorgeous his blue eyes were close up. His smile devastated whatever willpower I had to be calm. I blinked several times before I could say anything. "Oh, yeah, I'm Gena Reynolds, hi" I stuttered. I sounded like a stuttering buffoon. I didn't even shake his hand. Feeling a little self conscious of what I must look like right now, I worked my hands through my hair to make sure I didn't look like a deranged lunatic. What a bad time to be meeting someone. I don't even remember what I look like. I can't remember if I had taken the time do my hair. *What was I wearing?* Subconsciously I looked down at my clothes.

"Don't worry, you look great." he winked. There was that smile again. He was teasing me. "Did you have a rough night?" he laughed.

"No! Not the way you mean, I didn't sleep well last night. Excitement and all." I said with a little bit of agitation. My head started pounding again. I sat forward and placed my hands over my forehead above my eyes and massaged that area. I must really look bad, he thought I was hung-over. Crap, why didn't I just spent a little bit of time this morning to do my hair or something. It wasn't like I didn't have the time. This was not how I imagined my trip to Inuvik.

"Excited, huh. What's in Inuvik?" he teased. I was caught off guard with his question.

"It's a long story." I quickly tossed the aspirins in my mouth and gulped down the water. The pounding of my head was nothing I've experienced before. I grabbed both sides of my head and squeezed it hoping that would make the pounding stop.

"Gena, please lay back down and I'll go make you some hot broth. If your stomach is empty the aspirin is going to upset it. Just lay back and keep still." Margaret pestered.

With that she pulled Bradley out and closed the curtain. She returned afterwards with a cup of broth. I took the broth slowly than laid back down. I can see behind her he was staring at me. He probably thought I was some sickly girl who can't even fly to Canada without having to be drugged up and pampered to. When she pulled the curtains closed, I swear I could still feel his stare.

Moments later I heard the captain telling the crew that we were 45 minutes away. They were all whispering. I felt like an ogre. Everyone had to be very quietly because Margaret did not want me disturbed. What a day to be weak and incompetent.

Even though my head was still aching a bit, I sat up and pretended to be headache free. I pulled the curtain back. Immediately Margaret came over. "Gena, are you feeling better? Can I get you anything?"

"Yes, I'm fine. No I don't need anything." I said it loudly so that

Bradley could hear. All this attention was so uncomfortable and embarrassing. Margaret rubbed my back then left to go back to her seat.

I turned my seat to look outside the window. The clouds outside were thick and heavy, I was glad the sun wasn't peaking through. I could feel his eyes looking at me. Nervously, I kept my eyes down and tucked my hands under my thighs pretending to be preoccupied with the clouds.

"Are you really feeling better?" he whispered. I slowly turned to meet his gaze. Wow, he really is gorgeous. His blue eyes could pierce right through me. Keep your composure I said to myself.

"Are you calling me a liar?" I replied. Being defensive helped in keeping my composure.

He looked at me with one eyebrow pulled up and a crooked smile. His smile was unbelievably breathtaking. "No, I would never call you a liar, but your attempt to hide your headache is not very convincing." he stated.

"It's not as intense. The pounding is gone but the ache is still right here." I pointed to my left eyebrow. I was unaware that I was rubbing that area with the palm of my left hand.

"May I?" he asked. Before I could protest he placed his hands to each side of my face and with his thumbs, slowly massaged my eyebrows. He slowly moved his thumbs down the side of my temples, shifting his fingers and palms further back around the base of my head. I kept my eyes closed because I could feel his eyes boring down on me. I could feel the heat from his hands. I can feel his warm inviting breath against my skin. *God he smelled good.* Suddenly I felt his thumb over my lips. My eyes darted open, his face was inches away from mine. I was startled by his closeness, so I pulled back.

We sat there staring at each other.

"I'm sorry; I didn't mean to do that. Please I don't mean to be so bold.

I just got carried away. You're just so…um never mind, Sorry." he stuttered.

"No, that's okay. I feel much better now. Thanks." I said nervously. My heart stopped and restarted. I was so embarrassed by my reaction to his touch. I didn't want him to see how much I liked his hands over my face. I slowly turned back to the windows.

"What's in Inuvik?" He asked. I turned toward him but kept my eyes downward.

"Just visiting my family" I replied.

"This must be your first trip to Inuvik?" he guessed.

"Why do you say that?" I questioned.

"Well, I know everyone in Inuvik, and if you've ever been there I would have seen you." he said with confidence.

"So, you know all 3500 people, do you?" I kidded.

He laughed. "Who are you visiting?"

"The Burrens" I answered.

"Well, you're on the right plane than." he smiled.

I laughed. He is charming. "So, what's in Inuvik for you?" I asked.

"I'm coming home. I had to go check out some things for my dad. So where are you from?" he asked.

"I'm from Crew, Indiana. This is a short visit for me. I have to get back to start school." I said.

"High School" He questioned as he looked directly at me.

"I'll be a senior in High School." I replied.

"Luckily I failed Kindergarten; I'm starting my senior year too. School starts on Monday." He said blandly.

Before I could replied the pilot announced that we were about to land. I fumbled around looking for my seatbelts. Suddenly his hands shot across my lap and snapped the buckle together. As I turned to thank him, my lips brushed the side of his face. I could feel the smoothness from his newly shaved skin. In that one second our eyes met with intense fiery. Embarrassed by my reaction, I looked away. He quickly pulled back.

"Sorry, those seatbelts tend to get lost in between the cushions." he stammered.

"Thanks." I said quietly. God, he smelled good. I could still feel the tingling on my lips. He would definitely make Inuvik an interesting place for someone. My flight was definitely more interesting.

"Gena, how long will you be in Inuvik?" he asked sadly. He was looking down at his hands.

My heart skipped a beat when I heard him say my name. I have never heard my name pronounced so sweetly. He said it so naturally like we've known each other since birth. "I have to start school on August 31st. So I guess 2 or 3 days." I said.

"That is not very long. Will you come back again?" he asked slowly.

I wasn't sure what he was asking but I felt a little excited that he wanted me to come back. "Well this trip wasn't planned. Maybe I'll be back when I have more time." I responded.

"Well, if you need someone to show you around, I'd be happy to be available." He offered with a gentle smile. It was very distracting.

"Thanks, Corin. I may take you up on that." I said.

"Sounds like a date to me." He smiled.

The plane landed smoothly but it disrupted our conversation. I waited for him to continue with our conversation but I can see he was writing something on a card.

"Gena, we're here, is your head still bothering you?" Bradley asked.

"No, I'm fine." I replied.

"I will be right back for you, let me get your luggage out." He instructed.

Corin had already gotten up from his seat. He towered over me for a second, than he deliberately knelt down next to my seat. He took my left hand and turned my palm upward. With his other hand he placed a business card with his number on it.

"Don't forget our date, Gena." He said looking straight into the depths of my soul. Abruptly he walked off.

He exited the plane behind Bradley.

Chapter Four

I handed her my dad's business card but I wrote my number on the back. I had to stay calm. Don't scare her off. This was too important. This was nothing I'd encountered before. I knew when I entered the cabin that she was the one from my dreams. In the instant our eyes met, I felt the strange impulse to be near her. I was drawn by the depth of her haunting dark brown velvet eyes, soft fair skin, and taut rosy lips.

Was she related to the Burrens? She doesn't look like them. How is she related to them? How come she has never visited before? I didn't know the Burrens had family anywhere else. Her last name is Reynolds. Even her name is beautiful.

She probably thought I was an idiot; all I could do was stare. At first when, I saw her behind the curtain, I wasn't sure if she was real. It was like a ghost from my dreams haunting me. I have dreamt of her but I never thought she was real. She wasn't anything I could have dreamt up. My imagination wasn't creative enough to put together such a beautiful package. Her soft silky brown hair, her warm inviting breathe, she smelled good. When her lips touched my face, her caress hit me with enormous force. I had no idea such force existed. How can something so trivial be so powerful? If this is what she can do to me with a simple caress, what will happen when we kiss?

I have no doubt my existence is to be with her. I can't even see any future right now until I can secure the present with her. I had no doubt she will haunt me in my dreams. I could sleep forever if she was there with me. I have to tell her as soon as possible. I will wait for her to go see her family than I will come over tomorrow and talk to Rolfe. I will get her alone and tell her about my feelings for her. We can work out the details afterwards. I can't let her go back to Indiana without me. *Crew, Indiana.* Where the hell is that? Is there a clan there? Why have I not been there? I only have a few days to get this right.

The warmth coming from her *aura* was drowning me. I could breathe it, taste it, and feel it all around me. I have to get off this plane now, before I do something stupid. The urge to be near her was suffocating me. I'd already scared her when I lost control of myself and touched her lips. It was *really* smart to buckle her. She probably thought I was some weird stalker freak. I needed fresh cold air to clear my senses. Wow, I can't believe how hard it is to walk away. My heart is not working with my brain. As I got closer to the exit, I turned and stole another look at her. *Imprint her in your memory.* If I fall and lost my memory, I pray that I still have her stored inside my heart.

She has invaded and conquered me in a matter of one hour. I couldn't put up a fight even if I wanted to. Hell, I wouldn't put up a fight. I surrendered when I first saw her. I was hers from the very beginning. *I will see you again, Gena Reynolds* I vowed.

I ducked through the cabin door and let the cold fresh air cleanse me. If I had a choice I would rather be inundated with her scent but I had to slow down. I took a couple of slow deep breaths and let my senses clear. I heard my name being called, I recognized the voice but a small part of me was hoping it was her that was calling me back. I looked further down the tarmac and saw my dad.

"Corin, over here!"

"Hi! Dad. Thanks for picking me up." I said. No, I really wasn't thankful. If he wasn't here I would've asked Bradley for a ride and got to spend more time with her. To late now, as we were walking towards his car. Impatiently he started questioning.

"Tell me what happened in Quebec Territory?" he asked. He was serious now.

"They're all gone. The good news is that there were survivors, five or six. I tried to track them down to bring them here but I lost their scent at 10 miles out. I don't know if they made it. It looked like they were taken by surprise. They probably didn't see it coming." I recanted. I was the strongest and fastest of this clan. My parents' aura gave me those abilities. I was often sent in to see if there were any survivors. I could not fight the hunters by myself but I could get away before they even knew I was there. The memory of the destruction and carnage left behind by the hunters made me sick, they destroyed everything. They left no evidence that life was once there.

"I know you tried, if anyone could fine them it would be you. You tried. We have to get this information to Rolfe quickly. They may be working their way here. We need to be prepared. We're not as strong as we once were." He pulled out his cell phone and started to dial.

"Oh, who's that?" he asked. I followed his eyes over to Gena, now exiting the plane behind Bradley. God, how I envy Bradley right now? Bradley was holding her hands as she stepped down from the plane. I can remember the feel of her soft skin—warm and smooth. Even though I knew it was his job to assist her I felt a bit of jealousy and anger. *Don't touch her too long old man. She is mine.* I watched intently as she walked slowly down the ramp. When she almost tripped I felt compelled to run to her but Bradley was there.

I composed myself and responded "Her name is Gena Reynolds; she is visiting the Burrens for the weekend."

"Oh, I think I know who she is. Rolfe mentioned that Justin was bringing his fiancée to meet the family. They're all really excited that he has found his *concero flamma*. He met her while visiting some friend in the Midwest. Justin hit the jackpot, she is a beauty. Lucky kid." He sighed "I only wish the same happens to you guys, someday."

His words hit me like a ton of bricks. Everything stopped and slowed down to a coma-like stance. *She is engaged to Justin!* Of course, why else would she come to Inuvik? My hopes plummeted. The blood in my body left me. I felt cold and weak. I sat there sick and emptied. If I could be nauseous I would vomit buckets right now. My arrogance slapped me squarely in the face. I pictured many bad case scenarios but I didn't picture her with someone else. How arrogant of me. Of course she was taken, look at her. *Damn it, Justin, not her.* How could she belong to someone else? Was I wrong? No, I felt it on the plane. The thought of her with someone else... No, the thought of her being held by someone other than myself tormented me. This can't be right.

"How long have they been together" I questioned. But I didn't get an answer for he was on the phone with Rolfe. How could I be so wrong? No, I wasn't wrong. She is my soul mate. Justin is wrong. He has been wrong before. He's an idiot, he's always wrong. I felt angry and cheated. I don't deserve this. It was suppose to be definite. Find her and everything will fall into place automatically. Not find her and lose her to someone else.

I watched as she got into the black sedan. She smiled and waved back at Margaret. She didn't even look toward me. I was insignificant in her life. Wow, how that thought hurt me. Was I just another one of her admirers and Justin was the winner. The ache from this admission was slow and painful. I can feel it creeping up and piercing my heart. My moment of triumph was silenced by the crushing of my heart. I can see my future now—always watching, waiting and hoping. This was so grossly unfair.

I can't afford to see her again. I will only allow her to haunt me in my dreams. *You can get through this.* She's only here for two maybe three days, I can avoid her. I'll deal with their marriage later. Maybe my feelings for her will lessen once I'm away from her. What do I have to do to keep away from her? I would have to leave Inuvik. This town was not big enough. Deep down my fears surfaced. *Or I will be cursed to love her forever, waiting on the side lines, wanting her attention, and tortured by her happiness with someone else. This was not happening to me. God, the ache in my heart was crushing me.*

"Rolfe, wants us to debrief him tomorrow at noon. Did you say something earlier?" he asked.

"No, I was just talking to myself." I uttered painfully.

My eyes followed her black sedan all the way into Inuvik. As the sedan sped down Mackenzie Road and thru the town, it disappeared beyond the wooded trees that divided the town from the Burren estate. Even though our home was further down the same road, as her car entered the gated entrance I felt like I would never see her again. She was leaving me and there was nothing I could do about it. The ache in my heart worsened. I was watching my future dissipate before my eyes. Every breath was hard. Simple tasks were mundane and unimportant. I saw no beautiful bright colors just gray. How did my life change so quickly? I went from looking and hoping to lost and despair.

"Michelle wants to see you as soon as you get in. She said you haven't picked your courses for the semester. Do me a favor be nice to Mark, he is having a hard time with Ella. They can't seem to agree on anything, it's driving your mom crazy." He informed me. My dad has always been about keeping peace. When Mark announced he was marrying Ella, things went south fast. They couldn't agree on any wedding details.

As the car pulled up the gated entrance, I could see Michelle standing at the front door, tapping her feet. She was mad because she wanted me to help her choose the right courses with the right teacher. She always had problems with teachers. As I got out of the car and toward the door she walked up to me with her hand up. "You were supposed to be back yesterday, I had to sign you up for all your courses. I hope you like Human Sexuality and Home Economics. You're going to be spending a lot of time knitting and cooking while studying the human sex organs." She laughed. I ignored her and continued to my room. I didn't feel like dealing with her antics right now. "Hey are you okay? Corin!" she yelled from behind me.

"He's probably upset from what he saw in Quebec Territory, I wouldn't taunt him right now, Michelle." I heard my dad telling her. Little did they know my pain wasn't for the people that died in Quebec Territory but for the girl who just entered my life. Her face will haunt me.

I went into my room and flipped the stereo on. I wanted to be sane again. She was doing things to me I didn't think was possible. I remember her smile, her lips, the smoothness of her skin, the softness of hair, her scent and her breathe. The brief moment I had with her was so fulfilling. If the plane had crashed I would have been happy. Now, going back to my boring life looked even bleaker than before. How can I continue living my life now that I know that she exist, but I can't be with her. This was some sort of cruel sick twisted plot to destroy my sanity. I deserve better than this. I deserve her.

"Hey, hon. I heard you were back. Are you hungry?" my mother asked.

"No." I said quietly.

"Do you want to talk about it?" I looked up and saw my mother at the door. She could see that something was bothering me.

"No, I'm just tired. That's all." I said quietly.

"Well, Tristan and Cory called earlier; no doubt they want to hear all the gory details from the Quebec Territory. I have to go help Ella pick out some china patterns on the internet, so I will be at the Daniels' house." She sighed. "See you at dinner, glad your home."

"Sure, mom" I replied. I wasn't paying much attention to what she said. I didn't feel like talking to Tristan or Cory. I didn't want to talk about the Quebec Territory incident. I just want to sit here and dream about her. As painful as it may be, I just want to dream about her. I want to be near her. "Oh, mom! Can I ask you a question?" I quickly responded.

"Sure honey, what's on your mind?" She turned back to face me.

"You know that *concero flamma* thing that you and dad always talk about; can someone have two soul mates?" I asked.

"I don't understand what you're asking, what do you mean exactly?" she questioned. She looked suspicious of my question.

"Never mind, it's nothing I was just wondering that's all. Forget I asked." I knew that if I pursued with this question she was going to drag every bit of information out of me until she was satisfied that she had resolved my problem.

"Are you sure?" she replied.

I nodded and went back to listening to the CD that was playing. I started to think of her again. I didn't care if this was bad for me. All I know is that when I dream about her, I was happy. In my world, she was mine and nothing else mattered. We were together and I could talk to her freely.

I could kiss her inviting lips without any doubt of her affections. She would love me just as much as I loved her.

"Hey, dude. I heard you ask mom about a soul mate, did you meet someone in the Quebec Territory?" my brother Mark, always seemed to be at the right place at the right time. Nosy bastard

"No, Mark. It was just a question." I sarcastically replied.

"Hey, man. If it helps, Ella is not my *soul mate* but I care enough for her to want to marry her. Not everyone will find a soul mate. Sometimes I think it's a mythical dream that our parents talk about just to keep us straight. Look at Carl; he's forty and still waiting to find his soul mate. He's just wasting his life and not enjoying what's in front of him. No one really knows anything about this stuff. We're just told to keep our eyes open and wait, that's stupid man. Well, I'm going to keep my eyes opened meanwhile I'm going to have one hand in the cookie jar enjoying the sweets." He said scathingly.

"Mark, what if you marry Ella, than your soul mate shows up? What will you do?" I asked.

"Hey, man. I can't think like that. If we all think like that, we would all be single and lonely. That's worse, wasting your life waiting for some miraculous meeting." He smirked.

I didn't have a response for him. I just laid there. I didn't ask him what to do if you did find your *soul mate* but she was going to marry someone else. I was irritated with him. How could he marry someone that could someday be someone else's soul mate? How ironic? I was being punished for what my brother was doing.

"Hey, a bunch of us is heading out to Tuk Beach for one last bonfire before my wedding. Do you want to come? Justin, Max, Cory, Tristan will be there. Natalie will be there too. She asked if you were coming." He implied.

"I'll think about it, when are you leaving?" I asked.

"Around 9pm, we would leave sooner but Justin, Tristan and Cory have some family thing they have to do before they can get out there. Can I count you in?" he asked.

Hearing Justin's name, I knew if he came he would bring his fiancée. I couldn't deal with that right now. It's just too soon. I would probably end up making a fool of myself.

"I'm kind of tired, I'll skip this one." I said flatly. Justin is actually cool guy. I wonder if he feels that same way about Gena as I do. Does he think about her like I do? How can she be his soul mate when I am certain that she is mine? That's the problem, I am certain she is mine but she may not even see me that way. She obviously loves Justin if she accepted his proposal. I need to get out of this room. I need to run. I need to feel the wind and fresh air. This stagnate air was crushing me.

I quickly got up and left my house. Today I was thankful for the gift of speed. I wanted to disappear and in seconds I was gone. I ran through the thick forest. If I hit anything, I didn't feel it. The pain in my heart was worst. The air was cold. The sky above me was clear and beautiful but I couldn't enjoy it. I couldn't banish her face from my mind long enough for me to see anything else. Her face was everywhere at once. Her scent was drowning me.

I continued to run. I didn't pay much attention on where I was going or when I was going to stop running. My sense of direction was blurred. I could feel a certain pull to turn here and go left here and right there I wasn't aware of anything I was doing. All I can feel was this great need to go in certain directions. My brain could not comprehend what my legs were doing. Soon, I could see that I was heading in the direction of the Burrens' house but I could not stop myself. I came from the forest behind their house. Where I stood I can see the whole back of the house. I scanned through each of the open window and saw no one.

Get out of here stupid. I thought to myself. My brain was fighting with my heart. She was drawing me towards her. There was no other explanation. Everything we've been taught about *concero flamma* was happening to me. I used to think it was rubbish but look at me now. Look at where I am. From the moment I saw her, on the plane behind the curtain, I knew she was my soul mate. Her hold on me was strong. Was she even aware of her power of me?

She is only engaged to Justin. They're not married yet. I still have a fighting chance. I have to at least try for her. *Oh, but what if she did not share the same feelings for me, as I do for her.* Would that hurt more than I'm hurting now? What if she rejected me? Before I could continue with my thoughts, I heard someone coming through the back door.

My eyes did not fool me. She was standing right there. She had changed into a blue sweater and her jeans were replaced by a pair of khakis. They were simple colors but they were so beautiful on her. I wanted so much to come closer and touch her. She looked lonely and lost. Why was she out here by herself? Where was Justin? Did she sense me? Maybe she could feel me just as strongly as I felt her.

As I was lost in my own thought, I didn't realize that I was slowly moving toward her. But then she turned around and went back in. Frustrated with myself, I recoiled back into the woods. I ran back towards my house. I know what I must do but thinking about letting her go was killing me. She would eventually belong to someone else because she wanted to. Even I could not control that. I have known Justin all my life; this was not something I could do against him. He was a friend. He has never done anything bad towards me. We were like brothers. I wouldn't hesitate to steal her away if he was a stranger. It didn't matter now, she didn't choose me. She chose Justin. That thought silenced my heart.

Chapter Five

I watched him exit the plane. It seemed like he deliberately walked slow so I could enjoy staring at him. Just before he got to the door he turned and caught me staring at him. My heart definitely skipped, stopped and restarted. Then he left. I looked at the card he gave me. It was a business card.

Randell Security Company

John Randell

On the back he wrote his phone number. Next to the number was a symbol I had never seen before. Well, this would definitely give me an excuse to call him.

Bradley came back through the door and waved me to come. As I exited the door, I can see further down the tarmac that Corin was talking to an older man. This must be his father; they were a carbon copy of each other, except for their aging differences.

I took a step forward, missing a step all together. Luckily Bradley was near enough to catch me before I fell down the stairs and totally embarrass myself in front of the most gorgeous guy I have ever seen. I didn't realize how bright the sun was, until it triggered the pounding in my head. When I got down the stairs safely, I waved at Margaret and got into the car as quickly I as could, before the headache could get any worse. I didn't want to meet my new family being in a foul disposition. That would definitely get me kicked back to Indiana.

Bradley drove through Inuvik. We crossed the town so quickly, that if I'd blink I would have missed it all together. The town was so small it only had one intersection. I don't even know if you can call it an intersection since the light was a caution light and not an actual traffic light. From the window I could see the town was made up of basically 6 to 8 buildings. I saw one grocery store "*North Mart*". It must be a spin-off of *Wal-Mart.*

As soon as we passed the town, we entered a heavily wooded area. If I didn't trust Bradley, I would be afraid. The forest was so dense it hid the sun. After some time, I could see the steel gates with the scripted letter B on the railing. The gates opened as the car came towards it. Further down pass the gates, you could see a massive brick mansion that looked like something out of Europe, instead of Inuvik, Canada.

The car stopped in the front and I could see a large audience of people standing there waiting for me like I was some superstar at a premiere. This family was huge. I could count at least 15 people. They were all so beautiful. They all looked relatively the same but each had some distinct features. Everyone look so perfect. They must've gotten all dressed up for me. Looking down at my dark blue jeans, and creamed color v-neck shirt, I felt grossly under dressed. I should have thought more about my clothing. *How stupid can you be? You only have one chance to make a first impression dummy, and the impression they will have of you is this. Really smart.*

Without thinking, I opened the car door and got out quickly.

"Let me get that for you, Hi, my name is Cory."

"Oh, thanks. Cory, I'm Gena." Before I could stand, they all came towards me. So many people greeted me, hugged me, introduced themselves to me, I felt overwhelmed. I have never been around this many family members before. In Indiana, it was always just me and Uncle Josh.

"Please everyone, let her get inside and let's greet her properly." the deep loud voice from the door announced. I recognized that voice from the phone. This must be my Uncle Rolfe.

I was escorted in by twin male cousins named Cory and Michael. They were identical twins. "Wow, you are gorgeous, if we weren't related I would have to make a fool of myself." said Michael.

"Shut-up you idiots, you're embarrassing her." the voice coming from behind me, pushing Michael out of the way. She entwined her arms around mine. "Hi, Gena, I'm Dana." She looked to be the same age as me but she was definitely prettier. She had beautiful blond wavy hair that hugged around her face and stopped just short of her shoulder. Her skin was pearl-like and flawless. If Dana didn't make me feel self-conscious the other girls Lauren, Aimee, and Julianne definitely finished me off.

I barely notice the beauty of the grand entrance of this house because I was enthralled at the beauty of the people standing in front of me. I could hear one cousin name Preston, complimenting me but he obviously didn't see the rest of his family the way I see them. Maybe their just used to being beautiful and this is nothing new to them.

I was led to a large living room with plenty of room for this large family to all take a sit. Several of the older men stood behind their wives. The younger people sat all around me.

"Come sit here next to me and Lauren. Be careful Michael, you may drool on grandmother's couch." she chided.

I chuckled "Wow, I didn't know there were some many of you." I said quietly.

The room went silent, then an older woman came over to me and pulled me up from my seat and hugged me so tight, I couldn't feel my arms. She was joined by an older man. They both hugged me so tight; I had to fall back a bit to get some air. "I am so happy that you found us. I'm happy that you're alive." My grandfather cried.

My grandmother grabbed my face and whispered "My child, you don't know how many times I've dreamt that you were alive. You're as beautiful as your mother. I tried to tell them that I could feel you but after time, we lost hope. Yet here you are. You found us." She erupted into tears. I could not help but hold onto her and kiss her cheeks. Lauren moved from her seat so that I could pull my grandmother to sit next to me.

"Gena, I am you mother's oldest brother. My name is Rolfe, this is my wife Madeline. This over here is my oldest, Justin, Preston is my second and you've met my youngest daughter Lauren." I greeted each and every one of them with a smile and a nod.

When he was done, a tall beautiful blonde woman stepped forward "Gena, on behalf of my family, I want to welcome you. My name is Idelle, this is my husband Marcus. Over here is my oldest daughter Aimee and my son Lawrence. Your mother was my baby sister." She acknowledged.

When she was done, another family member stepped forward, "Gena, My name is Alain. We've spoke on the phone. This is my wife Judith. You've met my twin sons, Cory and Michael." They looked at me and winked. "There are two sets of twins in this family, so don't feel bad if you get us mixed up." he said softly. Blaine and I were actually adopted by Grandfather William when our parents died. My father was Grandfather William's younger brother. We lost our parents when we were babies.

"Gena, Alain is my twin. My name is Blaine. This is my wife Renee. You're sitting next to Dana my eldest. Behind you are Julianne and Will. We want to welcome you home." He ended.

I sat there absorbing everyone around me. They all took turns asking me questions about my life, where I live, what my likes and dislikes were and I answered and asked many questions.

"Bradley informed me that you have not eaten today. That will not do. We've just found you; we can't loose you to hunger. Why don't you get settle in and when you're done, come join us for dinner." Rolfe asserted.

"Come I'll show you to your room, where are all your lug gages?" Lauren said.

"I only brought two bags." I replied.

"Oh my god, Dana, Aimee we get to shop for her." She yelled to the other girls.

Laughter erupted from everyone in the room. "I knew you guys would love that, that's why I told her not to bring too much." Alain confirmed.

"Uncle Alain, you are a genius!" Dana yelled.

"Come let's get you settled and ready for dinner." She pulled me up the enormous spiral staircase. As she ascended the stairs, she spoke non stop about having another female cousin since they were out-numbered.

When we got to the third bedroom, she and Lauren dumped all my clothing on the bed and sorted through them to see what I could and could not wear due to the climate here. I was so embarrassed of my plain wardrobe compare to how they were dressed. They definitely did not get there cloths from *North Mart.* They must have everything shipped in. I could tell by some of the symbols on their clothing that they were high-end name brands. I can't pronounce them but I've hear of them.

"Gena, this is your room. Your bathroom is over here. This is your closet, which we will definitely help you fill." Dana informed. They were so happy to shop for me that I didn't have the heart to tell them that I wasn't going to be here that long.

The massive bedroom was triple the size of my bedroom at home. The bathroom was grander than any bathroom I've ever seen. *All this for one person* The closet was the size of my whole bedroom at home. When they placed all of my clothing in the closet, the closet looked even emptier than before.

"Gena, do you need to freshen up before you come down." Lauren asked.

"Yeah, just a bit. Do you guys know where I can get some aspirin? My head has been aching practically all day. I was so excited to come here that I didn't get much sleep last night and with the flying and stuff it just hasn't gone away." I explained.

They all stared at me blankly before Aimee stepped forward and said "We can have some sent up to you, we'll leave you to freshen up. See you downstairs okay. Welcome home. We are really glad you're here." They all came around and gave me a hug.

After I spent some time in the bathroom, trying to make myself look presentable, I rummaged through my clothes to find nicer things to wear. I settled on a fitted blue cashmere sweater and khakis. When I came out of the bathroom, I found some aspirin on the night stand and glass of water. I quickly took the aspirins and chased it down with the water.

I left my room and descended down the stairs. I didn't realize until I was at the end of the stairs that I had descended the stairs from the opposite side. This side of the stairs ended in front of long rows of French doors that led out to the backyard. Curiously, I stepped through the doors and out to the backyard. The backyard was so well kept, and the greenery was breath-taking. I stood there for a few minutes and enjoyed the fresh clean air. After a couple of breathes, I went back in.

"There you are did you get lost?" Justin said.

"No, I was just curious, the backyard is so beautiful." I replied.

"Well, it should be beautiful, Aunt Idelle and Aunt Renee spends thousands on keeping it that way. Are you ready to eat?" he responded while rubbing his stomach.

"Starving, let's go." I chuckled.

We entered the dining room together. "I've found her, she was trying to hunt her own food in the backyard, luckily I intervene, and she almost got a hold of the stone rabbits." he laughed. Everyone in the room, laughed. I can tell he is the one that makes everyone laugh. There is always one in the family.

After dinner, everyone moved to the library. The room was beautifully covered in rich mahogany and thousands of books. The rich dark reds and burgundy made the white grand piano look so beautiful.

"Do you play?" Uncle Rolfe asked.

"I play a little, but not talented enough to play one of these." I said shyly.

"Your mother played the piano beautifully. She composed her own music." He bragged.

"Speaking of my mother, you've answered a lot of question about her but I am also curious about my father. Do you know who he is?" I pleaded.

"Yes, we know who he is. Why don't you sit down and we'll explained a lot of things to you. Now, before we start, I want you to listen to the complete details before you interrupt with questions. It just makes it easier to recant. Okay?" he instructed.

I nodded "Okay."

"Gena, before we talk about your parents we have to tell you about our kind…your kind."

What did he just say? Did I hear him correctly?

"We are descendants of an ancient race not from Earth. Millions of years ago, our ancestors left our world, Tiamat, to come to Earth to live in peace. Our world was plundered in war and death, than eventually destroyed in the process. Our ancestors came here way before any civilization was even formed. Humans were present but they were unsophisticated and uncivilized."

He said humans like we weren't human. I look human. They look human.

"Our ancestors discreetly help shaped what humans have today. We live discreetly from humans to prevent discovery of our differences. The main difference between us and humans are that we have extraordinary strengths."

What strengths? I don't have any strength. Is there a candid camera hidden somewhere?

"Some of us have heightened senses. Some of us have super human strength. Others have the ability to travel at great speed. We all share the same weakness. We do not tolerate hot weather. That is why we live here in Inuvik.We can heal from any injury except decapitation."

Did he just admit to being immortal? Did they expect me to believe this?

"We age normally up to the age of 35 than the aging process slows down. Much so like comparing dog years with human years. We can live twice as long as humans. Because of our strength, nature's cruel way of controlling our population inhibits our female specie from producing more than three offspring and it must be done before she reaches the age of 25."

What did he just say? I looked around the room. All the parents were relatively the same age. The younger people were also around the same age. There were no small babies or younger children.

"Each one of us is born with a different aura specific to our strengths. When we are together, we absorb each others different auras, giving each other the ability to have combine strengths. Our aura also helps us heal from injury and disease. Are you following all this? Are you okay? Can I continue." he asked. I don't know what my facial expression was but I didn't want him to stop.

"No, please continue." I pleaded. *I wasn't sure if this was some sort of prank or poor sense of humor but the story was interesting. I don't have an aura.*

"Twenty years ago we noticed that some new births didn't have an aura. We assumed this was the natural order of evolution for our kind."

There he said it again…our kind. What does he mean by our kind?

"We realized that the aura is stronger in couples who marry their *concero flamma* or soul mate."

Soul mate? There is no such thing.

"The male species of our kind has an innate ability to identify their *soul mates.* If they are lucky to find each other, their union has a better chance of producing a child with an aura. Without an aura, these children's strengths are weaker than ones with an aura. Even though we are somewhat immortal, we are not free from dangers. The same cause of war and destruction that drove our ancestors to come here has also followed us here. Through the years we have been hunted by our mortal enemy who we call *hunters.*"

Mortal enemy? I don't have any enemies. Are these hunters aliens too?

"They are just as strong as we are but they do not heal an aura. As long as we remain strong, we do not fear them. But, with the changes of our species, they have managed to hunt our kind to the point of near extinction. The lost of so many of our kind prevents us from finding our soul mates. This is why we have had a lot of children birthed without an aura, leaving them defenseless against the hunters." He paused to see if I comprehend what he was saying.

"Did the hunters kill my parents?" I asked quietly. *I wasn't sure when I started to believe this story but the question came out so naturally, it frightened me.*

"Your parents union was very special, they were soul mates. However, their auras were strong before their union so it was to be expected that their offspring would have a *very strong aura.* We did not know how strong until you arrived today. Gena, we could feel your aura as soon as you landed."

I don't have an aura. He must be mistaken.

"Being around you now is a phenomenal experience. The strength from your aura transcends any *concero flamma* union. Preston, Lawrence, and Julianne were born without an aura, but since your arrival we can feel an aura coming from them. It is not as strong as the others but their senses have heightened. Gena, you were born with the *healer aura.*"

I have a what? An aura? What the hell are these people doing? Is this some sort of sick joke?

"Your strength is your aura. In order for you to develop the other strengths, you must be around your own kind. But since you have never been around us, your body must go through a transformation. Your body is reacting to the changes that are happening to you with the headaches and nausea. Don't worry it is temporary. In time, you will develop some defenses but the complete transformation will take some years—*maybe two or three years.* Of course, that is just a guess."

The complete transformation of what? How did he know about the headaches and nausea? Probably one of the girls told him. I continued to listen intently. I wasn't sure of my facial expressions but I definitely know my brain was screaming insanity. I was pretty proud of myself for being able to keep calm and composed.

"Ironically, our aura is harmful to humans. How the aura works is it heightens the genetic flaws in those around you. Since most human diseases are genetic flaws the aura will speed up their disease process."

What? My aura kills people. Did he just say that? Well that explains why so many people die around me.

"That is another reason we do not live in areas populated by many humans. In the same token, your aura heightens our disease—*which is our aura*—but instead of hurting us it makes us stronger. Your aura is unique even to our kind. Your aura heals those of us that do not have an aura."

"When the hunters heard of your potential birth, they hunted your parents and killed them. At the time your parents feared birthing you in Canada was too dangerous, so they attempted to get you as far away as possible. When we found your parents they were already dead. We assumed that you were also dead because we found no evidence that you were successfully birthed. Your father's name is Daniel Roese. His whole family was also killed in the struggle."

My parents were hunted down because of me. I certainly did not imagine that scenario. I felt ashamed for thinking that my mother left me because she did not want me. She died for me. My father and his whole family died for me.

"In the past eighteen years, we have managed to stay together as a clan to be strong enough to defend ourselves from the hunters. The hunters will not attack a large and strong clan. They only attack when we are separated or too weak to defend. There are hundreds of clans spread throughout this planet." He waited to read my facial expressions. I stared back at him, numbly.

"When you contacted us six days ago, we did not know if you were possible. When you told me about the jewelry box, we knew then somehow you were saved. We do not know who saved you or how you came to be in the care of strangers."

Someone took me from my mother as she lay dying and saved me.

He stopped talking. In my mind, I was still processing everything. My descendants were *aliens*. There are other aliens hunting us. This must be some sort of family joke or prank. I looked around the room. I looked at my grandparents, aunts and uncles, all my cousins. They looked human. Looking at myself, I don't have any extraordinary strength. They were all waiting for me to say something. But nothing came out. I was still trying to believe what they were saying.

"We know this is a lot of information to absorb at one time, but there really isn't a *best time* for this sort of thing." Alain said softly. He squeezed my hand. I could not feel any extra strength from his grip.

"So basically, you just told me that because of me, my parents were killed. On top of that, my aura killed my adopted mother, father, and my boyfriend Peter. The only person's death I'm not responsible for is my Uncle Josh. We are aliens from another planet. There are other aliens hunting us. Also I can heal people." I said slowly and sadly. I leaned forward and placed my hands over my face.

"Gena, you can not blame yourself. Your adoptive parents and Peter would have died anyway. Plus, you did not know that you could affect their lives that way. I am sure that you gave them more joy with you being in their lives than not." Aunt Madeline assured. She came by my side and rubbed my back. "Aura or not, you have managed to fill a hole that had been empty in this family ever since your mother died. Your presence here has given us much to be happy about."

"I second that and I don't like being called aliens." voiced Justin. He came over and gave me a bear hug. "Don't be sad cousin. Everything that happened is in the past. Now you're here and we want you to stay. That's all that matters." He stated.

"Well, I didn't know what to expect. I'm not ready to move here. I have so many things to deal with back home. When Uncle Josh died, I did not have time to take care of all his things before I came here. I have to go back and settle his estate, than I can come back here." I stuttered.

"Gena, we want you here with us. We lost you once; we are NOT going to lose you again. Plus I can't bear the thought of you living alone and defenseless." Aunt Idelle stated.

"Thank you, I do want to stay. I don't think I was in danger in Indiana. I just have to settle his estate and than *really move my things here*. Also I have to finish school." I told them.

"Well, you're in luck. Blaine is a family lawyer. He can take care of things for you from here. We can make arrangements for all of your things to be shipped here. You can finish your schooling here at Peterson Academy. You may not have been in danger in Indiana but you have no family there. You have family here and we've not had you for eighteen years. We want to make up for that." Alain explained.

"Is there something you need right now?" Uncle Rolfe asked.

A little embarrassed by my selfishness I whispered "My bike."

"You want us to ship your bike here. The Sears Roebuck catalog has tons of bicycles and even tricycles for you to choose from. Hell, I can probably carry you around faster than a bike. For your homecoming, I'll buy you a new one." Justin said laughing at me.

"It's not a bicycle, Justin; it's a Ducati Monster S4R Testastretta with a 998cc V-Twin engine and 130Hp." I said sarcastically.

"You have a Ducati? No way. Dad, you can't say no now, she's got a Ducati." Lawrence complained.

"I knew you weren't just any girl. How long have you been riding?" Preston asked.

"Since I was 14 years old" I bragged.

"I want to see you ride. Dad when can we get her bike here? Do you want me to take care of it?" Justin asked.

"We'll get Bradley on it as soon as possible." Uncle Rolfe said.

"We have to get you registered for school here. We can do that tomorrow." Lauren said.

Everyone started planning my life in Inuvik. Lauren, Dana, Julianne, and Aimee were in charge of my shopping needs. Justin could not get over that I can ride a motorcycle. Lawrence was so jealous. He wants desperately to ride my bike. Lawrence questioned me over and over regarding the torque and engine. Justin, Cory, Michael and Preston wanted to have a party to introduce me to everyone before school started.

"I have another question." I cautiously announced.

"Go ahead honey." Aunt Madeline said.

"Few days before I called you, someone came to my house and delivered plane tickets to Inuvik and my passport. I only saw the deliveryman but I did not see the person in the limo. The deliveryman was really big and looked Samoan. Does this mean anything?" I asked.

Everyone in the room looked at each other. It did not look like they knew anymore than I did.

"I want to make things perfectly clear to everyone in this room. Gena's aura is not to be discussed with anyone outside of this family. Until her senses can protect her, she is at great risk, someone evidently knew of her existence in Indiana." Uncle Rolfe warned.

"And also there was a key in the jewelry box." I pulled the key out of my pants pocket. "Does anyone know what's it to?" I asked.

"It's the key to your parent's house. It is near here. We can take you there in the morning. We all built our homes nearby." Uncle Rolfe replied.

"I would like that. Thank you." I responded

"Gena, a bunch of us are going out to Tuk Beach for a bonfire. We usually hang out, eat smores, do some kissing," Justin stated. "Do you want to come along?"

"Justin, you're so stupid. Gena, you don't have to go. It's usually all the guys in the clan out there raising hell. We don't normally go but if you want, we'll go with you." Lauren stated.

"Everyone will be there. I've never been but it could be fun. We'll introduce you so when we start school you won't feel so awkward." Dana said.

Everyone would be there. I thought about the beautiful blue eyes. Well here's my chance to ask him about the symbol on the card. "Hey, I'm new here; I'll do whatever you guys want. Why don't we go in separate cars just in case we get bore and want to leave." I replied. I was excited at the prospect of seeing Corin.

"I like you already. She's a sport. I can't wait to see you on a motorcycle. I bet you look hot." Justin said. He wrapped his arm around my neck and said "I'm glad you're here."

"We have to change; we'll meet you there, Justin." Aimee stated.

All the girls rushed me upstairs to change. "Okay, Gena you first. Wear jeans and something warm. The weather changes quickly here." Lauren said. I was so glad she said jeans. That I can do. I quickly grabbed my favorite pair of jeans and two long sleeve tees and layered them.

"Will this do?" I jumped out from my walk-in closet.

"Wow that looks great. How did you do that so fast? Lauren you should take some notes." Julianne laughed.

"Well, it's easy to look great when you look as good as Gena does. I was not so lucky, so I require lots of work." Lauren replied.

"Lauren, you're kidding right. I can spend all day and still not compare to you." I told her.

"Well she does spend all day, that's why she is just *gorgeous darling*." Aimee joked.

We all burst out laughing over Aimee's display of a Greek goddess' posture. It felt so strange to be this happy. I'd never had any siblings. I was an only child. It felt lonely sometimes but my parents always doted on me so I never felt like I was missing anything. Then, there was Uncle Josh. He was a single man. He spent a lot of time with me until I started dating Peter. I didn't have lots of close girlfriends. I hung out more with Peter's friends, than my own.

Weird, how that part of my life seem so distant now. This family is so much different than my other family. I now have grandparents, which I did not have before.I have uncles and aunts galore. I have cousins, all so close to my age, that it is just too easy to be happy.

I have just inherited a large loving family of aliens.

Chapter Six

"Mom, Dad, we're going to the house to get change. We'll see you later." Dana yelled.

"Don't stay out too late. Have fun girls." Aunt Renee responded.

We all exited the front door, just to see Justin, Cory, Michael, Lawrence, and Preston piled into a big red flatbed truck. It was all decked out with every accessory you could put on a F150 truck. Just to be a jerk, Justin turned on the high beams right at us.

"Justin, you moron, stop" Lauren complained.

"We'll see you guys out there. Don't take too long. Lauren." He chided.

It was just interesting to see the siblings pick on each other. I never had that so I have to be more alert and on guard when Justin was around. He particularly loves to put people on the spot. We all cramped into Lauren's little red convertible sports car. We left the Burren estate and drove 2 minutes down the main road and pulled into another gated entrance. I can't believe we even got into a car for that. We could've easily walked.

"Okay, Dana, we'll be back to pick you up." Lauren stated.

We repeated the same process to get to Aimee's house.

Once we got to Lauren's house, we drove through the gated entrance and got out. This house looked similar to my grandparents' house except not as big and grand. It was a smaller version of the original. Not that this house was so small. It was huge compared to most homes.

Lauren took some cues from Julianne and was dressed in under 30 minutes. To me she still looked overly dressed for a bonfire.

We retraced the route to pick up Dana and Aimee.

"Lauren, you know we're going to the beach right?" Aimee commented.

"Shut-up Aimee, I was under a lot of pressure to be quick." she replied.

We drove out pass Inuvik, and headed north. After 20 minutes we arrived at the beach. It was already quite dark but some people were already there so the bonfire was already roaring. She intentional parked as far away from the beach as possible so sand would not be tracked into her car. We crossed the parking lot and headed toward the boardwalk. The planks were so uneven; you had to be careful not to trip. Laurens' heels were not so kind. She had to remove them.

"Hey, stick close to us; we'll introduce you as we go okay." Aimee said. "Watch out, some of them will bite." She laughed.

"Well we'll just have to bite back." Lauren declared. We made it over to the fire without spraining anything. It was amazing to see. Against the darkness, there was this huge bonfire, but the fire was not orange, it was more blue and red streaks jumping upward. It looked magical. I whispered "Oh wow, the fire is different." I whispered.

"It's the salt in the wood. Hi, my name is Max." he said

Lauren came up and said "Hey Max, this is my cousin Gena." I watched her from the corner of my eye, she liked this guy Max. Her body language went from confident to shy and nervous. It's amazing what attraction does to people. I just hope I'm not as obvious.

"So, where are you from, Gena?" he asked.

"I'm from Crew, Indiana. I just got here today." I answered. I was not really paying much attention to him. My eyes darted around looking for Corin. When I didn't see him, I felt a little disappointed.

"Are you just visiting or moving here." He asked. He was a good looking guy, He had messy brown hair, blue eyes and he was rather tall. He face was nice to look at. I can see why Lauren liked him.

"Well, I didn't plan on moving here, but because everyone's been so nice. I decided why not, plus they're growing on me." I smiled.

"Well welcome to Inuvik." he started to ask me something before a bunch of guys came up and barged between us.

"Hey Max, don't hog her all to yourself. Let us have a turn. Hi! I'm Steven." he looked into my eyes. He took my hand and kissed the back of it lightly. I was a little embarrassed by his gentlemanly gesture.

"Guys, back away from her, you're going to scare her back to where she came from?" this coming from another guy further away. "Hi! I'm Joseph." He yelled.

"Hey, everyone, this is our cousin Gena, she is from Indiana. She just moved here today. Don't do anything stupid because she will be attending school with us this fall." Dana announced.

"Thanks, Dana. That was really subtle." Aimee said.

"Well it's better than her having to repeat everything over and over." Dana explained.

"Hey are we going to play football or are you guys just going to stand there drooling over my cousin all night." Justin yelled from the other end of the bonfire.

"Well, that was really nice Justin, you've just manage to put her on the spot… *Idiot.* Sorry Gena. We are civilized we just don't show it often enough." Lauren stated.

"That's okay, A little uncomfortable but okay." I laughed. I was just being pleasant. Since Corin wasn't here I didn't have much interest in being here. I'll just bide my time and fake being tired later. I looked around at each and every one of them. *Why are they even interested in me?* Looking at the girls, they each had differences in their hair color or style but they were all beautiful, stylish, and flawless. The guys were just the same. They were all tall, strong, muscular not a single one of them had weight problems, or acne or any deformities. The really popular girls from Crew High couldn't compare here. I was super plain compare to these people. This was going to be one uncomfortable Senior Year for me. *How did such a small crappy town attract so many beautiful people?*

The girls gravitated toward the fire while the guys played football. The fire was nice and warm.

As I sat there in front of the bonfire lost in my thoughts, I could hear Justin talking to some guy behind me. He was going on about his fiancée. I didn't bother turning around because I didn't want Justin embarrassing me again. I just listened.

"Justin, man you're pretty lucky. When is the big day?" He asked.

"We haven't made that decision yet but I can't wait. She can't travel here yet, that scene in the Quebec Territory really scared her family, I may have to move out there or bring her here. I don't care where I am as long as it's with her. I have to say Mark you look worn out, how's your wedding plans going?" Justin stated.

"It's going. She changes her mind constantly. If it was up to me I'd elope." Mark answered.

"Hey let me introduce you to my cousin Gena." He said.

"Oh, let me go get Ella. *Ella!!! Come over here woman.*" He yelled. They both laughed.

"You're going to get your ass kicked later." Justin commented.

I could hear them walking towards me, so I turned around and stood up.

"Hey, my name is Gena Reynolds." I said as I raised my hand up to Justin's face "You've done enough, thanks Justin." He roared out laughing. He bear hugged me and swung me around. "Oh you know you love me." He grinned.

"Hi Gena, my name is Mark. This is my fiancee Ella. Welcome to Inuvik."

"Put her down you idiot. You have embarrassed her enough today." Aimee said angrily at Justin.

"Hey Mark, where is Corin?" Lauren asked. When I heard the name I quickly looked at Mark. I didn't see it before because Justin was distracting me but Mark had to be Corin's older brother. They had very similar features.

"Oh, he may come by later. I think he's a little depressed over the Quebec Territory thing. He was asking stupid questions earlier, all depressed and stuff. He wouldn't talk about it. I guess we'll just have to wait until he debriefed Rolfe." He replied.

I sat back down. I was listening to Ella talk about her wedding plans. We had to move over to the opposite side of the bonfire because the wind was starting to blow the heat in our direction.

"Gena, our engagement party is next weekend. You are officially invited." she announced.

"Oh, thank you but I'm not sure about what's going on next weekend, plus I don't know anyone here." I replied

"Oh, if you need a date, I bet any one of these guys would love to take you." She assures.

"No, that's not it. We'll wait and see." I said. The only guy I really wanted to take me was not even here.

Off the corner of my eyes, I saw Corin walking toward Justin with another girl. They were holding hands. My heart sank. I didn't bother to look up. I turned inward toward Ella, pretending to listen to her talk about china patterns. Meanwhile, I felt like an idiot. I must have gotten all the signals wrong. I listened in on Justin's conversation with Corin.

"Hey man, hey Natalie. Glad you could make it." He said.

"Yeah, congrats man. I heard." Corin said quietly.

"You are so lucky, Justin." proclaimed Natalie.

"Hey, I heard it was really bad in Quebec. You got to give us details man." Justin begged.

"Not now man, I'll tell you guys tomorrow." Corin said.

"Oh, hey have you guys met Gena?" Justin said with excitement.

"Yeah, we met on the plane this afternoon." Corin said flatly. He did not sound excited about meeting me. I must have had dreamt the whole thing.

"She's great! Huh?" Justin bragged. God he was always going to embarrass me in anyway he can.

"Yeah, you guys are really lucky." Corin whispered.

"Yeah, well you know we just keep finding them and adding them to our family." Justin laughed.

"Well, I haven't met her. I'll be back Corin" Natalie said

I could see her skipping in the sand towards us.

"Hey, you're Gena right. I'm Natalie. Welcome to Inuvik."

Of course, she was prettier than any of the other girls. She had long beautiful silky blond hair that ended above her waist. Her eyes were so blue it almost looked artificial. She looked like an angel.

"Hi, it's nice to meet you, Natalie." I said nicely.

I shook her hand. She sat next to me asking Ella about her wedding plans. I glanced toward the direction she came from and saw Corin standing on the other side of the bonfire. He looked agitated. His hands were stuffed in his pocket. I saw him sit down, wrapping his arms around his legs. He was staring into the fire.

"Well Gena, I'll see you around okay." Natalie said before she got up and went to sit next to Corin. I nodded and smiled at her.

I kept myself turned toward Ella and Aimee. I pretended to be interested. I was caught off guard when I peaked and saw Natalie snuggled up to Corin, and then she kissed him on his neck. That was too much for me to handle.

"Hey Lauren, I think my headache is back. I'm just going to go sit in the car. I'll just wait there until you guys are ready to leave." I whispered.

"Oh, if you're ready to leave, let's go. I've had enough sand and smoke for one night. Let me go get Dana." She responded.

"Oh, don't ruin her fun. I can just wait." I said.

"Please Gena, fun is shopping and more shopping. This is not our idea of fun. We'll meet you at the car. Don't tell Justin, he'll do something stupid." she winked. Aimee confirmed.

"I have to go say goodbye to Max." Lauren said.

I got up and walk toward the boardwalk. I walked carefully on each plank. When I got to the parking lot, I stopped to empty the sand from my shoes. I made my way to the car. I stood there next to the car with my hand massaging my temples. I felt stupid and duped. *Wow, within 24 hours you've managed to have your heartbroken by a nice boy from a stupid town from nowhere with a population of 3500. Great start*

My thoughts were disrupted by the sound of sand grinding in the pavement. I turned and looked up and saw Corin standing 8 feet behind me. He looked defeated and remorseful. His hands were in his pockets. He was probably here to apologize. I could let him apologize but maybe it was my fault too. I was stupid and vulnerable when we met. I saw him walking towards me. I raised my hand up "Corin, its okay. Nothing happened. Let's just forget it, okay?" I said. I was going to take the high road. My pride was in jeopardy.

He stood there staring back at me. We were disrupted by someone coming so I turned around and got in the car.

"Sorry Gena, oh hey Corin. I couldn't get Max to give me the keys. Let's go. Justin is holding Aimee captive, so she will just have to go home with someone else." Lauren chattered.

I turned to smile at Corin than turn back. We managed to pick up Dana at the other end of the parking lot. I saw in the rearview mirror that he just stood there. He was probably stunned by me letting him off the hook. I laughed, I might have lost the fight but I definitely won this round.

Lauren chattered all the way back to the estate about Max. It didn't bother me because it made the trip much quicker. She dropped me off at the front door.

"Hey we'll see you tomorrow. We've got to get you registered for school. Also your wardrobe has got to be ready before school starts." they waved and sped off.

I entered the mansion. It was pretty late so I was trying to be super quiet.

"You're home early? Did you have fun?" my grandfather asked.

"I had lots of fun. It's just been a really long day." I responded.

"Gena, I'm really glad you're home." he said. He looked so calm and peaceful.

"I'm glad to be home also, grandfather." I gently hugged him and continued up the stairs to my room.

I was exhausted. As I lay in bed, I tried to summarize everything that happened today. I didn't get too far before I fell asleep. I woke up a bit disoriented. It felt like I slept for days. My body was heavy and achy. My arms and legs moved like they were weighed down with lead. I looked over to the clock on the dresser, *August 27th Friday 11:30 am.*

I quickly got up, showered, and dressed. I wanted to go see my parents' home.

As I descended the stairs, I was stopped by the familiar voice that I wanted to avoid. I didn't want him to see me, so I darted back up the stairs. I'll just wait here until he leaves. Just when I thought I was able to escape being seen I heard my name being called.

"Gena! We have to get you registered today. Come on!" Lauren yelled.

"I'm coming. Just let me get my purse." I yelled back.

I rushed down the steps hoping that he was gone and we didn't have to see each other. As I got to the last step I could see him standing at the door. Our eyes locked, but then we both looked away.

I walked toward the door and past him without looking at him. I sidled against the door frame to avoid touching him "Excuse me, Corin." I whispered.

His hand shot out and grabbed my arm. "Wait, Gena, can we talk?" he said silently.

"No, Corin. Really it's okay. I have to go." I took my free hand and pulled his hand away from my arm. "See you around."

He stood there for awhile than turned to go inside.

I got into Lauren's car. We drove off toward the school. "What's with Corin?" she asked.

"I don't know, maybe it's the Quebec Territory thing." I lied.

"I feel sorry for him sometimes. Daddy always sends him to check out the scenes left behind after an attack. They say it is because he is the fastest, so if he had to get away he could do it. God knows what he has seen." She stated.

I pretended to look disinterested. Thinking about him being near the hunters made me anxious. What if something ever happened to him? I had to stop thinking that. He belonged to someone else. His business was none of my business.

"So, what's the name of the high school?" I asked.

"It is Peterson Academy. It may sound special but it is the only school around, so everyone goes there. The senior class has 165 students. How many people were at your last school?" she asked.

"Crew High School had 1400 students. The senior class made up 540 of that." I laughed.

She laughed. "Oh my, you're going to feel claustrophobic here." She said.

We got to the school within 5 minutes. She wasn't kidding when she said claustrophobic. The school consisted of 2 three story buildings and a gym. She got me to the office to fill out some paperwork. All of the classes that I wanted to take were full, so I had to settle with the leftovers. With classes like Home Economics and Human Sexuality, I should graduate with honors.

As we left the school, I thought of my parents' home. "Lauren, can you take me to my parents' house?" I asked.

"Sure, are you sure you don't want my Dad to take you?" she asked.

"No, I think he is busy with the Quebec Territory thing." I explained.

It took us a few minutes before we were in front a beautifully custom built house. The house wasn't shaped like any of the other homes. It was stylish and modern.

"You know, your dad was an architect." She said silently.

I got out of the car and headed toward the front door. I took the key that I had buried in my jeans and inserted it into the deadbolt key hole. It turned easily so I pushed the door forward and went inside.

I stood in the foyer and looked all around.

"Gena, I'll come back to pick you up at 2pm for lunch." she yelled from her car.

"Okay, thanks." I replied. I closed the door behind me and consciously locked the door.

I turned the switch on the wall, and to my surprise all the curtains pulled back and allowed natural sunlight to come in. I walked around the first floor exploring each room, taking my time. I looked at the picture of my parents on the mantle above the fireplace. I could see my features in both of them. I had his brown eyes. They were a very attractive couple. Their death seemed more nonsensical now that I can associate a face to their death. I continued looking around the room. The colors were all light whites, blues, and crèmes. The living room walls were glass with curtains built inside two glass panels. My hands brushed over the crème sofas and rich dark mahogany shelves. I continued into the dining room. *Table for six* They wanted to fill this house with a lot of kids. I continued into the library. Sitting in the middle of this room was a grand black piano. *This must've been hers.* I sat down and looked at the piece of music that rest on the stand. *This was probably what she last played.* I touched the keys. I looked over at the music sheet. Slowly my hands started playing to the notes on the music sheet. It was crude attempt at this beautiful piece, but I knew she would like for me to learn this and play it well.

I continued into the kitchen. It faced the backyard. Again, the walls were made from glass. The kitchen was made up of rich mahogany and stainless steel. I stood out in front of the glass wall. Looking down I could see the entire back yard. It had been well maintained.

I retraced my steps and went up the stairs. Again the same mahogany, adorned the stairs. I could see standing at the top of the stairs; there were four bedrooms and a master bedroom. I entered the master bedroom and took in the beauty of this room. It was like being in the sky. There were no walls, just the glass and the glass had a hint of blue, which reminded me of the sky. The large bed in the middle of the room was white and soft. The rich mahogany made up the shelving. The master bathroom resembled the bedroom.

I lay on their bed. I took in their smell. I couldn't tell whether this was their scent or just the clean sheets. There was a humongous walk-in closet that looked more like a dressing room. In the middle of this room was a large leather ottoman. The shelves were of the same dark mahogany. You can live in this room. All their clothes were gone. I guess someone decided after 18 years it had to go. To the left of the closet was a grand master bathroom that was big as the one in my grandparents' home. There was a huge jet tub and a shower room that was big enough for 5 people. The giant vanity hosted two sinks and a long vanity cushion sofa.

I left the master bedroom and found myself walking towards another room. It was a nursery. *My nursery of* course, she decorated it in every pink there was. *She knew I was a girl.* I started to cry. Even though I didn't know them, I missed them. They risked their life for me. I sat in the rocking chair. It felt so comfortable being here. *This was my home. This would be where they wanted me to be.*

I decided I wanted to move in here. As much as I loved being at my grandparents house, this is where I really wanted to be. I sat in the nursery for quite sometime. I didn't realize that Lauren was at the front door waiting for me. She must've honked three times before I could hear her.

I went downstairs and turned the switch and watched as the curtains move all around enclosing the house in darkness.

I exited the front and got into the car.

"Lauren, do you think anyone would be upset if I wanted to move in to my parents' house?" I asked.

"Gena, no one here will deny you anything. They may ask that you spend dinnertime with them, though." She replied.

As we pulled up the front gate, I noticed that Corin's silver car was gone. Well that is one thing I don't have to worry about right now.

"We have to get to work on your wardrobe as soon as possible since school starts Monday. After dinner, let's go over to my place and start ordering stuff." Lauren babbled.

I didn't even bother arguing with her. She was going to change my wardrobe whether I like it or not. "Yeah sure" I said flatly.

Lunch with this family was a big fanfare. There were so many people that it felt more like you're eating at a restaurant than at home. During lunch I asked if I could move into my parents' home and everyone was silent for a few seconds, before they all started offering to help me move in. Lauren was right; they would not deny me anything. The aunts decided to update all the appliances in my home. I heard them talking about stocking the pantry and providing me with linens and stuff. It was really strange how accommodating this family was. Once they decide on something, they dive right in and made sure everything was taken care of. I really didn't have to do anything. When they were thoroughly satisfied with making sure I was taken care of; the conversation changed to the

Quebec Territory incident. They did not keep any secrets in this family. Everyone was informed.

"I am confident they will not attack us when we are strong, that would be suicide for them. But I still want your aura kept a secret. I don't want you to be a target for them." Uncle Rolfe warned.

Everyone agreed. If I was suppose to be scared I wasn't. I felt safe with them.

After lunch everyone scattered to what they were doing before. Lauren, Aimee, Dana and I left to go back to Laurens' place. They went on the internet and ordered all kinds of clothes for me. Everything was necessary. It was so weird to be dolled up by others. I just sat there and let them enjoy themselves at my expense. All I could think about was moving into my parents' home.

"Gena, this is the last weekend before school starts, what do you want to do?" Dana asked.

"We can have a slumber party at my house." I said.

"Oh my God, that's a great idea. Can we invite all the girls?" Aimee asked.

"We can help move you in and have a slumber too." Lauren said.

"You can invite whoever you want." I said.

They each got on their cell phone and started calling people. Within ten minutes plans were made.

Girls Slumber Party at my house Saturday.

Chapter Seven

What did she mean by nothing happened, let's just forget it? How can she think nothing happened? This was a blow to my heart. I could tell she was irritated when Natalie kissed me but why was she acting this way. What about her and Justin? How does she think I feel?

I didn't want to debrief today. I just want to see her. If she wasn't staying here I would have just told them what they wanted thru the phone and stayed home. I hate seeing stupid Justin. I couldn't believe he stayed at the beach when she went home. He doesn't deserve her, I do. Damn it, I do.

This house used to not bother me but now I find it so hard to come here. It has been 24 hours since I've met her and everything around me laid in turmoil.

"Hey, Corin, come on in." Rolfe said.

"Thanks Rolfe, is everyone here?" I said. My eyes were searching for her.

"Hey Corin, what's up?" Lauren said.

"Hey Lauren, just here to debrief about you know the Quebec Territory thing." I answered preoccupied.

"Gena! We have to get you registered today. Come on!" she yelled up the stairs.

"Lauren, why is Gena going to school here, I thought she was going back to Indiana?" I was curious about the sudden change in plans.

"Corin, she is not going back to Indiana. I have to go, see you later." She responded.

So, she is staying. That changes things. I looked up and saw her coming towards me. Wow, her eyes will haunt me again. I wasn't going to move away from the door. I wanted her to come to me and maybe I could touch her even if it was just by accident.

"Excuse me, Corin." She whispered. The way she said my name sounded so beautiful coming from her lips. I couldn't help myself.

I reach up and grab her arm "Wait, Gena, can we talk?" I whispered. The scent coming from her body inundated my senses. Her hair smelled so good.

"No, Corin, Really it's okay. I have to go."

What is okay? That I suffered? I felt desperate when she pulled my hand away. Her touch sent waves of sensation to my heart. I can't keep letting her leave me this way. I watched her get in the car and sped off with Lauren. I can't go on like this. I was thinking about her constantly. If I wasn't thinking about her I was dreaming about her. I dreamt about being with her, touching her, loving her. How much more can I handle without losing my mind? I was being destroyed from within and I enjoyed it. Torturing myself over her was better than not having her in my life at all. Would that be enough? Can I abstained myself from her if she was near? What are my options? Can I love her at a distance? Can I watched her belong to someone else, love someone else? No I can not. I have to talk to Justin.

"Hey Corin, don't just stand there. Come on in."

"Hey Preston, is everyone ready?" I replied.

"Damn, Corin you look sick. How bad was it?" he asked.

"It is pretty bad." I replied. I wasn't talking about the death and destruction I saw in the Quebec Territory. I was referring to the slow torture of my heart from a beautiful brunette with haunting brown eyes.

We walked into the conference room. After I gave them a detail account of what I witnessed, they started discussing future plans. I zoned them out. I excused myself than left. I looked around for Justin. I can feel my heart racing. I was ready to fight Justin. I can feel the hostility rising in me. I found him talking on his cell phone in the backyard. I hesitated confronting him. I needed to calm down. I went back inside and left through the front door. I needed to get some fresh air to think this through. I got in my car and drove around for a few minutes. I was willing to fight Justin for her. Did she want me to? Would I hurt her by hurting Justin? I found myself back at the Burren's estate driveway. I saw him standing in the driveway talking on his cell phone again. This was a sign. Talk to him.

"Justin! I need to talk to you." I yelled.

"Hey, just the man I was looking for. My dad wants to see us. It looks like you were right. There are survivors. We are rounding up a posse to go get them and bring them back here safely. Come on, they're waiting for you." He informed me as he continued back inside.

Frustrated I followed him back into the mansion.

"Dad! I found him." He yelled.

"Good, Corin! I want you and Justin to head towards the Manitoba province. Preston, you and Tristan will scout out the Saskatchewan Province. Mark, that leaves you and Max to scout out the Alberta province. Michael and Cory have already left to check out British Columbia. I want you guys to meet back in Yellowknife. Find them and bring them back here safely. Whatever happens, stay together and be safe." he ordered.

As frustrated as I was I knew this needed to be done plus I would be alone to question Justin.

"Corin, I know you're fast but you haven't seen me lately. My aura has been soaring. I know I can keep up." Justin bragged.

I rolled my eyes at him. *Eat my dust!* I thought to myself. "Come on, the sooner we get to them the better. Plus I got school on Monday." I warned. *Also the sooner I can get back to Gena.*

We all got into our cars and raced to Yellowknife. Traveling at over 160mph, we can make it to Yellowknife in almost 4 hours. That was a long time in the car with Justin. *Perfect!*

We all agreed to leave our cars in Yellowknife and go the rest by foot. Where we were heading, we probably couldn't get to by car anyway.

As soon as we got in the car Justin was fiddling with my stereo. Justin was a couple of years older than I, but age did not make much of a difference between us.

"Man, this is a nice stereo. Did it come with the car?" he asked.

"No, Michelle and Mark got it for me last Christmas. Don't you remember? Ella and Mark got in that big fight and she threw soda at him and it got all over my stereo, ruined the whole thing." I reminded him.

"Oh, yeah! I'm glad I don't have to worry about that crap. Hey, what happened to you last night? I turned around and you were gone." He asked.

"I was just tired." I answered flatly. He seemed confident about his relationship with Gena. I was beginning to feel self doubt.

"Really, that's the first time I've ever heard you say that." He replied.

"I had a lot on my mind." I stated quietly. *Yeah, I was thinking of your fiancée. I was thinking of how I was going to steal her away from you.*

"Yeah, I bet it was pretty gruesome in Quebec Territory. I'm sorry you had to go there alone. We would go with you but you're just so damn fast. But you know, since my engagement I've noticed that I am faster. I don't mean to brag but lately I have been flying. This *concero flamma* thing really heightens your aura." He stated.

I just sat there. So she really is his *concero flamma.* Only your soul mate can heighten your aura. Was he really faster or is he just bragging? What about me? My feelings for her have to mean something.

"What's going on with you and Natalie? I saw you guys getting pretty close last night. I have to tell you man, I didn't see that coming." He asked.

"Nothing man, she's always had a thing for me, but I just don't see her in the same way. Last night, Mark asked me to pick her up and she probably thought of it as a date. She kissed me, but I told her I didn't want her that way. *Yeah, I want your fiancée.* She got pretty pissed." I recalled.

"Yeah, she is really pretty and all but she doesn't do anything for me either." he replied.

I need to get my head straight before I talk to him about Gena. I wasn't sure if this was a good idea right now. We needed to concentrate on the danger ahead of us. If the survivors left Quebec Territory and made it to Manitoba, most likely we would encounter them and the hunters. Justin and I were sent to the closest province from Quebec Territory because Rolfe knew there was a good chance they would be in Manitoba. They would've been traveling for 36 hours by now. If they had injuries or if they were weak than my estimate is that they were in Manitoba too.

"Hey, man. Why don't you get some sleep? You're going to need all the strength you can get if you're going to keep up with me." I commented.

"I'm too juiced up to sleep right now. Anyway I told you ever since I met Rachel, my aura has been soaring. I bet I could take you." He laughed.

"You mean Gena, right!" I corrected him angrily. I was disgusted. How could he get her name wrong? What an asshole. He doesn't deserve her. I felt a great urge to knock his teeth back into his throat. You can't say "I do" when you don't have a voice. I laughed at the thought.

"How did you know about Gena? Who told you?" he said seriously. He almost looked angry.

"What do you mean? You're the one who told everyone!" I said. Dumb ass. He himself had been flaunting his love for her in my face all this time.

"I did not tell anyone about Gena. I would not risk her life. You tell me who told you, Corin!" he exclaimed.

"Risk her life? What the hell are you talking about? What are you planning to do to her?" I questioned. Was he going to hurt her? I would kill him before I would let that happen. Who is this guy sitting here?

"I don't plan on doing anything to her! What are you talking about? We were told to keep her aura a secret but evidently someone told you. Who told you?" He yelled.

He was really beginning to irritate me. "Why do you have to keep her aura a secret, everyone knows that if she's REALLY your *concero flamma*, that your aura will change. She is your *concero flamma*, right?" I asked. This was the question I have being dying to ask him. His answer here will either hurt me or free me. If he said she was not his soul mate than I will tell him right now that she was mine. If he believes that she is truly his soul mate than I will have to rethink my plans.

"What the hell are you talking about? Did you hit a tree while running?" he asked. He looked disgusted with me.

"I'm talking about you and Gena, you know your fiancée?" I can't believe I have to keep reminding him about her.

"Gena is not my fiancée, she is my cousin. My fiancée's name is Rachel. She is from Colorado. Where are you getting your information dumbass, Hey watch out!" he yelled.

I quickly jerked the steering wheel back to recover control of the car. His words hit me like a ton of bricks. "Gena is not your fiancée?" I was so excited I could barely contain myself.

"No, she is my cousin. Who told you she was my fiancée?" he asked. He was disgusted again.

"Forget it; I think it was a bunch of misunderstanding." I was so relieved. All this time, I tortured myself with the thought of her and Justin. My heart restarted. I can feel the life in me coming back. The heaviness that has been dragging me all this time was lifted in the instant he said *no.*

"You still haven't told me who told you about her aura!" he questioned.

"No one told me anything about her aura. When you spoke about your aura, I thought she was the one that strengthen your aura." I explained.

"So you don't know anything about her aura?" he asked.

"I don't know specifically what you mean but why would her aura risk her life?" I questioned.

"I can't talk about that man." He answered.

"Since when does your family keep secrets from the clan?" I asked. I was angry. Anything that risked her life I wanted to know about.

"It's just a family thing. It would not risk the clan. It's for her safety. Don't ask me anymore man." He said quietly.

"I have the right to know, Justin. I'm always the one sent to assess the safety of our clan. I have the right to know if someone in our clan is being targeted specifically." I stated angrily. I can tell I was getting angry at him. I wanted to know if someone was after her. I would kill anyone who tried to hurt her. If I had to hunt this planet for them I would.

"Corin, I know you're mad about being left out, but this is really a family thing." He said.

"I still want to know, Justin." I said. He was really pissing me off. If I have to pound it out of him I would stop the car right now.

"Look, I'll tell you this much, Gena is special. OK." he said.

"That I already know, Justin. You're not telling me anything new." I stared at him.

"Wait a minute, do you like Gena?" he straightened himself up from his seat. His face lifted up like he had just discovered a rare item.

"No, I love her." I confessed.

"Man, I knew it." Justin exclaimed. "I told Preston that your personality would be perfect for her. You guys are both quiet, serious, and do you know she rides a motorcycle? Not just any motorcycle but a *Ducati*. She is no dummy either; she knows the engine, torque and all that stuff. She's pretty proud about it." He continued.

"Don't change the subject man, you still haven't told me why her aura is a danger to her?" I sternly replied. I wasn't going to let him drop this matter. Whoever or whatever wants to hurt her concerns me.

"Do you really love her?" he asked quietly.

"That is none of your business but I think I already answered that?" I responded. He was stalling. There was something he didn't want to share with me.

"You know what I mean. Do you really love her like…soul mate love?" he questioned.

"I really don't know if it is or not but I met her on the flight from

Quebec Territory to Inuvik. The instant I saw her I was drawn to her immediately. You know I don't talk all that much but I found myself asking her all kinds of stupid things. She probably wanted me to shut up because she was having a headache but I could not stop from talking to her. Ever since meeting her, I have not gone a single minute not thinking of her." I confessed. It sounded so pathetic. But it was all true.

"Wow that is a lot coming from you. It sounds like you've found her. Man, you're the luckiest bastard. You're nineteen, and you didn't even have to travel around to find her. She practically came to you. I'm 21 and just when I was going to give up, I just happened upon Rachel by accident." He stated.

"You're still ignoring the main question. Justin, if she is in danger I have to know. Nothing can ever happen to her as long as I am alive. Think about Rachel. What would you do to protect her?" I reminded him.

He looked at me for sometime. I waited patiently. The wait was killing me. Finally he shared "Gena is my late Aunt Alexandria's daughter."

"How can that be? I thought she was killed before she could birth." I asked. I remember the stories told about her death. How the hunters hunted her and her husband down. I remember being told no one survived and even the Roese family was all killed.

"Well, that was true up until Thursday. Somehow she was birthed before Alexandria died. Someone took her and fled. She was given to a human couple. They adopted her and cared for her until they died. She then went to live with her uncle in Indiana. When she turned eighteen she was given Alexandria's jewelry box." He stated.

"Did my dad make the box?" I asked sadly.

"Yeah, so you know she's got to be Alexandria's daughter." He confirmed.

My dad's company, Randall Security Company, mainly builds security rooms or "panic rooms" for high risk influential people but we also manufacture unique security items for our kind. William Burren requested a jewelry box made for his wife as a wedding gift. It was adorned with four 5-carat diamonds at each corner. The box was made specifically for her and the only way it could be open was with her blood. She loved it so much she had one commissioned for each of her daughters, Idelle and Alexandria. Idelle's was adorned with emeralds and Alexandria's was adorned with sapphires. These were the colors of their eyes. Each box was also equipped with a blood scanner that will only allow the owner's blood DNA to assess the box. The fact that Gena was able to assess the box means that she had to carry some of Alexandria's specific DNA.

"Who gave her the box?" I asked. I was trying to take all this in at one time. To know that she was living in Indiana all this time unprotected was unbearable. She was my soul mate; she could have been killed before I could ever meet her. She didn't even know that she was in danger.

"She said it was left to her by her adopted parents. They told her that a woman name Alexandria Burren gave her to them." He recanted.

"How can that be, they saw the destruction left behind at the Roese' place. They even found Alexandria's and Daniel's remains. It was tested. The test confirmed it was her. There was also a fetus left in her womb." I questioned.

"Hey, we are just as shocked as you are but look at her. My grandfather almost fainted when he heard her voice on the phone. My grandmother hasn't stop crying. Even my dad is convinced that she is Alexandria's daughter, and you know how skeptical he is." He said.

I never really looked that closely at Alexandria's portraits but now that he pointed it out I can see the family resemblance. She didn't have blond hair like Aimee, Lauren or Julianne but she had her mother's facial features and her father's chocolate brown hair and brown eyes. They all shared the same contours and full lips but Gena's was smaller and softer. Of course that is just because I've been dreaming about those lips every minute since I met her.

"So is Alexandria alive?" I asked.

"My father thinks that someone helped Alexandria birthed and than took the baby away." He said.

"But they found a fetus in her womb." I said skeptically.

"Well Alain has two theories about that. He said by looking at her injuries, she was probably dead before she could birth but someone could've removed the baby. Because they assumed the fetus was Alexandria's, they never checked the DNA of the fetus. Someone could have planted a dead fetus in place to throw off the hunters. The other theory is that since twins run in my family, Gena survived and the other twin died. Regardless, someone took her and saved her from the hunters." He explained.

"So, this woman told them she was Alexandria Burren." I asked.

"Yeah, but we both know that is not true. Whoever this person is we owe them a lot. Gena's life was spared because she helped Alexandria. Gena thinks this person came to her house and delivered plane tickets to Inuvik to her." He said.

"What? So she's seen this woman?" I asked.

"No, she said a huge Samoan delivered the tickets but someone was in the car he was driving. She couldn't see inside the car." He flatly stated.

I was thoroughly confused. "So how did her adoptive parents get the jewelry box?" I asked. I had to ask one specific question at a time even though I was impatient to know everything.

"Well the woman who delivered Gena told them to keep her. She only requested that they make the video and not to say anything until she was eighteen. She must've known how to open the box, so she they left a video and Alexandria's house key in the box." He continued.

"So this mysterious woman was at her house." I asked

"Well, Gena thinks that. If you think about it, it has to be. Who else knew of her existence?" he confirmed.

"So how did Gena know how to open the jewelry box?" I asked

"Well that is another long story." He sighed.

"Justin, what else are we going to talk about right now? Do I look interested in you?" I stated mockingly.

"Well, Gena was trying to pry open the box with a kitchen knife." He laughed.

"Are you kidding me?" I laughed. But, the thought of her hurting herself stopped my laughing. I can't imagine what I would do if I found out she killed herself trying to pry open a box, ironically one made by my own father. That would be tragic.

"Well, she didn't know any better. So, the knife pricked her finger and some blood got on the scanner. Lucky, huh! What is the chance of that happening?" he acknowledged. I agreed. "Then she found the video and the key. We got to see the video. There isn't anything on there to identify the mysterious woman." He finished.

"I can't imagine what she was thinking when she saw her world change. So did her uncle send her here?" I asked.

"Well, let me finish. In late July, her boyfriend died of leukemia. Then few weeks later her Uncle was killed in a race car incident." He said.

"Wait, Reynolds that sounds familiar. Is her uncle *the* Josh Reynolds who died in the Allstate 400?" I questioned.

"Yeah, well his death left her all alone. Than she discovered the box and now she is here." He ended.

"Wow, she's had a lot of sadness in her life. Do you know anything about the boyfriend? Was she in love with him?" I asked. After the words left my mouth I felt like a jerk.

"I don't know anything about that. I know what you're getting at but that is something you need to bring up with her." He stated.

"I still don't understand why this would endanger her life." I questioned.

"Well, if you would stop interrupting me, I could get this out all at once." He said.

"Sorry, go ahead. I won't interrupt again." I said.

"My grandfather believed that Alexandria's strong aura matched with Daniel's strong aura would produce an offspring that would have a very unique aura, the *healer aura*. They claimed that they could sense that baby's aura while Alexandria was pregnant. This aura would help those born without an aura form one. Somehow the hunters found out about this and killed them. Alain said that since Gena has never been around her kind, her aura stayed dormant. Now that she's been around us, she is slowly absorbing our aura and we absorbing hers. That's why she has been having the headaches and nausea. Luckily it is only temporary. Right now, her body is transforming and that will take some time. But until then, she is defenseless and could be killed easily. That is why my dad did not want anyone to know about her aura or her lack of defense. He fears that if the hunters learn of her existence and her unique aura they would try for her again. I don't know if you felt anything when you were in the plane with her but I'm pretty sure your aura gave her the headache. Since she's been here Preston, Julianne and Lawrence have developed an aura. Why do you think my dad allowed Preston to hunt with us?" he explained.

I have been so self absorbed in my own world lately that everything he just said to me was now hitting home. Preston has an aura from being around her. I didn't stop to notice that Preston was hunting with us. He normally stays behind and provides information. I had to stop and think.

All the sensation I felt when I entered the plane, was that her aura or is she my *concero flamma?* She developed that headache because I came into the plane, and she absorbed my aura. That makes sense. I definitely feel something for her. I don't care if it's her aura or my innate ability to be drawn to her. It didn't matter. I want her, I need her, and right now I know that losing her would hurt me greatly so if that is love, than I love her.

As I sat there contemplating my next question, Justin tapped me on the shoulder. "Hey, I'm glad it's you. I know you will keep her safe." He stated. I felt a gush of pride. I can't believe I hated him just a few hours ago.

"Hey, we're here." I said.

As I pulled up to the depot, I saw Preston, Max, Tristan, and Mark getting their backpacks. It was strange to see Preston out here with us. He looked pumped.

"Hey, Corin, don't say anything about Gena, okay. Let me tell my dad why I had to tell you, okay?" Justin pleaded.

"Sure, man." I stated. We pulled in and I parked inside the depot next to Preston's Ferrari.

"Hey, I thought you were the fast one." Preston yelled.

"I am fast but my Audi can't go as fast as your Ferrari." I kidded.

Justin and I got our backpacks and met up with the rest of them. I charted the area to cover and they all agreed. We all agreed to check in every four hours. Once they were located, the closest team will join in and help bring them in. With that we wished each other luck and safety.

Justin was right. He is faster. He wasn't as fast as I was but definitely faster. At least he could keep up. We traveled through very dense terrain. We got to Churchill by midnight. We picked up their scent halfway toward Lake Winnipeg.

"We've got to hurry, Justin. If they cross over the lake we could lose their scent." I yelled.

"Hey, I phoned Preston and Tristan to meet us here. They're in Saskatoon. They're going head east towards the lake." He informed.

Justin was really good at strategies. He loved to whole search and rescue thing.

"Stop, Justin. Do you smell that?" I warned.

"Yeah, what about 150 miles southeast from here?" he acknowledged.

"Be alert, do you smell anything else?" I warned. I wanted him to pick up the other scent too.

"Oh, shit! Hunters! They're right behind them too." He confirmed.

"Let's go, we have to get to them before they do. You span out to my right, travel high and no matter what happens do not engage alone." I explained. He nodded. Justin was always good at following orders, even though he was older; he knows I've been doing this much longer. He has always respected that.

We took off in opposite angles to cover more ground. When I got to the east side of Lake Winnipeg, the scent got stronger. As I got closer to the Lake, I could see them. There were six of them. One of the females was injured. They were stopping by the lake to rest. They looked too exhausted to fend off any attack. I could see Justin 300 yards to my right. We acknowledged each other with a nod. We slowly descended on the survivors. As we got closer, the oldest male got up in a defensive position.

"I am Corin Randall; this is Justin Burren we are from the Inuvik Clan. You are being followed by at least ten hunters 100 miles from here. We know what happened in Quebec Territory. We were sent by our elder to aid you to safety. If you want, you can come back to Inuvik with us or we can escort you to safer grounds." I stated.

"I am Trey Dayfuss, this is my brother Derek. The other male is Brent Clinden. Over there is Trisha, Robyn and Tina. We are all that's left of our clan. Tina is seriously injured. We have been traveling for over 30 hours now. We thought we lost them at Lake Superior but somehow they managed to scent us again. We were headed to Inuvik. We would be very grateful for your assistance. Is there only two of you?" he asked.

"We have two more on the way here. They are less than 100 miles away. We have to get the injured girl in the water. Her injuries are giving your location away. The wind around this lake is not helping. Get her into the water. Wash out her wounds. Can she heal?" I asked.

"No, she has no aura. She requires medical attention." He said sadly.

"Okay, get her into the water. Justin, get all your spare clothes and let them change. Here take my back pack. Give me your old clothes. I'll buy us some time. When Preston and Tristan gets here, get them to do the same." I commanded.

I walked over to the female survivors. "Tina, I need you to undress. Give me your bloody clothes. Wash off as much as you can tolerate. I need you two to take these old clothes and wash her with them. Make sure you get as much of her blood on them as possible. Justin has some clean clothes for you to change into. We have two more coming, they will have more clothes. Try not to contaminate the new clothes. Do you understand? Please be quick." I calmly instructed.

"The clothes we brought along have been buried along side with grass, leaves, pine cones and dirt to kill any unearthly scent. This will deaden the hunters scent for at least two hours." I informed them all. "I am sorry Tina, but you will have to stay in that water until Preston and Tristan gets here. If we put you in clean clothing now you'll just end up contaminating it before we can move you. Why don't you give her your old shirt Trey? We'll get you clean clothes when they get here. Who else doesn't have an aura?" I asked.

"Tina and my brother Derek, doesn't have auras." Trey answered.

"Justin, you take Derek, Trisha, and Robyn and head towards Churchill. We will meet up there." I instructed. I could tell he wanted to argue because Rolfe's rule was to always stay together.

"Don't worry Justin, Preston and Tristan will be here soon."

"I will stay with my brother." Derek said.

"You can not help right now. Please we do not have much time." I warned

"Derek, you have to go. I will be right behind you. I promise." Trey assured.

"Justin, get them out of here. See you in Churchill." I said.

"Corin, be safe. Remember what you have at home." He said. With that said he took the others and took off from the same direction he came from early.

I smiled. He was right of course. I will do whatever necessary to get back to her. I gathered all of the old bloody clothes.

"What can I do?" Trey asked.

"Keep her warm. I'll be right back. Oh, Preston and Tristan will be coming from that direction. They are close." I said.

I scattered the dirty clothes at 50 miles out. I could smell the hunters really strong now. When I got back to the lake, Preston and Tristan was there. Trey had already changed into clean clothes. Preston was in the water with Tina keeping her warm. She looked exhausted.

"Okay, get her out of the water and dressed. As soon as you're done we can go." I ordered.

"Corin, I don't think she'll make it. We tied off the bleeding areas but she has lost a lot of blood." Tristan said.

"We can only do what we can. I'll carry her. If you guys clothes is contaminated with her blood than you'll have to change too. Hurry" I said.

"I will carry her." Preston announced.

"Are you sure Preston?" I said. I looked straight at him. He was not the same man that I saw this afternoon. The look on his face was genuine concern and fear.

"Let's go. She needs to see Alain as soon as possible." He stated calmly.

With that we took off for Churchill.

"Nhan, the area's been saturated with their blood. We can't distinguish a clear route. The lake is saturated with their blood. They have to get to the nearest town. Lucos wants you and Cron to head north to Churchill. Lucos and I will head to Winnipeg. If you find them, wait for us. Don't do anything stupid. Can we trust you to do this?"

Nhan nodded. The hunt for these survivors has taken too long. No one will stand in his way. This was his kill. He was so close, than they changed the way they traveled. What made them become smarter? No, someone had to be assisting them. Whoever this idiot was he doesn't realize he will die along with them.

The hunters got confused with the scent from the old bloody clothing. It had worked better than I hoped. We got Tina to Churchill. There we redressed her injuries. She was still bleeding but it was much less than before. Tristan and I gathered the bloody bandages and ran them back 50 miles to the west towards Saskatchewan. It doesn't hurt to be safe. I did not want any chance of them tracing us back to Inuvik. We layered Tina in more clothing to kill the scent.

I watched as Preston carefully dressed her. I had never seen him so attentive to anyone but himself. He looked truly worried. It was endearing. I wondered if he realizes what he is doing. I feared for him. If we don't get her to Alain in time, what would her death do to him? "Is she ready to go?" I asked.

"Yes, let's go." He responded. He looked exhausted. He winced when he lifted her.

"Why don't you let Tristan or Justin carry her? You've carried her for over 200 miles." I warned.

"I will carry her." He stated. He did not hesitate or waver so I did not contest. Justin and Tristan just looked at me. They would intervene if I insisted but I knew Preston would not yield.

"Okay, let's go." I commanded. We headed toward Yellowknife keeping a span of one mile between each other. I stayed closer to Preston and the girl. We had to stop frequently because the sprint motion was causing her a lot of pain. Every chance we got, we changed her and redressed her wounds. I took her bloody bandages and ran them west towards Alberta. This made the trip much longer. Preston was getting tired and his exhaustion was showing. Every time we stopped he would change her bandage and then sat down holding her in his arms. There they would wait for me to get back. Each time I had to wake Preston.

"Preston, we have to go. Let me carry her. We can travel faster. You are exhausted." I begged.

"No, Corin, I can do this. I don't know how much longer she can hold on. I don't want to let her go. Please just let me." He pleaded.

"Preston, I swear to you, I will get her to Alain. You're exhausted. Let me carry her. You will not do her any good tired." I said cautiously.

"Please Corin, I am strong enough. If she does not make it than at least I have this time with her. Let's continue." He said sadly.

"Preston, we will get her to Alain in time. She will be fine." I promised him.

I didn't know why I said those things to him. I was giving him false hope. Looking at her now, how could she survive? She had deep gashes all over her. Several of them were so deep, that we had to pack rolls of gauze inside them to absorb the bleeding. I felt bad for keeping her in the cold water at Lake Winnipeg for so long.

We got to the southern mouth of the Mackenzie River. While Preston tended to Tina's injuries, Justin, Tristan, and I took her bloody clothes and ran them into Alberta and British Columbia. We met up with Mark and Max. Justin phoned Cory and Michael. He sent them ahead to Inuvik to warn Alain of Tina's injuries.

"Hey, Corin, what's going on with Preston. He doesn't allow anyone near her. He is acting possessed." Mark questioned.

"What do you think?" I replied.

"You're kidding right? Her? Here? Now?" he hissed

"I don't think its something that he can control or choose." I said. *For me it was on a plane. For Justin he skied right into her. Too bad for Preston. He just met his soul mate while running from hunters, worst yet she is dying.*

"She's not going to make it. You know?" He concluded.

"Shut-up Mark, he'll hear you." I hissed.

"He's right you know. She has been steadily bleeding; her heart rate is thready and erratic. How much more can she take." Tristan added.

We crossed over the Mackenzie River and got into Yellowknife by midnight Sunday. We got to the depot quickly. Preston was changing out Tina's clothes. Mark and Max readied the car for travel.

"Preston, you have the fastest car. You go ahead. Mark will follow behind you with Trey, Derek and Brent. Max will take my car and transport Trisha and Robyn. Justin and I will continue the scent thru British Columbia and end at the Pacific Ocean. Don't worry about us, we'll get back to Inuvik when it's safe and the scent is completely lost. She'll make it. Be safe." I instructed.

Chapter Eight

This was my first slumber party. I left all the arrangements to Lauren and Dana. They were so enthusiastic about the whole thing they could not be controlled. Every girl they knew was invited. This was probably a big mistake.

The girls started coming over at 8pm. By that time, I had already moved all of my clothes into my parents' home. I moved into their bedroom. I wanted to surround myself with as much of their things as I could. Aimee and Dana helped me clean out the nursery. I guess I'm too old for a crib and change table.

"All this stuff is just so adorable. She brought so many clothes for you.Your mother was so good at this decorating thing." Aimee said.

"Yeah, and this house your dad built. It is so cool. It makes our house look bland. I love the glass walls." Dana confirmed.

"Yeah, I know. It just seemed like a waste that no one lived here for so long." I said sadly.

"How many bedrooms are there?" Dana asked

"Well there are 4 bedrooms and a master bedroom. There are 3 bathrooms upstairs and one downstairs. Do you think I have enough space?" I kidded.

"You're so lucky. You have this big house all to yourself. No curfews, no grounding, no need to worry about what your parents would do if you had someone over" Dana said. I saw at the corner of my eyes that Aimee bumped her shoulder into Dana,

"Oh! Gena. I am so sorry. I didn't mean anything." She said

"No, that's okay. I didn't even know them. But I'm sure if I did they would totally ground me for having such a big slumber party." I assured her.

"Hey, I hear someone in the driveway. Lauren! Get the door." Aimee yelled.

We all went downstairs just in time to greet everyone. I tried to remember everyone's names but it just got too complicated. I wish that they had some flaws so I could remember them by it but they were all beautiful and flawless. The only girl that I did not meet at the bonfire was Corin's sister, Michelle. She had his same color hair and eyes. It was amazing to see the resemblance. I guess if I can't look at him I can just stare at her all night long. She would probably think I was some kind of weirdo stalker but it was just hard to forget the intense blue eyes.

We spent most of night doing each others hair and make-up. I didn't help anyone. I was never a big fan of make-up. My idea of make-up was lip gloss on special occasions. Peter always said I didn't need anything, so I just never bother. Plus it wasn't like Uncle Josh could help me in that category. Who was I kidding? I didn't get into make-up because I was just too lazy to do all that work everyday. I was lucky that I didn't have acne problems. If I did have acne, I would probably wear make-up to hide it. My hair wasn't much to brag about. It was long, wavy and brown. Nothing too exotic. I never did any highlights or change the color of my hair because that would mean that I would have to continuously maintain it. Again, too lazy to maintain anything.

Lauren ordered pizza and we made all kinds of cookies. Some of the girls made cookies shaped like someone they liked. It was funny. I was lucky to produce something round and edible and they were doing delicate face construction.

"Lauren, does this look like Preston?" Michelle asked.

"No, it looks better than Preston." She laughed. "Maybe once it's cooked it will show his big head"

"Hey, be nice." Michelle said.

"Too bad, the guys got sent out, huh. If not they would probably be here bothering us." Dana said.

"Where were they sent to?" I asked

"Oh, you were here when my dad sent Justin, Corin, Max, Preston, Michael, Cory, Tristan and Mark out to search for the survivors from the Quebec Territory attack." Lauren said.

"Yeah, Corin told them he thought that there were signs of maybe 5 or 6 survivors. He lost their scent when they crossed the Hudson Bay into Ontario. Rolfe wants them to be brought here where they can be safe. Corin thinks that the hunters are still hunting them." Michelle recanted.

"Isn't it dangerous to go where the hunters are?" I asked.

"Well, yeah but someone has to go, so of course Corin has to go because he is the strongest and fastest. The other guys are strong and fast too. They'll be alright. They are very good at tracking. I think they like to go, it's a male thing." Michelle claimed.

"Natalie, does this look like Max?" Lauren asked.

"Yeah, hey that's pretty good. You should give that to him. That would really blow his ego up bigger." Natalie giggled.

"Are you doing one of Corin?" I asked. Of course I had to ask. I was always going to think of him with her.

"No, I've given up on Corin. He's just not worth my time anymore. I thought last night he was turning the corner but than he told me he didn't feel the same way about me as I did about him. He's back on the market girls. You guys can have him." She proclaimed.

"He was never off the market Natalie." Michelle defended.

"Whatever Michelle, what is he waiting for? His soul mate? Come on, he needs to look around. There is no one else. If he can't find his *concero flamma* amongst us, where is he going to find her in a Sears Roebuck catalog?" she said sarcastically.

"You're just mad because he doesn't want you. Why do you keep pursuing him? It not like he is the only guy here." Michelle said.

So, Natalie liked Corin but he didn't like her back. So what was that display on the beach? Was that to make me jealous? What kind of games was he playing with me? The next time I see him, I'm going to ask him. Now I have two reasons to talk to him.

"Okay, girls! Keep your claws in check. You're going to scare off Gena." Aimee claimed.

We all laughed. I watched Natalie as she continued with her cookie. She claims that she has given up on him but her actions show otherwise. The cookie had dark brown hair, blue M&Ms for eyes and she contoured the chin sharply like Corin's. Thank goodness, I wasn't artistic. They all looked at mine and decided that I was in love with Santa Claus or the Buddha statue.

"So Gena, do you have a boyfriend?" Michelle asked.

"I did have a boyfriend, his name was Peter." I replied.

"Did you breakup with him because you moved here or was it because he was human?" She asked.

"Michelle, can I see you in the kitchen, please?" Lauren sneered.

"That's okay, Lauren. I don't mind. Peter died almost a month ago." I said quietly.

"Oh. I'm so sorry Gena." She said remorsefully.

"Michelle, you're always putting your foot in your mouth." Dana said angrily.

"No, it's okay. She didn't know, Michelle its okay. Don't worry about it." I assured her.

"Group hug!" Aimee announced.

Everyone laughed and hugged each other.

"Okay put the movie on." Natalie said.

"Hey someone's in the driveway." Dana announced.

We all got up and looked out the front. There in my driveway was my *Ducati*. Lawrence was standing next to it. He was waving me to come down. I couldn't get up fast enough.

"When did Lawrence get a bike?" Natalie asked.

"It's not Lawrence's bike, he wished. It's Gena's." Aimee responded.

I ran out to the driveway in my flannel pajamas and Ugg boots. "Oh, Lawrence, how did it get here so fast?" I asked.

"Gena, Bradley had it expedited here. You are so lucky. It's gorgeous. I hope you didn't mind. Dad told me to wait and tell you tomorrow but I had to bring it to you tonight." He said coyly.

"You rode it over here? Okay you are forgiven just this once. Thank you so much." I hugged him.

I missed this bike so much. Many times I dreamt of riding it here.

"Tell them, I'll be right back." I said to Lawrence.

I got on my bike and took off. I didn't know where I was going but I just wanted the feel of the wind against my hair and face.

I recognized the road I was on, so I headed north toward Tuk Beach.

The wind here was much colder than in Indiana, but I didn't care about the cold right now. The complete blackness was scary but exciting too. Driving this fast was therapeutic to all my ills.

When I got to the parking lot of the Beach, I stopped where I remember Corin last stood. I closed my eyes and imagined him standing there. I imagined our conversation being different than the last time we were here. He had a lot to explain to me. I felt a little excited about seeing him again.

I rode back thinking about the things I wanted to hear from him. All I know is that I think about him a lot and I want to know if he does the same. I wonder if he does this to all the girls. He had Natalie wait around for him, *will I fall victim to the same fate*? I hope he doesn't think I am anything like Natalie. I will not follow him around, if his feelings for me weren't mutual. I have too much pride for that.

I decided I will not pursue him. He will have to come to me. I will not allow him to treat me like he did Natalie. I will not look into his blue eyes and fall madly in love and make a fool of myself. I will keep my feelings for him to myself. He will not have that advantage over me.

I smiled.

I got back to *my house* and continue slumbering with the other girls.

It felt like I've been asleep for a long time. My limbs were heavy and fatigued. It took a lot of coaxing to get my body to move. I looked over to the clock on the wall and saw that it was 11am. Did I get enough sleep? I got up slowly. Well at least I don't have a headache today. I quickly showered and went downstairs. I saw that some of the girls had already left. Lauren, Dana and Aimee were sitting around the dining room table talking.

"Hey, late sleeper! Wants some breakfast" Aimee yelled.

"No that's okay. I have lots to do today. Lawrence said that my things from Indiana arrived last night. So I need to get them moved over here." I said.

"Gena, Lawrence, Will, and Steven have been busy all this morning. All your stuff is here. We didn't know where you want things so we've been waiting for you. Does your head still hurt?" Lauren stated.

"Oh no, you guys didn't have to do that. You should have woke me. I feel so bad that you guys had to do everything." I said.

"Gena that is why you have a large family. Take advantage of that, will ya?" Lauren giggled.

"Anyway, the boys did it hoping you would let them ride your motorcycle around. That thing looks vicious. I bet you looked hot riding around in Indiana. Did the boys fall all over you?" Dana bragged.

"They never got near me. Even Peter was afraid of my driving." I confirmed.

"Well too bad for them. The boys here would drool to see a hot girl, dressed in tight leather, riding around in a motorcycle." Dana laughed.

"Ha, Ha. I don't own any leather clothes." I replied.

"Well, we will just have to change that. Let's shop!" exclaimed Lauren.

"Yeah, we've got to get you a dress for Ella's engagement party. We'll find you a date afterwards. It is always harder to find a great dress than a great date." Dana said giggling.

"You are so right. We have to order everything and have it shipped express. We can not take any risk." Lauren confirmed.

They spent most of the afternoon shopping for me. I was busy putting my things away. I had to do some laundry. I went thru my dirty clothes and found the card the Corin gave me. I need to look up this symbol in the internet when they were done shopping. I wasn't sure where the laundry room was so I went through the kitchen. I walked into the enormous pantry and saw at the end of the room was another door. Maybe the laundry room was behind there. When I got to the door, there was no door knob. I search around the space for a switch or a trick button but could not find one.

"That's a panic room, Gena." Aimee informed me quietly.

I was startled. "What's a *panic room*?" I asked.

"What do you think it means?" She replied coyly.

"Oh." I said quietly.

"There is a blood scanner to the left there. It's like your jewelry box. Do you understand?" She said.

"Oh,yeah. I understand. The blood thing" I said.

Well I did not feel like cutting myself today so I'll just left it alone. "Do you know where the laundry room is?" I asked.

"Lauren! Gena wants to know where the laundry room is." She giggled. This was obviously an inside joke that I was not let in on.

"Shut your mouth! We do not do laundry here. Every three days someone from the town will come by and pick up your clothes. They will return your clothes that same day cleaned. Its part of the mayor's *Keep the town employed* policy." She proclaimed.

"Ella Daniels' father is Inuvik's mayor." Dana informed me.

"Okay, I need you guys to give me as much information about everyone you know here because I do not want to step on any toes or say something offensive. Let's start with each of your families. Lauren you first" I stated.

"Okay, so you know my father is the oldest in the Burren family. He is also now the CEO of Burren Oil Distributors. You know Justin has a soul mate name Rachel. She is from Colorado. As soon it's safe, she will travel here to be with him. Justin works for my dad. Preston is at Aurora College this year. He doesn't know what he wants to do yet. Then there is me. I will be your most valuable asset at school." She laughed.

"Does Preston not have a girlfriend?" I asked.

"No, Michelle likes him but he just sees her as a friend. Plus, no one can put up with his moodiness." Lauren replied.

"And you like Max." I confirmed.

"You got that, huh?" She shyly replied.

"Okay, Aimee you're next." I said.

"Well, my dad also works for Burren Oil. He's the marketing director. My mother is your aunt. You know Lawrence will be a junior this year and I have been with Tristan Daniels forever. He is waiting for me to finish high school than we'll get married. That's it" Aimee replied.

I looked over at Dana. "Your turn" I said.

"Well, my dad is the Family Attorney. He does not work for Burren Oil. You know Will, he'll be a sophomore this year and Julianne will be a junior. I will be your most valuable asset in school and none of the boys here are good enough for me." She proclaimed.

We all laughed.

"Then you know Alain is the family doctor. His twin boys are Cory and Michael. Cory is the genius of us all. He graduated two years ago at age 17. He will probably go on to be a doctor like Uncle Alain. Michael is the total opposite. He is a senior this year too."

"The school principal is Thomas Redman, Max's dad. Max and Natalie will be seniors this year too. Steven is a junior. You know the story with Natalie and Corin. So that's it for them."

"The man who built your jewelry box and the panic room is John Randall. His oldest son Mark is marrying Ella Daniels, the mayor's daughter. Corin will be a senior this year too. There is nothing to say about Corin except he is always busy with doing stuff for my dad. Michelle is also a senior this year. She likes Preston. The youngest in the Daniels family is Joseph Daniels; he'll be a junior this year. So now you know everything." Lauren announced.

"Wow, it's like a soap opera here. A bunch of beautiful people, doing beautiful things" I said.

They all laughed. "What about you, Gena?" Aimee asked.

"Well, you already know the most interesting part of my life, coming here. Other than that it was pretty boring." I said.

"Do you mind telling us about Peter?" Dana asked. Lauren and Aimee glared at her.

"No, I don't mind. Well, Peter and I met when we were in junior high school. We became good friends. Then at the end of our junior year in high school we became more than friends. During the summer we got closer. He was a football quarterback. Good looking, tall and strong. After my birthday he went to Florida to get treatment for Leukemia. The treatment did not work and he died on July 18th. He did not want me to see him. I never got to say goodbye and that's it." I told them blankly.

"Oh my god, I can just cry. He wanted to protect you at the end." Aimee stuttered.

"Well, I didn't see that at the time. I was very angry with him." I confessed.

"Gena, you have experience more hardship than anyone I know, yet here you are so nice and kind. You're not angry or bitter." Dana assessed.

"Well, you haven't made me mad yet." I winked.

"Do you like anyone here?" Lauren asked.

"Well, I would like to look this symbol up. Then after I look it up, I will answer that." I stated. I drew the symbol on a napkin and handed it to Dana.

Dana looked at it, than handed it to Aimee. Lauren looked at it and shook her head. This was a good sign. I had feared that they all new the sign because maybe he writes it to everyone. They went over to the computer and put in possible words to match the image.

"The two eights have got to mean double infinity, right? Who wrote this for you?" Aimee questioned.

"If you help find out what it means, I'll tell you." I challenged.

The door bell rang. "It's Lawrence, again." Lauren annoyed.

I came outside. "How about that ride Gena, you owe me?" Lawrence said.

"Okay, you can go five miles and then back. If you wreck my bike, I will disown you." I warned.

"Gena, come back inside. We found out what it means." Aimee yelled.

I ran back inside. "Okay what does it mean?" I asked anxiously.

"Do you promise to tell us who wrote you that symbol?" Dana asked.

"I promise." I replied.

They were giggling. "It's the Mobius strip meaning *Everlasting Love*." They yelled.

I stood there awestricken. All my thoughts and goals to ignore and forget him last night flew right out the window. I smiled to myself.

"Okay, tell us who wrote this to you?" Dana begged.

"I was on the plane with Corin Randall. We talked about my trip here. He asked me how long I was going to be here. At the time, I thought I was only visiting. He offered to take me sight-seeing. He handed me a business card with his phone number and he wrote the symbol right next to it." I said smugly.

"Are you serious? Has he said anything to you?" Lauren asked.

"No, that's the thing. He hasn't said a word to me since I've been here except for the usual *Hi and Bye*." I said.

"Well are you going to ask him about this?" Dana asked.

"Well that's the problem. I am going to wait. I am going to let him come to me. I heard what happened with Natalie. I don't do well waiting around for people to come to their senses. So, I will pretend like nothing is going to effect me. I am starting a new school. I've got lots to think about right now." I said sarcastically.

"Oh,my God. That is the best idea I've ever heard. You are right, we should never piss you off." Aimee said.

"I should try that with Max. You know, I think I will." Lauren stated.

"Great you'll have every guy in school ignored by every girl in school." Dana said dryly.

I laughed. Corin Randall was going to have to win me over with everything he's got. I will not yield easily. I will be hard on him as he has been on me since I've been here.

Everlasting Love Symbol, huh. He's good. He definitely won this round. I smiled to myself.

We spent the rest of the day at the Burren estate. Uncle Rolfe was keeping everyone informed with what was happening in Manitoba. Everyone was so calm and confident. I wasn't sure if they were telling fairy tale stories or talking about eight men trying to save some survivors from some cruel sadistic hunters. I didn't understand this life they led. They worried but not like normal people. I had a lot to learn.

"They should be leaving Yellowknife by now. They will split up and travel the rest of the way on foot. My guess is that the survivor should be in Manitoba or if their lucky in Saskatchewan. They would be better off if they are in Manitoba, Corin and Justin will be there. Corin knows how to deal with this better than anyone of them." He spoke with confident like Corin was his son.

"Do we know how many survivors?" Thomas Redman asked. He was a good-looking man in his late forties. His hair was wavy with some grays. I can see some of the same features on his face as Max. He stood next to his wife who was sitting next to Aunt Madeline. His hand was on her wife's shoulder.

"We are guessing between five or six." John Randall replied. This was Corin's father. He had the same crew cut hair as both of his sons. Their facial structures were exactly the same. If this was what Corin would look like in 20 years he would be very lucky.

"Thomas, the boys will not be back in time for the start of school. Can you take care of that?" Alain asked.

"It's already taken care of. When will they be back?" Thomas asked.

"Well, we don't know yet. As soon as I know I will let you know." Rolfe repeated.

"Gena, Blaine would like to talk to you regarding your late Uncle's estate. He is in Grandfather's office." Lawrence informed.

I made my way to executive office across from the family room. Blaine was sitting behind the monstrous executive desk. The room was decorated to intimidate businessman. Leather and dark rich wood adorned this entire room.

"Gena, thanks for coming. Have you settled in your new home?" He asked.

"Yes, everyone did everything. Thank you so much." I replied.

"So, I spoke with Mr. Gaffney regarding your estate. He's retired you know. I think I interrupted his golf game today." He said

"Yeah, I think he told me that last time I saw him." I answered.

"Well, you have quite a trust fund."

"Yeah, I'm always the last one standing." I replied quietly.

"Mr. Gaffney told me what you wanted to do with the Reynolds Trust Fund, are you sure about that?" he asked.

"Well, given what I know now, I really feel guilty about taking the money." I explained.

"Would you like me to find out if there is any other family?" he asked.

"Oh, that would be great." I exclaimed.

"Gena, I would do whatever you want. Are you aware that your parent also had money? Since you are their only child it will automatically go to you. Would you like for me to make those arrangements?" He asked.

"They set up a trust fund for a fetus?" I asked sarcastically.

"No, it is actually their personal wealth. No one in the family needed any reason to take their money after they died, so it has just been sitting in a trust fund for eighteen years." He explained.

"I wouldn't know what to do with it. What do you think I should do?" I asked

"Don't you want to know how much its worth?" He asked. He had this devious look on his face.

"Does it matter? I have a $150 million dollar Trust Fund in my name already. What does a little more money matter?" I hesitated.

"Well, you don't look too excited about all this money." He questioned.

"You wouldn't feel so fond of it if you amassed it through people dying around you." I stated.

"You shouldn't think of it that way. Millions of people died everyday. I assure you not everyone gets left with half a billion dollars." He said flatly.

"That's a lot of money. I don't want the accounts combine. The Reynolds Trust Fund should go to someone that is a real Reynolds." I said sadly.

"Gena, you were a Reynolds in their eyes. But, I understand what you mean. I will take care of it. From now on anything you need will come from your parent's money. I will change it to the Gena Roese Trust Fund. Is that alright with you?" He asked.

"Can you change it to Gena Reynolds Roese?" I asked

"I understand. Of course I can." He replied.

"Thank you so much. Also Blaine, if there is no other surviving Reynolds, can I donate the money to the Leukemia Society" I asked.

"Of course you can. Alain would be very proud to hear that." he said.

"Okay, so that's it right?" I asked.

"We're done here. It's getting late. You have school tomorrow. I'll see you again." He said as he escorted me back to the family room.

Lauren and Aimee were still there waiting for me.

"Hey are you ready to go?" Lauren asked.

"Yeah, let me get my things." I responded.

I said goodnight to my grandparents and Uncle Rolfe. On the way back to my house Lauren looked distracted.

"Hey, Gena, will you be alright staying by yourself?" She asked.

"I'll be alright. I have always been kind of a loner all my life so this is just another extension of my new life. Hey you're welcome to come over and "slumber" with me anytime." I stated.

"Gena, that sounds totally perverted. In order for me to stay tonight I would have to get the moving van out and get my stuff. I require a lot of thing to get ready for school." she giggled.

"Okay, I'll be fine. You're welcome anytime though." I repeated.

As she dropped me off at the door she yelled "So I'll see you tomorrow at 8am."

"No, Lauren, I'm going to take my motorcycle to school." I said.

"Okay, I'll meet you there. Hey, we all park in the front lot, okay?" she informed me.

"Okay, I'll see you at school in the front lot." I confirmed.

I got home and switched to have all the curtains in the first floor closed. I went upstairs to my bedroom. The moon was so beautiful. The light did not bother me, so I left he curtains open. I looked over at the business card on the night stand. *At least we were sharing the same moon tonight.*

Chapter Nine

Getting to school here did not require as much driving as I was used to. It took me twenty minutes to get dressed, eat breakfast and ride two minutes to the school. *That has got to break some sort of record.*

I pulled into the front lot at 8am like Lauren instructed. Even though this school was small, the front lot had as many fancy exotic cars as a foreign auto dealership. I spotted Lauren immediately; she was standing in the middle of an empty parking space.

"Hey, I saved you a space." She smiled.

"Well, thanks for using your body as a traffic cone." I laughed.

"This will be your parking space from now on." She exclaimed.

"Now, are you going to stand there every morning?" I asked. I pulled into the space and removed my riding jacket and helmet. My hair scattered all around my face. *Got to remember to buy hair bands.* I quickly turned to store my things in my bike.

"Oh, my god, you look like a motorcycle goddess. Watch out drool alert!" Dana yelled from behind me.

I turned to find Dana and Aimee walking towards me. In the background I can hear Lawrence, Steven, Joseph, and Will whistling at me. Embarrassed, I turned back.

"You're related, idiot." Lauren sneered.

"We're not." Steven yelled back referring to him and Joseph.

"Worse, you're invisible." Aimee teased.

"My God, Gena you look hot riding your motorcycle. I want to learn to ride a motorcycle. I want to wear a hot riding jacket like that, and the helmet hair thing, just like in the movies." Dana announced.

"Okay, first of all, Gena looks hot already. She doesn't need the props. Secondly, you would probably fall off the bike and rip the fancy riding jacket to pieces before you could even making it out of the parking space. And lastly, I don't want to be on the same road, while you're riding." Lauren stated.

"Okay guys, I can teach you to ride but it takes a lot of time. The riding jacket and helmet is a must for safety reasons not for sex goddess symbol." I replied.

"Maybe I'll just wear a riding jacket and a helmet, who needs to actually ride a bike." Dana said jokingly.

"Yeah, you can wear the riding jacket and helmet and take the tricycle to school. Total superstar baby" Aimee laughed.

We all laughed as we walked towards the front door. Everyone was staring at us. It was weird to be the center of attention. I can definitely tell that Dana, Lauren, and Aimee felt like this was the normal thing but for me it was a bit uncomfortable.

I spent the majority of the day looking for my classes. The school consisted of two buildings, three stories high. I could identify the gym easily but the classrooms were a bit harder to remember.

I had Aimee in my first class, English Literature, so she walked me to the classroom. Each class had only 15 students. At Crew High each class had 25 students, sometimes more. Aimee introduced me to some other girls in class. I couldn't remember their names, so I just sat there and smiled.

My next class was Calculus; I didn't know anyone in this class. I sat next to a boy name Trevor. He was tall, skinny, and lanky. He had a full set of braces that made his upper and lower lips protrude forward. When he talked, he would constantly stop to suck in his saliva. It was really distracting. He was nice though.

My third period class was Physics. I didn't know anyone in there either except for Trevor. He waved at me but I had already put my books down at another desk. I sat next to a girl name Mandy. She was rather large, so she took up quite a bit of our lab table. She was really shy, so I had to introduce myself. That was basically our conversation.

After class, I met up with Lauren, Aimee and Dana at my locker. We all walked to lunch together. The lunchroom was half the size of Crew High lunchroom but it still looks big. Half the students ate outside when the weather was nice. Lauren doesn't like the weather messing with her hair so we sat inside.

My next three classes were electives I had to take to fill my schedule. It was all that was left so I wasn't looking forward to them.

Dana walked me to my next class Human Sexuality. I had already taken this class in my sophomore year but it didn't matter here. I needed to fill the credit. Natalie was in this class with me so, I didn't feel so lonely.

"Hey, Gena. You're in this class?" she asked.

"Yeah, it was the only thing left." I replied.

She introduced me to several people I couldn't remember. One boy in particular kept staring at me. *Stare much, stalker.* The teacher asked us to introduce ourselves and that was her way of doing roll call.

"Okay, is Corin Randall, Michael Burren and Max Redman not present?" she announced.

When I heard Corin's name I looked up hoping to see him but I remember he was away. So, I have one class with him. Natalie was also in this class too.

After class I met Dana at the locker. She showed me how to get to my next class which was French II. Lauren was in this class with me. The stalker guy was also in this class with me too. I made the mistake of telling Lauren. She turned around and stared back at him.

My last class was Home Economics, another elective that no one wanted. During roll call, I found out that Corin was in this class with me too. That will definitely help make this class a little more interesting.

Once the bell rung, people scattered to their cars.

"Gena!" I heard from behind the crowd. It was Thomas Redman, the school principal. Everyone looked at me like was about to get in trouble.

"Yes, Mr.Redman" I cautiously asked.

"Alain asked me to tell you they need you at your grandparents' place immediately." He announced.

"Is everything okay with my grandparents?" I asked.

"Yes, everything is fine. Please, I told him I would send you immediately so get going." He said breathlessly.

"Gena, we'll meet you there, go." Aimee said.

I felt a rush of fear. Something was wrong I imagined every scenario. *If there is a God please, don't let anything happen to this family. I am willing to give up my own life, please not them too.* When I got to the estate, I saw several people I haven't met before. Cory and Michael immediately came to my side. *They're back.* I could see Max, Tristan, and Mark but after quickly scanning the small crowd, I could not see Preston, Justin, or Corin. Something happened to them. The fear in my stomach was coming up in a bitter taste in my mouth.

"Where are Justin, Preston, and Corin?" I whispered to Cory. My voiced crack and ached when I said the names.

"Justin and Corin are in Alberta. They had to stay behind to throw the hunters off. Preston is inside with my dad. My dad needs you in there right now." He said quickly. They rushed me upstairs into one of the bedroom. As I made my way up the stairs, I could see drops of blood on the floor. *Something happened to Preston.*

I entered the room, Preston and Alain was standing over the bed. In the bed was a beautiful young girl, pale and fragile. There were piles of bloody sheets on the floor in the corner. She looked dead. Preston looked even worse. The look on Preston face reminded me of Peter's mother. Exhausted and defeated.

"What happened?" I asked softly.

"Oh, Gena, I am glad you're here. This is one of the survivors, Tina. She has been gravely injured by the hunters. I have done all I can for her. Gena, she doesn't have an aura." He said sadly.

"What do you want me to do?" I asked.

"We don't know exactly, but maybe if you stand near her and hold her hand." He asked cautiously.

"I don't know if me standing over her is so helpful." I whispered.

"Gena, please we have to try something." Preston pleaded. He looked like he was getting ready to cry.

I walked over to Tina and stood there for a minute. I can taste the bitter bile forming in my mouth. I felt like I could vomit. I took her hand and knelt down beside her. Her hands were cold but I could still feel her pulse. It was weak and erratic.

As we sat there, I was fighting off the waves of nausea. I slowly felt warm, even sweaty. My hands were sweating. I didn't think I was faintly toward seeing blood but maybe I was. The nausea got worst but it wasn't bad enough for me to vomit. Oddly, I looked at her, she seemed more relax and less pale. Even her hand felt warmer or maybe my warmth made it feel that way.

We sat there beside her quietly for what seemed like hours. Preston looked up at me. No, he stared at me like I was a monster. "Gena, your eyes are red." He alarmed.

"My eyes are what?" I asked. He was scaring me. I got up and looked in the mirror. The color of my eyes was no longer brown but dark, rich red.

Preston ran and got Alain. When he entered the room, he looked at Tina and than over at me.

"Are you alright?" he asked.

"I'm nauseous otherwise I'm ok. What is happening to me?" I asked. I was so scared.

"Your aura is coming from you and into her. Can you feel it?" He asked.

"The nausea or the warmth" I asked.

"Well the nausea is from your aura passing through you into her. The warmth is your aura." He answered.

"What is wrong with my eyes? Is this permanent?" I asked.

"Your eyes are red because you're filtering the death from her blood. It's like a dialysis machine taking blood and cleaning it. It is just temporarily. It will pass once you leave her side." He informed me.

"Preston, she is healing now. She will make it. You need to rest. Gena, you did your job. The nausea will not pass until you leave her side. If you're uncomfortable you can leave." He stated.

"I will not leave her. I'll stay here until she wakes up. Gena, thank you so much" Preston said. He hugged me and got back to Tina's side.

"Gena, come let's get you some shades." He chuckled.

I left the room with Alain. As I got further and further from her, the sweating and nausea dissipated. By the time I got to the end of the hallway, the warmth was completely gone.

"It looks like you don't need shades anymore. You're eyes are brown again." He stated.

"Thank goodness, I don't know if I could explain this to my classmates. So, I'm a dialysis machine?" I asked.

"Something like that." he chuckled.

"So, when I cleanse her blood of death, where does it go?" I asked.

"You healed it, changing death to life. For example, before you came Preston did not have an aura. This is like a disease for our kind. Since you've been around him, you healed him allowing an aura to form." He explained.

"So I am a healer?" I asked.

"You're a healer. Do you want a cape?" he chuckled. I smiled.

I came downstairs with Alain.

"There is a bunch of people in the family room, you should go meet them. Remember not to say anything about your aura." He instructed. I nodded.

The family room was packed with people. Beside the family, the Redmans, Daniels, Randalls, and some new faces were all there.

"How is she doing?" Uncle Rolfe asked.

"She is going to make it. Gena's experience working with people in the hospital was very helpful to me." He lied. He gave me a slight squeeze on my shoulder.

"Alain, you are so modest. You saved that girl. By the way Tristan described her wounds and the fact that she doesn't have an aura, I am surprised she made it." Edwin Daniels proclaimed.

"Let's just be thankful she made it." Uncle Rolfe said.

"Gena let me introduce you to some new members of our clan. This is Trey Dayfuss and his brother Derek. This here is Trisha Kinsey and her sister Robyn. This young man is Brent Clinden. The young lady upstairs is Tina Malfoy. They're the only survivors from the Quebec Territory attack." Uncle Rolfe said.

I nodded and smiled at each one.

"When will Justin and Corin get back?" John Randall asked.

"I just got of the phone with Justin, he and Corin will continue planting the scent all the way to the Pacific Coast. From there they will travel to Whitehorse. They'll probably stay in Whitehorse until it is safe then they'll travel to Dawson City. They should be home by Thursday night." Uncle Rolfe explained.

Everyone nodded their approval. I was a little disappointed that Corin would not be back until Thursday night but I was happy to hear that he was alright. For the next hours, the survivors shared their terrifying stories.

The oldest survivor, Trey recanted the story:

"They attacked around 3 am. There were at least twenty of them. Derek and I were coming back from Montreal, when we got there it was too late. We found Trisha and Robyn. They survived because they got into their panic rooms. Brent was also in his panic room. We found three of them attacking Tina. We were able to kill them and get Tina. But because we did not burn the remains, the pack started tracking us. We eluded them several times but Tina's injury kept them on us again. We are so thankful for your help." He finished.

"You all are welcome here. We are a very large clan made up of many families. We stay together and we take care of each other. You're all welcome to stay. We've made arrangements for you. Trisha, you and sister will stay here at the Burren estate until a house is built for you. Trey, you and your brother, and Brent can share the home next to Mr. Randall. Now, everyone needs to go get some rest. We will iron out the little details tomorrow." Uncle Rolfe announced.

I rode my motorcycle home. I was exhausted. If this was the first day of school, I can't imagine how exhausting the second day would be.

Tuesday morning was the first day I woke up without any headaches, nausea or heaviness in my limb. I felt great. I got ready in record time again. As I made my way through the parking lot, I was surprise to find my space available. I parked and store away my riding jacket and helmet. Max and Michael came to my side.

"I can not believe, we are related. Such a waste" Michael commented. Max showed his approval by giving Michael a pat on the back.

"Okay, guys. It's beginning to get uncomfortable." I said.

"Sorry, can't help messing with the beautiful." Michael stated.

"Are you guys bothering Gena, again?" Aimee yelled.

"Gena, just close your eyes and click your heels three times, they'll disappear." Dana laughed.

"Sorry, Dana, she is not a witch like you." Michael snickered back at Dana.

"You're so stupid; it was Dorothy who did that. What a waste of space you are." She added.

I ignored them all and proceeded into the building with Aimee and Lauren. When we got to our locker, I looked over at Lauren.

"There's that stalker guy looking at us again." I whispered. He was big, muscular, and stocky. At Crew High he would probably be popular and play football. But here he was ordinary and uninteresting to look at. What makes it worst is that he thinks he is worthy of attention. He stood across the hallway leaning against the lockers with his arms folded over his chest.

"He is not staring at me or Aimee, he wouldn't dare. Max and Tristan would take out his eyes. He's just staring at you." She said glaring back at him.

"Oh crap, he's coming over. Now you did it." Aimee warned.

"Hi, ladies. I noticed you were looking at me. So, I thought why make them wonder—*Whose that guy?* My name is Craig Morrow. You're Gena, right?" he asked.

"First of all we weren't looking at you. There was a fly near your locker. Secondly we would not care who you were?" Lauren insulted.

"Lauren, don't be jealous. I wasn't talking to you. I was talking to Gena." He glared at her.

"Well, too bad. Gena is not interested in you or the flies surrounding you." Aimee cut in. She and Lauren gave each other a high five.

"Gena, when you are ready to come see me, you know where I am." He said as he walked away.

"I think I'm going to be sick." Lauren said.

We all laughed.

Aimee and I made our way to English Literature class. Today the teacher was going over our reading assignment. The syllabus for this class was ridiculously thick. All these essay assignments were busy work for me. I had most of these essays in my laptop. This would be an easy class for me.

Calculus, on the other hand, would probably take much of my time. Trevor and I were math partners. When I got into class, he was sitting there waiting for me. Our major assignment for Calculus was written on the chalk board. He gave us three problems to solve using Stirling's Formula, Bertand Series, and Newton-Raphson Method. If we solved these three problems by the end of the semester we could exempt the final exam.

"Gena, you can come over my house and we can work on these problems together." He asked.

"Trevor, I don't think that's a good idea. Let's just work on them separately and compare answers in class. Okay?" I responded.

"Well, when I get the answer I will definitely share it with you. I think we make a great team." He promised. I had to stop this before he gets any ideas. He was nice but just not my type.

"Trevor, let's just keep to Calculus, okay?" I said.

My next class was no better. Trevor managed to get rid of Mandy. "Now we can be Math partners and Lab partners." He confirmed.

I didn't have a response for him. After class, I met Lauren, Aimee, and Dana for lunch. Our table was much fuller today. Michael and Max were back. They talked endlessly about the trip.

Max looked over at me and said "Gena, when did you learn to ride?"

"I've been riding since I was 14." I replied.

"Why a motorcycle, why not a horse?" he asked.

"I like her on a motorcycle. She looks hot!" Michael added.

"Okay, I'm leaving." I said.

"You guys have a one track mind. Too bad it is wasted, she's already taken." Dana announced.

"Dana, shut-up!" Lauren glared.

"Who" Max said.

"Sorry, guys. Lunch is over." Aimee said.

We disappeared into the crowd leaving the guys to wonder. I knew this was going to haunt me in Human Sexuality class because Michael and Max were in my class.

"Come on, Gena, who is he?" Max nagged.

"We won't tell." Michael added.

"It's none of your business. Please quit acting like a bunch of old ladies gossiping." I replied.

"If you don't tell us, we'll make assumptions and spread bad rumors. That's what old ladies do." Michael giggled.

"No one will believe you." I whispered.

"We'll say we saw things and heard things." Max teased.

"Trevor, Okay! Now, shut-up. He's very shy and if you say anything, he may shy away." I hissed. I don't why I said that but I didn't have much choice. They weren't going to stop.

"Railroad mouth Trevor?" Max asked. He looked disgusted.

"I like smart and nice guys." I whispered.

"Do you like them slow and drooling too?" Michael added.

"Okay, you said if I tell you, you'll shut-up!" I hissed.

They both backed away looking disgusted by the information. The rest of the school day went by without any drama. After school I went over to the Burren estate to ask about Tina. It looked like she was healing fine and I did not have to be near her. Preston was so tender and loving around her. I was really surprised. He just met her and he acted like they've been together forever. Just the way he moved her, or gently brushed her hair, and caressed her skin, it was very warming. His eyes were always on her. I left there feeling a little lonely.

It was just another school day on Wednesday, so I thought. Before I could make it off my bike Aimee had informed me that Max and Michael had told Trevor of my *feelings* for him. I glared at them as I passed them at the locker area.

They were snickering at me. "Gena, we just wanted to help. It just breaks our heart to see you alone." They mocked.

"Too bad, your uncle didn't teach you how to drive a Monster truck. You could drive over their little cars and flattened it to a size of a stamp." Lauren said.

I dreaded going to Calculus but since I made the mess I had to fix it. This was going to be a long day. I walked in and saw Trevor sitting there waiting for me. He looked tensed.

As I sat down, he got up and pulled the chair out for me. I almost missed the chair.

"Gena, I want you to know, I mean you need to know…wait hold on." he took out a piece of paper with something written on it and stared at it for a few seconds and continue " I went and got my library card so now I'm ready to check you out." He stated.

It took all I had to not laugh. "Who told you to say that?" I said.

"Some of the guys were helping me with some pick-up lines." He admitted embarrassed.

"Don't ever use that line again. Trevor, we are friends. You are my Math partner and my lab partner. That is it. I see you as a friend. If you think of me otherwise, you are taking advantage of our friendship. Are you willing to take that risk? If you want I can ask Mandy to be my partner." I lectured.

"No, I'm sorry. You're a good friend." He replied quietly.

I was very proud of Trevor. He didn't let that issue bother him. We continue to work on our math problems without any uneasiness. During Physics, we laughed over other people's mistakes in chemical compounds. By the end of the day, we were friends and only friends.

As, I walked with Lauren and Dana to my motorcycle, I looked and saw Craig Morrow, sitting on my motorcycle. *No one sits on my Ducati.*

"Gena, I was wondering can you give me a ride?" he said arrogantly.

"Oh, you want a ride? Why sure." I handed my books to Lauren. "Hold these for a second; get everyone out of the way." I whispered to Lauren. I walked calmly over to the motorcycle. I got my riding jacket and helmet on. I slowly straddled on to the seat. "Get on, now you have to hold me *really* tight okay?" I instructed.

"Don't mind if I do. Once I get a hold of something I like, I never let go." He whispered into my ears. *I have to remember to clean my ears out thoroughly tonight.* I just straightened up and smiled back.

I started the engine and backed up slowly. I rode slowly pass all the people staring at us. Once I got to the end of the parking lot, I turned back around. I hesitated for a few seconds then raced down the lane; I jerked the handle up causing the motorcycle's front tires to rear up, dejecting Craig onto the hard pavement.

I turned around and pulled up next to him. "Next time you'll think twice about sitting on my *Ducati*." I warned.

"You, bitch, you almost killed me." He yelled.

I inched my motorcycle closer to him. He got up quickly and ran off.

"Now, I want to learn how to ride a motorcycle." Dana stated.

I got my things from Lauren and drove pass Michael and Max, "you're next", I said as I drove off.

You're such a show off.

Chapter Ten

We reached the Pacific Coast by Monday evening. After we washed and changed. We headed up the Yukon Territory toward Whitehorse. There we would have to wait until we were sure the scent was completely lost.

Max let us know that they reached Inuvik by Monday afternoon. He could not tell us how Tina was doing because no one was allowed to see her except for Preston and Alain.

"That sounds bad." Justin said sadly.

"Yeah, I don't know if Alain could do anything for her. She doesn't have an aura to heal her. Most humans wouldn't make it this long. Let's hope she has enough of our kind in her." I replied.

"How long do we have to wait out here?" Justin asked.

"I'm not too sure. I thought I caught their scent back in Fort McMurray that's why I wanted to continue the scent farther west but I haven't smelled anything since. I just hope they continue west. If they end at the Pacific they will lose the scent altogether and will have to either drop the chase or decide to go into Alaska or down the US western coast." I stated.

"Man, I never knew how good you are at this." He complimented.

"Yeah, I'm real good at running and escaping." I said sarcastically.

"You know what I mean." He responded.

We waited out in Whitehorse for 24 hours. After checking the area, we felt it was safe to travel to Dawson City. We arrived in Dawson City on Wednesday morning. We were both exhausted. We stayed in Dawson City for the next 24 hours. We kept in touch with Alain by phone. Tina was going to survive. Alain was kind of vague about the details of her recovery but I was just so happy for Preston.

"We can't seem to get him to leave her side. He looks horrible but he won't leave her. We can guess what this means." Alain said.

"We noticed it when we were traveling. He was exhausted but he would not let anyone carry her. I am happy for him." I stated.

"Okay, I have to go she is waking up. I will see you two on Thursday. Be safe." He ended.

By Wednesday evening Justin was getting on my nerves. He snored when he slept so that means only one of us could sleep at one time.

"Hey, Justin! I think its clear why don't we head back." I yelled.

"Sure, whatever you say captain." He replied.

We burnt every piece of clothing that we had on. After we changed we made our way back to Inuvik. Just to be cautious we did not take the straight path to Inuvik. We traveled into the Alaskan territory towards Beaufort Sea than came back down towards Inuvik.

We got back to Inuvik by early Thursday morning. Justin headed toward his house.

"Corin, she's not at my grandparents' house anymore. She has moved into her parents' house." He said laughing at me. It was very obvious that I wasn't going straight home. I can hear him laughing at my expense, but I didn't care. I made my way to the only person I wanted to see right now. I knew she was asleep but I wanted to see her face. I wanted to assure myself that she was here, safe and I didn't just dream of her.

I reached her house and scaled the back glass wall to the master bedroom. She had left the curtains pulled back. I balanced myself on the ledge and sat and watched her sleeping. I have been away from her for 5 days now. She slept peacefully. Her dark hair was a tangle mess around her face. Her facial features were relaxed making her more beautiful than I remembered. Her small rosy lips slightly parted. Her hands displayed beautifully over her stomach and breast. Her slow deliberate breathes made her breast rise and fall in a smooth rhythmic motion. It was erotic and mesmerizing. Even in her sleep she took my breath away.

She bewitched me.

Her hold on me was eternal.

I was a happily doomed man.

I got home around 3:30 am. I had to get some sleep. *I have school tomorrow.* I smiled.

"Corin, is that you?" I heard my mother from her bedroom.

"Yes, don't get up. I'm just going to go to bed." I answered back.

"Glad, you're home honey." She replied.

I had to set my alarm clock. I was so tired, I could easily sleep for days but I didn't want to miss the chance to see her.

It seemed like I just closed my eyes, when the alarm went off. I got up immediately, if I procrastinate, I would go back to sleep and be late. I quickly showered and grabbed a pair of jeans and a blue oxford button down shirt. I raced downstairs to the kitchen.

"I'm off to school." I announced.

"Son, you don't have to go today. It's just the first week of school. I talked to Thomas, he will take care of things. Aren't you tired?" my dad expressed.

"No, I want to go. Thanks though." I replied and left. I wanted to get to the parking lot early and talk to her before she started her day. I didn't know what classes she had and I know I could not wait until the end of the school day.

I pulled into my usual parking space and waited in the car. I watched as cars started pulling in. I looked for Lauren's red Mercedes convertible. Why does she have to ride with Lauren, she is always late. As I scanned, I saw a silver *Ducati* motorcycle pull into a parking space. The rider got out and pulled off her helmet. At that instant she took my breath away. As she removed her riding jacket, I lost all thoughts on what I was supposed to do that day. *How can she possible look sexier?*

"Nice, huh" That's what I thought when I first saw her do that. I think every boy in this school has been coming to the parking lot every morning to watch her do that. It doesn't get any less sexy. I've been encouraging Lauren to learn how to ride a bike." Max chuckled.

I cringed. Since I've been away everyone has been looking at her. Not after today. Let them be warned.

"Hey, nice to have you back. Have you seen Tina? She looks great. I think Preston has found his soul mate. He has not left her side since that night. It's a miracle she's alive." He jabbered.

I didn't look at Max while he was blabbering on about things I already knew. I watched her. I watched as she pulled her hair back. She was talking to Lauren and Aimee. Before I could think of what I need to say my legs started moving towards her. I felt my phone vibrate but I wanted to ignore it. After a few seconds, I pulled the phone from my jeans and answered it.

"What?" I stated. I was annoyed and irritated for the interruption. I was about to meet the girl of my dreams and someone was interrupting my destination.

"Corin, it's Justin. I told my dad about you and Gena. He wants to see you right now." He demanded.

"This can't wait until later." I said annoyed with his demand.

"He says right now. It is really important. It's about Gena." he reported. I stopped walking when I heard it was about her.

"I'll be there in a minute." I confirmed. I watched as she made her way into the building. She was walking away from me again. How many times must I endure this slow torture? Preston gets his girl and stays with her. I meet mine, but can't see or talk to her for one minute.

I got back in my car and drove towards Rolfe's house. If he has a problem with me being with Gena, he will just have to keep it to himself. He can't tell me I can't be with her. He's not her father. She has never needed him.

By the time, I got to the house I was ready for a huge argument if necessary. I was fired up and highly agitated. I haven't had good sleep for 3 days. The only time I was feeling good I get this interruption. Justin met me at the door.

"Thanks, for coming, Corin" He said.

"It didn't sound like I had a choice. What's going on?" I asked.

"He wants to talk to you about sex?" he replied.

I stopped in the foyer and turned around to face Justin. "Are you kidding me?" I said angrily.

"Nope" He said stupidly.

"I am not in the mood for this crap, Justin. What are you hiding from me?" I questioned.

"Corin, let's talk about this in my office, please." I heard Rolfe yelling from his office. I walked further down the hall to the office, Justin followed.

When we walked into the office, Alain was standing beside Rolfe near the fireplace.

"When is it your place to talk to me about sex? You're about three years too late." I said sarcastically.

"Sit down, Corin." Rolfe said.

"I'd rather stand. What is going on?" I asked.

"Justin told us that you believe Gena is your *concero flamma.* Are you sure about this?" he asked.

I was rather annoyed. Why was he questioning me? "I know she is." I confirmed.

"Well, congratulations Corin. I am truly happy for you. You're a perfect match for her." He announced.

"You brought me here to congratulate me?" I asked. I was getting suspicious. If they didn't have a problem with us being together than what was this meeting really about?

"Gena, is rather special, Corin. As Justin told you, she has not been around her kind all her life. Her aura has been dormant for all this time. She is slowly absorbing the auras around her." He said.

"That's why she has the headaches and nausea." Alain interrupted.

"Yes, and even though her aura is strong to those around her, it has yet to transform her to be like us. It's like she is human except for she has our aura. So, until she is completely transformed, you can not put her at risk for pregnancy. The fetus would kill her before she can protect herself. Do you understand?" He said factually.

I was shocked. I haven't even got to touch her or kiss her, and they're talking about sex. I have to admit, I wasn't even thinking about sex. All this time, I was just hoping to be with her.

"How long will it take for her to completely transform?" I asked.

"We don't honestly know. This has never happened before." Alain answered.

"What if we use birth control or protection?" I asked. I can't believe I am asking Rolfe and Alain this in front of Justin. I heard Justin chuckled in the background. I will kick his ass later.

"Human contraceptions do not work for our kind." Alain replied.

"So, how will I know when she has completely transformed?" I asked.

"Well the most definitive symptom is when her heart rate drops below any viable human rate. Her senses will be like ours. She will be able to heal herself. You will slowly see some progression but the most important one is the heart rate." Alain informed.

"In other words, Corin, congratulations on finding the girl of your dreams but oops you can't have sex with her. Hope you like foreplay." Justin said joking. I didn't think it was funny. I glared at him. Alain and Rolfe smiled.

I know this was serious but I got the sense that they also thought it is kind of funny. I love her. I can't help myself. If I have to wait than I will wait. I don't really have a choice in the matter. I will not lose her over something as trivial as sex. She's too important.

"What is your guess on the time frame?" I asked.

"If I were to guess, maybe two years" Alain answered.

I can handle two years. I thought he was going to tell me ten years or something really ridiculous. I was feeling a little better about the situation.

"It's okay Corin, learn to knit or sew. I heard it is really relaxing." Justin joked.

"Are we done here?" I asked. Alain and Rolfe nodded. As I exit the office, I threw my fist right into Justin's guts and walked away. I heard laughter erupt from the office. I was relieved that it was something minor.

I thought it would be something horrendous like she was leaving or dying. I can handle anything but those two things.

I made my way back to the school. I had missed my first class. My second class was World History. Max and Michael were in this class with me. We sat in the back.

"Hey, Corin, where did you go?" Max whispered.

"Rolfe's" I replied. I didn't have to elaborate. They know what that usually means.

"Hey, there's Craig Morrow. You should have seen what Gena did to him yesterday. I would have loved to Youtube that." Michael whispered.

"What happened?" I asked.

They proceeded to tell me about how she dropped him off her bike, but all I thought about was him holding her intimately. He has held her and I have not. They said something about him stalking her. I'll take care of that. They also told me about Trevor. I'll see Trevor at the lockers. When class was over, I walked up to Craig.

"Craig!" I said.

"Uh, hey Corin, what's up?" he hesitated.

"You have very nice blue eyes." I commented staring down at him.

"Uh, okay? Whatever." He said slowly backing away from me.

"If you would like to have them pulled from their sockets and handed to you, then I will kindly accommodate that. If I catch you even looking at her shoes, I will give you the opportunity to hold your eyes in your hands. Do I make myself clear?" I growled.

He did not answer. "Oh, and if you ever touch her again, I will use your own hands to remove your eyes. Understand?" I added with a smile.

He stood there and did not move. *One down and one more to go* I walked out to the locker area and spotted Trevor at his locker, combing his nasty hair. He was the epitome of drool and greasy disgust. What makes him think that he could even stand next to her? I made my way over to the locker next to his.

"Trevor, how are the braces coming along?" I asked.

"Hi, Corin. My braces are fine. Why do you want to know?" he asked nervously and cautiously.

"Well I was thinking that if you so much as think of Gena in any other way other than distant, *I mean really distant* friends. I could straighten your teeth out for you faster. Do you understand? Am I making myself clear?" I glared at him. I wasn't sure if he understood. His face was frozen and I couldn't see any intellect coming from him. Satisfied I walked away.

Well I got what needed to be done, done. School has been exhausting. I continue to my third class, English Literature. The class dragged on forever. When it was finally over, I met Max, Michael, Lawrence, Steven, Will, and Joseph at our usual table. We got there earlier since our classes were nearby. I sat at our table which faced the entranced, anxiously waiting for her to come through the door. Just when I was about to get restless, she came gracefully through the door. She was laughing and teasing Dana over something. She looked up and met my eyes. I did not look away. She appeared nervous over me staring at her. When she looked away, I was disappointed. They were making their way towards us, when something got her attention and she went towards her right. She was talking to Trevor. I became impatient and jealous. I would count to 30 no 20 than I would go get her.

Ten seconds later, I found myself heading towards her. She had sat down across from Trevor.

"Well, I think I got the answer to the first one, did you get it right away?" She was talking to Trevor.

"Gena" I said quietly. I stared down at Trevor. I envisioned pulling each tooth out slowly and jamming it back into his mouth. He retreated back from the table.

"Corin" She replied. She was looking down at her tray.

"Gena, can I talk to you?" I asked through my teeth.

"Corin, I'm talking to Trevor, can this wait until later?" she asked. She didn't realize she was practically guaranteeing Trevor's makeover.

"Trevor, can I talk to Gena, privately?" I dared him.

"Gena, I have to go finish up some things. I'll see you in class as friends okay?" he stuttered. He picked up his tray and scurried off.

"Corin, that was really rude. I can't believe you just did that." she said scolding me.

"I need to talk to you privately, can we go outside?" I asked impatiently.

"Whatever you have to say to me, you can say right here." She said firmly.

I looked up and saw everyone at the table staring at us. I could also see that everyone at my table was also staring.

"Come on." I said quickly as I grabbed her hand and pulled her out of her seat and towards the exit. I ushered her through the exit doors toward the picnic tables. She was so angry, she tried to go back in but I pulled her along with me until we were passed the picnic area and near the trees leading into the woods.

"Corin, let go of my hand." She yelled. "You are the most arrogant jerk. You just dragged me out here like some caveman. Who do you think you are? First you flirt with me on the plane, leading me to believe that you liked me. Than I see you with Natalie. Then you stop talking to me altogether. Now this! You think you can just drag people's heart around and not take responsibility for the mess you leave behind. You are not the center of my universe, you know!" she blabbered.

I watched as she talked with her hands. The way her breathing became labored and faster. The frustration noted in her facial expression. I came up close to her. I braced my hands on either side of her face and slowly leaned forward.

"But you are the center of mine." I whispered forcing her eyes to look at mine. I could feel the warmth coming from her body. All I could think about was touching her. I wanted to breath in her scent, taste her lips, and feel her skin.

"Corin, what did you just say?" she whispered.

I looked at her face; my eyes went to her rosy soft lips. I have been dreaming about those lips since the first time I ever saw them.

"Corin?" she whispered. I watched as my name left her lips. It was bewitching. The way she caressed my name was intoxicating.

"Say that again." I whispered.

"Corin " It was all I heard before I grabbed the back of her head and rushed her lips against mine. My mouth came down hard over hers; I wanted absolute possession of her. She opened her mouth to protest, and when she did I took immediate advantage and swept my tongue inside her mouth. *God she tasted better than I could have ever imagined.* I couldn't get enough of her. I pulled her even closer, cupped my hands behind her neck and angled her head to one side so my tongue could make a deeper penetration. My mouth slanted over hers again and again. She tasted so good, so sweet and the little moans she made in the back of her throat destroyed all my control. I can feel her breathe gasping and labored. I started to stop to let her catch her breathe but then her hands came up and grasped at my hair forcing me to hunger for more. I pushed her up against the tree, when I heard her moan it sent waves of excitement throughout my body. I had never known kissing to be this erotic. I could not take in enough of her. If I was crushing her against the tree; she was not complaining.

Our moment of bliss was interrupted when we heard people jeering and whistling.

"Get a room."

"Corin, Trevor is going to get upset"

"Principal's coming"

"What happens in Inuvik, will be seen on Youtube"

They were all standing outside hooting and hollering remarks to embarrass us. To save myself from wanting to kiss her again, I hid my face in the crook of her neck. We were both dazed and overwhelmed. I could feel her heart pounding inside her chest.

"Will this happen every time I say your name?" she murmured. Her breathing was labored and rapid.

I looked up at her beautiful brown eyes. Her eyes were dark and sultry. Her lips were swollen from kissing."We can put it to a test? Come on." I said.

"Where are we going?" she asked.

"We're going to ditch the rest of the day." I explained. I couldn't wait to have her all to myself.

"I am not going to ditch school. You just got here today. You shouldn't be ditching either." She scolded me. She looked beautiful even when she was scolding me.

"What class do you have next that is more important than us?" I questioned.

"Nothing is more important than us, but I have Human Sexuality next and I believe you are in my class. If you don't show up I will tell on you." She mocked me.

"Well if Human Sexuality is our next class than you're right. School is very important. We should not be late." I answered enthusiastically. But what got me excited was not the class but when she said *nothing is more important than us*. I totally agree.

We pushed through the crowd and went directly to our next class. I held her hand the entire time. When we got to the classroom, she started to sit in the front of the class.

"No, Gena. I want you back here with me" I said quietly. I pulled her along with me to the very last row in the corner.

"I think you're a very bad influence on me. I may fail this elective because of you." She said.

"Well, you're in luck. I just happen to be the best Human Sexuality tutor ever and I am totally available to you at anytime." I offered.

"How much is this going to cost me?" She played along.

"I'll send you a bill." I warned with a smile.

"And what if I don't pay up" She mocked.

"I will come to collect." I winked.

She paid attention in class, while I sat with all my attention on her. I watched how her small body moved when she breathed. I watched as she pulled her hair back from her face with her hands. I found myself touching her hair without her even knowing it. Once, I brushed my knee next to hers on purpose just to touch her. It was the best Human Sexuality class I've ever taken.

"Gena, what's your schedule?" I whispered.

She handed me her schedule. I looked at it. I wanted every class to be like this one. I decided when she was in the next class I was going to have Thomas change my schedule to be the same as hers. I brushed my fingers over her hand under the table and placed the paper into her hand but instead of letting go I entwined our fingers. She looked down at our hands and than at me and smiled. I saw her glanced over at Natalie and dropped my hands.

As we walked to her next class I assured her "Don't worry about Natalie, she's easy distracted."

"You don't know that." she said quietly.

"I've known her all my life. She has no commitment to anyone for too long. I was a just a conquest." I informed.

"Conquest, huh? Am I you're conquest." she said.

"I've fought and battle for you. You're my prisoner for life." I winked at her. I can tell she liked that response. We walked to her French II class and I left her with Lauren. "I'll see you in Home Economics." I said before I brushed my lips over hers.

I wondered the hallway to the main office. After getting my schedule reorganized, I look over the classes she took. Calculus and Physics, no wonder she befriended Trevor. I guess I have some making up to do with Trevor.

When I got to Home Economics, she was sitting in the front with Mandy Toomes. I came over to her and said "Come sit with me or I'll make a scene." I warned with a slight pull on her shirt sleeve. She got up and moved to the back of the class with me.

"You're a spoil brat." She said.

"And you indulge me." I responded.

Baking oatmeal cookies was on the assignment today in Home Economics. She did most of the work while I messed with the equipment.

"Why did you take this class?" she asked.

"Michelle, signed me up as punishment for not being home in time last week." I answered.

"You couldn't help that." she defended. I liked it when she defended me. It was endearing.

"She waited and probably for the same reasons you're in here we find ourselves making oatmeal cookies. These look disgusting. Did you follow the instructions right? You know I'll be judging your cooking." I commented.

"They always look lumpy and brown. I've done this before you know. You may be surprise." She responded.

She doesn't know how she has surprised my total existence since she has come into my life. I can't remember ever being this excited to be with anyone.

Chapter Eleven

Thursday turned out to be the best day since meeting my new family. I didn't expect to see Corin until Friday, so I was surprised this morning when I saw his car in the parking lot. Then I was disappointed when he left in his car without saying one word to me. How does one person have so much control over someone's life that one minute I was happy and the next my joy plummeted.

Regardless of how things went this morning I am satisfied with the turn out. I laughed at myself. All the defiant things I was going to do and say to him, all went out the window when he kissed me this afternoon. I was a poor representation for free minded women. We were walking to my motorcycle with a plate full of oatmeal cookies. *How ironic.*

"I saw you on your bike this morning. You almost set off a crime wave." He said with a crooked smile on his beautiful face.

"Quit exaggerating. There is a guy over there with a motorcycle; I don't see a crime wave happening over there." I replied. I was flattered by his comment but I could not let him know that.

"He doesn't look as good as you do on your *Ducati*." He commented.

"You like my motorcycle?" I asked. He knew the name, so I was hoping he would appreciate the greatness of my bike. It was a bit of a show-off thing to fish for compliments for my bike.

"I like you on your *Ducati*. I don't think anyone else on a *Ducati* will have the same effect for me." He said with a smile. His smile could melt my heart any time.

"Can I come over?" he asked.

"Only if you help me eat these cookies, I told you, we made too many. It would really ruin my GPA if I fail Home Economics too." I said.

"Well, we'll just have to practice and practice a lot. Failure is not an option." He laughed. I smile when I heard the word "we" coming from his lips.

He helped me with my riding jacket and tucked my hair inside my helmet. "I heard what you did to Craig Morrow. If I asked you for a ride, would you dump me off too?" He asked.

"No, we would ride off into the sunset." I said. I was getting good at charming him. I was pretty proud of myself for coming up with that comment with him standing so near me.

"I'll see you in a bit." He said. I could feel him watching me ride away.

When I got to my house, the laundry I had left this morning was done and placed in clear plastic bags. *They dry cleaned everything?* I felt a little spoiled. I took the bags in and threw them over the stair banister; *I'll put them up later.*

"Today was laundry day?" he said standing at the door.

"That was fast." I said. I was a bit startled to find him there so quickly. I wanted to clean the house a bit but forget it now. "So, when is your laundry day?"

"I don't know, my mom takes care of that." he replied.

"Well, lucky you." I stated quietly.

"I'm sorry about your mom." he said as he pulled me to him. He looked down into my eyes with his intense blue eyes, he was hypnotizing me. "I don't want you to have to endure anymore heartaches in your life."

"That's quite a goal to set for me." I replied.

"We'll work on it together." He said as his hands came up to my face. His thumb traced my lips. His eyes came down to my lips, with the same longing and wanting as this afternoon. He kissed me so forcefully this time, without any hesitation. He was much more passionate and unreserved. When I parted my lips to allow his tongue to explore my mouth, he tightened his grip and pulled me against him. I clung to his body, feeling his hard muscles, returning his kiss with as much passion. When he finally broke off the kiss he just stood there looking down at me. Very deliberately and slowly, he caressed my face with his lips, inhaling my scent as he made his way down my neck. His hands slid down to the curvature of my back to hold me still while he explored the scent from my neck. "God, you smell good." He murmured in my neck.

"I think you're just a bit biased right now." I murmured. It was hard to come up with those words while he was caressing the front of my neck then rounding to the side.

"You are wrong. It isn't any perfume or lotion it just your natural scent. It really turns me on." He murmured.

"You are right I don't wear any thing. It irritates my skin." I told him.

"Good, I like the way you smell." He said.

Sensing that this was a good time to take a break, I pulled back and smiled. "I have a lot of homework and you're not helping." I informed him.

"Well, I changed my schedule to match yours so *we* have a lot of homework." He corrected me.

"Great, so you're taking Calculus and Physics with me. I already have a math and lab partner." I said slyly.

"Well, I'll just have to kill Trevor." He said sarcastically.

"Stop it, be nice. If we get the three problems in Calculus right, we can exempt the finals." I told him. We started walking into the living room. He fumbled with the switch to open up the curtains.

"Wow, that's not something you see everyday." He said as he admired my dad's architectural work on the glass walls.

"I know it takes a bit getting use to. Do you want anything to drink?" I asked.

"Sure. Whatever you have" He answered. He sat down on the couch and played with the books left on the coffee table.

I made my way to the kitchen and got two Cokes. When I came back he was resting on the couch. He raised his arms out to invite me to lie next to him. I placed the cokes down and sprawl out next to him on the couch. He held me in his arms, as I laid looking up at him. My face was position perfectly in the crook of his neck.

"Gena, I would ask that you stop breathing on my neck, but that would probably kill you. It is driving me insane. If you don't turn around I may end up doing some thing offensive." He warned.

I giggled but turned facing outward. I could feel his face submerged in my messy hair. He wrapped his arms around my chest and stomach. I caressed his hands and arms. It felt natural to be here with him, in his arms. After a few minutes, I felt his body relaxed. I looked up at the corner my eyes, *he was sleeping*. I laid there playing with the little hairs on his arms. When I felt he was deeply asleep, I eased myself off the couch and out of his arms. Looking down at him sleeping, he was divine. I don't know how I know it or when I felt it, but I know now I will always want this man.

I quietly cleaned the house and put my laundry up. I sat on the floor in front of him doing my homework on the coffee table. After awhile, I went into the kitchen to start dinner. I went into the pantry and looked around for something to make for our first dinner. I wanted something special but I didn't know what to look for. As I got closer to the end of the pantry I remembered the panic room. I remember the story of the survivors who fled into the panic room for safety. I thought about what I would do if I had to defend myself. I went back into the kitchen and got a kitchen knife. I walked back to the panic room door. I pricked my index finger and placed a drop of blood into the scanner on the left side of the wall. Immediately the door pulled back. It was so sudden and forceful that the room rattled. I took two steps toward the entrance.

"Gena! No!" I heard yelled from behind me.

I was so startled I turned quickly. "God, you startled me." I said frightened.

"I'm sorry, but don't go in there." He directed.

"I was just curious. I wasn't planning on staying in there." I explained.

"If you walk through the door it will automatically shut you in. You will have to scan from the inside to get out." He explained.

"Oh, well I could scan to get out so why can't I just see what its like inside." I asked.

"Gena, this panic room was made for our kind. If you notice there is no air ventilation going in or out. Until you have completely transformed, you will not be able to last an hour in there." He explained.

"Well, I wasn't planning to stay an hour either, but I'm glad you told me that." I said quietly.

"It was made like that to prevent the scent of the survivors from being picked up by the hunters. If they know you're in the panic room they will wait. They have the patience to wait for weeks, until you die of starvation or thirst. Even for us, it is uncomfortable to not breathe after 12-15 hours." He explained.

"Well, that is disturbing." I stated. I placed another drop of blood into the scanner and the door quickly closed.

I walked slowly out of the pantry. "Sorry, if I woke you." I apologized.

"No, I'm sorry for falling asleep on you. You made it so easy for me to relax. Plus, when I was away from you I couldn't sleep. I kept thinking about you." He explained as he ran his fingers through his hair.

"Stop enchanting me, if you haven't noticed you already have me." I hinted.

"I didn't know that at the time." he mumbled. "Why did you want to see the panic room?"

"Well I just thought if I needed it I should at least familiarize myself to it." I explained.

"Gena, I will never allow anything or anyone to hurt you. I promise." He said as he came over and wrapped his arms around my waist.

"Corin, you can not take that responsibility. You're not with me 24 hours a day." I reminded him.

"Well I'm working on it. I changed my class schedule, so that's 8 hours there. I'll be here until you ask me to leave. I don't have to go home. I can perched myself right outside your door if you like." He murmured as he nuzzled at the side of my neck.

"Will you be serious and what do you mean you don't have to go home?" I asked.

"My parents haven't placed any restrictions on me since I was 16 years old. I don't think they will start now." He replied. "Are you going to feed me? I am starving?"

"Well, I was working on that before you accosted me in the pantry?" I humored.

"Am I accosting you now?" he whispered as his lips started descending down the side of my neck. I can hear him inhaling my scent as he moved along. His hands massaged the back of my neck exposing my neck to him. "I don't think I can ever get enough of you."

"Corin, I thought you said you were hungry." I said, panting.

"I don't think I need food right now." He answered with his lips still on my skin.

"What do you need right now?" I asked, unconsciously.

"I don't think it's gentlemanly of me to say." He murmured. Instantly we felt the cell phone in his pocket vibrate. "I swear this thing is going to get tossed." He hissed.

"What!" he answered. I struggled against him trying to get loose but he wouldn't allow it. "I wasn't being rude, what do you want, Max? I'm at Gena's. Where?" he sounded irritated as he snapped the phone shut.

"What did Max want?" I asked.

"They want to come over, no they're here. I'll go tell them to leave." He said irritated.

"Corin, stop! You are being very inhospitable." I pleaded.

"Okay, but they can not stay long. I am not ready to share you yet." He stated.

I went to the door and opened it before they could ring the door bell. "House Warming Party!" they announced in unison.

"Max, I thought you said it was just you and Lauren." Corin yelled from behind me.

"Oops, I lied." He replied innocently.

"You're an asshole." Corin cursed at him.

"Corin, be nice." I pleaded.

"Yeah, Corin be nice. It's not your house you know. Thank you, Gena, for being such a gracious host. It is really hard to find good family and friends nowadays. I hope we aren't interrupting anything. We wouldn't want to do that." Justin said mockingly.

I had to hold Corin back. "Justin, behave or go home." I scolded. I could tell he was making a private joke towards Corin, mocking him. I will have to ask him about it later.

"We brought House Warming Gifts and food. Is it okay?" Aimee asked.

"It is fine. Corin is just a little irritable because he didn't get enough sleep." I said.

They all came in couples. Lauren and Max brought over a veggie plate. Mark and Ella bought over pizza. Tristan and Aimee brought over chips and salsa. Dana invited Derek over. Justin, Trey, Michael and Cory invited themselves for free food and drinks. Michelle came over with Brent.

It was a very comfortable get together. Everyone laughed and told stories. Justin continued to get on Corin's nerves.

"Gena, I am begging you to teach Lauren how to ride a motorcycle. If not, maybe just how to get on and off one. I'll buy her a riding jacket. Do you need a helmet if you're just getting on and off?" He asked as he winked toward Lauren.

"Max, I told you. I am not coordinated enough to sit upright on the thing." Lauren said sternly.

"Well, we'll just take some pictures with you in a tight leather riding suit and have you toss your hair around." He said.

"That sounds like fun." Lauren replied.

It was fun to seem them lovingly kid around with each other. Tristan and Aimee were somewhat similar. They were so easy around each other. They ended each other sentences. He was very polite and courteous of her needs. They didn't need to ask each other for any thing; it's like they knew what each other needed before anything had to be said. They ended everything with a gentle kiss, or caress. But it was really about how they looked at each other. No matter where she was in the room, he always found her.

"Gena, did Corin tell you why he was so ornery last week?" Justin asked.

"Justin, shut-up!" Corin snapped.

"Corin was lead to believe that you and I were getting married." He announced laughing.

"Who told you something like that?" Dana questioned.

"It was a simple misunderstanding." Corin mumbled.

I turn to look at him. I smiled and winked at him. He got up and went toward Justin. Max grabbed him by the stomach before he got there. "Okay, I think that's our cue to go." Aimee said.

"Come on everybody, party's over." Tristan announced.

Lauren and Aimee helped clean up a bit before they left. I was standing in the kitchen when Corin came back in.

"That was fun." I said.

"They would use any excuse to have a party." He replied.

"So, you thought I was marrying Justin, huh? Is that why you acted so distant?" I asked coyly.

"I'm sorry. I know my behavior was childish but I was not in my right state of mind. I met you on the plane. Then my dad told me he thought you were Justin's fiancée coming for a visit and I lost it." He confessed.

"Did you ever think to ask me? It would've saved you a lot of grief." I said.

"I know that now but back then I was hopeless. The thought of finding you and losing you all in one day was agonizing." He admitted as he came up close behind me. He was playing with my hair. I can feel the closeness of him. He slowly slid his arms around me and pulled me back into him. He rested his face in my hair.

"Corin, you said earlier that you did not have to go home. Remember?" I reminded him.

"Uh, huh." He murmured in my hair.

"Would you think badly of me, if I asked you to stay with me tonight?" I asked embarrassed by my boldness.

He stopped nuzzling my neck and turned me around to face him. "I'll go get a change of clothing." He rushed out the front door and was gone. All I could do was stand there and laugh.

He was back before I finished loading the dishwasher. I smiled when he came in. He helped straightened the living room. He hit the switch to close all the curtains. The artificial lights didn't seem to be romantic as when the curtains were open.

"Corin, leave the curtains open." I said.

"No, you never know there maybe some peeping Toms." He laughed.

I finished in the kitchen and went to join him in the living room. He was sitting on the couch.

"So, what do you want to do?" I asked.

"What I want to do and what I can do is two different subjects. Come over here." He requested.

"Do you mind if I ask you a personal question?" I asked as I settled on his lap.

"No, go ahead." He replied.

"You guys have the ability to find your soul mates, what about us girls? How do we know that you're the not just messing around? When did you know for sure?" I asked.

"Gena, what do you know about the *concero flamma*?" he asked.

"Well I don't really understand how it works but I know the translation from Latin is *twin flame*, which is also referred to as soul mate, right?" I answered.

"Yes, but it's a little more complicated than that. I want to start by telling you that I know with all my heart that you are my *concero flamma.* I knew that the moment I saw you on the plane behind the curtain. When I got on the plane, I was drawn by this undeniable urge to find you. Once our eyes met, I could not help myself. I remember you were having a headache but I could not stop bothering you. You probably thought I was rude and talkative but I did not care. I thought up a thousand ways to touch you. When you allowed me to touch your face, I was very close to stealing you away. It is a powerful feeling of wanting and needing. This power does not yield with distant or time. When I close my eyes, I could only see you. So, when I was told that you were Justin's fiancée, I nearly lost all my senses. Usually when, we meet our *concero flamma* we pursue them endlessly. That pursuit is what allows the girl to see the true person in us. We express our feelings without any reservations, and I think that is why the girl being pursued can not fend from loving back. Do you understanding?" he ended.

"Can you be wrong?" I asked.

"I have never heard of such. I don't know why a guy would fake such a thing. It is really important for him and his future. Because if he is wrong and one day she may leave him for her true soul mate. Why would you risk that?" He explained.

"Well it is just so definite. What if the girl rejects him?" I asked

"Well there is this undeniable draw that happens between two people that compels them to want to be together. It is almost like they can not help themselves. They really can't ignore it or control it. Like when we were on the plane, I could not stop myself from talking to you or sitting next to you. I hated that curtain. I was so irritated when you sat behind that curtain for 12 minutes." He expressed.

"You timed the minutes I was behind the curtain?" I questioned.

"It took you away from me for 12 minutes. I didn't have a lot of time, so 12 minutes was really agonizing." He said as he placed his hand on my face.

"All you had to say was that you loved me." I said sarcastically.

He laughed. "I love you, Gena Reynolds." He said. "How do you feel about me?"

"Well in the past 5 days, I have not stop thinking about you. I remember every word you've said to me. I remember when you touched my lips and my face. I dreamt about what you're kiss would be like. I wait anxiously to see you. I get very disappointed when you're not around. If that is love, than maybe I love you, too Corin." I ended silently looking into his eyes.

"I love the way that come off your lips." he whispered in my ear. He got up and started pulling me towards the stairs.

"So does everyone know about us now?" I asked

"Yeah, I think so. I told my parents earlier when I went home to get some clothes." He mentioned.

"What do they think of me asking you to stay over tonight?" I asked, feeling a bit guilty.

"We don't think of it like that. I would be unhappy when I'm not with you so what choice do I or they have? It is our destiny to be together, whether it is now or later. Now let's put you to bed. We do have school tomorrow." He stated. He pulled me upstairs to my bedroom. "Where do you want me to sleep?" he asked.

"Do we have to sleep? I want to continue talking to you." I asked selfishly.

"We can do whatever you want. Come on I'll talk you to sleep." He said.

I went and changed into my t-shirt and boxer short. When I came back into the room, he was laying on top of the covers. He had removed his shirt and still had his jeans on. I was struck by his handsomeness. I looked over him slowly. His body was overwhelmingly masculine, rock-hard and muscular but lean not bulky. His chest was wide and broad. The muscles running along his arms were strong and solid. Seeing him laying there was like having an extraordinary erotic dream.

"Come let's bore you to sleep." He chuckled.

I got into bed and snuggled next to him. I placed my hand on his bare chest and played with the fine hair that was on his chest.

"Gena, I'm 19. How old are you?" he asked.

"I'm 18." I responded.

"When is you're birthday?" he asked. I can feel his hand caressing up and down my right arm. I can't believe such a simple act was so sensual.

"June 28th. When is yours?" I answered numbly. I could not concentrate on anything but the way his fingers played with the skin on my arm.

"October 23rd." He replied.

"So in your eighteen years without me, how many boyfriends have you had?" he asked.

"I've had only two. One when I was sixteen. He gave me my first kiss. His name was Joseph. He moved away. Than there was Peter" I responded.

"How long were you with Peter?" he asked with a slight tone of resentment.

"We dated for 4 months." I answered.

"Were you intimate with him?" He asked quietly.

"No." I responded.

"Have you ever loved anyone before? Besides your family" he muffled from the back of my ears.

"Well, I guess I can say I loved Peter. We were really good friends before we got closer. I loved him but not love him. Do you know what I mean? He died this past July." I said.

"Do you miss him?" he asked.

"Yeah, he was a very kind, unselfish, easy to love kind of guy. You would've liked him." I said.

"Gena, I would like him just as much as I like Trevor. I'm just being brutally honest and possessive." He said with a smile.

"No, I think you would like him." I reconfirmed.

"I'm jealous of him now." He said as he kissed the back of my ear.

"Why are you jealous? After everything we've said to each other. I've confessed more to you than I have ever said to anyone." I said carefully.

"I'm jealous of the time he had with you. Don't think of me badly when I say this; I am thankful that you are alive to be here with me today. But I still wished that you were raised here. Imagine if we found each other at birth and never missed any time apart. We would probably be married and this would be us growing old together right now." He explained.

"That is a bit on the obsessive side." I said.

"I was dreaming of the possibility." He whispered into my ear.

"You would probably grow tire of me if that was the case." I said.

"I don't believe that is possible. I am lying here with you in my arms, yet I wished to have back your past eighteen years." He yearned.

"Well, unlike you I am thankful for what I have right now." I confirmed.

"I am thankful too; I'm just crazy about you. I am very impatient. I want to know everything about you. I want to know what you did when you were little. What were your favorite toys? What is your favorite color? You know all that stuff." He let out.

"Well, I like the color blue, like your eyes. My favorite toy was the Ken doll, because it reminds me of you. I like fast motorcycles. Your car would probably be something I like if I wanted a car. I really don't have a favorite flower because I like all flowers, just as long as it comes from you. I don't own any fancy jewelry or wear makeup. Maybe once in a while I'll put on lip gloss. I can read music and play the piano. I took ballet when I was little but I wasn't graceful enough to do anything with that. I wasn't into sports. Once I tried to play tennis but I sprained my ankles more than I could count. I was a cheerleader once, but the drama from being a cheerleader got tiresome. I watch football, whenever I was with Peter. I like to watch my uncle race his cars. I like riding my motorcycle. What else can I tell you? What about you?" I finished.

"Ken doll huh? Well, I have always lived here. You are more beautiful than any doll imaginable. I played with Legos and levers as a child. My favorite color is green but I do love your brown eyes and hair. I think we both like good fast mechanical things. A motorcycle is really hard to drive around Inuvik in the winter time. I have been searching for you as long as I can remember. I used to dream about what you would look like or be like and my imagination does you no justice. You far exceed my dreams. I am the fastest and strongest in this clan. I have been doing missions for Rolfe since I was sixteen. I like hockey and soccer but if you want me to play football, I would gladly accommodate you. I would love to see you in a cheerleading outfit. I like you just the way you are without makeup or lip gloss. I don't play any musical instruments. I can't even read music. I do love to see you play though. Other than that I am quite boring." He ended.

"You dreamt of me?" I asked flattered.

"I dreamt of the possibility of you. I guess in my heart, I knew you were out there somewhere." He admitted.

"What did you think I looked like?" I asked curiously.

"Well. Let's just say I got the brown hair and pink lips right." He chuckled.

"How many girlfriends have you had?" I asked.

"I have had no girlfriends in my life." He confirmed.

"None" I reiterated

"Well, I have had relationships with women but they were not my girlfriends." He corrected.

I was kind of embarrassed by that comment but I did ask. It was nice to know that he had never belonged to anyone else. *Now I was the possessive one.* I moved closer to him, placing half of my body over his chest. I could hear the faint beats of his heart. "You're heart beat is so slow. It's almost unbelievable that you are alive." I commented.

"It will be the same for you when you've completely transformed." He pointed out.

"If I had never discovered my real family, would I eventually become human?" I asked.

"No, you're aura will always be with you. It will stay dormant. But you may be hiking one day and if a hunter happens upon your scent he will kill you. You wouldn't be able to defend yourself because your aura has not been developed. They could pick up your scent from hundred of miles out. This happens to a lot of our kind who wants to leave this life behind and try to be human. We hear stories of them being mauled by bears, mountain lions, and so on but we know it isn't an animal. Sometimes you don't necessarily have to be hiking, there was a "satanic ritual" killing in New York City, where the whole family were beheaded. That family used to be from here. They left here wanting to change themselves. The son came back here looking for a wife once but could not convince someone to go back with him." He recounted.

"Why did he have to come back here for a wife? Can't he find someone in New York?" I asked.

"We don't have a clan in New York." He replied.

"Does she have to be one of us? Why couldn't she be human?" I asked.

"Gena, our kind can never be intimate with humans. If the human girl gets pregnant the fetus will kill her before the first month. Even if she didn't even know she was pregnant. It is nature's cruel way of keeping our kind in check. We can never integrate our species with the human species. It is the same way with the hunters. Not all of them are born with the genetic makeup of their kind. They could have three kids and only one has the gene, in some cases none. Nature can not allow two of the most powerful species to have unlimited resources." He continued.

"So, since I have not transformed yet, what about us?" I asked.

"That is what I was discussing with Rolfe and Alain today. They called me just before school this morning and asked to talk to me. Justin had told them about my feelings for you. So they had to warn me." He stated.

"Warn you about what?" I asked.

"Well, since you have not completely transformed yet, we can not risk getting you pregnant so no sex. I don't want to risk your life over pregnancy and I can wait. Don't get me wrong, I want you in every way possible, but I will not risk hurting or possibly killing you." He stated adamantly.

"Can't we use birth control or something? I mean not now but later when we want to?" I asked.

"Those only work on humans; they have no effect on our kind." He answered.

"How long will it take for me to be completely transformed?" I asked.

"Alain guessed two years maybe three." He responded.

"Are you okay with that? I know you have needs. You don't have to wait for me. I will understand." I said. It ache my heart to think of him with someone else but if he needed intimacy that I could not provide I would understand why he would chose someone else.

"You say that like I have a choice. Have you been listening to anything I've said? I could never want anyone but you. There could be beautiful women everywhere but my desire could only be for you. Knowing that you exist, I could never want anyone else. I have needs but my wanting to be with you far outweighs the intimate desires." He stated firmly.

"Are you sure?" I asked again.

"I don't want anyone but you. I can only love you. If anything ever happens to you, then I will follow you to the next life. Life would be cruel and unbearable without you. Before, when I didn't know that you existed, my life was just getting by each day. Now that I know you exist, life would not be the same for me if you were gone." He confirmed.

I felt selfishly relieved to hear those words. How can I not love this man with all my heart? He is everything I could possibility want and more.

It was a cruel joke to not be able to make love to him when we wanted to. Right now, I wasn't ready but I know deep in my heart that if I could, I would be willing to give him whatever he wanted even if he wanted it tomorrow. Who am I kidding, if he wanted me now I would probably give in to him. I had no willpower when it comes to him. I couldn't deny him anything. But right now he is willing to wait and that was so beautiful to me.

"So how do we know when I am ready?" I hesitated.

"When your heart rate is the same as mine" He answered.

"Two years, huh" I repeated.

"Gena, we can do many things besides making love." He rolled me over onto my back. He placed his body on top of me.

"We can do this." he kissed my cheeks.

"How about this?" he kissed my neck.

"I like this." he placed his hand inside my shirt and caressed my stomach.

"This is definitely a must do." he slid his hands down the side of my hips down my legs and pulled it over his back.

"But I like this the most" with those last words he covered my mouth with his. I can sense the hunger coming from him. When I moaned, his kissed became more intense and forceful. His tongue teased my lips until they parted so he could overwhelm my mouth with his tongue. It was a mixture of raw desire and yearning. Earlier I was worried that he may not be able to wait two years, now I question my ability to wait. He slowly pulled away and rolled on to his back pulling me with him. My breathing was labored and panting.

"Now go to sleep." He whispered. His arms tightened around my waist and shoulder. There I settled into a blissful sleep.

Chapter Twelve

"Baby, wake up." He whispered as he caressed my face.

"What time is it?" I mumbled.

"Its 6:30 am." He answered.

"Why are we getting up so early?" I asked as I turned over and cover my face.

"Don't you need time to get ready for school?" he asked tugging at the comforter.

"I only need twenty minutes. You're killing my beauty sleep." I murmured from under the comforter.

"Really? Twenty minutes." He asked astonished.

"Why do you want breakfast?" I asked pulling back the covers. I felt guilty. He was probably used to his mother making him a grand breakfast before school. Here I rarely ate. He would probably complain of starvation and run back home.

"No, I can do that myself. I just thought women needed a lot of time to get ready." I guessed.

"Not all women. What time did you wake up?" I asked as I turned back under covers.

"Just half an hour ago, I was watching you sleep." He stated without any hesitation.

"Anything interesting" I asked.

"You're interesting and beautiful." He commented as he nuzzled the back of my neck, inhaling the scent of my hair.

"You're being bias again." I stated.

"Since you're awake, I wanted to ask you something?" he asked.

"I knew you had an ulterior motive. Ask away." I answered.

"How do you feel about riding with me to school?" he asked.

"Is that what you want?" I asked.

"I was just thinking that I don't think I can continue to threaten every guy in school if you continue to have an audience in the parking lot, drooling over you." He explained.

"Corin, you are ridiculous. There is no audience. You imagination is crazy."

"I'm not the only one that thinks that way." He suggested.

"Max, Cory and Michael don't count." I answered.

"We're still men. We know what other men think and sometimes it isn't so innocent." He replied.

"You woke up early to worry about this. I am going to have to keep you busy so we will sleep the same hours." I said giggling.

"Are we going to sleep together every night?" he asked brazenly

"Do you want to?" I asked but selfishly I wanted him to stay with me.

"That is a stupid question. Of course, I want to. I was waiting for the invitation." He stated confidently.

"That was the real reason you woke me up early wasn't it?" I clarified.

"Yeah, while I was watching you sleep, I decided that I didn't want to miss waking up with you. Nothing in my bedroom compares to seeing your face first thing in the morning." He said bluntly.

"Well, what about the motorcycle thing?" I asked.

"Well, I figured once I got to stay, I would work the riding together angle." He admitted.

"You sure do a lot of planning and plotting early in the morning. I can barely decide what to wear." I answered.

"If you're adamant about taking the Ducati, than I will ride piggyback. Maybe if they see me riding piggyback, it won't be such a turn on." He stated sarcastically.

"You riding with me sound nice." I said silently.

"Yeah, I hear about those rides you give people. Trust me; I'm a little harder to buck off. I won't let go." He added.

"I am counting on that." I said.

"Come on, get up. I'll go make breakfast. I hardly see you eat." He noticed.

Begrudgingly, I dragged myself out of bed and in the shower. I showered quickly and dried my hair. Since he had on jeans, I got a pair of jeans and pulled on a long sleeve tee and covered that with a thin blouse.

When I got downstairs, I could smell French toast. I couldn't remember the last time I'd French toast. I was a lazy eater so it was easy for me to skip meals or just eat cereal. "You spoil me." I stated.

"I would make something fancier but you don't have much. I was lucky to find these things." He complained.

"Something fancier than French toast" I commented.

"You may fail Home Economics after all. I guess you will need a tutor in that as well. I'll tell you what. If you help me in those easy classes like Calculus and Physics, I take care of the harder courses." He laughed.

"You've got a deal." I played along.

"Here you're going to have to eat it without syrup." He handed me a plate.

"I didn't know you put syrup on French toast?" I confessed.

"You're hopeless. See how much you need me. I don't know how long you would've lasted in Home Economics. I think I'm getting the crappier end of the deal. Cooking, Knitting, Crocheting, Gardening, when will it end." He teased.

"I do need you, in many ways." I said as I came close to him. I pulled his face down close to mine and kissed him gently on the lips.

"Quit, trying to get out of eating. You eat. I have to go get ready. I have a lot of work to do if I'm going to be the smart one in this house." He said as he rushed upstairs.

I ate what I could and cleaned up. When he came down he was dressed plainly in jeans and a green t-shirt but he looked princely and majestic, it was the way he carried himself. I don't think I can ever get used to him.

"Well, I think this is the first time I've had the girl waiting downstairs for me to get ready. You are a pleasant surprise." He said as he descended the stairs.

"Ready?" I asked.

"Let's go to school. I want to show off the most beautiful girl in my arms." He exclaimed.

We left for school in his car. It was silver and sporty. I glanced at the back for the car's make. *Audi.*

"I've seen a lot of different types of Audi but what type of Audi is this?" I asked.

"Well, it is the fastest Audi made. It's a R8. You would appreciate this. It has a 420Hp V-8 engine. It may just rival your Ducati." He bragged as he opened the door and invited me in.

"Wow, 420 horse power. I may just have to buy me one." I said awing at the black leather inside.

"So you like going fast, huh?" he jest.

"I have a Ducati for that reason. But the Hp in my Ducati is 130 Hp, I can't imagine the power of this baby." I was salivating.

"If I had known this was all it took to lure you in I would have grabbed you off the plane and thrown you in my car." He laughed. I looked up and we were already in the parking lot. *I have to get one of these.*

"Hey, look there's Trevor. Please be nice to him. He is really a good guy." I pleaded.

"Okay, but no hugging, touching, or sharing of supplies." he warned.

"You're hopeless." I said as I reached over and kissed him firmly on the lips. He held me back and kissed me more passionately. "I'll see you in class." He whispered off the tip of my lips. I waited for a second to collect myself than exited the car.

"Hi, Trevor" I announced.

"Oh, Hi! Gena. Is Corin around?" he asked as his eyes scanned the parking lot for Corin.

"He's parked over there. Trevor, its okay. I talked to Corin about us being Math partners. It was just a misunderstanding. He knows we're just friends." I assured him.

"Oh! Yeah. I'm glad he knows that. Just friends, absolutely nothing else" He uttered nervously.

"I think I got most of the second question, did you work on it at all?" I asked

"Yeah, I did, here I made you a copy. What do you think, right?" he asked.

"I don't know Trevor, I got the same theory on part A but our answers are different on part B. I'll take a closer look at it tonight and get back to you, Okay?" I said.

When I got to my first class, Corin was sitting in the back. Aimee moved into the back roll too. I sat where he saved me a sit.

"Only deviants sit back here." Aimee said.

"Well, I am very good at corrupting the innocent." Corin whispered to me.

All I could do was smile. I was corrupted in a good sort of way.

The day went by as usual for except Corin was in all my classes and we sat in the back. He didn't really disrupt me from learning but once in awhile I would glance at him and he was definitely not paying attention to the teacher.

As we made our way to the cafeteria, I mentioned my observation. "Did you learn anything at all?" I said to him.

"I've learned a lot today. I learn that you tend to shift your weight when you know the answer and you want to be called upon. I know that you frequently play with your hair. I also learned that when you get frustrated you curl the corners of your paper." he continued.

"Okay, I got it. I meant were you paying attention in class at all." I interrupted.

"Yes, I was paying attention to you in class." he admitted.

"Corin, if you don't pass, how will you graduate and go on to college?" I asked frustrated with him.

"Gena, I don't want to talk about that, right now." He said as we got closer to the lunch table.

"Corin, that isn't fair. Your future is just as important as mine. Don't you think we should discuss it together?" I asked. He was quiet. "Excuse me, Corin, I have to go wash my hands. I'll meet you in the cafeteria."

I made my way to the bathroom. After washing my hands, I turned and saw Natalie standing at the doorway. "Hi, Natalie" I greeted cautiously.

"Hi, Gena. So you and Corin are an item huh? Don't worry it doesn't bother me. I gave up on him a long time ago. He is all yours now." She said.

"Sorry, Natalie. It just happened." I said.

"No, don't fret. We had nothing in common. He was always so serious. But you probably like that. You guys look good together. I heard you guys talking about college. That is something new." She said baiting me.

"Well, we're seniors. What's so weird about talking about college?" I replied.

"It's not weird for everyone, just Corin." She answered.

"Why is it weird for Corin?" I asked. I took her bait like an idiot.

"Did Corin not tell you?" she said cunningly.

"We haven't had a chance to discuss college. It doesn't matter to me if he wants to go to college or not. " I answered. It was true; last night was the first time we have been able to talk.

"Good, because I don't think he intended to go to college after graduation. He had other plans." She replied.

Embarrassed that I didn't know I asked "What plans?" I felt stupid for taking her bait but I really didn't know and the fact that she knew angered me.

"Well Corin family owns Randall Security Company. His father expects Corin and Mark to take over one day. Corin however has always dreamt of traveling abroad. He has even set aside a lot of money to do so. He was waiting to graduate than tell his dad that he wants to travel for the next two years. Once he returns he will make a decision on what he wants to do. Did he tell you about this? Knowing Corin he probably didn't want you to feel bad about trapping him here. Oh, I'm sorry. I didn't mean to say it like that. I'm sure he'll get over it. He has always voiced his displeasure to work for his dad. But I'm sure that now that you're here, thing will be different. Don't take this the wrong way but it is just tragic to see him domesticated. He has always been independent and free; it will just be weird seeing him settled down. But I'm sure you will make him too happy to think of anything else. You are his soul mate, after all. Hey why don't you travel with him? That would be perfect. You should definitely talk to him about it. It was really important to him at one time." She conveyed as she walked away.

I stood there in the bathroom thinking about what she said. I knew part of what she said was out of resentment but some of it could be true. She knows him better than I. He made those plans before he met me. I was trapping him here. Earlier, I didn't understand why he reacted so bluntly to my college question. He never planned on being here after graduation. Now I know he was just not going to tell me. He would never admit this to me. Trapping him here would be selfish and unfair of me. I didn't have a choice since I was not ready to leave here. But, if he waited for me to be completely transformed than; it could take two or maybe three years by that time it would be too late for him. He wanted to get married and start having children. After graduation was the only time he could have to himself. Meeting me really disrupted his plans. I was sort of angry that he didn't trust me with his plans. What else was he hiding from me? I watched him carefully during lunch. I kept a smile on my face to hide the fact that I was preoccupied. Every now and then he would take my hand and kiss it. By the end of the lunch hour, I was beginning to find it hard to keep up the pretense.

The distraction kept me quiet the rest of the day. I could tell Corin knew something was bothering me but every time he asked I told him I was fine. I did not want to see him go. I would love to go with him. I could not ask him to wait. There was really no way around this. I want him to have the freedom he desires and when he was ready come back to me. I would wait.

At the end of the day we rode home in silence. I pretended to be preoccupied with the Calculus questions.

"Are you going to tell me what's wrong?" he questioned.

"Nothing wrong, Corin. I just have to concentrate on these formulas." I responded distantly. By this time, my heart had sunk down to the pit of my stomach. This is what happens to me when I am bracing for some very bad news. I can feel the numbness in my heart forming; my protective shield was coming up. I knew what I had to do but selfishly I did not want to do it.

When we pulled up, I started to get out but he grabbed me by the hand. "Gena, I have to go see my parents for a minute. I'll be back." He said.

I nodded keeping my eye away from him and got out. I could feel him staring at me as I made my way to the door. I did not want to turn around. I could feel the heat coming from my heart rising slowly to my face and eventually welled up in my eyes. There were many delivered packages and boxes at the front door. I didn't bother to pick them up. I shoved them aside. I went inside and immediately went upstairs to put my things away. I stood looking outside through the glass walls. Telling him to go follow his dreams was the right thing to do, I know that. I did not want to be the one to trap him to this life until he was ready. I don't want him to live with that regret.

When did I become so needy and dependant. I can do this. I have lived through worse. I pulled myself together after losing my parents. Losing Peter was hard too and I managed to live. Uncle Josh's death was definitely harder but somehow I am here—living. I have always been a survivor. This was different. Corin wasn't dying. Knowing Corin he would not tell me what he wanted. I would not allow him to be unselfish. I want him to go. He deserves it. I will not be his prison. He has always been busy doing things for this clan, I don't want him obligated to do things for me. He only needed two years. By that time I would be fully transformed and I can go with him. I can occupy my time with getting to know my new family. I could start some college courses while he was away. This is the 21st century, we can always be in touch by phone, or email or whatever necessary. I had to pull myself together to show him it was okay for him to do this. I had time to get used to this.

I went downstairs and walked toward the kitchen. Before I got to the kitchen I felt drawn to my mother's music room. I haven't been in here since the first day I came here. I sat down at her piano and tried to play the piece of music she had on the stand. It was a very difficult piece. Frustrated I stop playing, tears were coming down my face. I remember the last time I cried while playing the piano. I was told by my instructor that I had to play a piece she picked out for my first recital. It was a difficult piece, so I was very upset that I could not perfect it. After months of practice, I was finally able to play it beautifully. I remember her saying "*this piece will come to you naturally one day.*" As if she knew I would be here today, I felt the music coming through my fingers to the keys. I played this piece over and over. My shoulders and fingers ached but I could not stop, until my tears became too much.

Chapter Thirteen

After I dropped her off at her house, I drove over to my house. *She was concerned about our future.* All this time, I profess to love her but never once did I tell her how I would take care of her. Of course, she would be concern. She was the responsible one. She has always taken care of herself. I felt like a love-struck irresponsible idiot. When I got to the house, my mother was sitting in the parlor cross-stitching. I greeted her and sat down next to her.

"Mom, where is dad?" I asked.

"He is at the office. He'll be home soon if you can wait. Is everything alright? Did she kick you out already?" she jested.

"No, she didn't kick me out but I want to tell you something." I answered.

"Go ahead." She replied.

"Well, after Mark announced he was giving up looking for his *soul mate* and marrying Ella, I thought that if I traveled to other clans, I would have a better chance of finding her. I have been saving money to travel abroad. I meant to tell you guys but I wanted to wait until after graduation. But now you know things have changed. I want to use that money to go to Aurora College. I know dad thinks it's a waste of time, because he wants me to work for him. Maybe one day I will end up working for him but right now I want to find what works for me. I really need you to support my decision and help me convince dad." I confessed. I watched as she looked at me. Her silence made me nervous.

"I can't believe how much you have changed since you've met Gena. I watched you go from a stubborn young man to a responsible adult. I am very happy for you. I know you're dad have been pressuring you about working for him. I will support you on whatever you want to do. You don't have to ask his permission. Let me deal with that. You go do what is right for you and Gena. If you need anything, all you have to do is ask." She assured me.

"I want to give her everything she deserves. Right now, I can't support her financially and I think she may be a little unsure of our future but I would like to work for dad while I am attending college. I just don't want him to assume that I will give up college if he asked me to." I said.

"You don't have to worry about him. I don't think you have to worry about Gena. She is not worried about money." She explained.

"How do you know she's not worried about money?" I asked.

"Well, when you announced your feelings for Gena, your dad was concern about how you guys would be able to support yourselves. Your dad did not want to offend you but he also knows that love doesn't pay the bills either. He spoke with Blaine to set up a trust fund for you and Gena, as an early wedding gift. But Blaine told him it was not necessary. Are you aware that Gena has a trust fund well worth over $500 million dollars? So, the last thing she is concerned about is money. She has also offered to establish a multi-million dollars fund for the Leukemia foundation. If she is concern about the future, it isn't about money. You need to go talk to her about those concerns." She advised.

"Thanks mom. I'll do that now. I'll be back this weekend to get the rest of my things. Don't let Mark take anything. Love you mom." I said as I walked to my car.

When I got back to Gena's house I waited a few minutes to gather my thoughts before I talk to her. I noticed all the boxes and packages were still left outside. I could hear from the door that she was playing the piano. I entered without her knowing I was home. I walked quietly to the music room. She was playing a piece of music that was so enchanting. I stood at the door and listened to her play. She looked like she was in a trance; except for I could see she was crying. I started to move toward her to comfort her but she stopped playing and placed her hands over her face and continued to sob.

"I am sorry." I said quietly. It broke my heart to see her cry. I was mad at myself that I was the reason for her sadness.

She looked up quickly and wiped away her tears. "How long have you been standing there?" she asked consciously. I went to sit next to her on the piano seat.

"Just a few minutes" I answered. "Don't cry. I hate to see you cry."

"The music just overwhelmed me, that's all. Did you go see your parents?" she asked.

"My mom. My dad was at the office." I told her. "I know something is bothering you, please talk to me."

"Do you remember this afternoon when I asked you about college?" she reminded me.

"Yes, and I have something to tell you about that but you go first." I responded.

"I don't care if you don't want to go to college. I want you to do what you want. You deserve to experience everything you've ever wanted. I don't want to tie you down if you wish to go somewhere, you know like far way." She stammered. I can tell she was having a hard time finding the right words.

"Where am I going?" I asked. I was confused by what she was thinking.

"I mean, if you want to travel and experience things." She was irritated.

"Are we going somewhere?" I asked sarcastically.

"Please, be serious. I mean if you want to travel abroad before you settle here with me. I don't want you to feel that you have to give up any of your dreams because of me. I don't want to trap you here. I want you to have the freedom you deserve to go see things, experience things, and enjoy yourself before you come back to me. I will understand if you need to do that. I will wait for you. I wish I could go with you, if you want, but we both know that's not possible right now." She finished.

"Where do you want me to go?"

"I don't want you to go anywhere. But I know that you've dreamt about traveling abroad after graduation and I want you to know that I am okay with that." She blurted out.

"Who told you about that?" I asked.

"Does it matter?" she stated quietly.

"Yes, it does. I've only told that to a few people and there was a motive behind me telling them that." I answered.

"What do you mean *motive*?" she asked.

"A year ago Mark announced that he was giving up looking for his soul mate. I tried to encourage him to travel with me abroad to keep searching because it would be a disaster if he married Ella and then later his soul mate show up. Ella is taking a great risk marrying Mark when she knows that one day this could happen. We started making plans and saving money for a two year trip going to different clans. It's prudent to be absolutely sure before you marry the wrong person. Then he changed his mind. Those plans I had to travel abroad were to find you. I just didn't know you were coming to me. I don't want to go anywhere without you." I explained. I took her hand and place my lips on her palm.

"Are you sure?" she asked softly. I wiped away her tears. "You're not just saying that to make me feel better?"

"Wherever you are is where I want to be. You're not trapping me here. I don't want freedom if it means being away from you. I happen to like this prison cell. I could complain about the meals but everything I want is right here." I assured her as I lowered my lips to hers.

I meant to kiss her lightly but I soon found myself wanting more. When she wrapped her arms around my neck, I pulled her tighter against my body. Her gasping and panting sent a physical jolt through my body. My hands gripped tighter, kneading her back. As I turned my head to taken in more of her lips, I heard her whimper. The sounds she made when I kiss her were erotic to my ears. I slid my hands slowly over her hip and pulled her legs up around my hip, pressing her into me. Before I realize what was happening, she moved her hands down my shirt to unbutton them. She broke the kiss and placed her lips on my neck going down my chest. I wanted her so badly I was ready to sell my soul. But I knew we had to stop or else it would get out of control and I would end up making love to her. Hating our predicament, I pulled her away from me. I placed her on her feet and braced my hands on my knees. We were both short of breathe.

"I'm sorry, but we have to stop right now." I reminded her.

"I know. I'm glad you have some will power because mine is somewhere on the floor." She labored. I smiled back at her. I was still trying to gain some control over my body.

"I don't think I have all that much. It is going to be the longest two years of our lives if we keep doing that." I said exasperated.

She laughed. I was happy to see she was no longer sad. "You still didn't tell me who told you." I reminded her trying to change the subject.

"It doesn't matter anymore. I'm just glad you're not going to leave after graduation. For awhile there, I plotted ways to prevent you from graduating. Just for two years until I could go with you." She said with a smile.

"Here I am tutoring you meanwhile you're plotting to get me flunked out. Left up to you I would be the oldest high student at Peterson." I played along.

"It was only until I could go with you." She justified.

"Well, luckily I have a plan B. I've decided that we should both go to Aurora College here in Inuvik. It is a very good college with a very diverse program. After two years, we can go to colleges near other clans. There's one in Colorado, Minnesota, and Washington. If you want to go abroad, we can go to France, Italy, Albania, there is a lot to chose from. What do you think?" I suggested.

"When did you think up Plan B?" she inquired.

"Plan B was always there it was just behind Plan A." I replied.

"What was Plan A?" she asked.

"Finding you" I replied

"I like your plans." She said smiling. She reached out and pulled at my unbuttoned shirt.

"Don't start that." I dared.

"I was just going to button them back up. We can't go the grocery store if you're flashing your beautiful body everywhere." She jested.

"Who's bias now? What are those packages outside?" I compared.

"They're my new wardrobe compliments of Lauren, Aimee, and Dana. They ordered all kinds of clothes for me because my current clothes were not up to their standards." She said annoyed.

"I'll go bring them in. Do you want to go through right now?" I asked

"No, not really. I think we have to go to the grocery store." She replied.

"Are you cooking tonight?" I asked.

"Well since you made breakfast, I would like to make dinner." She replied.

"Well, we only have one grocery store here, North's." I added.

"Let's go. If there is only one store in Inuvik, we don't want to risk not getting the very finest of things." she giggled.

We went outside and brought in all the boxes and packages, then got into the car. As we exited the driveway, I noticed her staring out the windows. I can't believe how lucky I am to have her in my life.

"Gena, I want you to know that I will take care of you." I assured her.

"What do you mean take care of me?" She questioned as she played with my fingers. She kissed each finger slowly.

"Quit Gena, do you want me to wrap this car around a tree?" I warned.

"Sorry, I was just trying to keep busy." She said with a smirk on her face.

"Make a grocery list." I demanded. "I'm going to take my dad's offer about a job. It's just while we're in college here. I'll think of something else later. I just don't want you to worry about that."

"I wasn't worry about that. Is this about money?" she asked.

"Well you know that saying *love doesn't pay the bills*." I replied.

"Do you have a lot of bills?" she asked simply.

"No, I don't' have any bills." I retorted.

"Than why do you have to work for your dad?" She questioned.

"To take care of you" I responded.

"Corin, this is the 21st century. I don't need you to *take care* of me. You sound like a sugar daddy." She giggled.

"Be serious, you know what I mean." I replied.

"I don't want you to work for your dad." She said quietly.

"Gena, I need to do this." I said.

"Is this a man thing?" she asked.

"No, it's the right thing." I answered.

"I want you to be very honest with me, do you really want to work for your dad?" she questioned. I can tell she already knew the answer but was challenging me to lie.

"It was not high on my list of things to do but I have new priorities." I said as I moved my hand over hers.

"Why can't we share this responsibility together? We're already sharing a life together. We are living together. We are practically sleeping together. So we can pool our resources together. I really don't want you to work for you're dad, unless it is something you absolutely want to do." She said caressing the back of my hand.

"I don't think it would be fair to you if we pool our resources together." I commented.

"Oh, you know about that huh." She said quietly.

"Yeah, Blaine told my dad when he was talking about giving us an early wedding gift trust fund."

"Are we getting married?" she asked sarcastically.

"Eventually, don't you want to?" I asked, worried that she may think I was rushing things.

"Is this your way of proposing? Because if it is I want a full refund." she gasped.

"No not formally. It just came out because of what we were talking about." I reminded her.

"Okay, if we are going to get marry later—*mind you I have not said yes because I refuse to remember this as how you proposed*—than we will pool our resources. I don't want you to work for your dad. It's me being selfish. I happen to like my time with you and when you're at work you're not with me. If you want me to be happy, please do not think of taking care of me as a financial responsibility but love me unconditionally." She politely requested.

"I do love you unconditionally. Your happiness is very important to me. We'll work it out and I will work on getting that *yes* from you." I promised.

We got to North's. The store is set-up like a Super Wal-mart but much smaller. I knew the clerk, so I set up an account for them to deliver groceries every week. We went over the items that we felt were always needed. She was very good at this. She took over the chore without any hesitation.

"Corin, why don't you get an extra house key made?" she directed.

"Okay, I'll be over there." I replied. She wanted me to have a key to her house. It's now permanent and real. After the keys were made, I wondered around the store looking at their displays. I was still feeling ecstatic at the prospect of us being married one day. She wanted a memorable proposal. That I know I could do.

We got what we needed and headed home.

"So what are we having for dinner?" I asked.

"I know this isn't as fancy as French toast, but over the years I have perfected macaroni and cheese." She bragged.

"We are practically professional chefs as far as I'm concern." I boasted.

"I have to call Lauren when we get home. She wants to know when the clothes get here. I think she wants to play dress up tonight." She said.

"I want to spend time with you tonight. Don't call her. You can do that tomorrow." I insisted.

"Looks like you're not going to get your wish." She pointed as we pulled up the driveway. Standing at the front door were Lauren and Max, Aimee, and Tristan, Ella and my brother Mark. I cursed under my breath.

"Gena, I brought over some of the packages that were delivered to my house. Did you get the other packages?" Lauren asked as we were getting out of the car.

"Yes, Lauren, I was just about to call you." She lied, looking over at me.

"Great, we need to see what you can wear to Ella's engagement party tomorrow night." She bossed.

"Lauren, we have not eaten yet. Can you wait until we get dinner done?" Corin said irritated.

"Did someone say dinner? We came just in time." Mark said

"Come on, now you want dinner." Corin complained.

"It's okay, Corin. The girls can help me." She assured. She grabbed my hand and pulled me towards the door. "Be nice." She whispered.

We all went inside. Lauren and Max brought in at least ten more packages. Aimee and Ella took the groceries from me and followed Gena into the kitchen. Max helped Lauren take all the packages upstairs. I stayed in the living with Mark and Tristan.

"Well grouchy, you landed yourself the catch of the decade. You got the girl and moved into to her house all in one day. That's fast even for you." Mark said boastfully.

"He is lucky. Aimee and I have to wait until after we are married to get our own place." Tristan added.

"Well, it shouldn't be too long for you and Ella." I commented.

"Oh, you didn't hear. Dad asked Ella if some of the survivors could stay at our new home until another house was ready for them. Trey, Derek and Brent is staying there right now. Hopefully they'll be in another place by the time December comes around. I hate to cross over the threshold with three guys living at my house." He said sarcastically.

"Well, that was nice of Ella. Are you okay with it?" I asked.

"Hey, whatever she wants. We have been arguing so much over the wedding stuff, I don't want to fight over anything else." He replied defeated.

"What is Gena making for dinner?" Tristan asked.

"She is making Macaroni and cheese." I replied.

"You guys are living together practically married and you're eating macaroni and cheese?" Mark said with a slight hint of mockery.

"I don't care what we eat. She makes everything taste good." I replied arrogantly.

"I happen to like macaroni and cheese. Throw in a salad and you've got a hardy meal." Tristan added.

"You guys are so disgusting. It makes me sick to see you guys whipped." Mark stated.

"I like being whipped." Tristan said laughing. I concurred by giving him affirmative nod.

"Are you ready for tomorrow's party?" I asked Mark.

"What's there to be ready about, all I have to do is show up. She didn't give me anything to do. Hey, you're tux is in the car. Mom told me to bring it to you. She wasn't sure you would remember." He stated.

We made our way to the car and got my tuxedo from Mark's Lamborghini. He went over to Gena's Ducati and stood there admiring it.

"Wow, when Justin told me she had a motorcycle, I didn't know she had a Ducati. You guys definitely have a thing for speed and silver. This thing is gorgeous." He commented.

"She looks good on it too." I bragged.

"I bet she does. I would love for Ella to do something like this but she is too reserved." He said quietly.

"Hey, are you alright man? You don't look like someone who's getting married in December." I asked.

"I don't know man, she has been acting weird lately. She snapped at me today over the color of the napkins." He said.

"It is just pressure from all this wedding stuff. Don't worry about it. You should be used to it by now. You guys have been going at it for 3 months now." I stated.

"This was different. It's like she was daring me to call off the whole thing." he said shaking his head.

"You're making this out to be bigger than it really is. Are you getting cold feet?" I asked jokingly.

"No, I'm just making an observation that's all. Maybe you're right." He responded. I could tell he was bothered by something but I didn't know if he wanted to continue.

"Hey, you guys thinking about stealing my motorcycle?" Gena teased as she walked toward us.

"Dinner is ready." She came up and wrapped her arm around my waist. I was really aroused by her possessiveness.

"When are you going to let me ride this thing?" Mark asked. His mood lightened up when she came out.

"Well, it depends on your driving record." She replied.

"She'll never let you on it now." I said laughing.

We got back inside. We had to get the extras chairs from the breakfast table to have enough room for everyone to eat in the dining room. I was very proud of Gena for being so accommodating. Somehow she made enough Macaroni and cheese to serve for 8 people. She also made a Greek salad to compliment the macaroni and cheese. We all gathered at the table and sat next to our mates.

"Wow, Gena this is so good. You've got to give me the recipe." Aimee complimented.

"Yeah, when Corin told me you were making macaroni and cheese I thought you were going to break out the kid's instant stuff. What's in here?" Mark asked.

"It's basically the same except I used Gruyiere cheese and heavy cream." She said modestly.

"This is gourmet stuff. What are we having for dinner tomorrow?" Mark mocked.

"I would place a deadbolt on the door, Corin. I don't think he's kidding. Gena this is really good." Lauren added.

"Ella, I heard you guys lent you're house to Trey and Derek." I asked. I noticed that she was really quiet tonight. She looked pre-occupied.

"Yeah, it's just until something is built for them. I feel bad for Trey. They're house was completely destroyed by the hunters." She replied.

"Well, that was really nice of you and Mark. Have you guys seen Tina and Preston? She looks really good. Uncle Alain said once her femur is set she can start walking. Preston is unbelievable." Aimee informed.

"Yeah, she is really doing well. I thought she was a goner when we were in Yellowknife." Tristan recalled.

"I just love the way Preston is being so caring around her. It is so sweet. I have never seen him like that with anyone." Lauren commented.

"I'm just glad she made it, I think it would crush him if she died. It would have been a tragedy to finally find your soul mate only to watch her die." Aimee said bluntly

We all agreed.

"Speaking of soul mates, what is going on with Dana and Derek? Is it true?" Max asked.

"I'm not sure. They haven't said anything to anyone." Aimee answered.

"They are so lucky. What is the chance of finding two soul mate matches in one week?" Max said.

"Three." I added entwining our hands under the table.

Suddenly, Ella got up and walked out. Mark followed after her. We all sat there silently waiting for them to come back in. We could hear that they were arguing about something in the driveway but we all pretended not to eavesdrop. Gena got up and started clearing away the mess in the kitchen. They all pitched in to clean up. We waited for them to come back but when we heard the Lamborghini engine roared out of the driveway we knew they'd left.

"Were they just trying to get out of doing the dishes?" Max said joking.

"Stop. Max. Gena, we need to check out the clothes upstairs." Lauren said.

I watched as Lauren and Aimee dragged Gena begrudgingly upstairs. After awhile, they came back down.

"Okay, Gena you're all set for tomorrow's party. Corin you're going to love what I picked out for her." Lauren boasted.

"I know I will. I love what she has on now." I confirmed. I gave her a wink. She smiled back.

"Okay, we have to go. Thanks for dinner Gena. Let's do it again soon." Aimee announced.

We watched them march off to their cars and drove off. I turned and looked at her. *Finally alone.* I moved slowly toward her and quickly picked her up and ran upstairs. Her giggling was music to my ears.

"It's a little early for bedtime don't you think?" she asked.

"I'm not planning on sleeping." I smiled devilishly.

"You know we can't do that either." She reminded me. I placed her on the bed and joined her.

"I was thinking about making out all night long until we both explode." I said as I descended on her lips.

Chapter Fourteen

Nhan, we've been tracking for two days now. They're not in Vancouver. I'm tired. Let's just drop it.

I will not. They will not get away. Have you forgotten what they did to Sopa? If you want to go back than go! I will head north to the Alaskan Territory.

Nhan, I am your brother I will not leave you.

Cron, go back or stop nagging.

Okay, how far do you want to take this?

I'll go as far as Beaufort Sea in Prudhoe Bay if I don't catch a scent, I'll come back.

I'll go with you but it will end at Prudhoe Bay.

We were lying in bed wrapped around each other. It feels odd that this was only our second night together. We were so comfortable together that it felt natural to be with him this way. No fear of being judged by those around us. His parents did not think anything of him moving in with me. I like this soul mate thing. It is so definite that you did not fear heartbreak or failure. As long as you both were alive that was all that was required. Finding one another was the hard part but once found you were complete. Thinking on my past relationships, there was always feared of rejection, heartbreak, infidelity, and even abuse. This was something totally different. Of course, it has its tragedies, if your soul mate dies before you ever met than were you doom to loneliness.

"What are you thinking about?" he asked while nuzzling the back of my ear.

"I was thinking about the *concero flamma* thing. It has its good and bad. I'm glad we have the good part. Do you think that is what's worrying Ella? " I noted.

"No, I think they are both just having a little cold feet thing. They knew from the start that they were not soul mates, what has changed?" he said as he slid his hand over my stomach.

"I know but if they both fear that they may have soul mates out there wouldn't that eventually be taxing on their relationship?" I asked.

"Maybe so but why worry about it now, if it wasn't an issue before. Don't get me wrong, I wished he would wait but he fears that he would be waiting for nothing. Ella also is worry because she is 20 years old now. She only has five years left before she can not have children." He pointed out as he lifted my shirt to expose my stomach. He caressed his lips over my belly button. It was distracting, but I knew what he was thinking when he went there. He was thinking about our own children. It is so ironic; normally girls my age would be frightened with the thought of being a mother so early. This was all so new and different than life as a human. There was no fear because you knew without a shadow of a doubt that this was the man you were supposed to be with.

"I still think they worry even though it didn't matter before. I mean this is what humans fear when in a relationship. I was raised as a human. Every relationship was filled with doubt, rejection, or abuse. It is not easy. Mostly for a girl, if we get into a relation with a guy who's a jerk, he would take what he wanted and leave." I said.

He quickly lifted his head up. "Did someone do that to you? Did someone hurt you?" He asked with concern.

"No, but that is what I used to worry about. Before you give yourself completely to someone, you want to be sure. Since there is no belief of a soul mate system, there is no certainty. It's pretty scary." I stated.

"Yeah, it is scary but at least humans can be with anyone they want. With our kind, you yearn for your soul mate. This is the only person you really want to be with. Any other relationship is filled with doubt. It's like being the "other choice". Who would want that? With humans, if their mate dies or leave them, they can start over with someone else and be just as happy. With our kind, we don't want to be with anyone else. No one can fill the hole left behind. Not even our children. So you spend the rest of your life waiting to be with them again in death. That is more tragic, don't you think?" he challenged.

"I guess there is a good and bad to both situations. Which one would you prefer, if you had a choice?" I asked.

"If you had asked me two weeks ago, I would have chosen to be human. Finding you now, it's almost like I can now go on with my life. I'm not searching, hoping, or worried anymore, just ready to live." He answered confidently.

"Yeah, my life was pretty bleak up until I met you. You have to agree we've had some kind of divine intervention helping us. In a state of grief and despair, I almost shoved my mother's jewelry box in storage. I was so frustrated that I could not open the thing. Then I remember something my uncle said about prying it open and something came over me. My curiosity mixed with anger was enough for me to risk amputation to get the box open, that's what started it all." I remembered.

"I remember Justin telling me that. I was laughing at first but then I thought about what could have happened if you accidently stabbed yourself and died. The irony of that would be heartbreaking. You don't know what it's like to have that fear. I mean searching for someone and never knowing if they are alive or dead." He added quietly.

"That is why we have to thank divine intervention." I said.

"I was coming. I would've search for two years at least." He replied.

"I don't think you would have come to Indiana." I stated.

"You're right, but that's what makes our situation so much harder than humans. We're lucky when we find our soul mate but we could spend a lot of time looking. If you weren't curious about the jewelry box, I would have been searching for two years and probably never found you." He confirmed.

"And, what would you have done after two years. Would you do what Mark is doing and settle down with Natalie?" I asked with a hint of jealousy.

"Are you jealous of Natalie?" he asked with a smile.

"Well, you did kiss her first." I acknowledged.

He came up to my face and secured my face in his hands. "She kissed me in the neck, and that is not a kiss. This is." He said before he covered my lips with his. I could feel his bear skin against my stomach; the little hairs from his navel tickled me erotically. I wrapped my arms around him holding him firmly against my body. We could do this forever and I would not be satisfied. He slowly pulled back and looked at me intensely.

"You don't need to be jealous of Natalie. I am here with you. Whatever or whoever brought us together, knows that we were destined to be together. That is worth thousands more than a kiss in the neck. " He whispered.

"Thank you for waiting for me." I said.

"Thank you for finding me. Now we have to get some sleep. We have an engagement party to go to." He replied.

I slept easily being near him.

In the deepest part of my sleeping brain, I felt fear. I was wake. I was cold. I was hurt. I can feel pain. I was weak. I was dizzy. I could not stand up straight. Where am I? What am I doing here? I saw flashes of my mother's face. I saw flashes of my father's face. What are they doing here? Looking around I saw flashes of darkness sprinting all around me. What are they? The air was cold and bitter. Looking up, I see trees swaying. Something was coming. Something was near. I could not see them, but I knew they were coming for me. I started to run. The bushes and trees were cutting into my arms. Someone help me. Corin, where are you? I slipped and fell hard into the hard snow. My hands were bleeding. My legs were hurting. I could not breathe. Breathing hurt so much. I could see I had gashes all over my arms and body. I tried to cry out for help but nothing came out. There was no where for me to go. I struggled but I could not get up. Death was coming for me finally. It had already taken my father, my mother, Peter and Uncle Josh. I had challenged it and now it was coming for me. I don't want o die now. Please I've changed my mind. I want to live. I've got a lot to live for now. Corin, please help me. Please come for me. I am here. I could feel the pain in my arms, legs, and on my chest. Something was crushing my chest. The air was escaping me and I could not get any in. The dark shadows were coming. They were all around me. The coldness was slowly leaving me. I felt a warm sensation coming over me. I was sweating. How could I be sweating? Redness came over everything. The sky was red. The trees and air was red. I must be bleeding to death. Bleeding or suffocating which one will take me first. Someone was calling me. I searched all around but could not see. The voice was familiar but I could not see where it was coming from. It was Corin. I tried to yell out but I had no air left. It was too late. He was too late.

I startled awake. I sat up quickly, pulling away from him. It was just a dream. I have never had a dream that seemed so real. I was in my room.

"What is wrong? Are you okay? Did you have a nightmare?" he

worried. He sat up and turned on the lights.

"Yeah, I just had a bad dream." I said as I placed my hands over eyes. It was so real, I just wanted to cry.

"Do you want to talk about it? Hey, look at me, its okay." He said as he pulled me to him. He looked down at me. His facial expression scared me. He quickly jumped out of bed and turned on the bright lights. He just stood there staring at me.

"What? What's wrong?" I stuttered. He was frightening me.

"Gena, are you alright? Are you hurt anywhere?" he asked.

"No, I don't think so." I said as I looked at myself. I don't feel any pain.

"Gena, your eyes are red. Get dress we have to go see Alain." He scrambled around looking for his shirt.

"Corin, I'm okay. I don't think Alain can do anything about it." I said coming out of bed and looking into the mirror. I watched him standing in the middle of the room in shock.

"You may be hurt, or something terrible is happening." He yelled. "Gena, please, let's go see Alain. We have to let him examine you. You could be sick or something, hurry."

"Alain has already seen this." I said silently covering my face with my hands.

"What? When?" he asked as he came over to my side. He pulled my hands away and looked into my eyes. I could see worry and fear in his eyes.

"It happened Monday when I was healing Tina." I answered.

"You were *healing* Tina, what does that mean? What the hell did he make you do?" he questioned. He looked worry and confused.

"Please don't get worked up. I am not hurt. When you were away, Preston brought Tina back in a very bad way. Alain asked me to be near Tina. She did not have an aura. Alain said my healer aura would cleanse the death from her blood. After a few hours, she started to heal but my eyes were red for a few minutes until I was away from her. Alain said I helped her develop an aura to heal. The redness in my eyes is the healing of her blood." I explained.

"If you healed her blood, what does that do to you? If you are absorbing the death, wouldn't that harm you?" he questioned.

"No, Alain said I wasn't absorbing the death. I was healing her blood. My eyes will be back to normal in a few minutes." I said as I raise my hand to cover them.

"I don't care if you have purple eyes, I was just worried. What made your eyes go red now? You're not injured. I'm not injured." He asked.

"I don't know. I had a dream about me dying and it may have triggered something." I said frustrated.

"Why would you dream about yourself dying? Are you sure you didn't absorb Tina's injuries?" he asked as he pulled me into his arms.

"No, I feel fine." I replied.

"Than why would you dream about dying? Were you sick?" he asked.

"No, I dreamt of being attacked and dying from injuries." I said silently.

"Who attacked you?" he questioned impatiently.

"I don't know. I think I have been hearing a lot of stories about the attacks and with my vivid imagination it just triggered a combination of scary things. Let's get back in bed. Sorry I woke you." I said calmly.

"You're eyes are brown again." He commented.

"Yeah, it scared the crap out of Preston when he first saw it too." I chuckled.

"I was scared. I thought you gouged your eyes out when you were having your nightmare." He said as helped me back to bed. He pulled me into his arms.

"Corin, gouge my eyes out?" I giggled.

"Are you really okay? Do you want to talk about it?" he mentioned.

"No, I'd rather not talk about it. It was just a dream. I don't know about you but I am exhausted. Changing eye color takes a lot out of you." I said joking.

"I still think we should go see Alain tomorrow, just to be on the safe side." He said.

"I don't think Alain can do anything about it. Why worry him?" I replied.

"Worry him? I worry. I don't like the idea of him using you as some sort of death sponge. He probably doesn't know what it is doing to you. It could harm you." He said

"I am fine and I am not a death sponge. You make it sound so bad. He said it was like a dialysis machine but instead of cleaning it, I was healing it." I assured him.

"He is just guessing. He doesn't know for sure. I don't want anything to happen to you. You may feel fine now but what happens if you heal too many people. What are you a filter? What happens if it gets too much? That has got to do something to you." He concluded.

"I am not a filter. Corin, your aura allows you to be strong and fast. Do you get sick or hurt from that? My aura heals our kind. It should not hurt me." I validated.

"You don't know that for sure. You may be right, but I just can't help feeling like it could hurt you; absorbing death. It just doesn't sit well." He worried.

"I don't worry about you running around at a ridiculous speed, so you shouldn't worry about me healing." I declared.

"Running around doesn't make my eyes red. You being the death sponge or filter do. I still want to see Alain tomorrow. I don't appreciate him experimenting on you." He complained.

"Corin, I am fine. We can talk to Alain about it tomorrow but please do not be rude." I warned. I watched as he ran his hands thru his hair frustrated. We lay in bed silently for awhile.

"So you have the healer aura, huh?" he pointed out.

"Yeah, I thought you knew." I said.

"Justin, told me but I didn't know exactly what that entails." He answered.

"Changing your mind about me?" I asked.

"No, you're not getting rid of me that easy. It's just in my lifetime and I think our parents there has never been a child born with the healer aura. I think it's been over a few hundred years. It's like legendary. Somehow that fits you perfectly. You're unique and legendary." He assured.

"I don't know about that. I am just a girl who got lucky. At the lowest point in my life, when living hurt more than dying, I found you."

Chapter Fifteen

"Wake up my little healer. We have a busy day ahead and I really want to go talk Alain today." I nudged at her. I can not get over being here with her. Waking up seeing her face was addictive. I can't get over how beautifully she sleeps. She doesn't make a sound. I like waking up early just to look at her sleep.

"Don't remind me." She murmured. She definitely would hate to know that I have been watching her for the pass hour.

"It's almost noon, Gena. We have to go see Alain. The engagement party is at three." I reminded her with a kiss to her shoulder. I caressed her arm with my lips. Her scent was intoxicating.

"Almost noon, why didn't you wake me earlier?" she distressed.

"Well, you didn't sleep to well last night so I thought you needed some extra time this morning." I reminded her.

"Oh, don't remind me. Nightmares really suck." She said disturbed.

"Did you have anymore?" I asked.

"No, it was just so clear. I can still remember it. Usually if I have a dream, I can't remember it by morning. Of all dreams to remember" She said troubled.

"Why don't you go get dressed? I'll make you some breakfast, and you will tell me about the dreams. I heard it helps if you talk about it." He suggested.

"Are we having French toast again?" she asked with a smile.

"French toast with syrup, coming right up." I declared. I watched as she went into the bathroom. I hated to see her having problems. She should not worry about anything. We have already been through the hard part, now we were suppose to live happily ever after.

I made my way to the kitchen and started making breakfast. It should be easy today since we have all the ingredients. I hit the switch to pull back all the curtains. I can't get over how much talent her dad had. I wish I could thank them for her. Without them, I would not be as happy as I am today. If she had died 18 years ago like everyone thought I would be searching endlessly for someone that did not exist. "Thank you Daniel and Alexandria Roese" I vowed silently.

"Are you talking to my parent's portrait?" she asked as she was descending the stairs. I can't get over how she can make herself so beautiful in just 10 minutes. It must be in her genes.

"I was thanking them for you." I praised.

She smiled and came over by my side. We both looked at the portrait together. "You look just like her except you have his eyes." I observed.

"Yeah, I always wondered where I got my brown eyes. If you didn't notice everyone in both of my families had blue or green eyes. No one except for me has brown eyes or red sometimes." She acknowledged.

"Come on, let's feed you." I said as I pulled her along to the dining room.

"Wow, you really spoil me. Flowers too! If you keep this up I'll be disappointed with anything less." She acclaimed.

"Well, I am the expert in Home Economics. This is what we call "Breakfast fit for a Queen." Please sit. May I serve you?" I gestured. She laughed.

"Okay, I want you to share your nightmare with me. I want all the details." I said.

"Well, I was in the forest I think. I was running from something but I couldn't make out what it was. But for some reason I believed it was death. I was injured badly. I tried to run but I could not breathe. It was so real, the pain and shortness of breath. I called out for you but I could hear you but I couldn't see you. Then everything went red. Then I woke up." She recanted.

"Yeah, that does sound like you're imagination using the survivors' story to scare you. Maybe you should not listen in on anymore debriefings." I said. This life was all too new for her. We were raised hearing these stories but she has only been here only few days, and already she's heard and seen too many bad things.

"Do we have to go see Alain?" she pleaded.

"Gena, it's just a precaution. He may just say the same thing I just said but he is a doctor, maybe he can give you some suggestion on blocking these images out." I assured her.

"I'm just so embarrassed about being scared. Everyone here is so brave and heroic." She said.

"We have been exposed to this all our life. You just got here. You shouldn't be embarrassed about anything. Look what you have had to endure within the past two weeks. You discovered a new family. You found out you're not even human. You go around healing people. You fall in love with your soul mate. I'm surprised you haven't had nightmares every night." I pointed out.

"Those things, especially falling in love with you, would not give me nightmares." She acknowledged. I love it when she says she loves me.

"Come on eat. We have to go over to Alain's house." I instructed.

She finished her breakfast and we loaded the dishwasher together. I caught her looking over at the panic room in the pantry. "Gena, I will never let anyone hurt you, okay? Your death will kill me too you know. Given what your parents had to do to get you here, I will not fail them." I assured as I pulled her to me. She didn't say anything. She just held me.

I called Alain to warn him of our visit. We pulled up to his driveway soon afterwards. Alain was much more practical than Rolfe. His home wasn't adorned with columns and museum-like topiaries. It was a simple colonial style home with white siding and black shutters. Even though it had 6 bedrooms, it didn't look pretentious and grandiose like Rolfe house. As we got out Cory and Michael came through the door to greet us.

"Hey, Corin, nice of you to come by and visit us. We haven't seen you since Thursday. Do you have to ask for permission to go outside now? Gena you need a date for the engagement party?" Michael teased.

"I am busy spending time with the most beautiful girl in the world. You guys don't stand a chance. Get your own date. Where is Alain?" I boasted.

"You lucky bastard. My dad is inside in his office." He replied.

We made our way to Alain's office. He was sitting at his desk.

"Gena, Corin, nice to see you two. You sounded distressed on the phone. Is everything alright?" he asked as he got up and greeted us.

"Hi, Alain, I had a nightmare last night." She said nonchalantly.

"Alain, it was so bad her eyes turned red." I expressed.

"Oh, now that is different. What was the nightmare about?" he assessed.

"Well, I dreamt I was dying and it felt so real, that I think I may have triggered my healer aura." She explained.

"That is possible but I also think that when you were healing Tina, you picked up her terrifying experience and made it your own. I noticed when I was caring for Tina that she kept telling me that she could feel the feelings you had for Corin. I think that made Preston a little jealous until she explained that it was your feelings not hers. It's like you guys melded during the healing process." He explained.

"Well, that would explain how vivid the dream was. It was probably like you were there when Tina was attacked. What should we do to prevent the nightmare from coming back?" I asked.

"Yeah, my eyes can't turn red whenever I get scared. How will I explain something like that?" she said anxiously.

"Well, I'm not a psychologist but I think it will pass with time and Gena, your aura wasn't triggered because you were afraid. It thought you were dying and it was there to protect you." He explained.

"Will this happen every time she heals someone?" I asked.

"Yes, but with more exposure to our way of life, the easier it will be for you. Don't forget Gena, it has only been 10 days since you came here. You've had a lot to deal with. Give it some time." He assured.

"Okay, Alain. I feel much better already. Thanks for seeing us." She thanked.

"Yeah, Alain, thanks." I reiterated.

"Anytime. I'll see you guys at the party tonight." He said.

We left Alain's office and headed over to my house. I had to get some of my things plus see how Mark was holding up.

"Do you feel better now?" she asked.

"I will feel better when this doesn't affect you anymore." I stated.

"I think it will just take some time." She said. I nodded to confirm what she said.

"Is that Mark and Ella's house?" she asked as we passed the two-story brick colonial.

"Yeah, Mark had it built after he proposed to Ella. It was just finished. They haven't had the chance to move in when all this happened. Now, there are three men living there. I don't think I can share you that way. I like our privacy too much." I said.

"Yeah, I like what we have too." She agreed.

We pulled up my parents' driveway and were greeted by Michelle. "Hey you guys. Gena welcome to our house." She announced.

"Hi, Michelle, how's Mark holding up?" I asked.

"Well, they haven't fought today. If that is what you mean. But the day isn't over yet." She said with sarcasm.

"December can not come quick enough." I sighed.

We walked in and greeted my parents in the parlor. My mother was getting a home pedicure and manicure.

"Oh, hi Gena, Corin. You didn't tell me you were coming by today. Gena, welcome to our home" She welcomed.

"Hi, Gena. Welcome to our home. You are welcome here anytime." My father greeted Gena.

"Thank you Mr. Randall, you have a beautiful home." She complimented.

"Your house is something too; I should know I was there when it was being built." He praised.

"Thank you." She said shyly.

"Oh, I want apologize for the misunderstanding about the Justin thing. Did Corin tell you it was my fault for telling him that?" he asked.

"No, it's alright. Everything worked out." She assured him.

"Yes, it did work out. I think Corin is very lucky to have you." He commended.

"Dad, you're embarrassing her." Michelle yelled from behind.

"Dad, I totally agree." I confirmed.

"Corin, what are you doing over here? You need to get Gena home so she can get ready for the party. Us women need a lot of time to get ready, you know. It is very important you respect that." My mother scolded.

"We're just here to get some of my stuff. Where is Mark?" I asked.

"He is over at Ella's house. Don't bother him today. He is not himself. Just get your things and go get ready for the party. It is 12:30pm already." She warned.

We went up to my room. I just realized she had never been to my room. I hope it wasn't too messy. "Welcome to my humble abode." I announced. She entered with a smile. She stood in the middle of my room taking everything in. She walked over to the stereo and looked over my personal CD collection. She then moved over to my bed. God, how many times did I dream of her lying on my bed and now here she is. I watched as she sat down on my bed and moved towards the middle of the bed.

"I believe we have never kissed in here." She said with a devilish smile. Her beauty overwhelmed me.

It took everything I had to not rush over and ravage her. I made my way over slowly trying to pretend to be in control. "I have had dreams of you on my bed but this it is much better in reality." I complimented as I sat next to her.

"You say that you've dreamt of me being here?" She questioned.

"Every day of my life than after we met, every second" I confirmed as I took her lips. Her hands locked themselves in my hair. I shifted my weight pinning her to my bed. Looking down at her lying on my bed, her brown hair spayed out, her lips parted and her eyes in a trance, how could I ever want anyone or anything else? "I love you, Gena." I said slowly and deliberately. She responded by pulling me back down to her lips. As she kissed me she ran her hands inside my shirt causing me to quiver. I slid my hands down to unbutton her shirt. When I exposed her, she did not stop me. I touched my lips on her skin between her breasts as my hand caressed her breast. When I felt her hands pulling at the buttons on my jeans; it jolted me back to reality.

"Gena" I said panting in her ear. "We can't." I fought with her hand. "We have to stop." I pulled her upright and fumbled with the buttons on her shirt. I watched as she moved her hand to help me.

"I'm sorry I got carried away." I said sadly. I watched as she looked at me with a smirk and laughed.

"What is so funny?" I laughed along.

"I think I'm being punished." She stated.

"You're not the only one." I said as I re-button my shirt.

"No, that's not it. Never mind" She said hiding something from me.

"Then what" I asked curiously.

"Do you really want to know?" she tempted.

"Yes, of course." I restated.

"Okay, but don't get jealous," she said. *Too late, that already made me jealous.*

"The last time I was with Peter he wanted to do this, but I told him no. I told him I wasn't ready. Now the tables have turned on me. I am ready but you're the one stopping me. You're the one saying "we can't". It is just ironic that's all." She said openly.

"Well, I'm glad you said no to him. But you have to believe me, I want to just as badly as you do. If your life wasn't endangered, I would not be so restrained. I would have probably taken you that day at school. But your life is so much more important than this." I confessed.

"I know. I don't know why we keep doing this to ourselves. Don't depend on me for the willpower to stop. I am depending on your willpower." She remarked.

"You are very hard to say no to. But losing you would be harder. So we will wait." I concluded.

"Oh, I meant to tell you I love you too before you distracted me." She added.

"Come on, we only have two hours to get ready for this party. Luckily we are fast." I said.

"What about the things you came here for?" she reminded me.

"I got what I need." I declared.

We rushed downstairs, waving back at my parents. When we got home she went upstairs to get ready. I pulled a small velvet box from my jean pocket and placed it on the banister. I went upstairs to another room to change into my tuxedo. I heard her call for my assistance. I quickly tucked in my shirt and carried my jacket and tie to her room.

"Gena, you need some help?" I asked.

"Please, I may need your help with this zipper?" she asked.

I came over to where she was standing and watched as she slipped the tight pink dress on. It fit her every curve perfectly. I took a deep breath. I am going to kill Lauren. It was a light pink strapless stretch satin dress. The neckline of the dress forced her breast together forming a perfect cleavage. The bodice hugged her every curve down her hips to the middle of her thighs stopping just above her knees. I had to stop myself from imagining what she was wearing underneath. I couldn't stop staring at her. She mesmerized me. I walked over and assisted her with the zipper.

She let her hair down in a wavy beautiful mess.

"I think Lauren is trying to kill me in these shoes. I don't know if I can walk around in these too long. They are so high." She complained. I wasn't looking at the shoes.

"Do I look okay? Maybe I should put on some makeup." She asked.

I didn't answer I just kept my eyes on her. She looked exquisite in that dress. I didn't know whether to thank Lauren or kill her. "You look excruciatingly beautiful. You don't need makeup." I said to her. I was utterly captivated.

"You're bias. Maybe I should put some lip gloss on." She suggested.

"I'll just kiss them off you." I remarked.

"Corin, don't start. I don't want to wrinkle this dress. Lauren would kill us both." She warned.

"Here let me help you with your shoes." I offered. I just wanted to touch her somewhere even if it was just to slip on her heels.

She giggled as she sat down on the bed. I took her heels and slid them on her feet. I inhaled her scent as I caressed the length of her calf with my lips. I looked up to see her smiling down at me tenderly. "You really know how to charm a girl off her feet." She complimented.

"I only want to charm you, no on else." I whispered. I took her hand and pulled her upright. I took one good look at her. "Perfect" I said.

"Thank you, can I help you with your tie?" she asked as she pulled at my tie drawing me close to her. She worked on it for a few seconds and produced a perfect bow tie.

"Wow, should I be worried that you know how to do that?" I teased.

"Not unless you're jealous of my father. He wore a bow tie every Sunday to church." She stated proudly. She always surprises me.

"Are you ready?" I asked.

"Yes, unless you think I need lip gloss." She answered.

"You took only 30 minutes to look this gorgeous. I can't imagine what you would look like if you took an hour." I proclaimed.

"You're bias again." she mentioned.

"No, it is a fact. Now come downstairs I have something for you." I said excitedly.

"What is it?" she asked, impatiently.

"Come down if you want it." I challenged.

I rushed downstairs before she could make it down. She wasn't as fast because of her heels. I stood at the banister holding the velvet jewelry box.

"Corin, what is that?" she hesitated as she descended the stairs to stand right in front of me.

"Do you remember that symbol I drew on the card I gave you." He asked.

"The Mobius strip sign" She answered. I was surprised that she knew what it was called. I opened the box and pulled a necklace with a pendant with the same symbol. The symbol was formed with white gold encrusted with tiny diamonds. I held it up to her.

"Oh, Corin it is so beautiful. When did you get this?" she asked in awe.

"I got it when I was in Dawson City this week. I was walking around one night when I could not sleep and there it was sitting in the store window. When I saw it, I knew immediately it was made for you. Here turn around." I said.

She turned so I could place it on her neck.

"You are my one and only temptation." I whispered.

"Thank you Corin. I love you." She whispered.

I smiled back at her. "I know. Let's go show you off." I said. We made our way to my car.

"So, where is the party at?" she asked as I held the car door for her. When she sat down the dress rose further up her thighs. I've seen her legs in shorts before but what the dress did for her legs was really tempting.

"At the North Chateau, a little south of here. You'll love it. It's like our hidden jewel. We've spent a lot of money on it. The North Chateau was a beautiful chateau built in the late 1920s' for the late Canadian Prime Minister as a gift for investing in Inuvik. In the 1998, Edwin Daniels, my dad and Rolfe bought it and restored it. Edwin and my dad love the Edwardian period, so it was restored with lots of Edwardian architecture designs." He boasted.

"I don't think I've seen anything like that here." She said.

"It's not something that is opened to the public. We normally use it for these kinds of events. Rolfe uses it to entertain the oil businessmen. If you haven't notice, there aren't any luxury hotels in Inuvik." He pointed out.

When we drove up the long driveway to the Chateau, I watched as she was awestruck by the building ahead.

"What do you think?" I asked.

"Wow, I would've never thought something this beautiful was here in Inuvik." She said.

The Chateau was a four-story building with 12 suites and two grand ballrooms. It has the charm and dignified style of the Edwardian Period. It is richly adorned with Italian Marble, crystal chandeliers, Wedgewood motif, and gilded architectural embellishment. The beautiful arched roofs and luxurious décor provided historical elegance. The picturesque landscaped gardens were done with the help of all the Burren wives.

When we pulled up, I handed my keys to the valet. I watched closely as he looked over Gena. I really couldn't blame him; I would probably do the same. This was going to be a long night. We walked towards a crowd of our friends.

"There they are." Tristan announced.

"Oh, Gena you look absolutely beautiful. We did well, huh, Corin?" Lauren fished.

"I think you did too well." I replied.

"Your sister is looking for you." Aimee informed.

"Shall we go in?" I asked Gena. She nodded but she was not really paying attention to me. She was still taken back by the building. I escorted her into the grand entrance. Mark and Ella's engagement brought in 200 guests from many different clans. There were some human friends and business comrades of my dad here too. There were a large group of men standing at the far end of the entrance. I saw how they immediately turned to look at Gena. She was not going to make this easy for me. If this wasn't my brother's party, I would not subject her to these people. The look on their faces only means for one thing, and I did not like it. I looked for Michelle but did not see her right away. Something is wrong. I don't see Mark or Ella. My parents were not here either.

"Gena, I have to go find Michelle, will you be okay? I want you to stay with Tristan and Aimee." I instructed. I didn't want to leave her but something was wrong. I felt I could trust Aimee and Tristan to keep her safe from the vultures in the room.

"Okay, is everything alright?" She worried.

"I'm going to find out. Be right back." I kissed her gently on her lips.

I ascended the enormous stairs to the second floor towards one the suites. I immediately saw Michelle coming out from one of the suites.

"Michelle, what is going on? Where are Mark and Ella?" I questioned.

"We've got serious problems. Mom and Dad are in there talking to Mark. Ella locked herself in the other suite." She explained.

"Are they fighting again?" I asked as I walked toward the suite where Mark was.

"Worse." She replied. I looked at her before I walked in.

"Hey, Mark! What's going on? Are we going to celebrate or not?" I tried to be light and cheerful but when I looked at Mark he was a mess.

"Corin, we need to talk. Mom, Dad can I please have some privacy." He pleaded.

I watched as my parents left. They were clearly worried and anxious. My mother looked like she was about to go into tears. When the doors closed, I watched as Mark pulled off his tuxedo jacket and loosen his tie.

"What's going on, Mark" I impatiently questioned.

"We can't go on with this." He said dejectedly.

"Come on, Mark. It's just nerves. You guys love each other." I explained.

"It's not enough, Corin." He said quietly staring in a daze.

"It has been enough for two years now, what has changed?" I asked.

"She told me today that she has found her soul mate." He said with agony.

I ransacked my brain for this person. Were they downstairs? There isn't anyone new. "Who is it?" I asked quietly. I knew this was a moot point because there was nothing I could do to help him. For years we were selfish and arrogant to fear that he made leave Ella for his soul mate never the other way around.

"Trey" He said quietly. "She said she knew right away when he came to our house. She thought she could fight it but the pull was just too strong. I saw her kiss him this morning but I didn't confront her. This afternoon we talked about it and I agreed to forgive her. But right now, when I see her I don't see the girl who once loved me. She isn't mine. I don't want to hurt her by keeping her away from him. The stupid thing is I'm not mad. You were right. I should've waited." He openly stated.

"Mark, I'm really sorry man. What are you going to do?" I asked.

"I'm leaving." He voiced.

"Where are you going?" I asked.

"I'm going to take that trip that we planned. You don't need it." He said flatly.

"Mark, are you sure? What about the party?" I reiterated.

"I've already broken off the engagement with Ella. She feels really bad. I can't face her right now. I'm leaving tonight. I would have left earlier but I had to see you. I love you, man. Take care. I'll be back. Hopefully with a Gena of my own. I am truly happy for you. You deserve it. Tell her I said goodbye. Why don't you use this opportunity to introduce her to everyone?"

I grabbed him and hugged him. "I'm going to miss you. Take care of yourself. Call me when you know where you're going first. If you need anything, you call me." I directed.

We walked out together. My parents hugged him. Michelle was crying, He pulled away and left thru the back hallway, from there he could take the elevator down to the kitchen and sneak out to the back. We watched as he disappeared. We didn't know how long he would be gone but hopefully only two years. I heard Ella open her door and closed it back.

"What about Ella?" I asked.

"Her parents are in there. We're just waiting to hear what they want to do." My mom stated. After a few minutes, Edwin came out and approached us.

"John, Diane, I am so sorry." He looked remorseful.

"Edwin, we understand. There is nothing we can do about the way we live. It is almost a curse sometimes, but it is part of who we are." My mother reassured.

"What do you want to do about the party?" my dad asked.

"Ella wants to leave now. We don't have any reasons to celebrate. Since everyone came from so far, why don't we just let them celebrate? I'll support whatever you want to do, Diane." He voiced

"You go take care of Ella. We'll deal with everyone." She asserted. We watched as he escorted Ella and his wife down the same hallway and left.

"Corin, have you and Gena talked about announcing your union?" my mother asked.

"Mom, I am living with her. But still I would like to talk to her before I spring something like this on her." I conveyed.

"I'll go get her." Michelle announced as she sprinted down the stairs. My parents walked toward another suite.

"We'll give you some privacy." My mother stated as she pulled my dad into the suite.

I was suddenly overwhelmed with nervousness. I saw her come up the stairs with Michelle. She walked gracefully toward me and gently squeezed my hand. I pulled her into the suite behind me. When the door was closed, I turned and carefully watched her. She stood in the middle of the room.

"What is wrong, Corin?" she asked. Even to this day, the way she said my name excited me.

"Mark and Ella have broken off their engagement." I said quietly.

"Oh." She whispered like she knew it already.

"Ella found out that Trey is her soul mate. Mark broke off the engagement and left twenty minutes ago. He is going on that trip that we planned long ago." I reminded.

"How's Ella holding up?" she asked.

"She just left with her parents. She'll be fine. Guilty but fine." I divulged.

"I'm so sorry. Are you alright?" she worried.

"I'm fine. My parents are a little surprised but there is really nothing we can do about it. We knew that something like this could happen. It just so happens it was today of all days. At least they weren't already married." I confessed.

"So, what happens now?" she asked

"That is why Michelle brought you up here." I said as I moved to stand in front of her. "I know with all my heart that you are my one and only true love. What we have is everlasting" I said as I pointed to her necklace. "I know we were going to announce our union formally one day but since we have this opportunity now, I would like to ask you for your permission to announce it tonight." He declared.

"I would love this opportunity to tell the world that you belong to me and I to you. You did not have to ask me. To be honest, I thought we already did that when you moved in with me. But this is just as good." She said warmly. I was so elated that I grabbed her face and kissed her forcefully and hungrily. I heard her moaned when I ran my hands over her hips and up her breast. I was messing her hair up by pulling her tighter into me. As abruptly as we started, I pulled away from her trembling lips and whispered "You make me so happy. I will love you forever."

"I am counting on that." She flirted. She pulled away and went over to the gilded mirror to straighten her hair. "You made my lips swollen; now I don't have to get fat injections." She teased.

"Don't you dare change anything on that beautiful face of yours?" I ordered.

"Oh, Corin. Don't think I will accept this as proposal either. I refuse to remember my proposal on this day when Mark and Ella broke off their engagement." She said sarcastically.

"I promise you when I propose, it will take your breathe away. You will not say no." I promised.

"I wasn't planning on saying no, but I want to remember it for the rest of my long life. If you mess it up, I will constantly remind you." She teased.

"I will never disappoint you, I promise." I reiterated.

"Okay, let's do this. I want to crush all the other girls' hearts when they hear you belong to me." She smiled.

"I will enjoy seeing the faces of all those tormented men in the room." I added.

"Okay, let's go break some hearts." She teased.

I followed her out the door. My parents were waiting in the hallway. I nodded to my mother. "Oh, thank you Gena. We hated to put you on the spot." My mother said apologetically.

"Diane, I am extremely happy for this opportunity. I should thank you." She divulged.

"Let's go do this." My father interrupted.

We all descended the stairs together. Midway down the stairs, people quieted down and looked up at us. My father made the announced about Mark and Ella's cancellation. Everyone was so surprised and disappointed.

"I want to thank everyone for coming because even though Mark and Ella are no longer getting married, I want everyone to stay and celebrate the announcement of my son Corin and his *concero flamma*, Gena." He said proudly. Everyone in the room erupted into cheers and congratulations.

I got to see all the disappointed faces in the audience. I looked over at her and pulled her to me. I kissed her proudly in front of all those afflicted.

Chapter Sixteen

We spent Sunday moving his things in. I could tell he was a little sad about his brother leaving but he didn't want to talk about. I felt sorry for his mother. She watched two of her sons leave within 24 hours. I could almost relate to the lost and despair. I watched from the bed as he aligned his CDs in order in our room. *Our room*, it sounded nice. After the announcement we celebrated into the night with all our friends. When we got home, he carried me upstairs like we had just gotten married and he was carrying me to our honeymoon. It was fun to dream about that.

"You're daydreaming again." He witnessed.

"I was just dreaming about us." I confessed.

"I don't have to be dreaming to think about us. I get to live it every second." He boasted.

"You always have to one up me on the charming." I noted.

"It is easy to confess my feelings to you." He conveyed.

"What is going to happen to Ella and Trey now?" I asked

"Well, as much as it hurts my brother, I can only be happy for them. This is something that is a part of who we are. There is nothing we can do about. I was so sure you were my soul mate that I thought about fighting Justin for you. I don't think I could stand by and watch you marry anyone else. That's why Mark didn't go through with it. Ella was willing to still marry him but he knew that she didn't belong to him. I think he will be alright. I just hope he finds what he is looking for. I think it will be harder if he came back empty handed. If that is the case, I don't blame him if he doesn't come back at all." He stated.

"You would fight Justin for me?" I questioned.

"I would either fight him or leave and never see you again." He said sadly.

"Well, I'm glad you didn't leave. That would be tragic for me." I confessed.

"I'm just glad things turned out for us. I was so miserable a few days ago; I would like to forget that all together." He shared.

Changing the subject, I asked "So what happens after the announcement?" I sat up in bed.

"Well, we will wait until after we graduate then we can get married." He planned.

"Well, since we can't even consummate the marriage why don't we wait?" I stated.

"Marriage to you is not about consummating, it is about making you officially mine." He declared as he came over and placed his hand on my face.

"I am yours in every way. I don't need any paper to know that." I said warmly.

"And I am yours but I want this and one day you will too. We can't go living in sin." He teased.

"Living in sin involves sex; we can't even get pass second base." I indicated.

"Second base isn't so bad." He pointed out as he caressed my lower lip with his thumb. He doesn't realize what that does to me. I pulled his lips down to mine.He grabbed hold of the back of my neck and forced our lips together. He kissed me ravenously while his hands caressed my neck, and then moved lower until he covered my breast. The wonderful heat coming from his skin combined with his irrestible scent drove me wild. My lips wanted to taste every inch of him. My hands wanted to roam all over him. But his control was phenomal. He eased himself away from me and stared down at me.

"What are you thinking about?" he asked quietly.

"Bad lustful thoughts" I admitted shamefully.

He laughed. "Me too"

"I was just wondering if I could survive making love to you if what I just experience was only a small part of what's to come." I admitted openly.

"Don't worry, I'll keep you alive." He said devilishly.

"Come on, we have to clean this up. Laundry day is tomorrow." he voiced.

"I'm going to shower then I'll fix dinner. Do you want to shower with me?" I dared.

"I don't know if I have the will power to see you naked. I'll go shower in the other bathroom." He said in defeat.

"Coward" I teased.

"I am a coward. I know what you can do to me and I know what I am capable of doing." He warned.

I walked into the bathroom smiling at him. I felt so powerful having this much control of him. He just doesn't realize; he has the same power over me. I quickly showered and went downstairs to start dinner. Tonight, I was making lasagna. I started a pot of boiling water to cook the lasagna strips. In another pot I simmered a mixture of pureed tomatoes, mixed herbs, olive oil and garlic. I went to the refrigerator to get the ricotta cheese. As I was about place the uncooked pasta into the boiling water, the phone rang.

I let it rang twice before I picked it up.

"Hello." I answered.

"Gena, It's Mark. How are you?" he replied.

"Mark, it is so nice to hear your voice. How are you doing? Are you okay?" I pleaded.

"I'm fine. Is Corin there?" he asked.

"Oh, yes. Let me get him." I said.

I ran up stairs with the phone. I found him in the bedroom dressed and rubbing his hair.

"Corin, it's Mark." I handled him the phone.

I left to give him some privacy. I went back downstairs to finish the pasta. Once the pasta was done, I assembled the lasagna and placed it in the oven. Satisfied, I went back up stairs to check on Corin. I could hear from the door he was still talking to Mark. I waited outside to give him privacy.

After some time, I went back downstairs to wait. To keep myself busy, I put together a small pasta salad with leftover lasagna sheets. I had to cut them into small bite size pieces and mixed them with cherry tomatoes, olives, olive oil and bleu cheese. I went to set the table for two then placed the mixed pasta salad down. When I returned to the kitchen to check on the lasagna, I heard Corin coming down. I pulled the lasagna out and walked over to the dining room table. I placed it down on a stand and started cutting into it.

"God, that smells good. I am starving. You really wore me out today." He commented.

"The day isn't over yet." I teased.

"Well, I better refuel. Lasagna, I love lasagna." He complimented. I gave him a square of lasagna and scooped some pasta salad onto his plate.

I watched him eat, before I started on my plate. He finished his piece quickly and helped himself to more.

"You have learned a lot in Home Economics, I am very proud of my tutoring skills." he chuckled.

I sat there quietly observing him eat. "How is Mark?" I asked.

"He called to tell me he is in Prudhoe Bay, which is the northernmost part of Alaska. He is going to learn how to ice fish." He said smiling.

"Ice fish?" I asked.

"It doesn't matter what he is doing. He sounded happier. Do you think?" he questioned.

"I don't know. I didn't get to talk to him much. You know him better than anyone." I said.

"I think he feels a lot of relief." He guessed.

"So, did he say when he was coming back?" I asked.

"No, but if he is happier out there than home can wait" He declared.

He ate all but two pieces of the lasagna before he declared he was full. I could not believe how he could eat all that and still walk. He helped me clear and wash the dishes. We went into the living room and put away more of his things. He had a lot of books on human anatomy and biology.

"You like Anatomy and Biology." I asked.

"Well, I am fascinated on how things work, whether it is machine or human body. The human body is the coolest machine next to ours. I wonder what gives us our abilities and them lack there of. It can't be that far off." he stated.

"Have you thought about pursuing this further?" I asked.

"What do you mean, in college?" he questioned.

"Yeah, like medicine or engineering." I pointed out.

"I thought more about mechanical engineering. What about you?" He declared.

"I want to go into Research Medicine. There are a lot of diseases out there that needs a cure. I have the money and the time; it just seems like the perfect fit." I informed.

"Yeah, I heard you wanted to donate money to the Leukemia Foundation. That is really kind of you. Is that how Peter died?" he asked.

"Yes, but that is not the only reason. My adoptive mother died of breast cancer and my adoptive father died of heart disease. It just seems a little unfair that we can live almost immortal but they can die so easily." I remarked.

"You would be the one to cure all disease for human kind. You were born to heal us. So it is just natural that you would find a way to help other specie." He noted.

We continued to unpack his things. After we were done downstairs, we went back to aligning the CDs in the bedroom. He had a remarkable collection of all kind of music. He was only 19 years old but he seemed older and wiser than the other guys here.

"Corin, do you ever get tired of doing things for my uncle Rolfe?" I asked.

He looked surprised by my questions. "You know that saying *'with great power there comes great responsibilities'* well that basically is my burden. When I was born, my parents immediately knew I had a very strong aura. Most of our kind are born with one extraordinary power whether it is speed, strength, or heightened senses; our aura makes our specific skill stronger. When we are around others of our kind, their auras help us heightened the other skills too. I was born with a very strong aura that heightened my speed and strength skills without the need of the others around me. Being fast and strong, make me the perfect candidate for clandestine missions. I've been doing this since I was 16 years old. Sometimes it is hard to go by myself but someone has to do it. This last trip was actually fun because I got to share it with the guys." He reminisced.

"I asked because you seemed more mature than guys older than you." I said.

"Well if you've seen what I've seen, you would age faster too." He stated.

"Why do the hunters want to hurt us?" I asked.

"Well, before our people came to Earth, which was called Gaia long ago, we lived on a planet far from this dimension called Tiamat. On Tiamat there was a three tier society. The first tier is the ruling class. They ruled the people and make the laws. The second tier is the defending class. They are like the military today. The third tier was the commoners, they comprised of workers, laborers, and hunters. Your aura determines the tier you're in. Like for example if we were in Tiamat, you would be in the first tier and I would be in the second tier. The commoners were born with no auras but they were strong and many. There was an uprising, like a revolution. After years of war and destruction Tiamat was finally left inhabitable. Some of our ancestors banned together and left Tiamat for Earth. The hunters blamed us for the destruction of Tiamat. They vowed to destroy us and some of them followed us here. Through the years we have evolved and they have evolved. We may be smarter and stronger but we need an aura. They are not as smart or civilized but they are strong and they don't need an aura. They prefer to live outside like animals. They can't live as long as we do but they can birth more than we can. Luckily not all of their births have the genetic ability to be super strong. Some are born as simple as humans. They can not heal either. That is our advantage. Does that answer your question?" he ended.

"Wow, it all seems so unreal. So, how many clans are here on Earth?" I asked.

"We don't actually know. You can spend years exploring Earth and still find places that have never been touched by man. As far as we know, we have met 120 clans. They're not all this big either. Some clans consisted of 2 or 3 families." He answered.

I sat there quietly finishing the labeling of his the CDs. I was absorbing all this information but I don't think it has really hit all the way home. I felt like I should have more questions or even cast doubt but for some reason everyone has been so trustworthy, I just accepted what they said as truth. With Corin, I would believe anything he says because I trust him completely.

"I think we are done for tonight. We have school tomorrow. Let's call it a night." He announced as he took the pen and CDs from my hand. I went and changed into my shorts and t-shirt. When I came back he was in bed with only his pajama pants on.

"Now, whose turn was it to get to second base?" he teased.

School was the only constant thing in our lives. The second week of school wasn't as exciting as the first week but we managed to get through it unscathed. With Corin beside me, I did not get the attention of any other guys. Trevor was the only guy that I socialized with beside our close circle of friends. Trevor was surprised to learn that Corin was pretty helpful in getting the answers for third question on Newton-Raphson Method. We were still working on the second question on the Bertrand Series. The other classes' assignments weren't as time consuming. At lunch, we found out from Joseph that Ella was still feeling guilty over what happened. She was ignoring Trey. Corin assured Joseph that his family had no ill will against Ella. It was just an uncomfortable situation. Corin kept everyone informed about Mark.

After school we spent time with friends. Our house was the new hang out joint for everyone. I didn't have to cook every night. Each night someone volunteered to bring over food to share. It felt like we were a bunch of neighbors doing pot-luck every night. I found out that Thanksgiving in Canada was in October and not November. By the end of September we had settled into a routine. Most of the time we spent time helping each other with homework and assignments. I was very helpful in this area, because a lot of their classes I had already taken. I rarely saw my grandparents because they traveled a lot. Uncle Rolfe was busy running the family business. The aunts were always busy arranging social and charity activities for the town and family. Aunt Madeline and Idelle were always doing gardening somewhere. Hockey season kept all the guys busy. There was a split on fans for the Maple Leafs and Canadiens.

Of all the family members, I spent most of my time with Alain and Cory. We shared a common interest in research. I had a theory that our blood could be used to help humans find cures for certain diseases. We spent a lot of time working on that theory. We took samples of our blood and used it to test diseases on animals. We were doing our own clinical trials on mice. We made no significant findings but it was interesting all the same. Lately, Alain was always at the Inuvik Union Hospital. He was now the Chief of Internal Medicine and Surgery so I continued with the experiments by myself, using my own blood. Sometimes Corin would be with me and he would volunteer his blood. I hated needles so I often gave a unit of blood all at one time so I didn't have to endure too many needlesticks. Alain's basement was a functioning laboratory, so many times I would be down there with Cory and Corin would watch hockey with Michael.

This life was what we dreamt of. This was our happily ever after. We talked a lot of our future and having children. We even had names picked out. We both wanted to have three kids but it all depended on when my transformation was complete. I hated my predicament but Corin was very accommodating. He had a plan for any situation. It felt like everything hinged on when my transformation would be complete. As soon it was safe we would rush to have three kids, I had only until I was 25 years old. Nature was cruel to our kind but it also provided us with some rewards.

It was October, the weather got colder so I rarely rode my Ducati. Snow covered all of Inuvik and I didn't want to leave my bike outside. Lawrence volunteered to have it stored in his garage. He was definitely in love with it. Lauren, Dana, and Aimee went thru my wardrobe to make sure I was set for the harsh winters of Inuvik. Corin was at Max's house watching hockey with the guys.

"I think you should at least get one fur coat." Lauren suggested.

"I'm not really into fur. I like wool or downy or I can layer a lot of things." I said.

"Gena, fur is in." she implied.

"When have I ever been in style, anyway I need you guys' help in doing something for Corin's birthday. It's October 23th." I asked.

"Do you want to have a surprise party?" Aimee asked excitedly.

"I wasn't thinking about a party but maybe a get together." I corrected.

"Gena, he is going to be 20. Its' got to be a party." Dana insisted.

"I thought that was the age of 21." I questioned.

"Maybe so, but 20 is very important too." She insisted.

"We could do surprise party that is small enough to be a get together." Aimee compromised.

"That sounds better. What do you guys have in mind?" I asked

"Well, we can have it here. We'll invite only friends over. We can have North's cater the food so we don't have to do anything." Dana suggested.

"That sounds nice." I agreed.

"You can get the house ready. I'll take care of the invitations. Aimee, you and Dana can take care of the catering." Lauren assigned.

"So, what are you getting Corin?" Dana asked.

"I don't really know? Any suggestions?" replied. Up until now, I didn't give it much thought.

"I wish Mark was here. He could help you." Aimee said quietly.

"Yeah, I feel so bad for him. Do you know when he'll be back? He's been gone for four weeks now." Lauren asked.

"He really didn't say. But Corin said he sounded happier, so that's got to be good." I answered.

"Deep down I hope he finds someone and brings her back here. It would make things much more comfortable around Ella." Dana said.

"Well, I wish he does find someone but right now he is learning to ice fish." I remarked.

"Ice fish? Where?" Lauren asked in disgust.

"Well, last we heard he was in Prudhoe Bay." I reminded.

"Alaska! There is no clan in Alaska. Matter of fact there is nothing there but old fishermen." Aimee joked.

"Maybe he is just finding himself. Corin is not worry so I don't think we should worry." I ended.

"Ella is just miserable. Trey has been trying to see her but she won't see him. It's heartbreaking. I hope they eventually work things out. Derek is worried that Trey will do something stupid." Dana said.

"What do you mean stupid?" Lauren asked.

"Well, Derek said he has never seen his so depressed and dejected." Dana informed.

"They need to get together and work things out. There is really nothing we can do about their relationship." I said.

"Great idea, Gena. We should get them together. What do you have in mind?" Dana asked.

"Oh, I didn't mean we should get them together. I meant they should get together." I corrected.

"They need some help. At this rate someone is bound to get messed up." Dana said.

"Well, I don't know. We probably shouldn't meddle." Aimee added.

"We need to do something. It is making Joseph and Tristan uncomfortable to be around people. Trey and Derek feels like they have violated the peace of the clan that saved them." Lauren added.

"Well, what do you guys want to do?" I asked.

"How about we invite them to one of our pot-luck things? Once they are here, they will have to address each other. They are soul mates; they can't ignore the force that will eventually draw them together." Dana planned.

"Let me run it by Corin first." I suggested.

"Oh, yeah. Definitely. Call me and let me know." Aimee added.

I nodded. I felt uncomfortable with the whole idea but the situation did warrant some outside help. We finished making plans for Corin's party. They left after all the details were ironed out.

Corin phoned and told me he was going to be late getting home. He didn't want me to wait up. I went to bed by myself for the first time since Corin moved in. It felt odd and strange to miss him for just a few hours. I did not have any problems falling asleep.

I am here again. Where am I? What am I doing here? Looking around I saw flashes of darkness sprinting all around me. What are they? Something was coming. Something was near. I could not see them, but I knew they were coming for me. I started to run. Corin, where are you? I slipped and fell hard into the hard snow. There was no where for me to go. I struggled but I could not get up. Something was holding me down. I can see hands that were big and hairy holding my ankles. I kicked at it but it did no good. The claws dug into my flesh. Blood was oozing out. The heat came over me. Redness covered the air, wake up Gena.

I woke up startled by the front door closing. *Another nightmare*, when will I get used to this. I laid there watching Corin come in quietly. He quickly changed and got into to bedroom. I pretended to stir when he came into bed.

"It's just me babe, sorry. Go back to sleep." He whispered.

I let him believed that I had fallen back to sleep but I just laid there in silence. I was afraid to go back to sleep. These nightmares were so vivid and detailed. I can't imagine what Tina had to endure. I only dreamt about it, she experienced. I didn't want to tell Corin. I didn't want him worrying about something he could not help with. Sometime during the night I fell asleep due to pure exhaustion.

I woke up when I felt Corin caressing my face.

"Morning, I've got you some breakfast downstairs. Do you want me to bring it up?" he asked.

"What time is it?" I mumbled.

"Well, it's almost noon." He informed.

"There goes Sunday." I said quietly.

"Are you okay? Are you coming down with something?" he asked I he felt my forehead.

"No, I just hate sleeping so long." I said.

"Did I disturb your sleep last night?" he asked.

"No, I missed you last night though." I replied. I wanted to change the subject but I didn't want him to pursue why I was sleeping so long.

"Sorry, for coming home late. Game went into overtime." He answered.

"Who won?" I asked

"The Canadiens. You go freshen up I will bring you breakfast." He said proudly

"No, I'll come down." I said as I made my way to the bathroom.

When I came down, I heard him on the phone. I went to the kitchen and saw him standing there talking. He waved me to go into the dining room. I complied. He has set-up breakfast. He was so good at making sure I was fed. He had pink roses in a vase next to the breakfast.

"Guess who that was?" he asked coming from behind me.

"Who?" I replied.

"It was Mark. He has met someone in Prudhoe Bay. He is not sure but he thinks she is our kind. He was asking me about how I felt when I first met you. He didn't tell me why, but his questions sounds like the same things I asked when I first met you." He explained.

"Aimee said there were no clans in Prudhoe Bay." I declared.

"Not that we know of." He explained.

"Do you think he has found someone?" I asked.

"I don't know. He wasn't that specific but I hope so." He hoped.

"Speaking of that, Dana and Lauren would like to invite Ella and Trey over for dinner here. They want to get them talking. I told them I would check with you first. If you feel uncomfortable, I will tell them no." I asked.

"I don't mind. They are destined to be together, there is nothing I or Mark can do about it. I personally know what Trey had to endure. Mark was to Trey as Justin was to me. I understand what Trey is going thru." He recalled.

"I love you, I am glad you did not give up on me." I said softly as I reached for his hand and kissed his palm.

"I don't think I have a choice when it comes to you. Your hold on me is eternal." He said lovingly.

Chapter Seventeen

"I have tracked the scent to Prudhoe Bay. There must be a clan here. We should stay in this area until we find them"

"Nhan the scent is not strong. It may not be a clan. We can find them and kill them I want to go home before the freezing temperature starts to come in."

"Cron, there was a group of them that helped the ones that escaped. Maybe the ones here can lead us to the larger clan"

"What if the clan is too large, we have to go back and talk to the elders."

"Why don't you go back and tell them what we've found? I will wait out here until I get more information."

"Nhan, don't do anything stupid. Wait for word. I will be back."

I continued to have nightmares nightly. Sometimes I would wake up and pretend to go into the bathroom so that Corin could not see my eyes. I did not want him to worry. The nightmares got more and more vivid. Sometimes they got too scary, so I would stay awake to prevent them from coming back. Corin was so good in the morning making sure I was ready for school. Some days I was so exhausted I had to nap as soon as I got home from school. He did not think anything of my exhaustion because I would tell him I was having a headache.

Friday after school, Corin and I went over to talk to Lauren about the pot-luck dinner. When we got there, Preston was there with Tina. This was the first time I got to see her without the bandages. She looked gorgeous. She and I shared the same shade brown hair and brown eyes but while my hair was wavy hers was perfect fine and straight. Corin and Preston haven't seen much of each other since that day. They excused themselves to let Tina and I get to know each other better.

"You are as beautiful as remembered that day" she said.

"Thanks, I didn't think you were even awake." I said embarrassed.

"When you touched me, I could see you and feel everything you were feeling. Corin is so lucky to be so loved." She said.

"Well, it looks like you and Preston are very comfortable together too." I added.

"It's ironic, huh? When I saw him coming into the water towards me I just knew. I was dying but I was so happy. Does that make any since?"

"You were happy to finally find him. Did that give you the will to survive the trip?"

"No, I was dying. We both knew that. Every chance we got to talk I would tell him that I was happy just to at least get to meet him. It tormented him but he would not give up."

"It is a miracle."

"Gena, if you did not help me I would be dead by now. Even if I willed myself to live for Preston, my injuries were just so devastating. Thank you so much." She thanked.

"I am glad I got to help even though I didn't know what I was doing."

"You did enough." She assured.

"Do you ever get nightmares about being attacked?" I asked.

"I have visions of being thrown and pushed by certain faces. I think I blacked out for most of it. When I came to, Trey was carrying me to safety. I kept telling them to leave me behind but they were very persistent. I had lost my family and they had lost theirs. We really did not know where to go, until Brent mentioned your clan. Trisha was afraid it was too far away but we had to give it a try. I don't think we would have made if you guys did not help us in Lake Winnipeg. Corin strategy with the de-scented clothes worked incredibly."

"So, in your visions, do you actually see faces or blurred darkness?"

"I see the faces of those who attacked me but I am not worried. Trey, Brent and Trisha killed them."

"It must be horrible to relive that."

"Well, I don't have those nightmares anymore. Preston has made my life so comfortable. He is tutoring me at home so that I can graduate next year. He has already asked me to marry him. My life went from tragic to fantasy in the course of over one month. I just wished my family got to see how happy I am now."

"I am sure they are watching over you. You have had some remarkable challenges to overcome, and you seemed to weather them fine."

"Thanks, I heard Alain saying that you have been having some nightmares because you healed me."

"Yeah, it is just my vivid imagination taking over. I'll be fine."

"I heard you guys are trying to get Trey and Ella talking." She mentioned. At the corner of my eyes I saw Lauren walking in to the parlor.

"Hey Gena, I'm sorry I'm late. I had to talk to Aimee about getting Tristan to bring Ella over tomorrow. I think we are all set. Tina, you and Preston should come too."

"Yeah, it would be fun. I am making Beef Wellington. I got the recipe from the internet." I encouraged.

"Wow that sounds like fun. I'll ask Preston."

"You don't have to ask Preston. Just tell him. That is what I do to Max."

"Who else is coming?"

"Well, Ella and Trey is definitely coming. Derek is making sure Trey comes so Dana will be there also. Aimee and Tristan will be there. Then it is us too." Lauren answered.

"Twelve people, do you have enough food. I can bring something." She asked.

"No, we have lots of food already. Just bring yourself." I said.

"Well, than we will see you tomorrow night. Thanks for the invitation."

"Okay, we will see you than. I'm going to go get Corin; we have a lot of food shopping to do. I'll see you two tomorrow."

I left the parlor and headed to the family room. Corin and Preston were watching hockey.

"Hi, guys." I announced as I walked over to Corin. He pulled me down on his lap.

"Gena, I just want to thank you again for what you did for Tina. I was telling Corin about it."

"I really don't know what exactly I did but if that is all I have to do to help, I am glad I could."

"I was telling him about how freaked out I was about your eyes. It is something to remember, huh?"

"I've seen it. Oh, babe, I invited Preston and Tina to the pot luck is that okay?" Corin added.

"That is so weird I invited Tina just now. I have to stop by North's to pick up some things, do you want me to come back by and pick you up?" I asked.

"No, I'll go. Preston, I'll see you and Tina tomorrow." He said as he got up and pulled me along.

When we got to North, we quickly got what we needed and headed home. I wanted to make him dinner since he was so good at making me breakfast. As we pulled up the driveway I saw the packages that Lauren ordered for my winter wardrobe.

"Lauren, really loves shopping." He said.

"I think she sees me as a pet project."

"What did she ordered this time?" he asked as we picked up the five packages and brought them inside.

"Winter clothes I think."

"From Secret Lingerie?" he asked with a devilish look on his face.

"I don't know. I don't remember us looking at Secret Lingerie catalogues, open it." I instructed.

"If I open it, will you wear it for me?" He said with a devilish smile.

"No one else is going to see me in them but you." I replied.

"I mean will you but it on right now." He repeated.

"I was going to make dinner for you first. Maybe we should wait until after dinner." I suggested.

"How fast can you make dinner?" he asked pulling me into the kitchen.

"I was going to make chicken pot pie. That should be two hours." I implied.

"Two hours! I want a peanut butter and jelly sandwich with a glass of milk." He rushed.

"Corin, I am not making you a sandwich. Stop thinking about the packages and let me get started with dinner." I declared. I pushed passed him to the kitchen counter. I quickly got all the ingredients into a pie dish and placed it into the oven. I was cleaning up when he came to stand behind me. He slowly slid his arms around my waist pulling me back into him. He was nuzzling my ear as he whispered "I opened one of the Secret Lingerie packages, and I really like it."

"You could not wait, huh?" I said as I turned to face him.

"It is like Christmas morning for me." He smiled as he lowered his lips to my neck and worked his way down my shoulder tugging at my t-shirt.

"Corin, don't start. I have the pie in the oven." I reminded him.

"Mm, I like dessert." He whispered as his hands came under my shirt.

"Corin, I am talking about the chicken pot pie." I stuttered.

"I meant I want my dessert first." He said as he descends his mouth over mine. His lips brushed over my lips softly as he drew in my lower lip into his mouth and gently sucked on it. He angled his lips and kissed me deeper, his tongue sliding inside my mouth touching my tongue. I wrapped my arms around him and kiss him back. Whatever I was doing before, I didn't care.

"You are the best dessert ever." He murmured in my neck.

I chuckled. "You're biased."

"It doesn't matter. My opinion is the most important. I'll get the pie out." He offered as he released his hold on me. "Come eat."

I sat and watched him eat. "Gena, I want you to eat. You're going to need the energy. I plan to experiment with you tonight." He teased.

"What do you mean by experiment?" I asked feeling a little nervous.

"Well, when you're done I will show you." He said waiting for me to finish eating. He was done eating and he was now sitting back looking at me.

Just to rile him I ate each piece slowly. He watched patiently as I got down to my last piece. Before I could put my fork down, he stood up swiftly, grabbed me from my chair and carried me to the bedroom. I laughed all the way up. His excitement was so thrilling. When we got to our bedroom, he put me down and went over to the bed and handed me the package. "I want my Christmas present now."

I took the package and ran into the bathroom. I pulled out a black sheer mesh slip with matching thong. It was so risqué I was a little embarrassed looking at it. But he wanted to see me in it, and I was willing to do anything to please him right now. "Are you sure you want me to wear this tonight?" I yelled from the bathroom.

"Come out let me see!" he demanded.

I slowly walked out into the bedroom. He was sitting at the end of the bed. He was still fully clothed. I stood near the bathroom door watching him. His eyes were dark and lustful. I watched as he took in a deep breath and closed his eyes. He slowly made his way towards me. "You look exquisite." He said in a deep and throaty voice. To my surprise, he handed me another package. "Now, put these on." He ordered. Smiling I took the package and went back into the bathroom.

The second package had a white embroidered eyelet baby doll slip with matching thong. It too was seductive. This slip hid nothing. The white lace heightened my skin color. I tousled my hair and walked out to the bedroom. Again, I found him sitting at the end of the bed. I watched as he gazed me over with his lazed eyes. "Beautiful." Was all he said before he came over and handed me another package. "More, please." He said silently. I loved the way he begged. I understood what he was doing now. He knew I could not wear these things to bed but he wanted to at least see them on me. He wanted his personal runway show. This excited me.

I took the third package into the bathroom and quickly changed into a light pink sheer mesh front slip with straps covering the back and the matching thong. This one was more risqué than the other two because it did not cover anything in the back. I slowly made my way out and towards him. He watched in agony. I could see his breathing become more labored and unsettled. I saw him leaned forward dropping his face into his hands. I stood right before him and gently pulled his head back to look at me. "In order to enjoy the show you have to look. Do you want me to continue?" I asked seductively. I saw him swallowed hard and handed me another package. I laughed and turned to slowly walk back into the bathroom. I can hear him groaning when he saw the back of the lingerie. Smiling I went back into the bathroom.

The fourth package contained a light blue satin flyaway baby doll with plunging neck line. It opened up in the front showing everything from under the bra to my navel. The panty was smaller than the others. This one should take his breath away. Proudly, I exit the bathroom and walked slowly to him. I watched as his eyes met mine. He stared back with tortured and hungry eyes. He braced himself and placed his arm out. I walked toward him until his palm touched my naked belly. "Please, stop." He whispered. I moved closer into his hand and watched as he looked up at me. "I can't take much more. Please put clothes on." he pleaded. Sensing his defeat, I returned to the bathroom and changed into my regular shorts and t-shirt.

I found him in bed with just his pajama pants on. I walked over and snuggled next to him. "What was that all about?" I asked smiling.

"I wanted my own lingerie catalogue stored in my memory so whenever I want to I can just remember each picture." He chuckled.

"Did you get everything you wanted?" I asked smugly.

"And more" He teased.

He drew me closed to him and we both fell into a blissful sleep.

Chapter Eighteen

This one is from the clan that helped them.

He brags about how they duped us with the clothes.

I should go out there and rip his head off.

What is he doing here all by himself?

He wants the girl to return with him to Inuvik.

So, the clan is in Inuvik.

Who is this leader Corin?

I will kill him personally for interfering.

Finally the information I have been waiting for. I will not kill this Mark right now. I need him to show me who this Corin is. If I can just kill him I will be satisfied.

Go back to Inuvik, you idiot.

I will scare the girl then he will take her back to Inuvik.

I don't need to wait for the clan for that.

I woke up alone. I was disoriented. Please God, don't let the past few months be only a dream. She is real. Kissing her is real. Tasting her is real. Her touching me is real. I looked around the room. She wasn't in bed. It was still dark outside. The clock showed 2am. I turned on the night stand light. She was gone.

"Gena!" I called out. I did not hear an answer. My eyes darted around the room. The bathroom light was on. I went over to the bathroom door. I could hear she was crying.

"Gena, are you alright?" I asked from behind the door. I was frightened. I could hear her sobbing but she would not answer me.

"Gena, please let me in. Are you hurt?" I pleaded. Still no answer, now I was frightened beyond repair.

"Gena, if you don't let me in, I will break this door down. Please baby, I just want to know if you're alright." I pleaded up against the door.

"Just give me a minute please." She said still sobbing.

"What's wrong? Are you hurt?" I questioned.

"No, please just one minute." She said tearfully.

"I know something is wrong, why would you be in the bathroom crying at 2am? Gena, please let me in. Maybe I can help?" I begged. Before I became impatient I heard the door unlock. I walked in to find her sitting on edge of the hot tub. Her face was buried in her hands. She was still crying. I walked over and wrapped her in my arms.

"Whatever it is, I promise I will make it better. Please tell me what's wrong?" I asked. She slowly lifted her face and turned to look at me. Her eyes were red.

"It is just a nightmare. I swear I will never let anyone hurt you. Do you believe me?" I assured her. I watched as she continued to cry. Her shoulders shook from fear.

"I will never let anything bad happen to you. You have to believe me." I reiterated.

"That is the problem Corin, you weren't there." She said sobbing.

"It is just a nightmare. I will always be with you." I coaxed.

"Corin, lately my nightmares have been getting worse. I keep seeing myself dying. But the worse thing is I keep calling for you and you're not there. Something must have happened to you." She said sobbing profusely.

"How many nightmares have you been having?" I asked with fear. She could have been in here every night crying her heart out and I would be stupidly lying in bed asleep. No wonder she feels abandoned.

"Almost every night" She whispered.

"Why didn't tell me?"

"I didn't want you to worry. There isn't anything you can do about it."

"At least you wouldn't be in here alone." I explained.

"Not all of them are this bad. This one was so real. I think I can see their faces. I just have a bad feeling something bad happened to you, and that is why you couldn't help me."

"I would never let anyone hurt. Do you understand?" I stated firmly.

"I know. It is just so real. I can see their faces, there were two of them." She recalled.

"It really doesn't matter those hunters that hurt Tina were killed. Remember? We can reconfirm that with Trey tonight, okay?" I reminded her.

"I know you're right, I just wished these nightmares would just go away." She said.

"Come, let's go back to bed." I said as I lifted her in my arms and carried her back to bed. I placed her gently in bed next to me. I wrapped my arms around her tightly.

"Don't fear for me Gena. I will not allow anything to happen to us. We have a lot to live for. I waited so long for you; I will not allow even death to keep us apart." I promised. She kissed my arm to confirm her trust in me.

I laid there and watch her sleep. She was exhausted. I promised myself that I would stay awake long enough to make sure the nightmare doesn't return. I watched as her breathing became steady and slow. Her face relaxed allowing her lips to part. I was aroused when I remembered her in each of the lingerie. I liked the pink one the most. I watched as she slowly wet her lips. I can't wait until the day we can make love freely. *I promise Gena, I will love you a hundred times more powerful than this.* It just seems so fortunate that we are together. I have always dreamt of her; prayed for her; wished for her. Here she is in my arms. Everything I have always wanted and more. I will protect her. No one will hurt her as long as I am alive. I would easily give my life for hers.

We were in the same position when I felt her wiggling in my arms. She turned and looked up at me.

"Good morning." She said with a smile.

"I think it is closer to noon time than morning." I corrected.

"I have a lot of prep work for the party. Lauren and Aimee will be here soon." She listed.

"Are you alright? Did you get enough sleep?" I questioned.

"I think I've had more sleep last night than all the past weeks combined." She noted.

"Gena, I don't want you to hide anything from me, again. Okay? I don't want to ever see you hurt or crying. You have to tell me. You are not alone anymore. I am here. If we are going to spend the rest of our lives together, I don't want any secrets between us."

"I'm sorry, Corin. I thought I could deal with it but when I feared your life, it became overwhelming." She explained.

"Losing you would hurt me more than death. Selfishly, I woke up and thought everything was just a dream. You don't know how scary that was for me."

"You can always evoke the Gena's lingerie collection. I never did ask you, which one did you like the best? She asked changing the subject.

"I really liked the pink one the most."

"You would. That one didn't cover much." She said.

"It doesn't matter; you were just as effective in your shorts and t-shirt. Those things were just eye candy." I declared.

"Eye candy, huh?" she asked with a smile.

"Yeah, my candy" I finished. "Come on, let's get this house ready for match making."

I was the first to make it downstairs. I went to clear away last night dinner left on the dining room table. I found the extra leaf extensions for the dining room table and added it to allow for 12 diners. When I got to the kitchen she was already there prepping for tonight's dinner. We spent most of the day playfully teasing each other. I didn't realize but she was a very good cook. She made a small version of beef wellington for lunch.

"This is so good. I think I may grow fat being married to you." I teased.

"If you haven't noticed, you have yet to propose." She snickered.

"Don't worry; it isn't like I don't want to. I've been threatened that it has to be magical or I may get a no."

"I don't think I've ever said no to you." She pointed out.

"That is why we get along so well." I smiled warmly at her. She smiled back. Her smile still takes my breath away.

By 5pm, Lauren and Aimee were over helping with the meal. I watched as Gena instructed over the meal preparation like a professional. Max showed up with Trey. I can tell he was little uncomfortable being around me.

"Hi, Corin. Thanks for inviting me." He hesitated.

"Hey, you're welcome. No hard feelings okay? It is the way we are, man."

"Man, I just felt so bad, because you guys helped us and all."

"Hey, it isn't like you could help it."

"The funny thing is I didn't believe in all that shit. Then when I saw her, I was almost blinded to everything around me. It was pretty scary." He remembered.

"We all know how you feel. Don't worry about Mark. He is fine."

"Thanks for making this easier for me." He replied.

"Oh, I wanted to ask you. When you guys came upon the hunters attacking Tina, you guys said you killed them all right?" I asked.

"Yeah, there were three of them. Why?' he asked.

"Did you remember what they looked like?" I asked back.

"They were all pretty young that's why it was easy for us. It was three male hunters, probably 16 to 18 yrs old. They all had long disheveled black hair. When we found them they were taking turns attacking her, she was already passed out on the ground. We thought for one minute she was already dead but luckily she made it." He recanted.

"Do you know if Tina, saw any of them before she passed out."

"She may have. But she was out cold when we found her."

"Well, Gena have been having nightmares about the attack. I didn't know if Tina could reassure her that the attackers are dead." I said.

"Why would Gena have nightmares over what happened with Tina?" Max chimed in.

"Well, she has had a lot of bad news in her life, than she comes here and hears all kinds of horrible stories. Alain thinks it is her imagination combining a bunch of scary stories and causing theses nightmares." I explained.

"Wow, is she alright?" Trey asked.

"She'll be okay. She is pretty tough. Do you know she rides a Ducati?" Max bragged.

Soon after, Dana and Derek arrived. Preston came with Tina. Lastly, Tristan brought this sister Ella. She started to leave when she saw Trey but the girls begged her to at least stay until dinner. We all convened in the dining for the Beef Wellington dinner. Gena was very proud of herself. Everything turned out great.

"Justin is leaving this week to go pick up Rachel. She is staying with us over the long Thanksgiving week-end coming up." Preston announced.

"Finally, we get the meet her. Justin has been a mess." Lauren added.

"When will she be here? I asked.

"Well he will leave tomorrow and they should be here by Friday. My mom is so excited. Justin's wedding will be her first wedding to plan." Lauren bragged.

"Ella, I think that you should stay and clean up since last time you dashed out of here." Max announced. Everyone at the table was staring at him.

"Ella, it's okay. Ignore him." Gena assured.

"I will help you." Trey announced.

"That sounds great. Ella, do you mind?" I asked knowing her guilt she would not refuse me. "Gena, has been slaving over the kitchen all day."

"I would be glad to Corin." She said through her teeth.

"Well that's settled. Why don't we leave them to clean up and let's watch some hockey." I declared.

We all pulled each girl out of the dining room. I knew Gena was going to kill me for doing that so abruptly but things were going too slow, Max and I had to step in. We all went to the living room and pretended not to listen in on Trey and Ella.

"So, will your dad announce them at the Thanksgiving dinner?" Tina asked.

"Yeah, they were going to wait and do another party but since winter is coming and it is so hard to get in and out Inuvik, they just decided to do it among the clan." Lauren replied.

"Hey, do you know what you're going to wear?" Aimee asked Tina.

"Yeah, Dana has been really helpful." Tina said.

"How about you, Gena?" Lauren asked.

"Well, I just received fives packages from Secret Lingerie last night, which are definitely not appropriate for a party." Gena remarked looking over at me.

"Did Corin like them?" Lauren asked quietly.

"Corin! Lauren wants to know if you liked the clothes she ordered for me last night." Gena announced.

I walked over to Gena, and gave her a warm hug around her waist. "It will definitely keep her warm during the winter season." I teased. They all erupted into laughter.

"Gena, you have really changed Corin. He used to be so boring and so serious." Dana remarked.

"I've always known him to be interesting and very romantic." Gena said with a gently kiss on my cheek.

"How did you guys meet?" Tina asked.

"We met on a plane coming to Inuvik. I was coming to meet my family and he was hitching a ride home." Gena answered.

"Yeah, she was having bad headache and here's this idiot who would not stop talking to her.?" I added.

"You? Talk too much. I don't believe that." Max commented.

"That is so romantic." Aimee said.

"Well, Tina, you guys have a very interesting beginning too." Lauren added.

"I would rather forget those circumstances." Preston said quietly.

"Oh, Tina. I have been meaning to ask you. Did you see any of the hunters who attacked you?" I asked.

"Yeah, they were young. There were 3 of them. But don't worry Trey, Brent and Trisha killed them." She answered.

"Tina, when you said young, how old were they?" Gena asked.

"They were probably 16 to 18 yrs old." She replied.

"Hey, I think Ella and Trey are coming." Preston whispered.

We all watched as Ella and Trey came from the kitchen. We weren't sure if they had work things out.

"Gena, Corin thanks for the wonderful meal. Everything is clean. I'm going to leave now." Ella hesitated.

"You're welcome and thanks. You really didn't have to clean up. I am really sorry for that." Gena apologized.

"Well, I guess we'll take you home." Tristan replied looking over at Aimee.

"No, that's okay. We're not too far. I'll walk." Ella replied.

"Mom would kill me if I let you walk home alone." Tristan

"She won't be alone. I'll make sure she gets home alright." Trey stated

Everyone in the room sighed with relief. We all waited as they walked away from the house.

"Thank God, I hope they work it out. I am so tired of looking at his sorrowful face." Derek announced.

"Oh, give him a break. He is in love." Dana replied.

"Well if things go okay, maybe we'll have two weddings." Lauren said excited.

“With Ella’s history, I hope they elope instead.” Max teased.

We all laughed and agreed. After the game, they all went home. When everyone was gone, I went over to sit next to Gena. I played with her hair. She was watching some cooking show.

“So, is this your secret to good cooking?” I asked as I nuzzled her neck.

“I am far from a professional; I am more like an experimenter.” She teased reminding me of last night’s experiment.

“Which part were you referring to?” I questioned as I entwined our hands and pulled her toward the stairs.

“Well, given that we are in the early stages of research we should double check our data and do a complete retest.” She teased.

“I totally agree with your research ethics. You should start with the pink trial first and if data is good, we will open the fifth package.” I played along.

When we got to the bedroom she rushed into the bathroom and changed into the pink lingerie. I waited for her at the end of the bed. When she came out, she stood at the door frame looking at me. I can’t believe how beautiful her body is. Every curve was soft and flawless. Her breasts were perfectly round and taut. When she let her hair down, it tousled down her back in a wavy mess that could arouse a dead man. I knew every time I let her parade around in lingerie, I was tempting my urges to no end. I told myself it was to build control. Right now, looking at her coming into bed, she controlled me. She bewitched me. I watched as she seductively walked towards me. I pulled her into bed and let her lay on top of me.

“I have dreamt of you wearing this all day and still you take my breath away. I love you, Gena.” I whispered quietly in her ear.

We laid there quietly holding each other, content and happy.

"Do you want to open the fifth package?" she teased.

"No, let's save that one for our honeymoon." I laughed.

Chapter Nineteen

Before Thanksgiving, school exams were all crammed into one week. Trevor, Corin and I were the only ones who took the Calculus questions seriously and worked on them. We got to exempt that exam. Corin had to take the English Literature Mid-term because he did not have perfect attendance. I exempted all my exams because I either made 90% or above or I had perfect attendance. I was a model student according to my English Literature instructor. Monday we didn't have any exams but I had to help Lauren during lunch with French. Corin was trying to cram in as much Shakespeare as he could before Tuesday's exam. I tried to keep myself busy so I wouldn't be a distraction for him. When we got home, I brought in the laundered clothes and put it away while he was in one of the rooms studying. Our bedroom closet was so massive that even with all my old and new clothes plus his clothes we couldn't even fill up one side of the walk-in closet room. Looking through our clothes, I smiled at our simplicity. We both liked t-shirts, jeans, crews, khakis, simple layered shirts, nothing fancy. The only fancy stuff in there was stuff Lauren, Aimee, and Dana brought for me. Thinking of that I had to pick out a dress for the Thanksgiving Party. I had already told Lauren that I was ready but I have no idea what I wanted to wear. The decision was made harder because they had ordered so many dresses, with matching this and that and accessories. *To me this was endless torture.*

I was thankful when the phone rang.

"Hello."

"Gena, hey how are you?" Mark announced cheerfully

"Hi, Mark! How is Prudhoe Bay?"

"Tolerable now. Where is my brother?" he answered.

"Hold on, I'll go get him. If he sounds grouchy it is because he has been cramming Shakespeare. It's finals week."

"Oh, I forgot. He can't cheat off you?' he teased

"Actually, he has to take English and Physics finals, everything else he exempted. I am very proud of my scholar." I said as I interrupted Corin.

"Corin, it's Mark." I said handing him the phone. I left to go back downstairs.

The one thing you can always count on being fresh here in Canada was seafood. Tonight I was making crab cakes with a creamy butter sauce along with some roasted vegetables. Paula Dean should be proud. Instead of frying the crab cakes, I placed them in the oven. I set the table and looked over my masterpiece. When Corin came down he was still on the phone with Mark. They were laughing, which was a great sign. Mark must have good news. Watching him talk with his brother was something I did not get to experience being an only child. The closest thing to siblings was my cousins. While still talking he came over and wrapped his arm around my waist as a gesture to indicate that he was referring to me in his conversations with his brother. I watched as he picked on the roasted vegetables. He was hungry and his brother was still talking. I took some roasted vegetables and fed him while he was on the phone. He continued to listen but he wasn't paying attention to the conversation anymore. He was playfully eating from my fingers. When he started to lick and suck on my fingers, I pushed him away and rolled my eyes. I walked into the dining room with the roasted vegetables.

"Do you want to skip dinner and go to dessert again?" he whispered from behind. He was off the phone and standing at the archway.

"Sorry, baby. But you have to eat and the only love you're getting tonight is from William Shakespeare." I smugly replied.

"I hate Shakespeare. I think he's gay." He retorted.

"Sit down; let me go get the crab cakes." I ordered.

"Wow, crab cakes, what's the occasion?" he smirked.

"Crab cakes is about as fancy as spaghetti here. In Indiana we couldn't get fresh crab so it would fancy there but not here." I replied as I made my way back from the kitchen.

"Gena, are you eating?" He teased as he counted the six pieces of crab cakes.

"Funny. So how is Mark?" I asked while fixing his plate.

"He has found his soul mate." He said plainly like it was no big deal.

"Really"

"Yeah, right now he is trying to convince her to come back to Inuvik. She is in some sort of band in Prudhoe and doesn't want to go." He remarked.

"You don't sound so excited. What's wrong?" I asked.

"I'm excited for him. I just don't know if she will come back here. He said she was singer in a band and she also teaches dance for the town children. It sounds like she is very rooted in the community there. She also has a brother that plays guitar for some rock band. He obviously travels a lot. So the whole town is her only family. That is very hard to replace." He explained.

"Wow, she sounds so cool. She is a singer and a dancer? I would love to meet her. What kind of band?" I said.

"She plays the guitar for some rock band that her brother used to hang out with before he made it big. He said she was singing at a bar one night and he was driving by and the draw was so strong he almost wrecked his car. He has been at that bar every night since. These are so good. You better hurry up and eat or I'll finish them off." He teased.

"Why are you not fat? You eat huge amounts." I questioned.

"I work out a lot." He teased with a wink.

"You are incorrigible. So did he mention when he was coming back?" I said.

"Well, that's the problem. He is not going to leave Prudhoe unless she comes with him. Like for instance, if you went back to Indiana, I would have to follow you because there is *no way* I can stay here and you be there. I would be miserable." He reminded me.

"You would hate Indiana." I said silently.

"I would go anywhere you are. I would love it if you loved it. Right now we are here because it is safer for you. When you have transformed, we can travel anywhere that is not hot and I would love it too. When we have children it is safer to be with the clan. It doesn't really matter as long as we are together." He responded firmly.

"You're so easy going and selfless. When I first found out about my family here in Inuvik, I was hesitant because everything I read about Inuvik was scary. Ridiculous cold weather, no sunlight in winter, too much sun in summer, and wild animals running around, does that sound good?" I said.

"What about now?" he asked.

"Well, I haven't experienced any of those things. The weather is cold but this house is always warm. Sleeping next to you helps. You make this place beautiful. I assume the sunless winter should be coming soon. I am still waiting to hate this place but I haven't found anything yet." I answered.

"Believe it or not, when you have completely transformed, the cold weather will not bother you. You would love it. It is the hot weather you will hate. Did you know our natural body temperature is 102 degrees? In the summer if it gets too hot which rarely happens here, we usually vacation somewhere colder like Greenland, Russia, Antarctica, or Northern parts of Mongolia. Usually it is only hot here 7 to 10 days in the summer." He stated.

"My body temperature will be 102 degrees? That is unbelievable?"

"Yeah, when you are with child, it can go up as high as 110 degrees." He declared.

"That is crazy. That is brain damage in humans. I learn new things everyday talking to you. These things don't come up when I am talking to the girls. All they want to talk about is shopping and clothes?"

"Are you complaining about the shopping? I happen to like your new wardrobe. Tonight we can take our research to phase three." He teased.

"Not tonight. After your Physics exam on Wednesday we can do anything you want but not until than." I scolded.

"Three days is harsh don't you think?" he pleaded.

"Well. If you do well in your English Literature final, we can work something out." I caved in. I can never deny him anything even if I wanted to. He doesn't know the full effect he has over me. If he said he wanted me tonight, I would surrender.

"What will I get if I make a 100?" he teased.

"Whatever you want?" I played along.

"That is a very dangerous wager you're putting up. Anything?" He dared.

"Anything you want." I dared back.

"You don't know all the dirty things I am thinking about right now?" he flirted.

"Well, does it have anything to do with the colors pink, blue, white, or black?" I teased.

"Nope, just the color nude" He winked back. His smile made my heart jumped.

"Go back and study please. I am getting uncomfortable." I pleaded.

He roared out laughing. He quickly grabbed me up and kissed me then left to go back to studying. I finished my dinner and clear the table. After the kitchen was cleaned, I watched some Food TV network; I am making fried chicken tomorrow. I got on the laptop and wrote down the recipe. I also looked up Corin birthday present.

After 8pm, I went over and called Blaine. I wanted to give him some information about what I wanted to get Corin for his birthday. He was heading to Edmonton on business, and I wanted him to check out what I wanted to buy. According to Dana, he was very good at these things. He was rather excited about it. I thought it would be weird to talk to him about buying such an expensive gift for Corin but he never indicated any disapproval. This new family is so different then a traditional family. They are very generous with their gifts and they don't think weirdly of me if I wanted to buy my boyfriend a car for his birthday. I might as well be asking for a tie. Blaine even encouraged me to by one for myself. But I told him I wanted Corin's. We agreed to talk again on Thursday.

I went to bed around 9:30 and Corin was still studying. I felt him getting into bed later. He was nice and warm.

"I love you." he whispered. I heard him and squeezed his arms tighter around me.

In the deepest part of my sleeping brain, I felt fear. I was wake. I was cold. I was hurt. I can feel pain. I was weak. I was dizzy. I could not stand up straight. I saw flashes of my mother's face. Looking around I saw flashes of darkness sprinting all around me. What are they? The air was cold and bitter. Someone help me. Corin, where are you? Are you hurt? Please don't leave me. I slipped and fell hard into a black room. My hands were bleeding. My legs were broken. I could not breathe. Breathing hurt so much. I could see I had gashes all over my arms and body. I tried to cry out for help but nothing came out. There was no where for me to go. There is no air. Oh, my God, I am suffocating. This is what it was like for Uncle Josh. I prayed for a quick death. I can't take much more of this suffocating. Something was crushing my chest, his hand was scarred. I looked up and saw his yellow eyes and his heavily scarred face. "I am coming for you, Gena! This time you will not escape me." He was big and muscular; his hair was long and in disarray. He had a scar on his face, jagged. He dug his claws into my skin, tearing my flesh like paper. The air was escaping me and I could not get any in. Corin! Corin! Corin! Please come for me. I can't get away from him.

"Gena! Wake up. Gena! It's just a dream." Corin was screaming and shaking my body to wake me up.

"Oh, God is my eyes red?" I asked as I sat up and grabbed him.

"No, they're not red." He answered

"I couldn't heal. This nightmare was different Corin, I could not heal. I saw his face, his scars, he spoke to me. This is not the same. He spoke to me." I spat out hysterically.

"Gena, it's just a nightmare. He is not here. He is dead. I spoke with Trey; he said they killed those hunters that attacked." He reassured.

"Corin, this hunter is not like Tina described. He was older. He had yellow eyes. He had scars all over his hand and face. He spoke to me. He said he was coming for me and this time I wasn't going to get away. He knew me Corin. He knows my past." I was so hysterical, I became nauseous. I got up quickly and ran for the bathroom. I was heaving in the toilet by the time Corin got to me. He held me in his lap and placed a cold towel over my face.

"You're trembling are you cold or scared?" he asked calmly.

"I'm not cold. I am actually sweating. Are my eyes red now?"

"Yeah, something is causing your aura to go into overdrive. Try to calm down a little. I'll stay up and make sure you don't have anymore nightmares, okay? Just like the other night." He comforted.

"No, Corin, you have finals in the morning." I said quietly.

"I don't care about the finals right now. I can make that up anytime. I just want you to try and focus on bringing you're body back to normal. Come on, let's talk about something else." He directed.

"Corin, I have been around a lot of people who died. My mother died protecting me. My father died defending me, my adopted father died of heart disease, my adopted mother died of breast cancer, my uncle josh died in a car explosion. Maybe it is not a coincidence. What if I bring death to my family or you? I can't handle that. If anything happens to you because of me. I can't deal with that." I repeatedly mumble.

"Gena! Stop. Those deaths are not you're fault. I don't know what these nightmares mean but I can only tell you what is real. I am real. You are real. We are real. I will never let anything separate us. Your family is very strong. Do not worry about them." He directed.

I sat there thinking quietly. I feared for him, I feared for his life. Maybe this was my aura trying to warn me that I was endangering his life, my family's life. I can feel him looking at me; trying to read my thoughts.

"Gena, do not even think of leaving me to protect me. You can not do that to me. I would rather die than be without you. Do you understand what I am saying to you?" he said in a very serious and cautious tone. All I could do was bury my face in his chest and cry. He read my face easily. Leaving him would be so painful. It showed on my face when it was only a thought. I could not leave him even if to save him. I was selfish and the pain would be unbearable. He carried me to bed and held me quietly.

"Gena, don't leave me. I can not bear it. I've waited all my life for you. Facing death would be easier than knowing that you don't want to be with me. Whatever this is we will face it together. We are stronger together. I am stronger when you are here with me. Please just don't think of leaving me." He pleaded. It broke my heart to hear how scared he was to lose me and not for his life.

"I can't bear it either. I am not as brave as you think. I love you so much it would probably kill me to leave." I said tearfully.

He pushed me back into the bed. Looking down at me he slowly kissed my face. He angled his lips to kiss me deeper. His passion was abrupt and strong. He continued to kiss me until I was gasping for air. His hungry mouth kissed a trail from my breast to my abdomen and down my navel. I was mindless. I fell back and let exhaustion take me. Barely conscious, I can feel him covering my body with his. When he was done, he pulled me against him and wrapped his arms around me. "I love you, Gena." He whispered.

I woke up and found him lying next to me fully dressed. I was wearing one of his shirts.

"Corin, do you need to get to school for your exam?" I whispered.

"I took it already. Let's go back to sleep." He murmured as he pulled me back down into him. I looked over and saw the time. It was almost 1pm. I slept the whole morning away. He was probably exhausted. I laid there quietly in his arms so I would not disturb him. It was easy to fall back to sleep in his arms. When I woke up again, it was almost 4pm. I tried to move from under his arms but he just kept pulling me back tighter. "No" he murmured.

"Corin, I am so hungry and thirsty. Aren't you hungry? I whispered.

"I'll go get you something." He said as he started to get up.

"No, Corin please let me bring you something." I said as I pushed him back into bed.

I got up and went downstairs. I made turkey and tomato sandwiches and brought it back to him. When I came in he was sitting up in bed.

"You look good in my shirt." He teased.

"I think you would say that even if I was wearing a plastic bag, anyway I don't know what happened to my clothes" I teased.

"Things disappear mysteriously all the time." He played along.

"I am so sorry for keeping you up last night." I apologized.

"Why? I'm not. If that is what keeps me awake, I would never sleep." He flirted.

"I'm talking about the nightmare. It was just bad timing. How do you think you did on the exam?" I asked hesitantly.

"Exams, I took the English Lit and I asked Thomas to let me take the Physics early. While you were asleep last night, I got a lot of studying done. We have the rest of the week to try to work these nightmares out of our lives. I think I did well enough to come out with B's."

"Corin, I am so sorry, you had to do that." I said tearfully.

"No, don't cry. I am glad I could do it. I was a little jealous that you didn't have to take any exams and you had all this free time, while I was studying." He reassured.

"Stop, you're just being nice." I said trying to blink the tears away.

"I just want to be with you, all the time. I am selfish. Come on we have a lot of free time. Do you want to spend it in bed? That's fine with me." He added.

"No, let's go downstairs. I want to make dinner for you. I had all this cooking planned for tonight." I said.

"Going downstairs is not going to stop me from thinking about last night. It was really hard to concentrate on the exams today when I could conjure up *that* every time I blinked." He smiled devilishly.

"Now, you're just embarrassing me." I said.

"It's just us here. I want you to know how much you affect me every second. Do you want me to describe in detail what it was like for me?" he teased.

"About last night, I want to ask you something and I want you to answer as honestly as possible." I said shyly.

"I will always be honest with you. What do you want to know?" he replied.

"How many women have you been intimate with?" I asked quietly.

"Why do you ask that?" He questioned.

"Well, you seem to know an awful lot. Who taught you?" I asked embarrassed.

"No one person taught me. It is a culmination of different things I learned being with different women." He answered cautiously.

"A lot of different women" I asked nervously. I really didn't know if I wanted to know the answer. I wasn't sure if it was important but there was a bit of jealousy and curiosity.

"Don't say it like that. There are clans out there that have women who are past the maternal age. Some no longer have soul mates and some never married. When we meet these women, we can satisfy our needs and theirs without hurting anyone." He said carefully. I can feel him looking at me.

"Oh, how many women have you been with?" I asked stupidly.

"I don't keep count." He answered nonchalantly as his made his way towards me.

"Oh, thanks for being honest." I said nervously.

"Gena, those women are my past. I no longer need or want them." He assured me. He lifted me face to look at him.

"I know I was just curious that's all." I said embarrassed. I started to look away but he held my face to him.

"Be honest with me. What is bothering you?" he asked.

"Well, I just thought that since I can't satisfy you completely that you might still need them." I whispered. I almost wished I didn't say it but it was too late.

"What makes you think I am not satisfy?" he asked.

"Well, I'm not too sure but I know that you have to refrain yourself when you are with me." I stated uneasily.

"I am very satisfied with you. I am very happy to have you in my life. I will never want anyone else. With you, I have felt things I'd never thought possible." He shared intimately.

"Are you sure I am worth the wait?" I said looking downward.

He pulled my face close to his making sure our eyes met. "You are worth it. I can wait forever for you, as long as you're with me." He said confidently.

"Corin, I am not going anywhere, so I will take that as a vow. Thanks for being honest. I have to take a shower. Eat your sandwich. I'll be back." I said. He reached out and grabbed me around the waist and pulled me back to him.

"The only thing I am hungry for is you. Before you go shower I want to tell you something. Please don't leave me. Please don't ever think that way. I was so hurt that you even thought of that. I could see it on your face, so don't try to deny it. As much as you think it would hurt you, it would crush me. That can never be the option. Our love is not conditional. Do you understand?" he avowed.

I nodded and kissed him. "I am sorry, for being stupid. You have to believe me when I tell you that I am not as strong as you think. You have my heart, forever." I reassured him.

"That is what I wanted to hear." He smiled.

Chapter Twenty

"Nhan, I spoke with Bron and Lucos. They will not move the clan this far north when winter is coming. They want you to be sure of the size of this clan and keep them informed. They do not want you to do anything stupid."

"I am still waiting for this fool to go back to his clan. The girl is a problem. He talks about this Corin. He must be the leader. If we take out the leader we can probably defeat the clan."

"Nhan, we can not take on the whole clan. That is suicide."

"Not the clan, just the leader."

"Nhan, he said to wait. Don't be stupid. I want revenge as much as you. You still don't know how big this clan is."

"What do you want to do?"

"We should follow them back to the clan. I want to know how big this clan is. We will use the unscented clothes techniques that they used on us. We should be able to watch them closely and not be scented. Once we have all the information we need, we can go back and talk to Bron and Lucos. We need the help of our elders if we are to attack this clan."

"Right now our problem is this girl. She does not want to leave Prudhoe Bay."

"Maybe she needs some persuasion."

"That is more like the brother I know. Come I have a plan."

After my shower, I went downstairs and found Corin on the phone. I continued to the kitchen to start dinner. I looked over the recipe and got all the ingredients to start. Corin came in and started to help with the flour.

"Do you mind if we have some company tonight for dinner?" he asked.

"You forget I am the nice one. You're the inhospitable one." I corrected.

"Well, I asked Trey, Trisha, Robyn, and Brent to come over. I also asked if Preston could bring Tina over. We really need to talk to them about what happened. If the hunter in your dream is not the ones who attacked Tina, maybe they can give us a clue on who he is?" he informed.

"Are they bringing dates?" I asked.

"No, I asked if they could come alone. I want this to stay as private as much as possible. Preston and Tina knows about your healing aura but the others do not. I tried to get in touch with Alain earlier but he is busy at the hospital. He will probably call back later." He declared.

"What do you want to know from them?"

"Well, Trey, Brent, and Trisha fought the hunters who attacked Tina. So they can describe those hunters. Tina must have seen some of the hunters. Each of them had to have seen something before they went into the panic rooms. Do you still remember the hunter in your nightmare?"

"It is very hard to forget." I said quietly.

"Don't worry we will get to the bottom of this. I don't have an explanation right now, but I have some theories?" he stated.

"What theories?" I asked.

"Well, I rather not start something I can't explain until I get some more information. It is better that way. Do we have enough food?" he asked.

"Yeah, I'll just get out more chicken. I was thinking about adding some biscuits and making some mashed potatoes with this. It will be a traditional southern meal." I said.

"That sounds good. Almost like in the TV commercials. What do you want me to do?" he teased.

"Just start on these potatoes and I'll work on the biscuits." I instructed.

"Real mash potatoes? You don't use the box stuff?" He questioned.

"Corin, you've never had real mashed potatoes?"

"Not really. My mother takes a lot of short cuts. Michelle can't cook unless there is a microwave." He informed.

"Well, I am going to spoil you baby." I teased.

"You already do." He answered back with a light kiss.

We worked together in the kitchen. When the chicken was done he watched me mashed the potatoes and add the heavy cream and butter. "Do you like it lumpy or smooth" I asked.

"Can you make it both ways?" he asked curiously.

I split the potatoes and handed him half. "Here, you work on these." I instructed with a masher. The other half I used the processor to get them smooth and creamy.

I watched as he picked at the potatoes and the biscuits. I used some of the seasoned flour and made some gravy for the mashed potatoes.

"Did you ever live down south?" he questioned.

"No, but Paula Dee is my favorite TV chef and she is from South Carolina. These are all her recipes. Do you like it?" I asked.

"I wish I could eat like this all the time. If the south wasn't so damn hot, I would move down there." He commented.

"If you eat like this every night, you would be as big as an elephant." I teased.

"I told you I exercised a lot." He flirted. He moved behind me, resting his chin on my shoulder. I can hear him inhaling the scent of my hair and neck.

"Yes, and I can appreciate all your hard work. You're body is very nice." I complimented.

"You have a nice body too." He tempted as he starting nuzzling my neck. I can feel the goose bumps raising everywhere his lips made contact with my skin. When his warm breathe brushed up against the back of my neck I could feel my knees weakening.

"Corin, someone is at the door." I stuttered.

"They can what." He murmured as his hands moved slowly inside my shirt. I braced myself against the counter when his hands slipped under my bra and cupped my breast. His fingers immediately rubbed at my nipples.

"I thought you wanted to be more hospitable?" I reminded him trying to regain control of the situation. My breathing sped up and each breathe was ragged.

"I'll let them in when I am done." He laughed as one of his hand slowly descended down my stomach towards my navel. Knowing that I had to be the one to stop him, I grabbed his hand and turned around to face him.

"You're helpless. Go get the door." I scolded as I pushed him away. He laughed as he walked away. I took a slow and deep breathe and shook off my arousal.

I went to set up the table. I watched as they all came into the dining room. Trey and Tina were very comfortable but the others have never been to my house. They looked a bit uneasy. The last time I saw Trisha and Robyn was the first day they came here. They both looked homesick and sad.

"Gena, is there anything we can do to help you set up?" Trisha offered.

"Absolutely not, you are my guest. Come take a sit." I declared. They all sat down as I went back in the kitchen and brought out the food.

"Everything looks so good. Is that fried chicken like from the south?" Trey asked.

"She even made buttermilk biscuits too." Corin bragged.

"Did you live down south?" Brent asked.

"No, I watch a lot of Food TV network." I said modestly.

"Corin, you are a lucky guy. Is it like this every night?" Brent said.

"I am the luckiest guy in the world." He winked at me.

"So, Robyn, have you started school yet." I asked changing the subject.

"Yes, Mr.Redman set everything up for me." She said quietly.

"Do you have any classes with Lawrence, Joseph, or Steven?" I asked.

"Every class has at least one of them; I think Mr. Redman planned it that way." She replied shyly.

"How about you Trisha?" Corin asked.

"I finished my senior year early. I was going to travel to France this year but I will wait for Robyn and we'll both go together." She informed.

" Brent, do you like Aurora College?" Corin asked.

"It's okay. I was going to go to Epitor in Ireland but things have changed." He said coyly.

"Is that thing called Michelle?" Trey teased.

"Trey is things working out with you and Ella?" I asked to change the subject since I could tell Brent was a little uncomfortable.

"Much better thanks." He replied.

"Tina, when will you be able to go back to school?" I asked.

"Well, Preston has been tutoring me at home. I kind of like that so, I'm not sure if I want to go back to school." She boasted proudly.

We all laughed. They were very likeable people in a difficult situation. They all lost their entire families in one night. Here they are with a new clan. Lucky for Trey and Tina they found their soul mates. Brent appeared conflicted with Natalie. But Trisha and Robyn have yet to find anything to help absorb some of their losses.

"Corin, you said on the phone that you wanted to go over what happened with the hunters. Is there something specifically you wanted to know?" Trey stated.

"Well, I wanted to know if anyone of you can describe what they look like. Not just the ones who attacked Tina but if you've seen any of the others." He replied.

"Why are they coming here?" Robyn asked anxiously.

"No, they would never attack such a large clan. It is just to be cautious. I like to gather as much information about my enemies as possible. Brent why don't we start with you? Tell me everything you witnessed before you got into the panic room" Corin said.

"Well, I was jet lagged from coming back from Europe. I woke up when I heard my mother scream. Before I could get to her, my older brothers grabbed me and threw me into the panic room. They told me they were going to do the same thing but they never made it to their panic room. The hunters must have been watching our clan for a long time. They knew where everyone slept and attacked while we were sleeping. They took out those with an aura first. They outnumbered us 2 or 3 to 1. My brothers were ambushed when they tried to save my mother. The hunters never even saw me. If one day you plan on attacking this hunter clan, I want to be apart of it." He vowed angrily.

"Thanks Brent. I know that was very hard for you. Trey did you see anyone?" Corin acknowledged.

"Well, by the time Derek and I got there, we saw what you saw. Everything was destroyed. First thing we did was checked the panic rooms in our home. We were about to leave when we saw Brent, Trisha, and Robyn coming out of their homes. We thought it was better to travel north into Nunavut but we heard Tina screaming. When we got there, we saw her being attacked by those three young ones we told you about. We quickly overtook them and got Tina out. I didn't see any other hunters." He recanted.

"I saw some of the older ones." Robyn said sadly.

"Can you describe them?" Corin asked.

"Most of the older ones, had long black hair. They are much hairier than the young ones. They have scars through out their body. They are very big and muscular." She described.

"Did anyone of them have scars on their face?" I asked carefully.

"One of the leaders had a scar that ran across his face. He was the most sadistic and ruthless one. He looked like he enjoyed torturing and killing. I think his name is Nhan." She recalled.

I looked toward Corin and saw him looking back at me. The fear that came over my face was enough confirmation for him. "Robyn, how did you see them without being attacked?" Corin asked still looking at me.

"Our panic rooms are located in the basement. My parents forced us into the basement and told us to wait. We watched from a small window embedded in the ground of our basement. We witnessed our parents being taken and killed." Trisha answered coldly.

"I'm so sorry." I whispered. I felt so bad making them relive the horror of their parents' murder. Corin sensed my guilt so he thanked them all for sharing their information and quickly changed the subject to something less painful. The dinner ended with us talking about non-trivial things from school to weather. By the time they left no one remembered the reason why they were asked to come over in the first place. I was in the kitchen cleaning up when Corin came in.

"Are you alright?" he asked cautiously.

"Yeah, I'm just a little sad about making them conjure up all those bad memories."

"Sometimes it is helpful to talk about this stuff. I think Robyn and Trisha needed that tonight. Did you recognize any of the descriptions? " He replied.

Before I could answer the door bell chimed. We both went to the door and saw that it was Alain. He was still dressed in his hospital scrubs and a white lab coat.

"Alain, I thought you were going to call. I didn't mean for you to leave work." Corin said apologetically.

"I'm actually heading home, so I thought I would stop by. Is that alright?" he answered.

"Absolutely, if you're too tired we can talk about this in the morning?" I said. I ushered him in and we all sat down simultaneously.

"No, I'm fine. So, Corin tells me you're having more nightmares." He started.

"Alain, I don't think there nightmares. I think there some sort of warning signs or even future sight." Corin informed. I wondered whether this was one of his theories.

"What makes you think that?" Alain asked.

"She has been seeing hunters that were not one of the ones that attacked Tina." Corin stated.

"According to Tina, her attackers were young. The one I see in my nightmares is an older hunter that Robyn remembered called Nhan. I have never talked to Robyn and this is the first time any of them has ever mentioned this hunter Nhan." I worried.

"How do you know about this hunter?" he asked.

"Well in my last nightmare, this hunter was the one attacking me. I could see his face and scars. When Robyn described Nhan he matched the one in my nightmares. Don't you think that's ironic?" I questioned.

"Well, that is different." He said silently.

"Have you ever experienced this before?" Corin asked impatiently.

"Well, in our history there were those that can foresee the future but I have not witnessed anything like this in my lifetime. I will get in touch with Rolfe. I think we should take Gena's nightmares very seriously and discuss this among the clan. I think it is time we let the clan in on Gena's ability." He declared.

"What about her safety?" Corin questioned.

"Corin, I don't see her being in any better hands than yours. But, right now the clan needs to be placed on alert. We have grown complacent and it is best to get everyone on watch. There really isn't a way of telling them about the nightmares without them questioning Gena's ability." He informed.

"I think he is right Corin. Everyone should know what is going on. It's only fair." I said.

"Alain, what if I take Gena away from here? What if we go to Europe?" Corin asked

"No, Corin, I don't want to run. What if they attack here and do what they did in the Quebec Territory? I don't want to be responsible for that." I pleaded.

"Corin, her parents ran and they are all dead. I would rather think that you guys would be safer with the clan." He reasoned.

"Baby, I just want you safe. That is my top priority. Everyone else can take care of themselves." Corin pleaded with me.

"I know but if they come here and hurt your family or my family, I couldn't bear the thought of us running and leaving them behind." I stated my case. This was the usual thing in my life—*being left behind.* I have always been the sole survivor. Right now, I feared it more than anything else in the world. I could not bear the thought of everyone dying to protect me.

"Corin, Gena is right. Running is not the answer. This clan is strong. We can fight them off." Alain informed.

I could tell from the expression on his face that he was not thoroughly satisfied with the choices. He wanted me far away from harm. He looked frustrated and annoyed. He ran his fingers through his hair deliberately. "What do we do in the meantime?" Corin asked quietly.

"Well, let me discuss this with Rolfe. I will get back with you tomorrow." Alain started.

"I want to set up parameters." Corin interrupted looking directly at Alain.

"What are parameters?" I asked.

"It's just precautions. No one is allowed to venture off by themselves." Corin explained.

"Like the buddy system?" I interrupted.

"Yeah, something like that. Let's meet with the rest of the clan before we do anything. Gena, are you having trouble sleeping? If you are I can give you something." Alain confirmed.

"No, Alain, if my nightmares are future visions, I want to be able to remember as much of it as possible." I said.

"Well, just let me know. I have to get home. Rolfe is in Switzerland. I have to get him before he gets into meetings. I will see you guys tomorrow." He said as he made his way to the door. We watched as he got into his car and left. I watched Corin as he walked back towards the living room.

"What's wrong? You look like you're not too happy with what Alain said." I asked.

"I don't like the idea of you being here if a hunter is coming after you. I want to take you away from here." He complained.

"Corin, I am not leaving. If something ever happen to them, I will never forgive myself." I shared.

"So, you rather stay and be bait; sacrificing yourself?" He yelled. He was furious but in a concerning way. I stood there looking back at him. I had never seen him angry before. I didn't realize what he was thinking all this time. While I was thinking about all the bad things that could happen to the clan; he was thinking about what could happen to me. This was hard on him.

"Corin, I am not bait. We don't know anything about this hunter. We don't even know if he is really after me. He may be after the survivors." I stated calmly.

"Gena, you said the hunter knew you. He even said *you would not get away this time.*" He recalled

"Yes, but Corin it's just a dream. I don't know any hunters. I'm pretty sure if I have met one I wouldn't be here right now. My aura could just be warning me because it is supposed to protect me." I explained as I came closer to him. I reached up and caressed his face. He held my hand to his face and kissed the inside of my wrist. His lips were so warm and soft.

"I'm sorry for yelling at you. Helplessness is not one of my strong suits. I feel like I should do more to protect you. The possibility of losing you is condemning." He said silently as he pulled me closer to him.

"Please don't think like that." I said as I entwined our hands and led him upstairs. He followed easily. I ascended the stairs backwards keeping my eyes locked on his.

"You are enchanting when you look at me like that." he gazed back at me. He thought I enchanted him. He has no idea what he does to me.

"You're not too bad yourself." I whispered. His blue eyes were just as powerful now as they were that day on the plane. They bewitched me. They held and controlled me. I could easily lose myself in the depths of his eyes. I watched as he produced a crooked smile that easily mesmerized me. He brought my fingers to his lips and kissed each one of them slowly and deliberately. I was captivated by him. I knew no matter what happens in my life this man would always have my heart and soul. I have so many doubts in my life but with him these things I knew for sure; my body wanted him in everyway, my brain can never decide against him, and my heart belonged to him and only him.

Chapter Twenty-One

I woke up with the scent of her on my mind. I can smell her in the air, on my hands and on the sheets. I was intoxicated by her scent. She was wearing my shirt again. Looking at her sleeping now was one of my favorite things to do in the morning. I can't remember ever wanting to wake up early for anything before. Nowadays, all I wanted to do is wake up early just to watch her sleep. She was so beautiful while she slept. Her face was relaxed and calm. Looking at her lips, they were so inviting, soft, and parted. Just thinking about her lips brought back memories of what she can do to me with them.

"Do you ever sleep?" she murmured against the pillow. I wasn't sure when she woke up but she knew I had been staring at her in her sleep.

"God, you're like a dream come true." I managed to whisper from my dry throaty voice. "How did I get so lucky?" I said silently as I pulled her body over me. I cherished her lips and mouth. My hands slid underneath her shirt and searched until I found her breast. I caressed her until I could hear her moan inside my mouth. "I love it when you make those noises." I revealed.

"You keep doing that and we will never leave this bed." She warned sensually.

"Is that a threat or a promise?" I clarified. "Because I do not mind being here" Before I finished that thought the phone rang. "Damn it, I hate the phone." I hissed.

"Right now, I hate it too." She said as she reached over and picked up the phone. "Hello. Oh! Hi. Mark. No, it's okay. He is right here." She answered. She quickly handed me the phone and got out of bed. I tried to grab her and pull her back but she fought off my hands and ran for the bathroom before I could get another chance at her shirt. *My shirt. Wow, she looked so good in it.*

"Bad timing, Mark. What's going on?" I answered.

"Sorry, man. I know its pretty early but listen, remember when I told you about the girl here. Well, her name is Leah. It turns out her parents used to live in Colorado. She knows Rachel, Justin's fiancée. After her parents died her brother moved her here. Her brother felt the town would take care of her while he was away. Small world huh?" he shared enthusiastically.

"Does she know that Rachel will be here this Friday? Justin's family plan to announce their engagement during the Thanksgiving dinner, will you come home for that?" I informed.

"I don't know. I'll tell her about the engagement party, maybe she'll agree to come to Inuvik with me." He responded quickly.

"Why don't you ask her to come down for the Thanksgiving dinner and she can see Rachel and meet Gena. Gena is really excited to meet her." I said as I watched her come out of the bathroom and rushed towards the bed, landing across my lap. She sat up with her legs folded under her and her thighs fully exposed taking the phone from me.

"Mark, please bring her here. She can stay at our house." Gena said excitedly into the phone. I was distracted by her position. I attempted to unbutton the shirt but she grabbed the shirt closed with her hand.

"Mark, I would love to meet her. Can I talk to her now?" she said. I watched as she pleaded on the phone with Mark, I was busy feeling up her legs. She kept swatting my hands away but I kept up my attack until she glared back at me.

"Hi, Leah. I'm Gena, Corin's girlfriend. I would love to meet you. Corin tells me you sing and dance." She spoke carefully while glaring down at me. *Girlfriend. She was practically my wife.*

"It really is nice to hear your voice. Please come. I am new here too and it would be so nice to meet you. You can stay with us." She said. I took advantage of her preoccupation and caressed her thighs. I giggled when she almost dropped the phone.

"Um, how long will it take for you to get here?" she said carefully one word at a time. I loved what I was doing to her. She was trying to pretend like she was listening on the phone, but her eyes were closed and she was biting her lower lip. "That sounds great. I can't wait to see you. Okay. It was really nice to talk to you." She said abruptly and handed me the phone. I nodded no but she shoved the phone up to my ear.

"Yeah, Mark." I said. I watched as she lowered her lips down to my chest and abdomen.

"Well, that sounds great. I'll tell Justin." She showered my chest with little kisses until she got to my navel. I almost threw the phone across the room. I laid there in agony as my brother spoke about things that I could not comprehend at this moment. All I could do was watch her lips brushing up against my bare skin.

"Well, I'll make sure Mom and Dad knows. No. I'm alright. I am doing something right now, so maybe I can call you back later." I tried to sound normal but my stuttering was pretty evident. When her tongue glazed over my naked skin, I could no longer think rationally.

"Okay, Mark. I will see you soon. Okay. I have to go. Okay Bye." I threw the phone on the floor and moan out loud.

"Hard to talk on the phone when someone is distracting you huh?" she said with a smile. She quickly jumped out of bed and ran for the bathroom. I was too absentminded to react quick enough to catch her.

"You're going to pay for this." I threatened out loud. I could hear her laughing behind the safety of the bathroom door. This morning has been one of the most memorable days of my life since meeting her. I laid there satisfied with my life. I can't remember ever feeling this much love for someone. I watched as she came out of the bathroom fully dressed in jeans and two stretch t-shirts.

"Do you think just because you're dressed you are safe from me?" I threatened with a smile.

"Get up. Alain should be expecting us soon, remember?" she reminded.

"Yeah, I remember. Come over here and give me one more kiss before we go over there." I tempted.

"No, Corin. I know what you're trying to do. Pay back will have to wait until tonight. If you want a kiss you'll have to come over here." She dared.

I shot out of bed and ran toward her. I grabbed her up and kissed her passionately in the lips. I pinned her against the bathroom door and lifted her legs up around my hips. "Never dare me baby. I am fast and strong enough to do this anywhere. It does not have to be in bed." I groaned in her ear.

"My God, you're fast. Okay. You win. Please stop. We have to go." She pleaded.

I gave her a quick kiss than let her go. "Tonight" I warned as I went into the bathroom to shower. She laughed and went off downstairs.

I quickly showered and got dressed. When I got downstairs, I heard Gena talking to someone in the kitchen. I made my way toward the kitchen and found Justin standing around the kitchen counter drinking coffee.

"Hey, man. I wanted to come see you guys before I left for Colorado. Alain told me what happen last night., since I can't be at the meeting this afternoon, I thought I could at least talk with you guys before I left. So, nightmares huh?" he stated.

"Yeah, but hopefully we'll work it all out before you bring Rachel here. You just worry about getting her here, so we can meet her." Gena declared. She was frying up some eggs.

"Hey, I talked with Mark this morning. He has met his soul mate and you won't believe it but she knows Rachel." I announced.

"My Rachel?" he responded surprised.

"Yeah, her name is Leah. She used to live in Colorado. When her parents died her brother moved her to Prudhoe Bay." I informed.

"No, shit. Thanks Gena." He accepted the toast and eggs from her. "Is there a clan in Prudhoe Bay?" he asked.

"I don't know, but by the way Mark talks about her, it doesn't sound like there is a clan. He is bringing her here for the Thanksgiving Dinner. She will be staying with us while she is here." I continued. Gena handed me a plate of toast and eggs. "Thanks babe" I watched as she started to put up the frying pan. I consciously stopped her and pulled her over to my plate. "You have to eat. I'll make some more." I watched as she started to protest but Justin caught her attention.

"You guys compliment each other perfectly. I don't think I have ever seen Corin give up his plate for anyone before." He chuckled.

"Maybe he doesn't like the way I made his eggs." She teased.

"No, maybe. I want you to eat more. Justin, she hardly eats. I don't know how she managed to survived this long on the small amount of food she eats." I complained.

"She managed 18 years without us. Maybe you're just a worry wart. That happens sometimes when you can't do *other things*." He teased.

"Justin!" Gena gasped. I laughed. Justin has no idea the *other things* were unbelievable.

"Sorry, Gena. I couldn't help it. Listen. I have to go. Don't worry. I'll be back with Rachel Friday. Thanks for the breakfast. Hey take care of my cousin." He instructed.

I didn't see him to the door. I waited for Gena to come back to the kitchen. When she came back, I pushed he breakfast plate towards her. "Eat babe. I want to see you eat three meals a day." I instructed.

"You're being ridiculous. I have managed to live 18 years without you." she said.

"I know, and I don't know how you managed to do it. You are too tiny to be missing meals. Anyway you have been exercising more lately so you need the energy." I teased.

"I guess if you put it that way. Thanks for taking care of me." She replied.

"I just want us around for a very long time." I added.

When we were done with breakfast, I helped her clean up and we went to the living and curled up on the couch.

"We need to ready one of the rooms for Leah." She said.

"I'll take care of that later. It was very nice of you to offer her a place to stay." I said.

"Do you mind sharing this house with a guest?" she asked.

"You don't have to ask me. I am just warning you that Mark will probably be here the entire time also. I think we need to ready two rooms." I warned.

"That's fine with me. I am very nice to guests. You're the grumpy one." She corrected.

"Mark is very annoying and he snores." I warned.

"Well, I don't plan on sleeping in the same room with him, so why should that affect me." She announced.

"Don't even say such a thing. I meant he snores so loud you could probably hear him from another room." I answered.

"Really?" she responded.

"Sorry, babe. I hate to admit it." I said.

"Well, we will have to make louder noises or we can exercise until we are too exhausted to care." She tempted.

"I like your ideas. I have to say you are very creative. I like the way you think." I said as I moved toward her.

"Corin, don't start." She warned as she put her hand out to stop me.

"Don't start what? We weren't finish earlier." I moved over her. She giggled underneath me. I tickled her neck with my mouth as my hand grabbed at her side. She wiggled around laughing, and pleading for me to stop. We stopped immediately when we heard the door bell.

"I hate the door bell, too." She complained.

"We'll just have to get rid of the phone and the door bells, make a list." I said as I got up and went to the door.

I opened the door for Alain. "Hey, Alain. Come on in. What some coffee?"

"Oh, yeah. Thanks. I heard Justin came over earlier, so you know that we have a meeting at 2pm today." He informed as we walked toward the kitchen. Gena, had already poured him a cup of coffee and handed it to him as he entered the kitchen.

"Thanks Gena, Did you have any problems sleeping last night?" he asked.

"No nightmares last night, thank goodness." She replied.

"I spoke with Rolfe and he will be flying back here by noon time. Blaine is coming back early too. Oh, he told me to tell you to call him on his cell phone whenever you have a chance." he said to Gena.

She nodded. "I hate that everyone has to come back here for a meeting about my nightmares." She exclaimed.

"The nightmares are a warning for the entire clan. It is very important to our survival. I'm just glad we have some sort of warning system. I just hate that you have to suffer." He stated.

"So, you believe the nightmares will come true?" I asked.

"Well, I talked to my parents and they can recall a person they knew that had the ability to foresee the future through her dreams. She didn't have the healing aura but she was able to forewarn her clan of impending danger." He told.

"Is she close? Can we talk to her?" I asked.

"No she passed away many years ago. But at least we know this was something we can depend on. Well I have to start my morning rounds at the hospital but I should be done by 2pm. Gena, I have some samples in the lab for you to look through. I think you would find some of the slides pretty interesting. Oh and if you need any more blood samples, I left a sample in the refrigerator. Okay. I will see you guys later." He finished. I walked him out and went back to the kitchen. She was standing at the far end of the kitchen looking out to the backyard thru the glass wall.

"Are you alright?" I asked.

"I was hoping that these dreams were just my imagination. Now he is saying that I can see the future. How come I can't see our future? How come it can't be things like our children or Justin's wedding or things that are nice? Why does it have to be something horrible?" she ranted.

"I think it works to protect you from dangerous things." I said quietly as I moved to be near her.

"Everyone is just guessing. No one really knows. I hate the uncertainty. Why can't it just be happy ever after?" she said frustrated.

"Everything is going to work out. I promise. I won't let anything take our happiness away." I assured her. I pulled her into me and held her there.

Just before noon we went over to Alain's lab to look over the slides. We could see that her blood cells actively healing the infected mice blood cells.

"Look Corin, I can heal influenza." She said cheerfully. I loved to see her light up like that.

"Well, I knew you blood was special but this is really cool. What are these other slides?" I asked.

"Well, we got samples of blood from mice that were infected with other diseases but I don't see my blood being effective with these other diseases. My guess is because influenza is not a genetic flaw. I'm going to ask Alain to get more strands of bacterial and viral diseases." She explained.

"None of these things can hurt you right?" I asked.

"Corin, we can heal remember? Anyway I'm not going to drink this stuff. Oh, shoot. Alain's blood sample is not enough. Could you check in the refrigerator if I have anymore blood left?" she demanded.

I walked over to the refrigerator and found her unit of blood stored on the top rack. "There is maybe a quarter unit left. Is that enough?" I asked.

"Yeah, but I will have to give some more later. I hate needles." She replied.

"I can give you some of mine, if that would help." I offered.

"Maybe later, right now I have enough. I'll just spin down the rest of this blood and use the serum. That is all we can do today. What time is it?" she asked.

"It's 1:00, we'll have to go soon." I directed.

"Okay, let me spin these down quickly and we can go." She said as she placed the tubes of blood into the centrifuge. I helped her decant the serum into falcons and labeled them before we placed them in the freezer. We worked quietly so we were done within 30 minutes.

We left the lab and drove over to the Burrens estate. As we pulled up we noticed everyone was already inside. We had to let the butler park the car since there was no other parking space. When we got inside everyone was already adjourned in the library. It was rather crowded but the room could accommodate many people so it wasn't too claustrophobic. Gena saw her grandparents and went over to hug them. I followed behind her. My parents were at the far end of the room. I excused myself and went over to tell my parents about Mark. My mother was very happy. My father was relieved. I kept my eyes on Gena. I watched as she made her way over to talk to Blaine. She left the library with Blaine. I started to follow her but Preston started talking to me about Mark. I had to repeat everything I had just told my parents. Everyone started listening in on the conversation so it was hard for me to get away. Moments later Gena came back into the library and came over to stand next to me. I was relieved she was back. I hated to not have her within my sights.

"I want to thank everyone for being here today. I know it was very short notice but something important has just come up. Now, I know everyone has met Gena, but what most of you don't know is that Gena is my late sister, Alexandria's daughter." He waited as many people turned to look at her in wonder.

"How is that possible Rolfe, I was there when we recovered what was left of Alexandria's body?" Edwin Daniels asked. I felt a bit of anger in his doubting tone.

"Let him finish, Edwin before you start with the questions." I heard my dad yell out. I will have to thank my dad later.

"Well, somehow she was saved by someone possibly from the hunter clan. She was taken to Dawson City and given to a human couple. This human couple cared for her until they died. Gena inherited Alexandria's jewelry box and was able to open it with her own blood. So, John you can confirm that at least she has her mother's genetic DNA to open the box. When she opened the box, she was informed of our existence and from there she found her way here. Now we have kept her past a secret because someone else knew of her existence in Indiana."

"Why would anyone hurt her?" Trey asked.

"Well, Gena's parents were killed because the hunter knew that her birth was very special. Gena has the healer aura. She helped Tina heal from her wounds. Also since she has been here Preston, Lawrence and Julianne have developed an aura. I'm pretty sure Michelle, Steven, Ella, and Natalie have felt some changes too." He waited as people started talking among themselves.

"I don't understand why your family chose to keep this from the clan." Thomas Redman asked.

"Thomas, we thought we lost her once. This other person knew of her existence in Indiana and we did not. We weren't sure how this would pose a threat to her." Rolfe stated angrily.

"Thomas, because she has not been around her kind, she can not defend herself. She can heal us but she can not defend herself from an attack." Alain added.

"So, why are you telling us now?" Edwin asked.

"For the past few weeks, Gena has been having nightmares about the hunters. At first I thought she had inherited the visions from healing Tina, but recent developments have led me to believe that she may be foreseeing the future." Alain explained. Noise erupted in to room. Everyone started looking at Gena and asking questions among themselves. I naturally placed my arms around her pulled toward me. I hated everyone talking about her as if she wasn't here.

"Gena, what do you see in your nightmares?" my mom asked kindly.

"Well, the first few dreams were very vague but lately, I can see the hunters clearly and after talking to Trey and Tina, I believed the hunter in my dream is named Nhan. I remembered the scars and yellow eyes. Each time, they were attacking me and the experience is so real that it sets my aura off." She explained calmly.

"What do you mean when you say *set your aura off*?" Thomas asked.

"Her eyes will turn red. It happens when she is healing." Preston replied protectively.

"Gena's aura goes into overdrive when it sense that she is in danger. Because her dreams are so realistic, her aura is triggered." Alain explained.

"So, are we expecting a pending attack? When will this happen? How do we know this isn't just her imagination?" Edwin asked.

I felt angry. Gena could sense this, so she held me tighter so I won't go over and clobbered Edwin Daniels for his stupid doubting comments. I looked down at her and smiled.

"Trust me, Edwin. We wished it was her imagination. I have witnessed these nightmares of hers and they are pretty real. I have questioned Trey and the others regarding their knowledge of the hunters. Gena could describe the hunter Nhan down to the very detail. She didn't get this information from Tina because Tina did not see him. Robyn saw him. Now, Gena has never encountered a hunter in her life so how did she come to know this information? Now, we waited to tell everyone this information because we did not want to falsely alarm anyone. We had to make sure." I explained as calmly as I could.

"Nhan is a ruthless killer. I watched him torture and kill my parents and others from our clan." Robyn announced.

"Gena, do you have any details on the timing of this attack?" my dad asked.

"Well, in my dreams, it was always night time and there was snow on the ground. The temperature was very cold. Other than that I can't tell you anymore." She explained.

"Right now it is coming to her vaguely. We just wanted everyone to be on guard and be careful until things changes. When I was a young child, our clan had an older woman who had the same power. She was able to warn us of impending tragedies. She could only tell what was coming but not when. This is very similar to Gena's abilities. We should be very thankful for her gift. It has been over two hundred years since I have witnessed this phenomenon." Gena's grandfather delivered.

Everyone in the room was silenced by his wisdom. He was considered the elder clansman. He has kept this clan safe for many years so there was a great deal of respect towards him. Rolfe was to take over when his father retired into his older ages but Rolfe did not have the patience nor the experience William had. Rolfe refused to take full responsibility for the clan. He wanted every father to participate in the welfare of the clan. He saw to it like a democracy where everyone had a voice on the welfare of the clan. The lost of Alexandria made him doubt his ability to solely care for everyone.

"Gena, I am sorry for doubting you. It has really been a trying day. This is quite a bit of information to get all at once." Edwin apologized.

"I assure you I know exactly how you feel Mr. Daniels." Gena replied nicely.

"Gena, I am sorry also. We are thankful for you and happy that you are here." Thomas added.

She gave him a smile and turned to face her grandfather. I was thankful for him. I hated to see him leave the clan again but he was older and his time was valuable to him and his wife. He no longer had to worry about others. This was something I hope for Gena and I one day.

"We will keep everyone updated if Gena sees anything new. Meanwhile we want everyone to abide by the parameters set in place by Corin. It is very important that everyone pay close attention to his instructions. I will now yield the floor to you Corin." Rolfe announced.

"The parameters are within 200 yards of everyone's backyards. No one should leave the area unaccompanied. Bradley will establish the checkpoint to the entrance of our neighborhood. If you are expecting any outsiders, I ask that you please register them with Bradley. All visitors will have to go through Bradley. Edwin, we want a full history on all the town employees involved with the laundry and delivery system. Please give them to Bradley. We will also establish security details at the schools and hospitals. If anyone sees anything suspicious or different please inform me or the security detail. Nothing is taken lightly. Lastly, I want everyone to pick up one of these tracking bracelets. They must be worn at all times. (Everyone in the room moaned there displeasure.) Does anyone have any questions?" I ended looking at Gena. She looked overwhelmed but I will have time to go over this information with her again later.

I watched as she moved to get a bracelet from Bradley. "No, Gena." I said quietly. "This one is yours." I said as I slipped the black tracking cuff around her small wrist and tightened the snap.

"How come mind is different from everyone else?" she questioned.

"Your bracelet is linked specifically to mine. If something happens and you need me right away, I want you to press this button. Don't take it off, because the alert will go off. If you accidentally break it I can still track you just don't try to take it off." I instructed.

"Obsessive much?" she teased.

"Only for you" I whispered. I planted a light kiss on her forehead.

"Well if no one has anything to add. Maggie has prepared a feast in the dining hall. Please have some lunch with us and make this a pleasant get together. My parents will only be here today and will return to France in the morning." Rolfe announced.

I watched as everyone left the library and headed toward the dining hall. Thomas Redman left to go back to the school.

"I knew you were special when I first met you." Tristan said to Gena. He gave her a quick hug before leaving with Aimee.

"You just keep on surprising us every time." Steven added.

"Hey can you tell me who wins the Stanley Cup this year?" Cory teased.

Everyone busted into laughter. The only thing missing was Justin's comments. I looked over at Gena. She didn't look to comfortable being the center of attention.

"Are you alright?" I whispered.

"I really don't want to be here." She said quietly through her teeth.

"We can leave anytime you want." I replied.

"I just want to say goodbye to my grandparents." She indicated.

I walked her over to her grandparents and watched as they congratulated our union.

"I am very glad it is you Corin. I have always wanted the very best for you and now you have my granddaughter." Her grandmother claimed.

"Thank you Beatrice. She is the very best." I responded by hugging Gena.

"Corin, you two are well matched. I couldn't have asked for anyone better. We will be back here for weddings and great grandchildren only. Do not keep us waiting too long." Her grandfather announced.

"We will definitely get on it as soon as possible." I promised. I watched as she hugged both of her grandparents and gracefully excused ourselves from the older crowd.

We made our way through the crowd and out to the car. The drive home she was quiet and distracted.

"What are you thinking?" I asked.

"I was thinking of how nice it would be to grow old with you. My grandparents look happy, don't they?" she commented.

"It will be like that for us. That is our destiny." I promised.

She looked back at me and smiled. This was the same smile that took my breath away from the very beginning. She was definitely my destiny.

Chapter Twenty-Two

I had to place the laundry outside the front door this morning. I was embarrassed at the amount of linens and clothes two people required to launder in three days. I just hope they don't inspect the linens too closely. As I dropped the laundry, I looked at the black tracking bracelet on my right wrist. It looked like a digital watch but plainer. The screen was black but you could see a faint blinking light. To the side of the screen there was the blue button used only for emergency. I prayed I never have to use it. Worse I pray I don't accidentally depress it. It took a bit getting used to. I have never worn anything permanent on my wrist. It was a bit comforting knowing that we were linked together; even though we rarely left each others side.

I was very proud to see Corin in action. He was very good at taking charge of the care of this clan. Rolfe relied on him more than anyone else even his own sons. Since the meeting Corin has been busy giving out orders and instructing security personnel over what he wants done and how he wants it done. No one questioned him or second guessed him. His attention to details was remarkable. Bradley and Carl were much older than Corin but they followed his orders robotically. I didn't realize how many people were involved in the security of this clan until they started reporting in with Corin.

We spent Thursday rearranging furniture to ready the two bedrooms for Leah and Mark. Some of the bedroom furniture came from Mark's house. After talking to Mark, Corin assumed responsibility over the house. Edwin Daniels felt financially responsible for the cost of the house Mark built, so he bought it. Corin signed over the house to Ella and Trey. All the furniture was removed and some were taken to storage. Brent, Trisha and Robyn moved into the new house next door. After talking with Trey, Corin placed him in charge over the security details over the schools and hospitals.

Some of Mark's furniture was used to replace the bedroom furniture in one of the bedroom in our house. Corin said Mark required a rather large bed and the one I had was not big enough. I didn't want to ask why he required such a large bed. But looking down at it now made me wonder why his bed was so big. It was definitely custom made because even king size beds weren't this big. His mother had to give me the linens for this bed because I had nothing that would fit it.

"Babe, where did you want this cabinet" Corin asked. I can't get over how strong he was. Moving furniture to him was more like moving chess pieces.

"Over here between the windows." I said. I watched him move gracefully across the room carrying the cabinet effortlessly.

"I didn't know these were windows." He said as he inspected the glass panel that opened up into the backyard. After he was satisfied with the window he walked over to me. "Are you wondering why he has such a big bed?"

"Do I want to know?" I hesitated.

"He has very vivid dreams." He laughed as he wrapped his arms around my waist.

"Ugh, now I won't be able to look at him without that thought." I said disgusted.

"Don't make me jealous. I don't want you looking at my brother at all." He murmured in my hair.

"Trust me; I don't see him the same way as I see you." I assured.

"And how do you see me?" He mumbled as he nuzzled at my neck. "God, you smell good."

At the same time we heard two rings.

"Phone" I said.

"Door" he added.

"I'll get the phone, you get the door." I instructed.

"Hello" I answered.

"Gena, its Mark" He responded.

"Hi, Mark. What's up?"

"Hey, we just wanted to tell you we'll be there tomorrow around 4pm. Is that alright?"

"Of course that is alright. That will work out great. Justin and Rachel will be here around noon time. We just spent the day setting up your rooms." I said. I got up and cover myself with a towel.

"Thanks. Okay, I have to go. Tell Corin, I said thanks for taking care of my personal business. We'll see you guys tomorrow. Bye."

"Okay. Bye." I replied.

I quickly showered and gathered my hair in a ponytail. I put on a pair of jeans and grabbed the first shirt I could find. As I made my way downstairs I could hear many familiar voices.

"There she is, Corin you said she was sleeping." Lauren complained.

"I was, but it's time for me to get up." I replied.

"Why are you sleeping at this time? Are you okay? Is it the nightmares again?" Aimee worried.

"No, I'm fine. I haven't had another nightmare." I reassured.

"Gena, you can tell us. You don't have to deal with this alone. We are your family. Don't be embarrassed." Aimee pleaded.

"Aimee, what am I chop meat?" Corin interjected.

"Okay, I'm fine. We have just been really busy moving furniture around. I just took a little nap." I mediated.

"Who was on the phone?" Corin asked.

"It was Mark. He wanted to tell us that he and Rachel will be here tomorrow around 4pm and he wanted to thank you for taking care of everything." I answered.

'That's great! Justin and Rachel will be here at noon. This is getting better everyday. I am just so happy everyone will be home." Lauren exclaimed.

"We're here because Finals are over. We brought food. We even brought in your laundry. Can we stay?" Dana begged.

"Of course, you guys are always welcome." I proclaimed. I looked over at Corin's displeasure.

"After we eat, we can go over what you should wear to the dinner party." Lauren declared.

We all made our way to the kitchen. They had brought over the leftovers from the buffet yesterday. Corin was too hungry to be irritated with them being here. We didn't bother sitting down to eat. Everyone just ate over the kitchen counter. After the food was thoroughly picked through, we discarded what was not eaten and continued to clean up the mess. The guys convened into the living room to watch a hockey game.

"I'm so excited to finally meet Rachel." Lauren declared.

"Me, too! I want to know how Justin will behave when she is around." Dana asserted.

"I am a little excited about meeting Mark's girlfriend, Leah." Aimee added.

"I talked to her yesterday. She sounds really cool. Do you guys know she is in a rock band? She also can dance. Isn't that cool." I said excited.

"Really?" Dana said enthused.

"How did Mark find someone so cool?" Aimee questioned.

"Corin said Mark heard her singing in a bar one night and he was hooked immediately. She teaches dance to the town children too." I exclaimed.

"That is so beautiful. Does she play or just sing?" Lauren expressed.

"I think she plays the guitar in the band. Her brother plays for some professional band." I provided.

"I bet she looks really cool rocking a guitar. I hope Max doesn't hear about this. He is going to want me to play the guitar riding on a motorcycle." Lauren teased.

We all laughed at the thought. We continued our conversation upstairs in my room. Lauren and Dana went through my clothes to decide what I should wear to the dinner. I was very thankful for their expertise because I had no idea what to wear. If left up to me, I would probably be either over dressed or under dressed.

"What happened to these shirts?" Dana cried holding up the two tees that Corin had ripped early.

Trying to not look utterly shocked I nonchalantly waved it off. "I don't know. It came back from the laundered service that way." I prayed that I didn't get anyone in trouble for that lie. "It doesn't matter, it was old anyway I really need to get some new clothes. I don't think I can get away with layering shirts to keep warm here." I recovered quickly.

"Did you say shopping?" Lauren perked up.

"Definitely. I need shirts, jeans, and whatever you could think of. Just no furs." I lied but this got them distracted enough to forget the torn shirts.

Aimee continued to help me pick out a dress for the dinner. We settled on the strapless dark blue dress that had a sweetheart neckline and ruche bodice. The skirt was fitted ending just above my knees. To keep warm Lauren would lend me her mink wrap. I wasn't worried about staying warm, the stilettos that matched this dress was more terrifying than anything I have ever owned.

"Do you want me to help you with your hair?" Lauren offered.

"No, I'm just going to wear it down. It would be warmer that way." I added

Satisfied, we went downstairs to use the laptop. Lauren and Dana immediately went through the online stores and ordered more clothes for me. Aimee and I wondered to the living room with the guys. I went over and sat on the floor between Corin's legs. He bent down and wrapped his arms around me. The hockey game was still on so we couldn't ask any questions while they concentrated on the game. Even though I didn't care for hockey, I could follow the game without any problems.

"Do you understand the game?" he whispered.

"Enough not to ask questions" I replied quietly. He chuckled. I felt his lips on the side of my face. During the commercials he would turn his attention to me but when the game started again he was like a little boy watching cartoons. When the score was so lopsided and time was running out, the guys lost interest in the game. Corin was happy for his team.

"Corin, is Mark going to be alright with Ella and Trey being at the dinner?" Tristan asked cautiously.

"Yeah. I think he has found his soul mate." Corin replied.

"Really, that was quick. You Randalls go from no soul mates to two in one year. What is the chance of that?" Max commented.

"I was pretty lucky. Gena came looking for me." Corin teased.

"Corin was really lucky. If it wasn't for my determination to open a jewelry box, we would've never met." I conferred.

"I don't know Corin was pretty determined to find his soul mate." Max added.

"Would he have come to Crew, Indiana?" I asked.

"No, I guess you're right. Corin you must have someone watching over you." Max admitted.

"No, Max. I think someone was watching over me. When I was at the lowest point in my life, I discovered a box that led me to this family. I came pretty close to storing that box away or possibly discarding it. If I had discarded that box, none of this would be possible." I pointed out.

"Isn't it ironic how things work out? You guys have a fascinating story but look at Mark. Who would have guessed that his soul mate was in Prudhoe Bay? What made him go there? There is no clan there. Look at Preston and Tina. They met under the worst conditions. Our kind is blessed with some outrageous circumstances along with some difficult situations." Aimee deliberated.

"I love it when you deliberate like that. You're so smart." Tristan complimented.

"I think every species are blessed with some good and bad situations. It is just a matter of how you look at it." Corin added.

"Gena, if you had a choice which would you chose?" Derek asked.

"Well, if you asked me two months ago, I would've said human. At that time, I had just lost my uncle. I was the last of my family. It was pretty bleak and lonely for me. I was praying for a short life. Now, I want to live as long as possible." I said looking up at Corin.

"I promise you a long and happy life." He vowed. I kissed him lightly.

"What's it like to live as a human?" Derek asked.

"Believe it or not Derek, humans are very similar to us. They may not have super skills but they have other advantages." I commented.

Lauren and Dana came into the living room with pictures of what they ordered for me. I pretended to look interested and excited. Corin laughed at my horrible acting skills. He helped by pointing out the ones he liked.

It was after 8pm when they left. Corin and I finished getting the rooms ready for our guests tomorrow. There wasn't much left to do but it kept us busy until 10pm.

"Babe, do you need any help in here?" he asked.

"No, I think I'm done. How does it look?" I asked.

"Very comfortable" He complimented as he took my hand and led me out of the room and to our room. "Let's go to bed."

"I had to lie to Dana when she found those shirts you ripped up earlier." I told him.

"What did you say?" he smiled.

"I blamed it on the laundered service. I distracted them by letting them shop for me." I said.

I heard him laughing. I quickly put on a t-shirt and a pair of boxer shorts. Exiting the bathroom, I found him standing on the side of the bed changing into his pajama pants. I walked over and wrapped my arms around him.

He picked me up and carried me to the bed. We laid there wrapped in each other arms.

"Did you really wished for a shorter life?" he asked quietly.

"I thought I was alone. It is really hard to be the last one standing." I explained.

"Would you ever take our own life?" he questioned.

"No, I am not too fond of pain. Accidently maybe but not purposely" I responded.

"Well, I'm glad you didn't get your wish. I can't imagine a life without you in it. I don't know what I would do if anything ever happen to you. I don't even want to think about the possibility." He confessed sadly.

"Don't think about it. Why dwell on something that is not real?" I replied.

"Because you're too perfect to be real. I fear sometimes that you're a figment of my imagination and when I wake up you'll be gone." He admitted.

"Do you need me to pinch you?" I teased.

"Trust me; I've already done that many times." He professed.

'Well, I am real. Our love is real." I declared.

"I believe you. I just can't imagine being left behind. It makes me so sad to hear how tragic your life was. I wished things could have been easier for you." He said sadly.

"Well, those tragedies led me to you. I can't imagine a life without you either. I certainly don't want to be left behind either. I think I can live but not happily." I professed

"I don't even know if I can live." He admitted.

"Don't say that." I scolded.

"Well, I'm just being truthful. If I didn't find you in the two years I allotted myself, I could have just lived but not happily. Now that I've known love; life would not be worth living if you weren't with me." He admitted.

"Well, let's just keep each alive forever so we wouldn't have to deal with that possibility." I said lightheartedly.

"I love you, Gena." He professed. I smiled. I could never grow tire of hearing those words from him.

"And I love you, Corin"

Chapter Twenty-Three

"I am coming for you, Gena!"

I jolted upright. My eyes scanned the darkness. That voice was so real. Was he here?

"Gena! What's wrong?" Corin worried

"Did you hear anything?" I trembled. My breathing was unsteady and erratic like I had been running. I rolled over to turn on the lights. My eyes continued to scan the room.

"No, Gena, there is no one here but us." He reassured pulling me back down.

"No, Corin. I heard him. He was here." I said frantically. I was scared. Somehow he had managed to get close to me.

I watched as Corin got up and inspected the room. He checked the bathroom. He left the room for some time and came back frustrated. "Gena, no one is here." He concluded.

"I am going crazy. I could have sworn he was here. His voice was so real. I am so sorry. I think I am losing it." I was terrified. How could I have imagined his voice? He was getting into my head. I felt nauseated. My stomach churned. I had this unsettling feeling that something bad was coming. I could not share it with Corin because I didn't know exactly what it was. I tried to take deep breaths to settle the nausea but when I tasted the bitter bile; I ran for the bathroom. As soon as I reached the toilet, everything I had eaten came rushing out. I felt Corin at my side. He held my hair and handed me a cold wet cloth. I rested my head on the toilet seat.

"What can I do?" he whispered.

"Nothing just let it pass." I replied. He handed me a glass of water to rinse my mouth out. He sat down next to me, rubbing my back.

"Was this nightmare like the others?" he asked.

"There was no nightmare; just his voice. It was clear as a bell and it was so close. I could have sworn he was next to me." I confessed.

"I am so worried about you. I hate that I can't do anything for you. I am supposed to protect you but I don't know how." He said with a lot of guilt in his tone.

"I can't believe how I've complicated your life. You would have been better off without me." I cried.

"Hey, don't say that. I welcome this complication. I will take whatever comes with you." He said as he lifted my chin to face him.

"How much more can you take? I know I am at some sort of breaking point. Corin, I am hearing things. That is not normal. What next? Hallucinations? Eventually you'll have to declare me insane and lock me up." I declared trembling.

"You're not going crazy. You have had a lot of things happen to you in a short amount of time. Think about it. How many people you know have endured what you've had to in the past three months?" he pointed out.

"Just don't leave me. I don't think I can endure that. Don't give up on me either. I am usually really boring. I don't have nightmares. I don't usually have people chasing after me or wanting to kill me. As far as I know there is no psychosis in my family." I claimed.

"Now, you're crazy. I would never leave you sane or insane." He vowed as he picked me up off the floor and carried me back to bed.

"Before I came and invaded you life, you didn't have to worry, you got 8 hours of uninterrupted sleep, you were fed well, and now you're constantly worried about me and my dreams. You haven't had a good night sleep. You're barely getting three meals a day." I bantered.

"Gena, at the end of the day, I have you. I will take whatever baggage comes with you. I could care less about sleep if you weren't next to me. Food would be tasteless and bland. I worry about you because I love you, and can not bare the thought of losing you. Now you have to get some sleep. Someone has to be nice to our guest, remember I am the grouchy one." He teased as he pulled my lips to his.

I woke up when I felt him moving in bed. He was sitting on the side of the bed with a huge tray of food. Of course, I was hungry but I can't imagine eating all this food by myself.

"Breakfast for my queen" He said quietly.

"Your queen will be a whale if she eats all this." I commented.

"You vomited a lot last night. I want you to eat as much as possible and I will help you with the rest." He pointed out as he buttered the toast and handed it to me.

He fed me, toast, scrambled eggs, some bacon than forced some strawberries and blueberries into me. When I begged to stop he handed me a glass of milk. "Every calorie is important, even if you have to drink it." He added. I drank the milk while he finished the breakfast.

"What time did you wake up to make this?" I asked.

"I've been up since seven. I like to watch you sleep. It has become a routine for me." He admitted.

"What is so interesting about me sleeping?" I questioned.

"It's silly but sometimes, I just want to make sure you're real. I've dreamt about you for so long, sometimes it's hard to know the difference between my imagination and reality." He confessed.

"I haunt you in your dreams too?" I said dryly.

"You do not haunt me. I've dreamt of your existence for as long as I can remember. Meeting you fills the gaps in my dreams. I like the idea of falling asleep with you and waking up with you in my arms." He said openly.

"I take too much of you. I don't deserve you." I said quietly.

"I gladly give myself to you and in return I'll take all of you." He said smiling. All I could do was smile back, because his smile left me speechless.

"I love you." I finally spoke. It was all I could think to say. I had no other thought but that. It was the most fulfilling three words out of my mouth. His face lit up and that made those words more meaningful.

"I should bring you breakfast more often." He teased.

"No, I should do it for you. You're too good to me." I returned.

"I'll do breakfast and you make lunch and dinner. Deal?" he exclaimed.

"That's a deal." I agreed.

"Rolfe asked us to meet Justin and Rachel at the tarmac, so we need to get moving. I'll take care of this and you hit the shower." He commanded as he took the tray away and left the room.

I was blow drying my hair when he came back in and stood at the bathroom door looking at me.

"That's all it takes to make you look beautiful." He commented.

"You're just biased." I replied.

"Maybe so, but my opinion is the most important, right?" he asked.

"It's the only one I care about." I responded proudly. I moved to meet him at the door. He smiled down at me than lowered his lips to mine. His kiss was soft and gingerly. He trailed his lips down my neck lingering in my hair. "Um, you smell so good." He murmured. When I felt his hands tugging at my shirt, I had to stop him. "Oh no, these are my last two long sleeve tees. The new ones are not here yet." I protested fighting off his hands. He chuckled in my hair.

"What if I promise not to tear them off?" he teased.

"You don't have the patience to make that promise. Anyway it is eleven. Now, go get ready." I scolded as I pushed pass him.

"I have an unlimited supply of shirts to choose from, you're welcome to them." He teased pulling me back by my shirt.

"I don't look good in them." I complained freeing myself from his grip.

"I like you in my shirts." He smiled devilishly walking towards me. He was so fast he got to the door before I could even turn around.

"Corin, please get ready. I'll be waiting downstairs." I pleaded with my hand holding him at bay.

"You sure do know how to use your magic words." He teased as he stole a quick kiss then let me pass. "Give me five minutes."

I went to do a quick check on the two guest rooms to make sure I didn't miss anything last night. I took another look at Mark's bed and laughed to myself. *Vivid dreams. I wondered if he has crazy nightmares like mine.*

We got to the tarmac around 11:30. Bradley had already arrived with the black sedan. Corin got out and chatted with him a bit before he came back in. I waved at Bradley from the car. It was too cold for me to stand outside chatting with anyone.

"The runway is pretty icy, so I told the crew to salt it down." He explained as he got back into the car. "Are you warm enough?"

"As long as I don't have to go outside" I replied.

"Here we are again. Back to the beginning" He remembered as he took my hand and pressed it against his lips.

"Headache and love at first sight." I teased.

"Love at first sight and heart break." He reminisced.

"Heart break" I questioned.

"Yeah, it was right here when my dad told me you were Justin's fiancée. My whole world came crashing down right here, in this very same parking spot." He recalled.

"Well, I wasn't too happy when I saw you at the beach with Natalie." I reminded.

"Mark asked me to pick her up and she mistook that as a date. Seeing you at the beach was hard too. I thought you were Justin's fiancée and that pain consumed me. It was worse when you sat across from me and did not say one word." He recalled painfully.

"Well when I saw you holding Natalie's hands at the beach, I thought maybe I read you wrong on the plane. I didn't want to get you in trouble with Natalie. Plus at that time, I had already agreed to stay and I didn't want to start my life here in such a bad way." I explained.

"I wasn't holding her hands. She tripped and I was helping her." He declared.

"Well, it looked like you were holding hands. What about the kiss?" I said with a hint of jealousy.

"Okay, I'm sorry for that. I should not have allowed that but I was so consumed with jealousy and rage that I could not think straight. Why didn't you talk to me?" he asked.

"I was too embarrassed. I thought that you led me on or I misread your hospitality for something else." I said admitted.

"You won't believe how crazy it was for me when I first saw you behind the curtain. Every single emotion that my heart could have, rushed through me drowning my logic. I was scared and excited at the same time. It is really magical how this works." He fantasized. I smiled and nodded agreeing with him.

"Is that their plane?" I pointed at the jet in the sky.

"I think so. I'll be right back." He said as he exited the car. I watched as he made his way over to Bradley. They were talking and laughing about something. It was endearing to see how well Corin got along with people twice his age. I watched as the plane landed safely and the cabin door opened up. Corin came back and escorted me to the exit stairs. I watched as Justin came out escorting a beautiful girl with long beautiful red hair. Her red hair made her skin look creamy and soft. She had green eyes that almost looked like jades. When they got down, we greeted them.

"Hi, Rachel. It is so nice to finally meet you. We've heard a lot about you. Welcome to Inuvik." I said kindly.

"You must be Gena. I had heard a lot about you and Corin." She replied as she reached out and shook both our hands. "Justin said you were beautiful but that word is just not enough."

"Thank you. I was just thinking about how unbelievable you look. I absolutely love your hair." I said astonished.

"Well, Corin you absolutely look super fine and I can't help but stare at myself." Justin kidded. I watched as Corin laughed at him.

"How was your trip?" Corin asked.

"It wasn't so bad. I got to sit next to the most beautiful girl in the world." Justin boasted.

"Come on; let's get you home so you can meet the Burren clan." Corin instructed.

Justin and Rachel got into the black sedan with Bradley as Corin and I followed behind in his Audi. The trip to Uncle Rolfe's house was short and quick. I got to see from a different view how the Burren clan greets new family members. They overwhelm people with their love and hospitality. I watched as they each impatiently took turns hugging and complimenting her. How could anyone resist loving this family?

We spent most of the afternoon getting to know Rachel. It was strange to see Justin behave more maturely and tenderly with her. We excused ourselves from the gathering to go home to cook for Mark and Leah. Corin said the trip from Prudhoe Bay to Inuvik did not have any food vendors on the way. Knowing Mark he would be starving. Rachel and Justin promised to stop by for dinner.

We returned to the house around 2:30. I quickly went into the kitchen to start on the chicken parmesan. I started on the tomato sauce first. Corin came in to help me pound the chicken until they were roughly 1/3 inch thick. He enjoyed playing with the meat. It was fun to see him laugh at his task. I seasoned the chicken then covered them in regular flour before I dipped them into an egg wash then finally coating them with breadcrumbs. Corin watched intently.

"You do it like a professional." He commented.

"I watch a lot of Food TV shows." I replied as I fried the chicken on a skillet.

"I watch it too but I can't go into the kitchen and just whip things out like you." He answered back.

"Corin, I have been cooking since I was 12 years old. My mother got sick and I had to help her during Chemotherapy. When I came to live with

Uncle Josh, he had this wonderful chef that taught me a lot of things. His specialty was American Italian and American dishes. The first thing he taught me was to make my own pasta. The second most important thing was the tomato sauce." I told him as I got him to taste the tomato sauce.

"He should be very proud. I love your cooking. My mother cooks but she takes a lot of short cuts. Her specialty is actually desserts. She would spend ten minutes on dinner but two hours on desserts." He stated.

"I would love to learn how to make desserts. I know how to make cookies and stuff but not fancy desserts. Maybe I should spend some time with your mother." I said excited. I placed the chicken, sauce, and mozzarella, parmesan and pecorino into an oven dish and placed it into the oven.

"That would make her really happy. Michelle has never been interested in learning anything in the kitchen. Just don't pick up any of her bad habits with dinner." He teased.

I smiled at him. It sounded nice to be around a mom after having not had one for 4 years.

We knew immediately when they arrived because of the roaring sound of Mark's Lamborghini.

We came to the door and watched as they got out of the car. Leah was a tall, statuesque beautiful blond goddess. Her hair was long wavy and a perfect color blond with no dark roots or imitation to it. She was almost the complete opposite of Ella. While Ella, was a medium height, beautiful brunette with brown eyes. Leah was a tall, blonde, with green eyes. She walked gracefully alongside Mark towards us. She appeared a little nervous, keeping her eyes downward.

"Hey guys, welcome to our home." Corin announced. I watched as the brothers embraced each other lovingly.

"Thanks for letting us stay with you guys." Mark said. "Leah Lenning this is Gena and my brother Corin." He said proudly.

"Welcome to Inuvik, Leah." I said warmly. "Please come in. I am so happy to finally meet you." Corin and I gave her a welcoming hug and ushered them inside.

"Thank you so much. Your house is so beautiful. I have never seen anything like it. It looks like something out of the Architectural Digest." She asserted.

"Wait until you see the inside." Mark bragged. We all walked inside. I watched as Leah's eyes were awestruck by the design of the house. Mark flipped the switch to show her the curtains inside the glass walls. She was so surprised.

"Oh my God, that is so cool. Are all the homes like this?" she asked.

"No, just this one" Corin added as he placed his arms around me. "I hope you're hungry. Gena made chicken parmesan." Corin stated as he took their lug gages.

"I am starving. Chicken parmesan sounds heavenly." Mark proclaimed. "I am tired of nasty Alaskan food. "

"I heard you're a great cook." Leah announced.

"I don't know about great but I do know some things. Let's get you guys settled then, we can feed you." I instructed. Corin and Mark followed us upstairs. I showed Leah to her room and helped her unpack.

"I hope this is alright. I have never had to get a room ready for a guest before."

"I hope you don't think I am weird for saying this but you are so beautiful." She complimented staring at me.

"Thanks, I was thinking the same of you. I can't believe how silky your hair looks. I bet you stand out quite a bit in Prudhoe Bay." I returned.

"Well, Mark said you were naturally beautiful but I really didn't know what that meant. I have always worn make-up, so I can't imagine going natural." She admitted.

"Wow, I can't tell that you have make-up on. It is very light." I replied.

"Its mineral make-up but how I wished I didn't have to wear make-up at all." She shared.

"I don't wear it because I'm too lazy to invest the time in myself." I divulged.

"Well, you definitely don't need it. Do you mind me asking, how old you are?" she asked.

"I'm eighteen. How old are you?" I replied.

"I just turned 20 last month." She declared.

"So, you and Rachel are the same age." I added.

"Yes, I can't wait to see Rachel. We were good friends when I lived in Colorado. It's been almost 5 years since I last saw her." she said.

"Well, she is excited to see you too. They'll be here for dinner tonight. We kind of have this pot-luck thing at my house most nights." I said.

"You ladies need any help?" Corin smiled from the door.

"Did Mark like his room?" I asked.

"I love it, when can I permanently move in." Mark announced from behind Corin.

"Forget it, I will feed you and that is it." Corin teased. As we all made our way downstairs.

"Corin, stop. You guys are welcome to stay as long as you like." I said as I watched Corin rolled his eyes.

"Thanks Gena, I am so glad you have a good leash on Corin. Let's eat. I am starving." Mark announced.

"I haven't had chicken parmesan since I left Colorado. There really isn't an Italian restaurant in Prudhoe Bay." Leah stated.

"They don't have any edible food in Prudhoe Bay. " Mark complained. "Look how much weight I've lost since I left."

"Gena, Mark has been complaining about Prudhoe Bay since the first day I met him." She declared as she sat down next to Mark.

"I believe that. You should be worry when he is not thinking about food." Corin teased as he handed Mark and Leah their plates.

"Gena, please teach me how to cook. Leah rarely eats, so I will have to be the one to keep us alive." Mark stated as he waited for us to sit down with our plates.

"Gena, rarely eats too. She just cooks because of me. I make breakfast and she makes lunch and dinner." Corin declared.

"This is so good, Gena. You have to teach me how to make this." Leah begged.

"Leah, please tell me you cook because Mark can't cook. Remember when we tried to make Mom breakfast. You almost set the house on fire with the bacon." Corin chided.

"Corin, I was 13 years old. I think I can handle bacon now." Mark added. Corin nodded to concede to Mark's comment.

"Trust me, this just looks complicated, but it is really easy." I asserted.

"Yeah, Gena makes everything look easy." Corin added as he squeezed my hand.

"So, Gena you're from Indiana? I didn't know there was a clan in Indiana." Leah asked.

"I'm from Crew, Indiana and as far as I know, there is no clan in Indiana." I replied.

"Gena was raised by humans." Corin declared.

"Really" Mark said surprised.

"Oh, yeah you weren't here when we had that clan meeting. It's a long story." Corin said flatly.

"What did I miss; I've only been away for 6 weeks." He questioned.

"Do you want me to tell him or do you want to do it?" Corin asked.

"No, you go ahead." I resigned.

"Gena, is Alexandria's daughter." Corin announced boldly.

"Alexandria is alive?" he asked surprised.

"No, before Alexandria was killed by the hunters, someone saved Gena and gave her to a human couple, Frank and Mary Reynolds. When they died she went to live with her uncle Josh Reynolds." Corin recanted.

"Josh Reynolds, the NASCAR driver?" Mark interrupted.

"Yes." I answered quietly.

"Gena, I am so sorry." Mark apologized.

"That's alright. Leah, my uncle died in August during a race." I filled her in.

She nodded "I'm sorry too. If this is too much for you, you don't have to talk about it."

"No, I'm alright. Corin go on." I directed.

"Well, she inherited Alexandria's jewelry box on her 18th birthday and that is how she found out about us." Corin finished.

"One of ours" Mark asked.

"Yep, she accidentally opened it." Corin added.

"Wow, so is it true? Do you have the healer aura?" Mark asked me.

"Yes, I have the healer aura." I said quietly.

"You have the healer aura?" Leak asked surprised.

"She is the one who healed Tina." Corin boasted proudly.

"Wow, I can not believe it. Corin, when did you find out about this?" He asked.

"Justin told me on the way to Yellowknife. I wasn't allowed to tell anyone." Corin said.

"Do you know who saved you?' Leah asked.

"No, but I would love to thank them personally. I could have easily been killed if it wasn't for this person." I stated.

"You know Leah, fought off a hunter attack when she was 15 years old." Mark boasted.

"Really, what happened?" I asked.

"Well, when I was 15 years old. My family moved us from Colorado to International Falls, Minnesota. We were staying with a friend when we were attacked. One of the hunters took me. His name was Cron. For some reason he did not kill me right away. He brought me to some cave deep in the middle of this heavily wooded area. Before he was going to kill me, I distracted him and was able to escape." She recounted.

"Tell them how you distracted him." Mark smiled.

"I told him I was a virgin, and asked him to have sex with me before I died." She said shyly.

"Oh, my God, really" Corin replied shocked.

"Yeah, so when he was getting undressed, I hit him in the head with a rock and ran. My brother and I were the only survivors. My brother moved us somewhere he thought was safe and that is where I have been since." She added.

"Why didn't you return to Colorado?" Corin asked.

"My brother hated Colorado. He found work on a fishing boat and moved us there because it was isolated." She shared.

"I can believe how smart you were at 15. I would have been killed already. How did you think to do that? Weren't you scared?" I asked astonished.

"I was scared to death but luckily I watched this policewoman talking about self-defense on TV and I remembered that she mentioned that distracting the assailant was the best way to buy some time." She recollected.

Mark and Corin roared out laughing. "When she first told me, I didn't believe her." Mark chuckled.

"Hey, you guys are strong enough to fight them. We have to be creative and if I have to throw my body at them to survive, I would do it again and again." She expressed firmly. I nodded in agreement.

"Leah, I would never let anyone hurt you." Mark said seriously.

"Speaking about that, we have reinstated safety parameters." Corin shared pointing to our tracking bracelets.

"Why, what has happened?" Mark cautiously asked.

"Well, evidently we found out that not only can Gena heal, but she can foresee the future too." Corin revealed.

"I have nightmares about being attacked by a hunter I have never met before. When I described the hunter in my dreams, Robyn identified him as the one called Nhan. He is one of the ones who attacked there clan in Quebec." I divulged.

"Gena, you are full of surprises. I can't believe I missed all this." Mark expressed.

"How long do you guys plan to stay with us?" Corin asked.

"You're kicking us out already?" Mark jested.

"No, I am just asking because if you plan to be here long, than you have to wear a bracelet. You know the rules." Corin said dryly.

"Is it alright if we stay long enough for Gena to teach me how to be an excellent cook?" Leah stated nervously.

"Leah, you guys can stay as long as you like. I would love it if Mark comes home permanently but if you're not ready than we will cherish the time we have with you now." I said kindly.

"Thank you so much, Gena. Corin." She replied softly.

We all left and went over to the Randell's house so Leah could meet John and Diane. John and Diane were so welcoming that at one point Leah became tearful and overwhelmed with emotions. Her display of emotions was not surprising as Mark's reaction to her. Mark instantly became protective and tender. Even Corin was surprised to see his brother's loving behavior. During the visit, I got to talk to Diane regarding some baking tips. I also found out that Corin's favorite cake was the red velvet cake. We had some discussions on what I wanted to do for his birthday cake. She was delighted that I wanted to make the cake instead of buy one.

On the way to North's we stop by to pick up a couple of tracking bracelets for Mark and Leah. Corin went over the instructions with Leah. Since Mark was our guest, he decided what he wanted for dinner.

"I remember talking with Corin one night this week and he mentioned eating crab cakes. I have been thinking about crab cakes for days now. That is what I want tonight. Do you mind making that tonight?" he asked.

"That is the easiest thing to make. I thought you were going to ask for a seven-course meal." I replied.

"Leah, come I will show you how to make this so you can make Mark happy." I instructed. We walked around North's going over the supplies needed. After we gathered what we needed, we made our way home. Mark and Corin immediately went to the living to watch a game. Leah and I went directly into the kitchen.

"I can not get over how beautiful this house is." She said with awe.

"Yeah, it takes a bit getting used to. So what's it like in Prudhoe Bay?"

I asked as I dump all of the lump crab meat into a large bowl.

"Well, it is pretty much just me. My brother, Kyle, is on tour right now with the band Code. Have you ever heard of them?" she explained.

"Yeah, I have a couple of their CDs. That is so wild. So Mark said you're in a band too." I asked,

"Yeah, but Kyle doesn't want me to do that for a living. Ever since my parents' death, he has been overbearing and super over protective. When I told him about Mark, he thought I was insane. He doesn't believe in the *concero flamma* thing." She said sadly.

"Well, do you believe in it?" I asked her.

"Well, I wish I had as much faith in it as you do. When I first saw Mark, I felt the attraction so strongly that it took my breath away. But I am not sure if it is physical attraction or something else. I tried to talk to my brother about it but he doesn't believe in it, so it's hard to know. How do you know?" she asked.

"Well, as you know I was raised by humans, so I would've probably been more skeptical than your brother. When I first saw Corin on the plane, of course there was the immediate physical attraction but then there was this strong undeniable obsession that follows. I really can't describe it but the force of the desire, longing, attraction can not be disregarded. Corin can probably describe it better; he suffered quite a bit thinking I belonged to someone else." I explained.

"Why did he think that? I mean looking at you two, I can't see how that is even possible." she pondered.

"It's kind of a long story but he was basically led to believe that I was Rachel. Luckily things got cleared up before something stupid happened. It's his fault." I replied as I mixed the crab cake mixture together.

"That was easy. What do we do next?" she asked referring to the crab cakes.

"I told you cooking was easy. Next we scoop each patty onto this baking tray and then into the oven. This should make at least 50 cakes. Just remember when you make this again that there aren't 12 people coming. We should make a salad to go with this." I instructed.

"Now, that I can handle. Who's all coming?" she said as she started on the salad.

"Well, Justin and Rachel definitely. Then there is Justin's sister Lauren and her boyfriend Max, than there is Aimee and Tristan, and finally Dana and Derek. Aimee, Justin, Dana and I are cousins. Hopefully you'll get a chance to meet everyone Sunday at the Thanksgiving Dinner." I informed.

"I just hope I don't crack up like this afternoon. It has been a really long time since I've been around my own kind. I really missed being around family. In Prudhoe Bay, the people were really nice but they are humans so I was really afraid to be close to anyone. I didn't want to hurt anyone with my aura." She said quietly.

"Don't worry about that. I think Diane really likes having such an emotional meeting. It makes her feel more motherly." I pointed out.

We were disrupted when her cell phone went off. She excused herself and went into the music room. I finished scooping the cakes onto the baking sheet and placed them in the oven. I was cleaning up when she came back into the kitchen. She looked distracted and lost in her thoughts.

"Is everything okay?" I asked concerned.

"That was Kyle. He is not too happy that I am here." She admitted.

"Why would he be upset that you were spending Thanksgiving with friends and family? Would he rather you be alone?" I asked irritated.

"He rather I not associate with another clan." She said sadly.

"Leah, do you want to be here?" I asked simply.

"Yes, I want to be here. I want to be with Mark. But I don't want to choose between my brother and Mark." She said sadly.

"Why don't you invite your brother here too?" I asked.

"He won't come." She answered quickly.

"Well, why don't you let me invite him? I think once he gets to know us; he would be more comfortable with you being here. Better yet, he may like it here." I suggested.

"Gena, thanks but you don't know him. We left Colorado because he offended a lot of people. He does things to get us ostracized. Things only got better when we left the clan." She explained.

"Leah, do you want to be here?" I asked firmly.

"Yes." She answered quickly.

"Than we will be extra nice to him; making it hard for him to offend anyone. Now call him for me." I said boldly.

She hesitated for sometime while I had my hand out for the phone. She finally caved in and called him. She handed me the phone as soon as she heard him pick up.

"Now what?" the voice on the phone answered.

"Is this Kyle?" I asked.

"You're not Leah, who is this?" He asked rudely.

"You're right. It is not Leah. I am Gena Reynolds. I am you sister's friend. I would like to invite you to my house for Thanksgiving." I responded curtly.

"I don't care for Thanksgiving. Where is Leah?" he questioned sharply.

"Well, Leah will be staying with me for awhile. If you're not too busy spending time with you're road crew you may come by and visit her." He started to cut me off. "And she is in love with a wonderful man. My address is 1810 Discus Manor in Inuvik. You are welcome to come by but don't expect Leah to follow you back to that lonely hole you call home in Prudhoe Bay. I am trying to convince her to stay here permanently. Maybe you could take some time off and spend it with the only family member you have left. This is important to you right?" I finished sarcastically.

There was a brief silence over the phone. I thought for a moment he hung up but than I heard him sigh.

"Well, she knows how to reach me when she wants to come home." He said slowly than he hung up. I felt a tinged of guilt for the whole conversation. He sounds so disconnected and cold. I looked back at Leah.

"Well, I invited him. He didn't really refuse. But at least he knows you're here and safe. All we can do now is wait. Don't worry Leah, he'll come around." I said.

"Yeah, I hope you're right. I think your guests have arrived." She declared.

"Come let's make some friends." I said confidently.

We came out to greet everyone. Mark immediately came to Leah's side and introduced her to everyone. I was very proud of my family. They were very welcoming and polite. During dinner Rachel and Leah shared stories about Colorado and the clan that lives there.

"How big is your clan Rachel?" Mark asked.

"Well we are made up of 4 families with total of 20 people. We are small but we are very close. The only problem is in the summertime we have to go further North because of the heat." Rachel answered.

"Gena, you have got to give me the recipe for these crab cakes." Aimee pleaded. I nodded to her request.

"Corin, you are a spoil man." Max expressed.

"Hey, I make her breakfast." He said as he kissed my hand.

"Leah, you're in a band?" Lauren asked.

"Yeah, I sing and play the guitar." She replied shyly.

"Lauren, I am adding this onto the list of things I want to photograph you doing." Max teased.

"Her brother plays the guitar for the band Code." Mark added.

"Really! They're famous. Will he come here to visit too?" Derek asked.

"I've invited him but he did not confirm so we'll just wait and see." I answered cautiously.

"When did you talk to him?" Mark asked.

"While we were cooking, he called and wasn't too happy about me being here. So, we thought it was a good idea to invite him here." Leah asserted.

"Why does he not want you to be here?" Corin asked.

"He's just worry about Leah's safety." Mark answered briefly.

"Well, he shouldn't worry, she has you now and being here is safer than being in Prudhoe Bay, all alone." Corin responded.

"Well, I tried to tell him that but he's not too happy about Leah being out of Prudhoe Bay." Mark answered.

"That doesn't seem fair. He gets to go all around the world while you have to stay in some small town wasting your life away. What will happen to you if Mark didn't come to Prudhoe Bay?" Aimee asked.

"He doesn't think that way. Ever since my parents' death, he was been really protective." Leah explained.

"It doesn't matter if he thinks to protect you or not, you're still in Prudhoe Bay by yourself, no family or friends." Justin added.

"Kyle was never comfortable with clans anyway." Rachel added.

"It just seems grossly unfair of him. The least he could've done was take you on tour with him." Aimee commented.

"We tried that once after I graduated from high school but that life was a little too wild for me. They do a lot of partying, drinking and drugs. Also he couldn't trust his band mates around me." Leah confessed.

"How often is he away?" Lauren asked.

"He is away pretty much all year long. He comes home for 2 or 3 days a month." She said sadly.

"That is so sad. Please tell me your staying with us Leah; I can't bear the thought of you being in Prudhoe Bay by yourself." Aimee pleaded.

"She will not be by herself. If she wants to return to Prudhoe Bay, I will go with her. I will be where she is." Mark said proudly.

"Thanks, Mark. I really don't want to go back to Prudhoe Bay but I don't want to lose my brother either." Leah said tearfully. I gave her a warm hug.

"That is why I invited him here. Maybe once he sees she is happy and safe, he will not make you choose. He doesn't have to stay but he can at least approve of you being here." I announced.

"That is such a great idea. Gena you come up with some great ideas." Dana admitted.

"So when is he coming? Do you need our help with anything?" Lauren asked.

"He declined my invitation but I did give him our address so when he misses you he will know where to find you." I affirmed.

"That was a good idea, baby. I can't imagine anyone turning you down." Corin complimented giving me a light kiss.

"Well, we will just have to wait and see." I ended.

We finished dinner and continued into the living room. Rachel and Leah talked about Colorado and we filled them in on life here in Inuvik. The clan in Colorado was much younger with children between the ages of 14-16 years old. Rachel liked being in this clan because there were more people her age. She was torn between staying in Colorado and moving to Inuvik. Justin didn't care as long as they were together.

"So, what are you wearing to the party Sunday?" Rachel asked Leah.

"Well, I can show you what I have and maybe you guys can tell me what's appropriate." Leah stated cautiously.

"Now, that is what we like to hear." Lauren voiced happily.

"Why don't you guys go help Leah, I'll go make some coffee and beignets." I instructed. I did not want to be stuck up there trying on clothes.

"I'll help you. I've had enough of clothes to last me a life time." Aimee confessed.

"Thanks." I whispered.

Aimee and I went into the kitchen and started on the beignets. I took out the recipe that I found on the internet and started on the dough. Aimee was really helpful. She wanted to learn how to cook just as badly as I did.

"Babe, can I talk to you a minute?" Corin asked as he made his way in from the living room.

"I can help her finish, Gena." Tristan said standing behind Corin.

"Am I in trouble?" I asked nervously.

"Lots" He giggled.

"Is this about the invitation to Kyle?" I asked anxiously.

"Nope" He responded quickly as he ushered me up the stairs and into our room. He quickly kicked the door shut and turn to me with a devilish smile.

"Corin, we have guest upstairs and downstairs." I reminded him.

"I know, but I miss you so much today." He confessed as he gathered me into his arms.

"Where have you been? I have been with you all day." I struggled in his arms.

"I know but not like this." He murmured in my hair. "God, you smell good."

"Corin, we have to get everyone home than we can be alone." I promised.

"Okay, I will kick them all out right now." He rushed.

"No, Corin. Please be nice. They will go home soon." I pleaded holding him back.

"Okay, but I'm going to be really grouchy after two hours." He warned. He forcefully pulled me into him, pressing me tightly to his chest. He hungrily placed his lips to mine. His passion was greedy and ravenous. I encouraged him by grasping at his hair and tightening my grip on his hair. His hands wondered up and down my spine. I lost all control when I felt his hands covering my buttocks. He lifted me up and pulled my legs around his hips

"We have to stop. Now we have to look presentable. You have messed up my hair. Thank God, you didn't tear anything. Come on baby, get yourself together." I instructed.

"I hate guests." He complained as he helped me straighten out my shirt and hair. I fixed his hair and we both giggled at our impatience. To pretend that we were not upstairs doing something devious, I let him go downstairs first while I pretended to check-up on the girls in Leah's room.

"Hey is everything alright?" I asked.

"Yeah, do you want to see what Leah's going to wear?" Lauren asked. I nodded pretending to be interested.

"Wow, that is gorgeous. Mark is going to like that." I complimented. "We have coffee and beignets downstairs whenever you guys are ready."

"Okay we'll be down in one second." Rachel announced.

I skipped down the hallway and downstairs. I gave Corin a quick smile as I passed him in the living room. I could smell the aroma from the beignets in the oven.

"Aimee, you did a great job. Sorry for deserting you. Corin had to talk to me about some personal stuff." I lied.

"Don't worry about it. Tristan helped me. I like it when we do stuff together. I think he is so sexy in an apron." She giggled.

"Well than it all worked out." I confirmed. When the beignets were done we plated them and brought them to the living room. Everyone reconvened into the living room. We enjoyed each other's company but once in a while I caught Corin looking at me. Tempting fate, I went to sit on his lap. He placed his chin on my shoulder and wrapped his arms tightly around my waist. It was erotic to hear him inhaling my scent. The conversation around us was uninteresting and it slowly dissipated because all I could think about was him and his body heat. I kept a smile on my face but my thoughts were lost in a daydream about him.

In my mind, we were alone and that was all we needed.

Chapter Twenty-Four

"Nhan, this clan is huge. We have to go back."

"Cron, I don't plan on attacking the whole clan. I just want that one called Corin. I want to teach him a lesson."

"How do you plan to kill him without setting them off?"

"We will wait until we can get him alone He lives in that glass house."

"How long do you want to wait?"

"As long as it takes."

"I am tired of all this chase for one Tiametan."

"Do you see his woman? She looks very familiar. I've see her before."

"Which one?"

"She is the one with brown hair, look at her."

"She doesn't look familiar to me. They all die the same."

"Cron, I have seen her before."

"Nhan, you have killed every Tiametan you've met so how is that possible?"

"I don't know, but I have seen the girl before."

Watching her sleep was addictive to me. She wore one of my oxford button down shirts to bed because she didn't want to lose anymore clothes to my impatience. I was aroused because I knew underneath the shirt she was completely naked. I toyed with the idea of looking underneath her shirt. Instead I watched as the hem of the shirt lay crunched up over her perfectly round hip. I could see just enough of her buttocks to fantasize about her.

She didn't sleep soundly tonight. I felt her twitch and startle herself many times but she never woke up. Maybe the dreams weren't so bad. I wish I could read her mind so I could find out what was going on in her head. I was supposed to protect her but all I can do was lay here and watch as her dreams scared her. She is so beautiful. How can she be afflicted with so many painful memories and still be sane? *There she twitched again.* I wanted to wake her up but I was afraid it was for nothing.

She was so quiet when she slept. She didn't snore or make any weird noises. I watched as the rise and fall of her chest begin to quicken. Her perfect displayed hands were now clinched together in a fist. The muscles on her arms tensed. Her head turned from one side to the other. She looked like she was about to speak but than she slowly relaxed her features. Suddenly her eyes flicked opened and she gasped for air.

"It's okay, baby. It's just a dream." I whispered comfortingly. I held her tighter and closer to me.

"Wow that was really scary. I dreamt they were near and that there were two of them." She said silently.

"Well, if it is only two of them than we have nothing to fear." I assured her.

Looking up at me she sighed. "Corin, please don't do anything rash. I don't want you hurt." She said sadly.

"I am merely pointing out that two is easier to kill than a whole clan." I stated.

"Were you watching me sleep?" she asked.

"I told you I loved to watch you sleep." I admitted.

"You're making me self-conscious now. Aren't you tired?" she asked coyly.

"Not right now but I want you to go back to sleep." I whispered.

"I wish I could dream about you instead of hunters." She stated.

"Do you need me to help you?" I whispered in her ear.

"What can you do sing?" she asked sarcastically.

"I can make you sing." I teased.

"Sing huh? I don't think our guest would be too happy with us." She replied.

"Well, while you were asleep, I heard Mark sneaking into Leah's room." I confessed.

"You're lying?" she accused.

"Do you want to go check? I can go demand him back into his room if you like." I teased.

"Really?" she repeated.

"Yes, and I bet they are doing the same thing we are doing." I murmured in her hair. I was slowly unbuttoned her shirt.

"Gossiping, eavesdropping and being nosy?" she replied.

"No, kissing and touching." I corrected as I kissed a path down her neck and to her breast.

"Dream about me baby" I whispered into her ear.

The light coming into our room did more than any alarm clock could ever do. The sun slowly worked its way into our room with deliberate brightness with each passing second. I watched as she hid her face against my chest to avoid the sun hitting her eyes. I couldn't tell whether she was completely awake or just subconsciously avoiding the brightness. When I felt her lips on my chest, I smiled. She was awake and another day with her in it was beginning.

"Wake-up sleepy head" I whispered.

"How do you stay awake all night and still manage to wake before I do?" she murmured against the skin on my chest.

"I didn't stay awake all night long. I went to sleep right after you did." I reminded.

"Did you dream of me?" she asked.

"I told you I don't have to be dreaming to think about you." I reminded her.

"I love it when you say that." she whispered.

"I think its time to get up, we do have guest you know. I'm going to make you some crepes this morning." I promised her kissing her shoulder.

"Crepes, that sounds good. What time is it?" she asked.

"It's almost 9:30. Do you want me to start a bath for you?" I tempted her.

"A bath? I haven't had a bath in years. Why didn't you offer me one last night?" she teased.

"If you can remember, I was a bit impatient." I noted.

"Well, I don't have the time to linger in a bath this morning but maybe tonight?" she suggested smiling.

"Okay, I'll start your shower than." I compromised.

"I think we better hurry up. We have guests you know." She reminded.

I went into the kitchen to start on my mother's crepe recipe. I had helped my mother make this many times but this time it was more important then making it for my family. I wanted to impress the girl of my dreams; she was the most important person in my life. I was plating the crepes when Mark came down.

"Look at my brother the domesticated boyfriend." He teased.

"I know how to impress my girl. Do you?" I provoked.

"I impress her in many different ways." He said with a smirk.

"What ways do you impress her, Mark?" Gena asked sarcastically as she came to my side. I gave her a quick kiss.

"That is something you'll have to talk to Corin about." He replied.

"Is Leah awake yet?" Gena asked.

"Yeah, she'll be down in a minute." He responded.

"Corin, these look great." Gena complimented.

"It's my mom's recipe." I admitted.

"There's my baby." Mark announced.

"Crepes. I am so jealous of you." She said looking at Gena.

"Corin made them." Gena corrected.

"Now, I am more jealous of you." She added.

We each got our plate and sat down at the dining room table. "Juice or coffee?" I asked. When the door bell rang, I looked at Gena. "Did you invite someone?" teasing her. Gena volunteered to go answer the door and came back with Justin and Rachel.

"Just in time for breakfast." Justin playfully announced.

"Gena, I am so sorry for not calling first. He is hopeless." Rachel said apologetically.

"No, it is perfectly alright. We're used to Justin showing up to eat. Here take my plate. Can I get you some coffee?" Gena said handing her plate to Justin.

"No, take mine. I'll go make some more. Gena, you eat." I directed.

"Corin, I would like more fruit and powdered sugar." Justin playfully teased.

"Justin, stop it. You are so bad." Rachel ostracized.

"I love having breakfast with Gena and Corin; they always have the best food." He bragged.

"Hey, Corin. I have decided for your birthday I am going to get you a humongous LCD TV. No offense Gena, but your TV sucks." Mark yelled out.

"That will be so great. You should get one of those 50' SONY LCD. Hockey would be so great on one of those." Justin added.

"I happen to like our TV." I replied coming back into the dining room with a plate for Rachel and myself.

"You're joking right. That thing is 20 years old." Justin pointed out.

"It works just fine." I replied.

"I don't care. I'm going to get you one anyway. It's my gift to you, so I can get whatever I want." Mark finished.

"So, what are we doing today?" Justin asked.

"Hey let's take the girls to Tuk Beach." Mark suggested.

"That's a great idea. I want to play some football." Justin roared.

Gena helped me clear the dishes while Justin and Mark called the others to invite them to Tuk Beach.

"It's going to be really cold; do you have enough warm clothes to wear?" I asked her.

"I will layer some shirts together and I'll wear my parka, is that enough?" she replied.

"I'll bring along my parka too, just in case." I suggested.

The plan was to all meet at Tuk Beach at noon time but we ended up getting there after one. It is funny how simple life was for us guys. When we wanted to go somewhere, we just got in the car and took off. Now because we have girlfriends to take care of us, we had to pack food, drinks, blankets, and even silverware. Gena made turkey and ham sandwiches.

Leah made some potato salad. Rachel pitched in some cookies. Lauren agreed to bring drinks and glasses. Aimee volunteered chips and vegetables. They've made this simple trip to the beach a Martha Stewart nightmare. I was waiting for someone to volunteer the picnic table.

When we got to the beach, I immediately got the bonfire started because I knew Gena would be cold. The girls had already spread the blankets all around the fire.

I took off my parka and wrapped it around her. "I want you to tell me if you get too cold." I directed.

"I'm fine, Corin. The fire is really nice." She replied.

I missed playing football with the guys. It has been too long since we last got together like this. The last time I was here, I wasn't in the mood to celebrate anything. I looked back at Gena, sitting near the fire with her beautiful brown hair dancing in the wind. She was giggling and talking to Aimee. She looked happy and that was more important to me than anything else in the world.

"Hey, she'll be fine." Mark remarked.

"I know." I said quietly.

Football, Inuvik style was played in the cold water. Similar to football played in the US in the harsh cold snowy weather, we played football, in the freezing water. We played in our jeans and t-shirts. The cold weather did not bother us. The water temperature was a perfect 40 degrees. I was always the receiver because of my speed. Justin had the best arm so he usually played quarterback. Michael and Max were known for their cheap and dirty blocks and hits. Cory was the fair one so he usually referees the games. We have been playing together since we were kids and it never changes. We always ended up splashing around until football became an underwater sport. Someone would toss the ball up and everyone would make a dive to get it first. There was no goal post or touchdowns, just tossing the ball around until we were exhausted or hungry, so after a couple of hours Mark and Justin were hungry.

We came over to where the girls were sitting and started drying off. I didn't dare touch Gena because the freezing wetness would probably kill her. I stood next to her and dried off over the fire.

"Did you have fun?" she asked.

"I did. It's been a long time. Are you warm enough?" I replied.

"Yes, are you hungry?" she asked.

"I could eat, but don't get up, I'll go get us something to eat." I responded quickly.

It was odd to see Gena all huddled up in layers of clothes while everyone dressed lightly. Even the girls wore only a light jacket. Lauren wore her fur coat just to show off. I can't wait until the day when Gena's body completely transformed to protect her from the harsh weather in Inuvik. I hated that she was so vulnerable. I got us a plate of potato salad and sandwiches. I fed her while she stayed tucked inside her blanket. We sat around the bonfire and told embarrassing funny stories.

Each couple shared how they met each other. Aimee and Lauren were pretty lucky. They were raised around their soul mates. Mark started by retelling the story of Leah's heroic escape from the hunter name Cron. Each time he exaggerated the attack or the beating Leah gave. She was embarrassed by his exaggeration. Everyone was so enthralled over her escape. The story was nothing short of miraculous to us, because none of us has ever been attacked. We lived a sheltered life here. Our clan was big and strong. After what happened to Gena's parents, we became well organized and always prepared for any danger. We develop protocols for certain scenarios and learned from other's mistakes.

"I can't believe how extraordinary your story is. But I think how you and Mark met is even better." Lauren admitted.

"You guys make it so real. All my life, I have always doubted the *concero flamma* thing but seeing you guys together really have me believing again. I just wished Kyle can witness this." Leah said sadly.

"He'll come around." Mark assured.

"Still our story is not as remarkable as what I heard about you two." She shared looking at Preston and Tina.

"Are you kidding? If you were here 6 weeks ago, you wouldn't think that." Justin announced.

"Well, I know Mark was getting married but how is that extraordinary?" she stated.

"Well did you know that Ella's soul mate is one of the survivors?" Preston asserted.

"Just before the announcement of our engagement, Ella met Trey who turned out to be her soul mate. I really did not have a choice in the matter. So to avoid everyone's pity I took off. I drove mindlessly towards Prudhoe Bay. I had never been there before and as you know there is really nothing that would have attracted me there but for some I found myself there. Then I found you. Our story may not be scary or life threatening but the circumstances of our chance meeting is nothing short of miraculous." Mark explained.

"Yeah, I tried to explain it to Kyle, but he doubts everything about it." Leah said sadly.

"Trust me, Leah. I had doubts to. I was going to marry Ella. It is really hard to believe in something that you have never witnessed for yourself." Mark explained.

"Yeah, the hopeless pursuit of your soul mate will test the will of any men. You're shrouded with doubts; what if she's already dead, hurt, raised by humans, or if you're really unlucky she belongs to someone else." Justin expressed.

"Yeah, I had given up hope of finding you. I was scared of waiting around for nothing." Mark said to Leah.

"I didn't believe in it until I saw you in the water." Preston admitted to Tina.

"I shouldn't have been on that slope that day. I don't know how to ski. I almost stayed home." Justin confessed to Rachel.

"I much as I would have searched I don't think I would have found you. I am just glad you came to me." I looked at Gena.

"I think in some weird comical way we were all meant to be here. Like it is our destiny to be the next generation of our clan; how else would you explain all the circumstances that brought us together?" Aimee finished.

When it came to how Gena and I met, I tried my best to describe how I felt on the plane but Justin was more interested on how Gena came to be on the plane. Rachel was the only person to have not heard the entire story so of course Justin started from the very beginning. He did a remarkable job telling our story because we did not have to correct him.

When it came time for Preston and Tina, things got serious. Rachel and Leah were so surprised over Tina heroic survival. Preston tried to explain how he felt when he saw Tina in the water but Tina stopped him before he got upset. The mood got lighter when Preston described how he reacted to seeing Gena's eyes go red after healing Tina. For once Justin did not have anything to say.

"Does it hurt Gena?" Rachel asked

"No, I only feel hot and sweaty." Gena described.

"Do you know how special you are? I don't think there has ever been a healer aura in our generation." She said with respect.

"I don't think there has been one in our parents' generation either." Preston added.

"This will make your clan much stronger. Others may come and want to be a part of this clan." Rachel confessed.

"Rachel, we don't plan to make it public knowledge. Gena's life may be put at risk if this information was discussed worldwide. Right now this clan knows and you may share it with your family but because she has not completely transformed yet. I don't want any chance of her being singled out." I explained.

"Transformed, what do you mean?" Rachel asked.

"Rachel, Gena was raised by humans. Her aura laid dormant all her life. Though she can heal us, she can't heal herself. Didn't you notice that she is the only one here wearing two parkas and a blanket?" Aimee pointed out.

"So, you don't have the ability to heal and right now you're not like us? How long will it take for you to completely transform?" Leah asked.

"Well, Alain guessed 2 to 3 years." I finished.

"Can you have children?" Rachel asked.

"Yes, we just have to wait until my body is ready." Gena responded quickly. We turned when we heard Justin clear his throat. I glared at him.

After some time, I was dry enough to sit with Gena. I kept the blankets close around her. Sitting next to the fire, holding her, with my chin on her shoulder, I nodded off.

"Corin, why are you so tired?" Justin asked.

"He didn't get much sleep last night." I heard Gena whispering.

"What are you doing keeping him awake?" Justin teased.

"I have nightmares Justin. He stays awake to make sure I get some sleep." She said scolding him.

"Oh, well I knew it had to be something else. We know it can't be sex." He blurted out.

"Justin, I can't believe you just said that." Rachel scolded.

"Justin, I am going to kick your ass." I warned.

"Justin, what they do in their bedroom is none of your business. You know what they say about those who talk about sex all the time. They don't get any." Mark defended.

"Mark, shut-up." Leah scolded.

"That is alright Leah. Justin needs a dose of his own medication." Rachel added.

"Okay, I'm sorry. I just can't help it. Rachel, I promise I'll be good." Justin pleaded.

"That will be the day." Lauren said rolling her eyes.

"We should bury him in the sand." Aimee thought.

"That is a great idea." Gena agreed.

We all gathered around Justin and trapped him. Mark and I held him down, while Gena and Rachel tied him up. Leah gagged him with paper towels. Everyone took turns covering him in sand until he was completely buried. We dug deep enough so he could not get out. Lauren wrote funny markings on his face. Dana completed the scene by covering his head with a brown bag. We took some pictures with our camera. Cory captured in on his video camera and promised to download it on YouTube. We kept him like that as we packed up the cars. Only when, Rachel could not bare it anymore, she dug him up. By that time, we were long gone.

On the way back we laughed at the pictures of Justin.

"Corin, your birthday is next Saturday. What would you like to do?" Gena asked.

"I would like to spend quality time with you, no one else." I answered honestly.

"You have lots of family and friends that would like to celebrate it with you." She pointed out.

"I know but you asked me what *I* wanted to do." I corrected.

"Fair enough but you know we're going to have to celebrate with them." She replied.

"I know but maybe we can save some time for ourselves." I suggested.

"I am having a really hard time thinking of something special for you. Can't you help me out?" she asked.

"Everything I have always wanted is sitting right here. You are my birthday present. I can never ask for anything else. I have spent all my wishes on you and it was well worth it." I said as I held her hand to my lips. I watched as she smiled at me. I loved that smile.

Chapter Twenty-Five

"Did you hear that Cron? I told you I've seen her before. Her mother is the one we killed in Dawson. How did she manage to be alive?"

"Bron killed the fetus, so how is this possible?"

"This changes things. We will go back and talk with the elders. They will have no choice but to launch an attack on the whole clan to kill the girl. We can not let her live. Her powers will strengthen them. If we get her now, than our kind will have a chance of annihilating them once and for all."

"Nhan, you go back; I will stay behind and learn all I can about their schedule. Plus, I have some unfinished business here."

"Cron, this is my hunt. I want the healer and her boyfriend. You can kill the rest."

"Right now, I just want one."

"Corin, I think my breast has gotten bigger or maybe I'm getting too big. Look at this shirt." I asked him as he was getting out of the bathroom. He had to shower to get all the salt water off him. I had to change because of the sand in my clothes.

"Well, you're not going to hear any complaints from me if your breasts are getting bigger but I know you're not getting fatter. I know every inch of your body." He teased.

"No, look at this and the last two buttons are missing. I think the laundry service is mad at me." I pointed out. I was wearing my favorite dark green blouse. The first button was stretched tight because of my cleavage. *Was I still growing?* Then, the last two buttons were missing allowing my belly button to be exposed. I though about wearing a camisole underneath but the only clean one was pink and it would not look good under a dark green shirt. Since my jeans lay just below my hips, a great deal of my abdomen was exposed. I looked around for a pin but could not find one.

"Well, it still looks good on you. I like green on you." He complimented peeking from the door.

"Be serious, it's a little provocative don't you think?" I asked.

"No complaints from me." He yelled back from the bathroom.

"I think I'm going to have to rip up this shirt and use it as a rag." I added.

"Hey, you leave the ripping to me. Keep it on. I want to rip it off tonight." He teased from the bathroom door.

"You're impossible. I guess it will be okay tonight since its only girls here." I murmured looking at my breast. Cory and Michael invited the guys over to watch hockey on their 52' plasma TV. My little TV could not compare to that. The girls were coming over to look through all the clothes that were ordered plus I had to make the final preparations for Corin's party.

"I will be at Cory and Michael's house for the game. They promised to feed me so you don't have to cook. I should be home around midnight. Justin said something about playing poker. If you need anything, you call me. Don't forget, I am only staying away this long because I don't think I would be too comfortable playing dress up. I really rather be with you." He asserted as he made his way out of the bathroom.

"I'll be fine. Anyway Leah will be here. You go have fun. I think I am just going to make some recipe cards with her. Wake me up when you get home." I said with a wink.

"I'll do more than wake you." He teased back.

Leah and I watched as the guys left for their night out. We had already made some French cookies called palmiers earlier so we were ready for our little girls' party. We went back inside to look over some recipes she wanted to learn. I had a large collection of recipes I got from the internet and off the cooking shows. She was so eager to learn that she offered to cook dinner while she stayed with us.

"That is a great idea. You can cook the dinner and I will learn to do desserts. We can have Diane over. Corin said her specialty is dessert. Plus I have to learn to make her Red Velvet Cake for Corin's birthday party. This would be really great because school starts again on Monday and that would be so helpful." I said.

"Please be very honest with my cooking. I want to be good not just get by." She instructed.

"Of course. You'll be fine. I think the girls are here. Can you get the door?" I asked as I gathered the recipes and placed them back in my folder.

Lauren brought over her mink wrap for me to wear Sunday. It was so luxurious and fine. I felt a little gaudy but I knew my parka didn't look appropriate with the dress and stilettos. Lauren had brought over some of the packages she ordered for me. It was delivered to her address because the retailers knew her address really well and she usually get things within 24 hours.

"I really like these shirts on you. The design is called baby dolls. Aren't they cute?" she said.

"They don't look too warm. Can I wear something underneath them?" I commented.

"Oh, shoot, I keep forgetting. Sorry Gena." She answered frustrated.

"I can wear them when the weather changes. Right now I need these. Will you guys look at the shirt I have on? I think my breasts are getting bigger?" I pointed to my shirt.

"I thought that was how you were supposed to wear that blouse. I don't see anything wrong with it." Dana mentioned.

"Maybe so, but I usually wear them buttoned up and sometimes with a camisole underneath, but are you looking at my breasts? Either the shirt has shrunk or my breasts are growing." I stressed.

"You wish. I have been hoping my breast grows bigger since I was 16. I think 18 is the stopping point." Rachel said kidding.

"Maybe I'm getting fatter; wouldn't that make my breasts bigger?" I asked.

"Well you're jeans look fine. I think your breast grows if you're pregnant. That is definitely what I am waiting for." Aimee said dreamingly.

"You have to have sex to get pregnant, right?" I responded dryly.

"Sorry Gena. That is the only thing that would make your breast bigger. Maybe you are still growing or transforming." Aimee explained apologetically.

"What are you going to transform into a porn star? I will be so jealous if your transformation gives you bigger breasts. That will just be unfair. Anyway we know you and Corin aren't doing *it*." Dana pointed out.

"Shut-up Dana that is none of your business" Aimee defended.

"Oh, don't worry about it, Thanks to Justin, I think everyone knows." I replied.

"Is it hard? I mean you guys sleep together; don't you get tempted to do something? I know when Max and I are in his room, he is all over me. I can't imagine us having our own place." Lauren admitted.

"Well, we do some things but we just have to control it. He doesn't want to risk anything. You know how over-protective Corin is. How do you guys not get pregnant?" I asked embarrassed.

"Well, we can get pregnant. The only thing is our body can sustain pregnancy. We are very careful about when we do it but if I get pregnant I would not die like you would." Lauren pointed out.

"Knowing Corin, just the possibility of endangering your life, he would abstain." Aimee said.

"I don't know how you do it. Don't take this the wrong way Gena but Corin is really hot. I used to have this huge crush on him before Natalie claimed him. She used to tell me how she crushed on him too. She would follow him around like a sick puppy. He could have had her anytime if he wanted to but he was always so serious. I think that's what made me loose interest in him." Dana confessed honestly.

"Well, I am glad I don't have to fight you over him. I can't imagine you as my competitor." I said

"I don't think there is any competition when it comes to you and Corin. We saw his transformation as soon as you came into his life. Remember that day in the lunchroom?" she recalled.

"What happened in the lunchroom?" Leah instigated.

"Well, it was so romantic. Corin wanted to tell Gena how much he loved her but she was sitting with someone else. He was so jealous he pulled her outside and kissed her in front of everyone." Dana fantasized.

"You didn't tell it right. Corin was led to believe that Gena was engaged to Justin." Lauren started.

"What?" Rachel interrupted.

"Bad information. Anyway, he went for days thinking that he had found his soul mate but she would marry someone else. Then when he found out she was not Justin's, he was called away for 5 days to rescue the survivors, so by the time he got back he was so revved up with all this emotions, then when he finally had the opportunity to tell her, she stupidly goes and sit next to this guys who Corin hates." Lauren continued.

"Corin does not hate Trevor." I corrected.

"Yeah, now he doesn't but trust me he hated Trevor that day." Aimee implied.

"When he saw her sitting there, he flipped. We all witnessed his crazy behavior. Max told him to wait and talk to you later but he could not contain himself. We were really surprised to see Corin act that way. He is normally serious and restrained. Nothing really rattles him. Then when he went over to your table, Max was worried for Trevor. We were relieved to see Trevor leaving with his teeth still intact." Lauren explained.

"So, what happened after that?" Leah asked interestingly.

"Well, I was mad because he was so rude. He asked to speak with me privately but I would not leave with him. He then pulled me outside." I said plainly.

"Tell me what did he said to you before he kissed you." Dana asked nosily.

"He said I was the center of his life." I replied quietly.

"Corin came up with that!" Aimee said astonished.

"He is very charming. You guys don't know him like I do." I boasted.

"I guess we don't. I've known him all my life and he can probably go for days without saying ten words to me." Dana said.

"Well, I believed it when we found out what that symbol meant. Than when you told us it came from Corin, I knew than that he found you." Aimee added.

"What was the symbol?" Rachel asked.

I lifted my pendant and showed her. "It's the Mobius Strip. It means everlasting love." I said with pride.

"When did you get this?" Lauren asked.

"Right before Mark's engagement party. He said he got it when he and Justin were in Dawson." I remembered.

"That is so beautiful. It is just so weird to see this side of Corin." Aimee said.

"Tell them what you're getting him for his birthday." Dana remarked.

"I am getting him the new Audi R8. Hopefully he will give me his old one." I said shyly.

"You got him a car?" Leah yelled.

"Gena is loaded." Lauren informed.

"Okay, I don't want to talk about me anymore." I announced annoyed.

"I think my brother Mitch has a car like that. Corin must like to drive fast." Rachel said.

"If he drives like Corin, we should all be very afraid." Aimee warned.

"Mitch doesn't know how to drive slower than 80mph." Rachel informed.

"Keep him away from Corin." Lauren advised.

"I happened to like Corin's driving. It is very exciting." I shared.

"Yeah, you drive the fastest motorcycle. You guys are perfect for each other." Aimee declared.

"Okay,we have to iron out the party arrangements, remember?" I reminded them.

"Oh before I forget, Dad said that the car will be here on Wednesday. It will be stored in our garage but you will need to sign for the keys that day." Dana announced.

"Also, we picked out a bunch of different foods, but you have to go to North's to finalize exactly what you want by Friday. I can go with you." Aimee informed.

"I would like to go too." Leah added. I nodded to accept her offer.

"Okay, so Wednesday, I'll stop by after school and sign for the keys for the car. Then Friday after school we can go to North's to finalize everything. I need someone to get Corin out of the house for me to decorate it." I planned.

"I can help you decorate the house." Rachel added. I nodded graciously for her help.

"I think there is a game on Saturday afternoon. We can have the guys get him over Cory's house for that." Aimee suggested.

"You know what, Mark ordered Corin's TV and I think he has to pick it up in Dawson. We can have them pick it up on Saturday, which should give you plenty of time to decorate." Leah suggested.

"That is brilliant. Will you make sure Mark is in on it? You guys, I think that is it. Thank you so much." I said graciously.

"Well we have to go. We need our beauty sleep to look good tomorrow." Lauren announced as they all got up.

"Oh, Leah, I forgot the shoes you need with your outfit." Rachel said.

"That's okay; I'll just go with you to get it now. I'll take Mark's car." Leah responded.

"Do you want me to go with you?" I asked.

"No, I'm good. Anyway if I am going to be living here, I might as well familiarize myself with everything." Leah replied.

They all left as quickly as they came. It was nice to have the house nice and quiet. I went into the kitchen and placed the leftover palmiers into a plastic container. I poured myself a cup of the hot chocolate and went back into the living room to go over the recipes that Leah had picked out. I wanted to copy them on index cards for her. I was on my fifth card when the door bell rang. I was a little hesitant to check the door because it was after 9 pm and I wasn't expecting anyone. I didn't think it was Leah, *why would she ring the door bell?*

I stood at the foyer looking out to fine a young man with messy blond hair standing at my front door. I couldn't tell how tall he was because he was leaning his head against the door. He had on shades and he looked tired.

"Can I help you?" I yelled from the door.

"I'm looking for my sister, Leah. Is she here?" he mumbled. I could barely comprehend him from the door.

"I'm sorry, who are you looking for?" I asked nervously.

"Are you Gena?" he yelled rudely.

"Yes." I yelled back.

"You invited me, remember?" he yelled back annoyed.

I quickly unlock the door and pulled it open. He almost fell inside because he was leaning against the door.

"I am so sorry. I couldn't hear you at first. Are you Kyle?" I asked. I could smell the alcohol coming from body. He stood looking down at me, waving back and forth trying to maintain his balance. He was completely inebriated. He could barely focus his eyes on me. He looked me over perversely and ended with a wicked smile.

"Hello there?" he slurred coming closer to me. He placed his hands on the door way to balance himself.

I was disgusted by the lustful way he was staring at my breasts. I hated that I had this shirt on right now. Unconsciously, I pulled my shirt together. I backed up into my foyer and watched as he tried to move into the house without falling. "You're drunk." I said repulsed.

"My God, you are beautiful. If I had known how beautiful you were, I would have been here sooner. Thanks for the invitation, sweetheart. Now where can we go for some privacy?" He slurred. He was standing in my foyer now, swaying over me. I paid no attention to his disgusting compliments; they were worthless coming from someone whose appearance sickened me. How could he show up and embarrass Leah this way.

"I think you are mistaken. I invited you here to spend time with your sister. You obviously don't care too much for Leah to show up here looking like this. If you were anyone else, I would have you thrown on the street. Why don't you go sit down over there and get sobered up before Leah gets back. She should be here any minute." I scolded him slowly.

"I like you. You're very saucy. I like my woman saucy." He leaned into me. I pushed him back with my arms but he grabbed me around the waist and held me against him. I was sickened by the odor of his intoxication, so I pulled my face away from him to prevent from being nauseous. He suddenly kissed my neck and started putting his hands inside my shirt. Shocked by his advances, I slapped him as hard as I could and pushed him back. He tumbled backwards and fell over the couch and onto the floor.

"You're disgusting. Do not touch me again. Just sit there." I said breathless and angry. I watched as he started to get up but fell back down, but this time he hit his head hard on the coffee table. I ran over and helped him stable himself. When he was righted on the couch, I was shocked to see him looking at my breasts again. I pulled my shirt together and sat back.

"Look do not move. I'll go get something for your head." I instructed.

He sat back defeated. I went over to the kitchen and got some ice and wrapped it into a kitchen towel. When I came back into the living room he was gone. Before I could scan the room, he was standing behind me. I was startled by him.

"I may be drunk, but I still know what I want." He said as he grabbed my waist and pushed me up against the wall. My head hit the wall so hard that I had to blink to refocus. I tried to push him back again but he overpowered my arms. He pulled my arms up and over my head, pinning both of them with one hand. I tried to bring my knee up to kick him but he forced my legs apart with his legs.

"You smell so good. I bet you taste good too." He said lustfully. When he tried to kiss me, I clamped my mouth tight, so he squeezed my jaw until I opened my mouth from the pressure. He quickly intruded my mouth with his tongue. I tried to bite him but I was only able to nip at his lower lip. Making it bleed.

"So, you like it rough, huh?" he warned pushing his body harder against me.

"Please stop, you're scaring me. You're drunk. Leah is going to be here any minute. Please stop." I pleaded. I didn't know when my annoyance changed to being scared but the lustful look in his eyes made me realize he was too drunk to distinguish between what was right or wrong. He was not listening, my pleads only encouraged him. I felt him rubbing his body against me.

"You invited me here. I am only obliging you." He murmured in my neck. I felt his hand sliding up my shirt. Frustrated he yanked at the shirt until it ripped, exposing my breasts.

"Very nice. I am going to have to keep you around longer." He breathed into my cleavage.

"Please stop. I don't want you. You have to stop. Leah would be very angry." I tried to reason with him. I was trying to reach the button on my tracking bracelet but he held my hands so tightly together I could not feel for the button.

"Do you know who I am? Every woman around the world wants me. Right now, you are the luckiest girl in the world, because I want you." He boasted as he bit my breast.

"Please, I don't want you. You are hurting me! My name is Gena Reynolds. I am Leah's friend. I have a boyfriend. He will kill you if you don't stop. Please if you stop now, I won't tell anyone. I promise. Please." I begged. I felt nauseated.

"I like the way your mouth moves when you talk." He said intoxicated. I struggled against his grip until I managed to turn my wrist to where I could depress the button on my tracking bracelet. I felt him rubbing himself against me. His hand squeezed my breast until I screamed. "I like that." He said devilishly.

"Please my boyfriend will be here any second. I have a tracking device and I just pressed the alarm. You must stop." I yelled breathlessly. I swallowed hard to control the nausea.

"I don't mind sharing you with him." He teased as he tugged my bra upward and lowered his mouth over my breast. I screamed for him to stop but it only made him press harder. When he bit my nipple, I felt tears running down my face.

"Please stop." I begged tearfully. He did not stop; instead I felt his hand tugging at the button on my jeans.

Suddenly, every part of my body screamed out in fear. He was going to rape me and I could not stop him. I struggled against him. The nausea and heat was forming. I was jolted with relief, when I heard the screeching of brakes in the driveway, I screamed out Corin's name.

Within seconds I felt an abrupt force ripping Kyle's body away from mine. I saw Kyle thrown to the opposite side of the living room like he was a mere rag doll.

Corin turned to look at me. "Gena, are you alright?" he bellowed breathless. I nodded as I slumped to the floor. My arms ached from being held over my head so long. I quickly pulled my shirt together, when I heard Mark come in.

Corin leaped over to where Kyle was lying and started pounding his face with his fist. "I will kill you for touching her." He snarled with a vicious hateful tone that scared me. I realized than that Corin would kill him and Leah would be devastated.

"Mark, stop him. It's Kyle." I screamed.

Mark hesitated for a second than turned to stop Corin. I watched as Mark made several attempts at pulling Corin off Kyle, but Corin would not yield. I quickly ran over to Corin, and attempted to reason with him without getting in the way of his rage. If one of his punches were to hit me, I would probably not be conscious for days.

"Corin, please. Its Leah's brother. He's drunk. Please baby stop." I pleaded. I pulled at his arms to no success.

Luckily Justin, Cory, and Michael came through the door. It took all of them to pull Corin away from Kyle.

Meanwhile Kyle face was unrecognizable, but he was still alive.

"Get him out of my house, or I will kill him." Corin roared. I placed myself up against him. He held me but his body was forcefully trembling. His face was ravaged in anger and disgust. He tried to comfort me, but I knew he was trying to control himself. He took my wrist and fumbled at the tracking device to disarm it but he was trembling so much he could not focus on the task at hand. "Corin, I'm okay. Please look at me." I pulled his reluctant face to mine. I held his face there until his body relaxed. He suddenly pulled me into a tight grip and buried his face in my hair. "I was so scared." He whispered in my ear.

"Gena, why don't you take Corin upstairs? We'll take care of this." Justin advised.

"I want him out of my house." Corin warned as he followed me upstairs

When we got to our room he pulled me to him and held me there. He buried his face in my hair and I could feel warm wet tears coming from him.

"Corin, I'm sorry for scaring you." I said softly.

"You should not be sorry. I just thought I was going to lose you. Did he hurt you? Tell me." he worried.

"He only scared me. He came to see Leah. I didn't know he was drunk until I had opened the door. When he came in he thought I was one of his groupies. I managed to push him off me the first time but then he caught me off guard when I went to the kitchen." I explained.

"He attacked you twice, why didn't you call me?" he said angrily.

"Corin, he tried to kiss me, but I was able to push him away. He fell onto the coffee table. I thought he would stay down. I didn't want to alarm you over some drunken idiot trying to kiss me. I though I could handle it. I went into the kitchen to get him some ice for his head, and when I entered the living room he grabbed me from behind. He was clearly too drunk to reason with and when he wouldn't stop, I panicked." I described.

"Gena, he could have raped you. I don't care if he is drunk or not. You should have called me. You can't reason with drunkards." He explained.

"Well, I know that now. It just happened so quickly. I'm sorry." I said sadly.

"I am not mad at you. I was just so scared. When the alarm went off, I feared the worst. When I got here and saw him all over you, I just went ballistic. I have never felt such rage towards anyone before. I could have killed him and not think twice about it." He admitted still trying to control his anger.

"I'm sorry you had to see that, I really did try not to press the alarm." I said apologetically.

"No, I want you to use this alarm. That is what it is there for. I just wished you had pressed it earlier. What if it was a hunter? It took me 18 seconds to get to you but in that time a hunter could have killed you." He said pain stricken.

"Corin, I knew who he was. I promise you, I would have set the alarm off if it was a hunter. How did you know it only took 18 seconds?" I asked trying to assure him.

"When I disarmed it, it shows the response time." He explained calmly. He was conflicted with whether he wanted to continue arguing with me or not. Frustrated he stared down at me. "Don't ever hesitate to use the alarm again. I don't care if it is a false alarm or not. I don't care if you know that person. If anyone is touching you in anyway that you did not agree to, you have to press this button. Do you understand?" I nodded. "Promise me." He demanded.

"I promise." I answered. I watched as he slowly let himself calm down.

When his body was less tense, I kissed him gently on the lips.

"Come." I lured him. I entwined our hands and pulled him to bed with me. "Just hold me. Let them deal with him. I just want you to hold me." I said.

He repositioned me on top of him and held me tightly. We lay there quietly.

We could hear when Leah came home. We heard her crying and yelling at her brother but we could not make out her exact words. The only voice we could make out was Justin's. He was directing Kyle's care. Rachel was helping Kyle with his injuries. Mark was trying to comfort Leah but she was hysterical over her brother's actions. We heard many hurtful things hurled at Kyle but he was probably not conscious enough to understand them. Cory and Michael offered to take him to their place and sober him up. After a long time, we heard them leave. Mark and Leah were still talking. Mark tried to assure her that I was okay but she wanted to see for herself. Mark was finally able to persuade her to wait until morning. We heard them cleaning up the living. When things went silent, we looked at each other.

"I want to take a bath." I whispered.

"Okay, can I wash you?" he asked tenderly.

"I want you to." I replied warmly.

He got up and walked over to the bathroom and started the water. He came back and helped me with my torn shirt and jeans. When I was completely naked, he picked me up and gently carried me into the bathroom. He smoothly placed me into the water. He gently pulled my face to him and lovingly kissed me.

"Lay back and relax." He instructed. He dotingly washed my back and shoulder, caressing each area with his lips.

"Corin, I don't want anyone to know about what happened tonight." I asked quietly.

"Why?" he asked softly.

"I am just thinking about Leah. I want her to stay here with Mark. If this gets out, I think she would feel really uncomfortable here." I explained calmly.

"I understand but she will have to understand that he is never allowed in this house. I will not tolerate him being alone with you and if I ever catch him drinking in Inuvik, I will personally take him back to Prudhoe Bay. And if he ever touch you again, I will kill him." He vowed.

"I will agree to that. Personally, if it wasn't for Leah, he can go to hell for all I care." I spited.

"I will be glad to send him there, all you have to do is ask." He affirmed.

"I am done." I said. I quickly stood up and allowed him full view of my body. He looked at me slowly and smiled. He assisted me out of the tub. He went and got my towel from the opposite end of the bathroom. He sat down on the vanity chair and stared back at me.

"You are beautiful." He said lovingly. "I love you, Gena."

Easily, without any conscious effort, I repeated "I love you, Corin, always."

Chapter Twenty-Six

I woke up earlier than usual because of what happened last night. I wasn't sure what to do with Kyle. A part of me wanted to kill him but the other part only wanted to disable him for life. I knew if I saw him again, it would be too soon and I would end up killing him. I tried many times to erase the memory of seeing her assaulted by that monster, but each time I closed my eyes it haunted me.

I can remember sitting at the poker table with the guys when the alarm went off. I sped off in my car with Mark barely inside, when I got to the door; I heard her screaming for me. If the door wasn't so well made, I was sure it would have been ripped off its hinges. The sight of her held against the wall and him molesting her body, sent waves of rage and hatred through me. I was numb with anger. Beating him did not satisfy me, I wanted to kill him. I wanted to hit him hard enough to destroy every cell in his being. When they pulled me away, I still could not think or see straight. The only thing that kept me sane was her. Knowing she was safe, allowed my numb body to feel again.

The incident last night was my first glimpse at the fear of losing her. In the 18 seconds it took to get to her, I was engulfed in fear. The visions of losing her crushed me and destroyed my sanity. When I heard her scream, I was a little relieved that she was still alive. The brief respite was quickly destroyed when I saw him on her body. The rage and hatred that came afterwards was not from the thought of losing her but from a man seeing the love of his life being raped by another man. No words can describe that feeling. Stupid as this may sound, I was thankful that it was Kyle not a hunter. Though it did not give me much comfort to think that, it stopped me from killing him.

I quietly got up and called Justin, I wanted to get to him before he told everyone about what happened last night. I was very thankful for his assistance last night but if we wanted to keep the incident a secret we had to start with Justin. After I explained Gena's request to him, he agreed that it was the best thing to do until Kyle could apologize. Surprisingly, he had already talked to Cory and Michael about not talking about what happened. I think Rachel may have played apart in his decision. The only other person that was let in on what happened was Alain. They had to wake him up to treat Kyle. Justin boasted that Kyle had 18 stitches across his left eye, he also has a broken jaw, two cracks in his left orbital bone, his nose was broken in three different places, he lost four teeth (only three were found, he might have swallowed the fourth) and he would not be able to use his lips for at least two months. He joked about Kyle being fed by a straw. When I was tired of his ranting, I cut him off and thanked him for last night. After I got off the phone with him, I eased myself back in bed next to her. I wanted to get some more sleep before we had to deal with Leah this morning. I knew Gena would be dreading it more than anything but Leah's guilt and remorse would be far worse.

It was well after 9:00 when I felt her getting out of bed. She thought I was still asleep. I watched her rubbing her wrist.

"Is the bracelet bothering you?" I said quietly trying not to startle her.

"It's nothing. I didn't mean to wake you." She replied.

"Let me see." I requested politely.

"Corin, really it's nothing. I'm going to take a shower." She responded slyly.

I quickly reached for her. She fought to keep her wrist from me. "Corin, don't get mad." she pleaded.

Both her wrists were red and excoriated. Her forearms were covered in bruises. I felt the heat of anger rising in me. How did I miss this last night? "You said he didn't hurt you." I grit under my breath.

"I bruise easily, Corin. Please don't get upset." She reassured me.

"What else are you hiding from me?" I accused. I was angry at myself. Last night I was more concerned with the possibility of her being sexually assaulted, I never thought of the possibility of him physically hurting her. Did he hit her? Nothing could stop me from killing him if he did.

"I am not hiding anything from you." She said angrily.

"Did he hit you?" I growled. I found myself out of bed standing over her. I was looking at her intently looking for signs of abuse. There were no signs of injury to her face.

"He did not hit me." She said quietly but I could tell she was hiding something from me. She was looking downward avoiding my eyes.

"What? Gena tell me or I will check you myself." I warned.

"He bit me." She murmured embarrassed.

"Where?" I said disturbed by her admission.

She unbuttoned her shirt and revealed a bruised bite mark over her left breast. I studied it intently trying to keep my composure. I inspected the mark carefully with my fingers. "Does it hurt?" I said sadly.

"No, I can feel it but it doesn't hurt." She admitted quietly.

"I'm so sorry that this happened to you. Are you really alright? Do you want to talk about it?" I comforted her.

"Corin, this is not your fault. I am very thankful that you got to me in time. The last thing I want to do is talk about it, which I know I will be doing soon with Leah anyway. Please let's just drop it. The only thing I want right now is breakfast and a shower." She concluded.

"Okay. I'll get started on your breakfast." I promised. I watched her walk to the bathroom. She was so forgiving and kind. I wanted so badly for her to give me permission to go pound Kyle some more but I knew she would not want that. She has had so many horrible tragedies in her life and now this; yet she was still kind and forgiving.

I quickly changed and went downstairs. When I got to the end of the stairs I saw Leah's luggages next to the door. I went into the kitchen and found Mark and Leah sitting quietly at the kitchen counter bar.

"Corin, I am so sorry." Leah said tearfully. Mark was holding her.

"Leah, this is not your fault. You can't be responsible for your brother's actions." I assured her warmly.

"I am the reason he came here." She cried.

"That doesn't make you responsible for what happened." Mark interjected.

"How is Gena?" she asked tearfully.

"She would be more upset if you leave." I declared.

"I can't stay here. I feel so bad." She exclaimed.

"She has grown very fond of you. It would upset her to know that you are in Prudhoe Bay because of this. I am sure you wouldn't want to carry that guilt around." I acknowledged.

"I just can't believe he would do that. Why would he do that to her? He has never had any problem with women." She bawled.

"Well, when he has sobered up we will ask him." Mark added.

"Leah, please don't upset Gena by leaving. She does not blame you. I am asking you to not upset her today." I said firmly.

"What about you?" she said sadly.

"What happened is between me and Kyle. I will not kill him if that is what you're asking. Now please don't let her see your luggages." I directed.

"Okay, I won't upset her." She said tearfully.

"I'll go put up your luggages." Mark remarked.

"No, I want to do it." She stopped him. We watched her leave the kitchen still crying.

"Corin how's Gena?" he asked.

"Surprisingly, she is better than Leah." I commented.

"She feels really bad. I am really sorry man. I didn't know he was like that." He said remorsefully.

"I don't think she did either." I added.

"So, what do you want to do with him?" he asked.

"What I really want to do to him would really upset Gena and Leah. I talked to Justin this morning. Alain saw him last night. Let's just let him sober up than we'll deal with him later." I instructed as I fried some eggs.

"Man, I thought you were going to kill him last night. Hey, I don't blame you. I would probably do the same thing if it was Leah. When I saw you toss him across the living room, I was shocked. You were crazy." He whispered.

"Man, I can't tell you how much I wanted to kill him. What the hell was he thinking?" I questioned angrily.

"He was too drunk to think but I bet he is wondering how he got his face rearranged this morning." He laughed.

"Justin said he will have to eat thru a straw for at least a month." I chuckled.

"Good, I hope Alain didn't give him any pain medications. He doesn't deserve any." He added.

"Hey, Gena doesn't want anyone to know. She doesn't want to alienate Leah with the clan. I talked to Justin this morning. He agrees to not tell anyone. So only you, Leah, Cory, Michael, Alain, and Rachel knows about this incident and no one else, agree?" I instructed.

"Thanks, Corin. That would make Leah feel much better. I dreaded going back to Prudhoe Bay this morning." He admitted.

"Hey, I think Gena was thinking about that too. She has a funny way of dealing with tragedies. All she wants from Kyle is an apology." I confessed.

"She is a good person. She makes everyone around her good. I am glad you have her." He complimented.

"I totally agree." I concurred.

"So how are you going to explain why we have a disfigured person in Alain house?" He posed.

"Well, if anyone asks we will just say he got into a brawl at a bar in Prudhoe Bay and got his ass handed to him. Leah just brought him here so she could care for him." I explained.

"Well that is going to be a problem, since Leah refuses to see him." He pointed out.

"We'll just say she is mad at him for having a drinking problem." I suggested. I looked at my watch. It's been an hour and Gena hasn't come down yet.

"That will work. Are you expecting something?" he asked.

"Gena doesn't normally take this long to shower. Maybe I should go check on her." I wondered.

"Women always take a long time to get ready. Leah takes in one hour just to decide what to wear." He disclosed.

"Gena can shower and dress in less than twenty minutes." I bragged.

"Really? She is full of surprises." He declared.

I left him in the kitchen and carried a plate of toast and eggs upstairs. When I got to our bedroom door, I could hear Leah and Gena talking. I turned and went back downstairs. Looking at the living room for the first time since last night, I noticed that the coffee table and one of the end tables were missing. Along with an apology, I will make sure Kyle pays for this. I went back into the kitchen.

"She rejected your cooking?" he chuckled.

"No, Leah is in there talking to her." I informed.

"Oh, you are better off down here. She was crying all night long. I was completely helpless. How did you deal with it last night?" He divulged.

"Gena was more worried about me. Even this morning she was trying to cover up the bruises on her arm to not upset me." I declared.

"Did he hit her?" he asked shockingly.

"She denies it." I answered.

"Man, now I want to kill him." He confessed.

"Leah would probably be really upset with you." I concurred.

"You're pretty sane about this." He noted.

"She keeps me sane." I revealed.

I decided to keep her breakfast warm in the oven until she was finished with Leah. Mark and I went into the living room to look over any damages. When it was closer to 1pm, I decided I had to intervene. I knew she was just too polite to stop Leah's tearful ranting but I did not want her to miss any meals. I went upstairs and walked into our bedroom with an egg sandwich and a glass of orange juice. They both looked at me.

"Gena, I brought you something to eat." I mentioned.

"Oh, Gena, I'm sorry. God, I am just so stupid today." Leah abhorred by her absent mindedness.

"Leah, it is alright. Corin has this obsession with three meals a day." She said sympathetically.

"Well, it's almost one, so you've already missing one meal." I pointed out.

"Leah, maybe you should get some sleep. You didn't get any last night." Mark revealed from the door.

"That is a good idea." I agreed.

Leah left with Mark. I handed Gena her breakfast and sat down next to her. "Thanks for saving me. She just could not understand that it was not her fault." She indicated as she started on the egg sandwich.

"I think this is the first time I have ever seen you hungry." I smiled.

"Comforting someone takes a lot of energy." She said as she finished the sandwich and sipped on the orange juice.

"I think you've helped Leah a lot. She was a mess this morning." I commented.

"I don't want to talk about it anymore. I have more important things to think about today." She indicated.

"What?" I asked.

"We need to talk to Justin before he starts blabbing his mouth." She reminded.

"Baby, I took care of that at 6am this morning." I boasted.

"Darn, I thought I woke up before you did for once." She said disappointed.

"Nope, I beat you again." I jested.

"Thank you, now I have to find something else to wear for the dinner. I don't want anyone asking me about the bruises. Oh and Leah have not seen these, so don't say anything." She instructed.

"Well, I can give you my opinion if you put on a show." I teased.

"Well I only have four dresses that have long sleeves so it shouldn't take to long. You have to be really honest okay?" she warned as she went into the dressing room.

She finally came out wearing a black fitted jersey dress. The sleeves were long enough to cover the bruises but the scoop neck line showed the bruise on her breast. I pointed to her breast. Flustered she went back into the dressing room closet. After some time, she came back out wearing a cream cashmere turtleneck sweater dress that hugged every bit of her curve. The hem was higher than the other dresses but right now I did not mind. The dress had a thin gold chain that wrapped around the hip. The cream color accentuated her skin tone and brown hair.

"I think my favorite color on you is crème." I confessed.

"This was the only one that covered everything. Is it alright?" she questioned.

"You look absolutely stunning. I am having a hard time controlling myself." I admitted.

"You are bias. I just wish it wasn't so short." She said tugging at the hem.

"That dress looks really good on you. I want you to wear that one." I said eyeing her lustfully. I walked over and played with the chain on her hips.

"Well, than it's settled. Thank you for your input." She said playfully as she wrapped her arms around my neck.

"Well, let's take it off so we don't wrinkle it." I teased as I nuzzled on her ear.

"Corin, it is cashmere, I don't think I have to worry about wrinkling it." She pointed out. "But this chain is very delicate, we don't' want to accidently break it."

"You are absolutely right. Let me help you." I murmured into her hair as my hands slowly pulled the hem up over her hips.

"No, Corin let me do it. You'll probably rip something." She said walking back into the dressing room.

I followed her into the closet and watched as she slowly eased the dress down and stepped out of it. She was wearing a white lace bra with matching panty. She turned and indicated with her finger for me to come into the room. Mesmerized by her beauty, I felt like I glided toward her.

"You look so peaceful right now." She whispered.

"If I die right now, I would die a happy satisfy man." I declared.

"Don't die on me. I am still waiting on many things from you." She implied.

"Are you talking about the magical proposal?" I questioned.

"Yes and the phenomenal love making." She said boldly.

"Those two things I can deliver. I promise." I vowed.

"I am holding you to it. Don't' disappoint me." She warned.

"I would never disappoint you baby." I promised.

We left our room and went downstairs. I pointed out the missing pieces of furniture. She wasn't too distraught over the lost of the furniture. I went into the kitchen and grabbed the first aid kit. She patiently let me treat her wrist. She caressed the abrasions on my right knuckles.

"Does that hurt?" she asked quietly.

"No, it will disappear soon." I replied.

"I was a little scared seeing you beat him. I can't imagine if you wanted to kill someone." She admitted secretly.

"I did want to kill him. But I was stopped." I confessed.

"Where is he now?" she asked.

"He is staying at Alain's house. Cory and Michael will keep an eye on him. We will tell anyone who asks that he was beaten up at some bar in Prudhoe Bay and Leah brought him here to care for him." I instructed.

"How long will he be there?" she asked.

"Well, he has a lot of facial issues. Two months?" I said unsympathetically.

"Facial issues, you mean damages." She corrected.

"Yeah" I confirmed.

"Well what about my lab?" she questioned.

"Well, if you have to go than I will go with you." I said openly.

"Are you alright with that?" she questioned.

"As long as he behaves, I don't have any reason to hurt him." I declared.

Justin and Rachel came over around 5pm. Mark and Leah was still napping. I went over the story with Justin and Rachel. They agreed to the plan. Rachel could not believe what Kyle had done. She remembers him being rowdy in Colorado but never criminal. Justin boastfully described Kyle's injuries until it became obnoxious. Rachel brought over the shoes for Leah. I was glad when they finally left at 6pm.

We woke Mark and Leah up to remind them of the dinner. Gena and I went into the kitchen and snacked on the left-over palmiers. When we were done, we went upstairs and got dressed. We took our time, unlike Leah and Mark they were scrambling around looking for this and that.

"You look absolutely stunning." I complimented her as she came out of the dressing room. She wore the necklace over the fold of the neckline. Her hair was worn down in its natural wave.

"Thank you." She replied coming closer to me.

"Lip gloss, huh? What's the special occasion?" I playfully teased.

"Just something different" She pointed out.

"Too bad, I'll just kiss it off you." I teased.

"I can always reapply or you can be kind and avoid my lips." She said playfully.

"Sorry, baby. I can never avoid these beautiful luscious lips." I confessed as I nibble at her lips.

"Well there goes my only attempt to look good." She surrendered.

"You're kidding right? You're the only woman here that can wake up looking beautiful without any conscious effort. Do you know how many women would love to be able to do that?" I declared.

"Speaking about women, I found out last night that you had some admirers before I came." She taunted.

"Mute point now." I replied nonchalantly.

"Just thought I let you know how attractive you are to other women beside myself." She added.

"Your attraction is the only one that matters." I said confidently. "This lip gloss makes you lips look sultry."

"Sultry, huh?" she fished.

"Yes and tempting" I breathed. Our face was so close; I could taste the lip gloss. Her breathe was warm and inviting.

"Can we be late for this dinner?" she said breathlessly.

"Yes, but it will really be embarrassing to walk in late." Our lips caressed with every word.

"People will spread rumors." She played along licking her lips.

"My reputation will be tarnished." I teased nudging her lips apart.

"Your reputation? How about mine" She laughed. Her laughter was music to my ears.

"I was a good boy until you bewitched me." I jested.

"I am sure you were the perfect role model. Come we have to go. We can't let Mark and Leah beat us there." She challenged.

When we got to North Chateau, we were greeted by Alain. He was obviously concerned with Gena.

"I know you want this kept a secret but I just want to know how you are doing?" he whispered.

"I am fine Alain. Corin got there just in time." She assured him.

"Corin, thank you so much. I don't know what we would've done if you didn't get to her in time. His alcohol level was 4 times the normal. He wouldn't have stopped. I've got him heavily sedated right now, but even that is too good for him. You did a number on his face." He boldly complimented.

"Thanks for holding him there. We don't know what to do with him yet but your house is the safest place." I thanked.

"Glad to do it. Gena if you need anything don't hesitate." He rushed off when he saw Lauren and Aimee making their way over.

"Gena, you look great. What happened to the blue dress?" Aimee commented.

"I wanted her to wear this one because this dress showed more of her legs." I teased.

"Well, she looks good anyway." Lauren added.

"It is warmer and the stilettos with the blue dress gave me the creeps." Gena confessed.

"You have to wear them to get used to them." Lauren advised.

"Maybe when there is no show and ice. You can wear it with your bikinis in the summer." Aimee mocked.

"That sounds good to me." I flirted. Taking her hand and escorting her inside.

This was the first Thanksgiving Dinner that William Burren did not reside over. It was seen as a changing of leadership in this clan. Everyone understood that Rolfe was reluctant to take on this role since the death of his sister but it did not stop people from expecting it of him. We watched as he took the seat that once belonged to William Burren. It was expected of him to deliver a speech on the future of this clan but instead he thanked each and every member of the clan for their individual efforts to keep us united and strong. I was rather impressed with his words of wisdom. He wasn't William but he had his own style and ideas. He involved everyone in the care of this clan and that is something that can be interpreted as strength for a clan of this size. Of course there were some that would like for there to be only one person taking full responsibility for the safety and welfare of everyone but we were evolving and if we didn't adapt the future of our specie may not survive.

North Chateau was beautifully decorated with Thanksgiving décor. The large dining table was covered with beautiful plate setting and center pieces. The wives in this clan really put a lot of their personal touches in the care of this set-up. After Rolfe's speech, he announced Justin's engagement. Everyone was happy for Justin and Rachel. When the announcement was thoroughly appreciated, he focused in on the welcoming of the Quebec survivors. He paid tribute to those that died in the clan. He also made sure to include the welcoming of Leah and her brother. Deliberately he welcomed Gena last. During his address regarding Gena's arrival he became tearful and Alain had to continue. It was obvious that the death of Alexandria still weighed heavily on his shoulder. No one really knew what lead Alexandria and Daniel to leave the safety of the clan to birth their gifted child somewhere else but I was pretty sure the Rolfe would take that to his grave.

When the floor was yielded to those who want to express a specific thanks Leah stood up.

"I want to express a tremendous amount of thanks to destiny for saving Gena's life, bringing Trevor and Tina here, and guiding Mark to me. For years I have doubted the belief of a soul mate but tonight I sit here and get to witness the perfect union of so many miracles. Thank you." She delivered. Mark stood up and kissed her. He raised his glass and paid tribute to *destiny*. Everyone chimed in.

I watched as each person added their thanks. This year has been very kind to our clan. Many unions have form this year, guarantying the strength of our clan. Selfishly, I didn't care about any other union except for mine. Looking at Gena, I knew what I was thankful for. I was thankful for everything that brought her to me. No other person had to go through what she did to be here today. I reached under the table for her hand and entwined our fingers. She looked back at me and smiled. Without words, we knew what we were thankful for.

Chapter Twenty-Seven

After having a week off from school, getting back to the same routine was hard. Monday was especially hard. The week seemed much longer when Monday was long. Trevor was much more comfortable around Corin. I just hope he never find out what really happened to Kyle. Corin was giving Trevor advice on how to talk to girls. Evidently, Trevor has his eyes set on some girl in his Biochemistry class. During Calculus, Trevor talked more to Corin than to me, *his math partner*. In the beginning Corin tolerated Trevor on my behalf but lately he has been more than generous with his time. He even invited Trevor to sit with us during lunch. Having Corin in all my classes was nice but a bit distracting. Every time I look over at him he was staring at me. I would complain but it didn't affect his grade so why fix what wasn't broken. During French class, Corin wrote me love notes in French. We passed it back in forth, he said it was a good way of learning. After school, I met Corin's mother for lessons on how to make the Red Velvet cake. The cake part was fairly easy but the butter crème frosting was the tricky part.

"I am so happy that you decided to make his birthday cake. It just adds a personal touch when you make it yourself." She said warmly.

"Well, I just hope I don't ruin it." I responded.

"I think you'll do fine. Corin tells me you're a great cook." She complimented.

"Coming from Corin, I think he is a bit bias" I replied.

"My son rarely compliments my cooking. How long have you been cooking?" She revealed.

"At age 12, I started off with simple things when my mother got sick than when I went to go live with my uncle, he had a chef that taught me the basics."

"So you have pretty much been caring for yourself since 12." She reconfirmed.

"I guess you can say that."

"That must have been very hard on you." She acknowledged

"I learned to grow up pretty fast."

"You and Corin are very mature for your age. Did you know I knew your mother?" She pointed out.

"No, really" I said surprised

"She was a few years younger than I was but we still got along fine. You look a lot like her."

"I've been told that."

"You know, I introduced your parents."

"Really? You know my dad?"

"Edwin and Daniel were very good friends. Daniel and his family were from Great Britain. Upon one of his visits to Inuvik, we introduced him to Alexandria. Within a year, he moved his family here to be close to your mother. They were married as soon as she finished high school. He built her that house as a wedding present." She told.

"So the Roese family is from Great Britain? Do you know if he had any other family left in Great Britain?"

"Your father had a younger brother. I don't believe there is any family left in Great Britain. I think you are the last to carry his genes."

"That happens to me a lot." I said sadly

"Don't be sad Gena. I am a very happy mother. Destiny saved you for my son. If you had died than, Corin would live his life searching for a love that did not exist for him. That would break any mother's heart." She admitted.

"I am very happy but I just wished I gotten to know my parents. I don't understand why they left the safety of the clan to birth me somewhere else. Isn't it safer to be here?" I wondered.

"Gena, they left because they didn't want to jeopardize the clan. At that time, we had a lot of small children. You don't see that now because they have all grown up. They didn't want anyone to die for them. There was a big argument between Alexandria and your uncle Rolfe. I don't know exactly how things ended but Alexandria was stubborn and one night her and your dad left. There was a serious effort made to find them but by the time they were found it was too late. I don't think Rolfe ever forgave himself." She recalled.

"So how did the hunter find out about me?"

"It was actually our own stupid fault. When we found out about your gift, we spread the news among clans. We do that to help other clans and also to reinforce the strength of ours. A child with the healer aura was not just special to her clan but to our entire specie. Do you understand that?" she declared.

"So, what about now" I asked

"When you are completely transformed, you will have the abilities to protect yourself from eminent danger. Until then, we will not make the same mistake again. We will not share this information among other clans. Your safety is vital to us all. Right now, my son takes on the responsibility of protecting to you even at the risk of his own life." She declared.

"I don't want anything to happen to him." I said sadly. The thought of losing him and left behind to live without him tugged at my heart.

"He has love and strength on his side. I don't worry about him, so you shouldn't either. Now come let's finish this cake." She ended.

We worked quietly making a dozen Red Velvet cup cakes. When were done, she drove me home. I invited her in but she had other plans with Aunt Idelle and Aunt Madeline. I thanked her and went inside. When I entered the house I smelled chili. Leah had lived up to her word about cooking for us. I found Corin and Mark in the living going over some new equipment they brought.

"Hey babe, how was cooking with mom?" He asked as he got up and kissed me.

"It was nice. I brought you something. What are you guys doing?" I asked.

"We found out the TV was broken. So Mark got his TV from the storage unit and we are going to use it for the time being. We have to update the wiring system. Are these red velvet cup cakes?" He said as he took the cup cakes from me.

"Hey don't spoil your appetite." I scolded.

"I'll only have one." He claimed.

"Hey give me one too; I'm working hard over here." Mark yelled.

After they each took one, I took the rest to the kitchen. I found Leah working in the kitchen. "I smell chili. That is so nice on a cold day." I verbalized.

"I am also working on cornbread. You're recipe cards are so easy to follow. If this doesn't taste good, I am entirely to blame." She admitted blatantly.

"I am sure you did great. I have dessert so we make a great team." I claimed.

"Gena, I feel so at home here. Did Mark tell you, I have decided to stay here?" She said excited.

"That is great news. I love having you here."

"Well, Mark has already made plans to build a place for us. Rachel told me last night that she intends to stay with this clan. You guys have just inherited two more clansmen." She boasted.

"I am so happy for you guys. Are there wedding bells in your future?" I asked.

"He hasn't said anything but I am quite overwhelmed with everything, so I'm not even thinking about that right now." She divulged. I could tell it was bothering her even though she denied it.

"Knowing Mark, he is planning something really big and surprising. I would be prepared if I was you." I advised.

"I am taking things one day at a time." She declared as she placed the cornbread mixture into the oven.

"That is going to smell heavenly when it comes out. Thanks for cooking. Don't spoil me too much. I'm going to miss it when you move into your own place."

"I just hope it comes out alright." She said nervously.

"You are better than you think. You did a great job with the palmiers. Oh! Talking about palmiers, I have to get Aimee that recipe." I remembered.

"I guess Corin didn't tell you, Aimee and Tristan are coming over for dinner." She said.

"He was a little preoccupied with the cup cakes. My sweetheart has a sweet tooth. Well that's even better. She can go over the recipes she wants and we can help her get them on cards."

"I hear Justin's voice." She whispered.

"I don't doubt it. Your chili probably brought him here." I mocked as we both made our way into the living room.

"This house always smells so good. " Justin said loudly.

"We're having chili and cornbread tonight, do you care to join us." Mark asked.

"Careful Mark, once you invite Justin he will move in." Corin joked.

"I love chili. Do you have enough?" he asked me.

"Leah made it so you will have to ask her." I deferred.

"There is plenty, where is Rachel?" Leah asked.

"She is in the car talking to her parents about her plans to stay here. I am so damn happy about that. We should celebrate." He boasted.

"Well, we can start with dinner than have some of Gena's Red Velvet cup cakes for dessert. They are so good." Mark bragged.

"My stomach did not fail me; I knew this was the right place to be." He admitted.

"Guided by his stomach, only you would admit to something so crazy." Corin rolled his eyes.

Rachel came in with Tristan and Aimee. "Something smells so good." Tristan announced.

"Leah made chili and cornbread." Justin voiced.

"Gena, I promise once our place is built, I will return the favor and invite you guys over every night to make up for Justin's intrusions." Rachel vowed.

"Don't worry Rachel; I am keeping a running tab." Corin joked.

"Consider me the entertainment." Justin declared.

"We have a TV for that." Corin replied dryly.

"You got the new TV already? Even better, now I can come over for games and food." He said sarcastically to annoy Corin.

"No, Gena's TV died, so we had to put Mark's in temporarily until my present comes in. Maybe you can make yourself useful and help us install the surround sound system." Corin said.

"I will work for food." He boasted proudly.

During dinner the guys discussed the plots of land that Mark and Justin wanted to build their homes. Justin wanted the plot next to my house but Leah begged him for it. At the end, Mark and Leah's house will be built next to mine, than Justin and Rachel's will be next door and finally Tristan and Aimee's place next to theirs. There were two more plots before it reached around to Edwin Daniels house. There was some discussion on whether Uncle Rolfe would eventually move into my grandfather's house leaving his house to Preston. Justin did not want his dad's house—*it was too grandiose*—he said. The building of both houses would take a little over three months. The Inuvik townspeople needed the work and Edwin Daniel's work program really kept the community prosperous. Due to the close proximity, Corin wanted to check every contract worker out for himself.

"Leah, that was unbelievable. The cornbread was so moist." Rachel complimented.

"It was Gena's recipes. I only follow instructions." She said modestly.

"Speaking of recipes, I want to go over you collection tonight." Aimee stated.

"So, Rachel how did your parents take it" Tristan asked.

"They were pretty disappointed because they thought Justin would make a great fit in Colorado but I told them it would be easier for me to adjust here than Justin to go somewhere else. He can't get free entertainment and food in Colorado like he does here. Really, I told them I liked it here and when we eventually have children, they would be safer here. They understood. My brother Mitch and my sister Elizabeth will escort them here for the wedding." She teased.

"Maybe they can move here." I suggested.

"I don't think that is possible, their clan is small enough as is." Justin replied.

"Yeah, it's hard seeing everyone move away but Colorado takes some getting use to." Rachel pointed out.

"So when is the big day?" I asked making a point to bring up the subject in front of Mark.

"I really like the idea of having a Christmas wedding. Madeline said she could pull that off, so we are looking at December 25th which is a little over two months away. I am so excited. After seeing what they did to North Chateau, I can't wait to see what they can do for a wedding." She exclaimed.

"They are very good. I think they are meeting today because Diane told me she had plans with Aunt Idelle and Madeline." I informed.

"When those three get together, big things are going to happen." Justin warned.

"I just hope they are available when it comes to mine and Leah's wedding." I said nonchalantly. I knew I was putting Leah on the spot but I didn't know how else to continue this conversation.

"My mother lives for this stuff. She would probably take over and you wouldn't be allowed any decisions." Mark teased Leah.

"Have you proposed, Mark?" I asked looking directly at him.

"Of course, I asked her the first day we met, remember?" he reminded.

"I thought you were kidding." Leah chuckled.

"So, Mark you're planning all this stuff and Leah hasn't even accepted. Priceless. Leah I would turn him down just to see what he would do." Justin poked.

"Gena hasn't accepted mine either." Corin admitted.

"It is because he hasn't done it right." I chided.

"Maybe I should teach you Randall boys how to do this." Justin boasted.

"No thanks Justin, I'll get my yes." Corin vowed.

"I'll get mine too." Mark winked at Leah. Leah looked at me and smiled.

"I had it so easy. Aimee wrote me a love letter when she was 10. I checked the yes box and everything was settled. I still have that letter as a contract." Tristan bragged.

"That is just so cute." Leah gushed.

We ended the meal with the cupcakes. Justin and Corin took the two extra. The guys spent the rest of the evening working on the entertainment system. We stayed in the dining room going over the recipes. Eventually I left them and went to my bedroom to get started on my homework. Corin came in while I was working on my Calculus homework.

"Need any help?" he asked.

"No, I'm almost done. Did you do your homework already?" I asked.

"Yes, while you were learning to make desserts. Thanks for the cup cakes. That was very nice." He massaged my shoulders.

"You're welcome. Are they all gone?" I asked.

"No, Justin and Rachel are still here. They're watching a game." He answered as he pulled my shirt sleeve up to inspect my arms.

"It's fine." I quickly reassured him. The abrasions on his knuckles were already gone.

"Justin said that Kyle has been asking for his sister. Maybe you should convince her to go see him." He suggested.

"Why me" I questioned.

"Well, you brilliantly brought up her proposal without making it obvious that she wasn't properly proposed to, so I just thought you could sneak in another ploy." He teased.

"You got that, huh? She told me she wasn't proposed to." I confessed.

"Mark can be absent minded some times. He needs a little help every once in a while." He admitted.

"We may have two weddings to look forward to." I said.

"I only look forward to one." He smiled before kissing me.

By Wednesday, school became a routine again. We had several huge English Literature interpretations due so Corin spent most of his time on the computer. I had most of these interpretations done from being in Advance Placement English back in Indiana. Today, I got Diane to drop me off at Blaine's house. I signed for Corin car. Dana and I took it for a ride around the block. It was really smooth. It was silver with black leather interior. It looked just like Corin's older model but this one was loaded with all kinds of toys. Blaine did a really great job of getting exactly what I wanted. After we returned the car back into the garage, Dana asked Will to place the big plastic bow back over the car.

"The key for this car is so big." I complained.

"Yeah, I think it has something to do with the computer chip inside. All Audi keys are like that." She pointed out.

"You can take someone's eye out with this thing." I claimed.

"Just so long as you don't leave it in their eye. It cost two grand to replace these things." She warned.

"Really, well I guess I will have to use something else." I said. Consciously I shoved both keys deep inside my pocket. I had planned to place the keys on top of his birthday cake but it just didn't feel so safe now.

"Gena, did you hear about Leah's brother. He is staying at Alain's house because he had gotten into some brawl in a bar. Derek said he was pretty messed up." She gossiped as we got into her car.

"I heard something like that. How is he doing?" I lied.

"Well, he is asking for Leah but she is so mad at him. Evidently he has a drinking problem. He probably does drugs too." She rumored.

"Well I don't blame her for being mad at him. This is probably really embarrassing for her." I hinted.

"I know but he is the only family she has. They need to work this out. Has she said anything to you?" She milked.

"No, I think she will eventually see him. She is really not a mean person. It just takes some time." I concurred as we pulled up the driveway.

"Well, do you want me to go with you on Friday to North's." she asked as I was getting out of the car.

"Only if you want to, Leah and Aimee are already planning to go with me." I informed.

"Okay, I'll see what Derek is doing Friday and let you know." She planned.

I entered the house to find Mark and Leah arguing over Kyle. Corin was standing in the kitchen doorway.

"I can't forgive him for what he did." Leah yelled tearfully.

"Leah, he is the only family you have left. I don't condone what he did to Gena, but he has a problem. He is going to need her to heal." Mark explained.

"What is going on?" I asked cautiously. I watched as Corin came over to my side and Mark and Leah turned to look at me.

"Kyle is asking to see you and Leah." Corin responded coldly.

"He wants to apologize to you. But Gena, I can not forgive him for what he did to you." Leah said tearfully.

"I didn't know he was awake, what did he say?" I asked.

"He was drunk and he had also being doing drugs." Mark said.

"I know that, what else?" I was irritated.

"He is not healing like he should." Mark said slyly.

"What did Alain say?" I anxiously guessed.

"His body is going through withdraw and it is interfering with his healing." Corin said coldly

"What does Alain want me to do?" I said quietly.

"Gena, you don't have to heal him. He deserves to suffer longer." Leah said.

"Leah, I was given the gift to heal. It would be unethical for me to choose who I want to help and who I will not. You however can choose to forgive him or not but like Mark said he is your only family. You should at least help him through this crisis. When he is completely healed, you can discuss how he can either be a part of your future or not." I explained softly.

"I know you're right but are you sure you can handle this right now?" Leah asked.

"Leah, I am fine. Trust me; I've been through worse pain than physical pain." I assured them.

"I will go with you. I don't want you alone for one second with him." Corin offered coldly.

"Are you okay with this?" Mark asked him.

"As long as he behaves, I will not hurt him." He repeated.

"I'll call Alain." Mark said as he got on the phone.

"Gena, why did Dana drive you home?" Corin asked.

"She offered and I accepted. Why?" I responded slyly.

"Right now, Gena I want to know where you are and who you're with at all times." He directed.

"Corin, I was with Dana." I defended

"Gena, you promised to be cautious. Any changes please, I need to know." He said frustrated.

Angrily I walked off and headed for the kitchen. I knew he followed after me but I did not say a word to him until we got into the kitchen.

"Gena" He called out softly as he reached for me. "I know I can be over bearing but please I only want to protect you."

"Corin, you are worrying yourself to death. Trust me to know the difference between a hunter and Dana." I explained.

"I'm sorry. It is just that I fear losing you more than anything." He confessed as he buried his face in my hair.

"Corin, I am not going anywhere. If you continue to be like this for the next two years, you are going to age horribly. I can't be seen with some old guy who everyone will think is my grandfather." I teased. I felt him chuckling against my neck.

"I'm sorry. I will try to not be so possessive. Are you saying if I grow old and ugly you wouldn't want me anymore?" he jested.

"I will always want you, and sometimes your possessiveness is nice." I whispered against his lips. He lowered his lips to mine. He buried his hands into my hair and hungrily crushed our lips together.

"Ahem, Alain said we can come over right now." Mark announced and walked off.

"Three months until he gets his own place. I would pay to have them work overtime." He murmured against my lips.

"We can pick this up later." I lingered against him.

"Promise" He vowed with a quick kiss.

Alain met us at the door when we pulled up."Gena, are you sure you want to do this now?" he asked.

"I am fine about this." I was rather annoyed with everyone challenging me.

"Leah, hold off on talking with him until Gena is done. He probably won't be able to comprehend anything anyway. Come lets get started." He ushered us into the house and up to the guest room.

Judith was trying to give Kyle some water while Cory was holding him still. He was shaking and trembling so violently that he choked up the water and was gagging. Leah immediately ran over to her brother and helped him. His face was covered in bandages. When he finally stopped gagging, Alain indicated for me to come closer. Corin was a bit hesitant since Kyle was still shaking and Cory was holding him down.

"Alain, shouldn't we tie him down?" Corin asked worried.

"The tremors and spasms are from his withdrawal. His body is starving for the drugs right now. Why don't you take over Cory's place? Gena, you come over here and hold his hands." He instructed.

"Why does she have to hold his hands?" Corin hissed under his breath.

"Corin, maybe you should step outside." Judith suggested.

"No, if she has to be near him, I will be with her." He said firmly.

"Okay, let's get started. Corin hold him down. Gena you come over here." Alain instructed.

Cory slowly released his grip on Kyle's right shoulder and arm while Corin got into the same position. When it was safe, Alain moved out of the way and I sat down next to Kyle's bed. I reached out cautiously and took his left hand. His grip was weak and sweaty. I did not look at him but I could feel his eyes on me. After some time I could feel my hands sweating. The shaking and tremor became less and less, as his grip became tighter and more intimate. Corin watched uncomfortably. At some point our fingers entwined as his body became ridged and tense. I could feel the heat and nausea coming over me. I closed my eyes and took deep breaths to calm the waves of nausea. The bitter taste in my mouth became nasty, I was afraid to swallow. I could feel heat throughout my body. I kept my eyes closed and let the warmth take over. I could feel the perspiration around the bridge of my nose and over my upper lip. The heat was almost unbearable; breathing in the hot air was difficult. Then there were the flickering of light and images. I don't remember experiencing this before. There was also a faint sound of voices. The sound became clearer and clearer. It wasn't a sound but one voice. That voice was familiar but distance. I concentrated on the voice, than I heard it.

Gabriella

Gabriella

Gabriella

With a lot of concentration, the flickers became clearer images. I heard Kyle's voice calling out for Gabriella. The images were of a young girl with long wavy brown hair. I couldn't see her face clearly but she looked familiar. With every flicker, I felt a tug at my heart. Then I felt an enormous void or lost. She was gone. The ache that was left behind was unbearable. I took a deep breath but the air didn't satisfy my lungs. When I opened my eyes, I immediately felt eyes on me. Leah was staring into my face. "Leah, who is Gabriella?" I stuttered.

"Your eyes are red." She uttered stunned by my appearance.

"Leah, Gena asked you a question." Corin tapped her on the shoulder.

"What was that?" she reoriented herself.

"Who is Gabriella?" I repeated.

"I don't know any Gabriella." She replied dumbfounded.

"Are you sure? She had long brown hair. I think something bad happened to her." I tried to focus on the bits of information I could see.

"Well I think there was a Gabriella from the International Falls, Minnesota clan. I didn't really know her but she was killed during the attack. Why?" she asked curiously.

"Was she Kyle's soul mate?" I said sure of myself.

"What?" I heard from several voices. The waves of nausea and heat came over me again. I had to brace myself and took some deep breaths.

"Gena, are you alright?" Corin worried.

"It's just the nausea. It is really hot in here." I whispered through the nausea. Judith handed me a cold wet towel. I washed my face but the heat immediately dried the wetness. I finally noticed that Kyle was no longer trembling or shaking. His body looked more relaxed and subdued. "I've got to stop." I whispered.

Corin immediately jumped up and came to my side. He pulled Kyle grip from my hand and assisted me to the far end of the room. Leah stayed at her brother's side.

"Corin get her outside, she'll recover faster." Alain instructed.

He assisted me to the hallway and continued to wipe my face with the wet cloth. The nausea and heat immediately dissipated. I knew exactly when my eyes went back to normal. Michael was standing next to Corin when I was finally able to talk without the nausea.

"What?" I asked.

"That is just so wild. Your eyes are unbelievable." Michael said in awe.

"Well, I'm glad I could entertain you Michael." I replied dryly.

"I still can't watch you do this without wondering if it is hurting you. You looked really uncomfortable in there." Corin expressed with worry.

"It is just the nausea and the heat. It is like being nauseated in the middle of a hot summer day with humidity of 100 degrees." I described.

"That has got to be torture." Michael said with disgust.

"Just unbearable for a while. I had to stop. Do you think that was enough to help him?" I reassured.

"I'll go ask Alain, if not than he will just have to suffer. I don't want you to do that again tonight." Corin said as he went back in the room.

Moments later Corin and Alain came out. "Gena, his vital signs are perfectly normal. His aura should heal him from now on. It was different this time, wasn't it?' Alain asked.

"Yeah, I could see images and voices. It was like I was in his head. I could feel his pain. He lost his soul mate I am sure of it. The void and lost was unbelievable. Her name is Gabriella. She looked like she was maybe 14 or 15 years old. She had long wavy brown hair. I could actually feel his pain." I explained.

"Well, we will have to ask him when he comes to. You should go home and get some rest. It is probably better if you take Leah too. I don't expect him to come to tonight." Alain suggested.

It was close to seven, when we got home. I was utterly exhausted. All I wanted to do was sleep.

"Baby, I'll bring you something to eat. Go take a shower." Corin instructed.

I didn't want to eat but I wasn't about to argue with him either. The shower was refreshing. It washed away all the sticky sweat that covered me. When I came out, he was there with a tray of food.

"Leah roasted a chicken. I think she said it was your lemon herb butter chicken and some steamed green beans. I also got you some creamy mashed potatoes. Come eat with me." He invited.

"It looks nice." I said warmly. He fed me the chicken and mashed potatoes. Afterwards, he tucked me in and left. I fell asleep immediately.

For the first time, since we've been together, I woke up before he did. It was a little after five. He was sleeping like a baby. I can see why he likes to watch me sleep; he was adorable. His face was relaxed and calm. He was more handsome than when awake. No, handsome was not enough, he was gorgeous. His lips were full with a slight pout when he sleeps. I lightly touched his stubbed chin. It was nice to see him unshaven and coarse. His chest was muscular and wide. I remember thinking the same think when we first met. I followed the small line of hair that trailed down his muscular abdomen to his navel. Slowly I eased myself over him and placed my lips on his abdomen. I felt him stir but he did not wake. I kissed a path downward until I reached his pants. "I like this dream." He uttered in a throaty voice.

"Good morning." I greeted him from below.

"You don't know how good it is." He said sleepily.

"I beat you this morning." I contended.

"If this is second place, I forfeit every time." He surrendered.

"Go back to sleep, I just have to do some homework." I instructed as I got out of bed.

"You're kidding right? How can I go back to sleep after that?" he exclaimed.

"Sorry, I couldn't help myself. I really tried to behave this morning but you're awful tempting when you are asleep." I said as I made my way into the bathroom.

When I came out of the bathroom, he was not in bed. I went downstairs and found him in the kitchen. My school books were laid out on the kitchen bar counter and a plate of eggs and toast. I smiled at him. "Is this my reward?" I teased.

"No, I hate to stay in bed without you. I put your homework out. If you're not up to it, you can copy mine. I just didn't know if you want to do that or not. Come eat." He admitted.

"Thank you, but I take pride in my own work. Anyway I can't have you spreading rumors about me cheating off you." I teased. I started on my homework as he ate next to me. Every few minutes he would feed me some eggs or toast.

When we got to school, everyone was talking about Kyle's recovery. Michael and Max had a different respect for me now. Corin and I spent lunch time explaining what happened last night. We did not talk about Gabriella but we talked about his recovery. When school ended, we met Mark and Leah at Alain's house. I did not check on Kyle, but instead I went to the lab. Corin stayed upstairs with Mark and Leah. I had to donate some of my own blood for research. I brought down a glass of orange juice and placed it next to the "phlebotomy" chair. After I pierced my arm vein with the donor needle, I released the clamp to allow the flow of blood into the bag. When the bag was full, I pulled the needle out and held pressure. I drank the orange juice and placed the bag into the refrigerator. I was glad that was over with, I had been dreading it.

Corin and I left and went back home. It was nice to have the house to ourselves for awhile. True to her word, Leah made lasagna. We quickly ate and started on our homework. We were in bed when we heard Leah and Mark return from Alain's house.

Luckily school went by really fast on Friday. During lunch Aimee concocted some story about going to North's to buy some bridal magazines for Rachel, I pretended to be interested so I could convince Corin that I wanted to go with them.

"We are just going to buy some girly magazines than we'll go straight home. Corin, you can come because I think Rachel wants to look at cakes too." Aimee gambled.

"No thanks. I have to finish the Bronte interpretations anyway." He declined.

"Well, I'm glad. I was going to buy your birthday present anyway." She teased boldly.

"At a grocery store Aimee?" he questioned sarcastically.

"There are a lot of things you can get at a grocery store." She jibed.

"Whatever Aimee" He said annoyed with her teasing him.

After school, I gave Corin a quick kiss and got into the car with Aimee. I called Leah and told her we were on our way. Dana declined our little trip. When we pulled up in my driveway, I noticed Justin's car in the driveway. Leah met us in the driveway.

"What is Justin doing here?" I asked Leah.

"We've got a problem. They picked up the TV today, so we have to think of something else to get Corin out of the house tomorrow." She said breathless.

"I thought you were going to talk Mark." Aimee reminded.

"Well, I have been really busy with Kyle in all, I totally forgot." She said apologetically.

"Don't worry we'll think of something. I signed for Corin car Wednesday. Will you guys look at the size of this key? " I said changing the subject so Aimee would not ask about Kyle. The last thing we needed to do was upset her today.

I showed Aimee and Leah the big key for Corin's Audi.

"I was going to place this on the cake but it is so huge. What do you guys think?" I asked.

"It's big but I still think it's a good idea to place it on the cake. He can have the cake and eat it too." Aimee mocked.

"I like that. Okay. I just hope it doesn't sink into the cake." I laughed as I buried the priceless key deep inside my pocket.

When we got to North's, I went straight to the manager's office to go over the catering list. Aimee and Leah lingered in the magazines area. I was looking over the catering order when suddenly a wave of nausea and warmth rushed over me. I knew instantly, that my eyes were red. I didn't dare look up at the manager.

"Ms. Reynolds is everything okay. Did we miss something?" she asked nervously.

Keeping my eyes downward I anxiously responded "Oh no, I think everything is okay."

"Well we will need you to sign the form and then everything will be delivered to your address tomorrow." She said.

I quickly signed the form and handed the form back to her keeping my eyes downward. I grabbed a pair of sunglasses from my purse and put them on. "Thank you so much, Janice." I said abruptly and left. I raced over to the magazine rack and found Aimee by herself.

"Aimee, we have to go where is Leah?" I whispered anxiously.

"She went to the bathroom, are you okay? What is with the glasses?" she asked nervously.

"Aimee, my aura is acting up. My eyes are red." I answered quickly tilting my glasses down to show her my eyes.

"Okay, I'll go get Leah, you go to the car." She instructed.

Before we could act, we heard a bloodcurdling panic stricken scream from the end of the store. We knew immediately it was Leah's. Foolishly, we both ran toward the screaming and found Leah being strangled up in the air by a huge man with messy long black hair. She was thrashing frantically around his grip but he was too strong to fight off.

I immediately press the blue button on my tracking bracelet. Aimee picked up cans from the shelf and hurled them at him, hitting him directly in the back and head. I copied her but my cans did not come close to hitting him. He howled in pain and dropped Leah. She fell to the floor and gasped for air.

"Gena, get out of here. I'll hold him off." Aimee ordered.

Before I could answer her, he leaped in front of us and back handed Aimee, sending her flying across the back of the store. She forcefully slammed into the concrete wall and was knocked unconscious.

"Stop Cron, your fight is with me. Leave them alone." Leah yelled from the floor.

He did not pay any attention to her. He was staring at me with vicious hateful black eyes. I turned to run but I instantly felt my hair yanked backwards. He threw me against the shelf. Before I could even move, he grabbed me by the neck and lifted me into the air. His hand covered my entire neck leaving me no room to pry at his grip. I clawed at his hand but it was useless. Suddenly he dropped me, allowing me to grasp for some air. Leah had jumped him from behind and was clawing at his face. He grabbed her by her head and hurled her into a can display. When I fell, I felt the key in my pocket poke at my groin. I quickly dug for the key but before I could get it out he had me by my neck again.

"Your eyes are red healer. But you will die before you can heal anything." He snarled hatefully

When I felt the key free from my pocket I held it firmly in my hand and sent it right into his eye. He howled in pain, grabbing at his left eye. The instant he dropped me I scrambled for the front door. I didn't get too far before I realized he had leaped on me, sending me crashing to the floor. My knees burned from being abraded in the floor, I felt my ribs and left arm crushed by his weight. He grabbed me by my head and slammed it into the hard floor sending me into complete blackness.

Chapter Twenty-Eight

When I pulled up the driveway, I noticed Justin's car. *Looking for food again* I thought to myself. I walked in to find him, Tristan, and Mark installing my new TV. It was huge.

"Hey Corin, like your birthday present" Mark boasted.

"Wow, yeah. That thing is huge. Where is your TV?" I said excited.

"We just got that installed in his room. We had to go all the way to Dawson to pick this baby up." Justin bragged.

"How big is that thing?" I asked.

"Sixty inches baby. Now we can *really* watch the games." Tristan asserted loudly.

"Where is Gena?" Justin asked.

"Oh, she went to North's with Aimee to get some magazines for Rachel." I answered.

"Yeah, Leah went with them too." Mark replied.

"Did Gena see the TV?" I asked

"No, they just pulled up. Leah met them in the driveway." Mark answered nonchalantly.

"What magazines does Rachel want?" Justin asked curiously.

"Bridal" I answered.

"Oh, God how many does she need? Just pick a dress and let's go." He complained.

"Hey, this is her special day. If she needs every magazine in the world, give it to her." Mark advised.

"Why do they all have to go?" Tristan asked.

"It's like the bathroom thing, when one goes they all go. Haven't you noticed?" Justin teased.

"Hey, I heard Gena healed Kyle Wednesday. What's his story?" Tristan asked.

"Alcohol and drugs" Mark remarked. Tristan did not bother to ask for any additional information. He was already disgusted with the thought.

"Hey you guys have anything to eat?" Justin asked. We all chuckled.

"Leah made paella. I'll go get you some." Mark said.

"I can go for some paella." Tristan joined in.

We all went into the kitchen. I stood over the bar counter watching Justin and Tristan eating while talking about last night's game.

The instant the alarm from my bracelet went off I responded. I ran for the door with Mark, Justin and Tristan right behind me. As soon as my car ignited, I gassed out of the driveway and headed north into town. Mark was on the phone trying to reach Leah. He took my phone and tried Aimee and Gena simultaneously. When we got no answer, I was filled with horror. I knew it wasn't Kyle, so it had to be a hunter, why else would Aimee and Leah not answer. *Please don't let anything happen to her.* My sanity was challenged with every second that went by. My heart felt like it was racing faster than my car. I could hear Justin's car swerving recklessly against the icy road to keep up with me. *Gena hold on. Please hold on, I am coming.* I kept repeating those words in my head like I was trying to will it to her telepathically.

Frustrated Mark slammed the phone against the dash board. It broke into tiny pieces. We were both insane men; trying desperately to pass the long seconds to get to the women we loved. We both could not console each other. The silence in the car was filled with horror and fear.

When we finally got to the turn, I jumped the curb and accelerated towards the front door, barely avoiding the humans that came rushing out of the store. Before my car could stop, I got out and crashed through the glass door.

There he was crouched over her, bashing her head into the floor. The rage and hatred roared inside me, ripping whatever sanity I had left to shreds. I leaped into the air and grabbing him from behind, forcing us both to crash into the floor. I quickly got up and grabbed him from his neck. My hands tightened around his neck, slowly crushing it. I tightened my grip until I felt his throat crushed. I sent him flying into the brick wall. The brick wall collapsed around him. Unsatisfied, I dug into the rubble and pulled him out by his hair. I could hear him gurgling for air. I grabbed a hold of his head and with one quick motion I twisted it completely all the way around until only the skin kept it intact.

I ran over to Gena's body. Justin was sitting next to her trying to find a pulse on her neck.

"I'll get Alain here." He panicked. He got on his phone as he ran down the aisle to help with Aimee and Leah.

She was motionless. There was pool of blood behind her head. I was afraid to move her. Tears flooded my eyes blinding me. I tried to feel for a pulse on her neck, but I was trembling so hard, I didn't know if it was her pulse or my trembling.

"Gena baby please don't die. Don't leave me. Gena if you can hear me please hold on." I kept pleading.

I placed my ear over her heart to listen for the beautiful rhythm of her life. When I heard the faint beats, I didn't trust that I wasn't hallucinating. I kept my ear close to her chest listening until I was sure I wasn't hallucinating. *She was still alive.*

"Gena, can you hear me?" I pleaded in her ear. "I am here, Gena." Every cell in my body lit up when I saw her lips move.

"Baby, I am here." I assured her. I kissed her face and lips wetting her with my tears.

"Corin" She uttered. Her voice could surpass any angels singing right now.

"I am here. Don't move. Where are you hurt, baby?" I asked as I scanned her face and body.

"Everywhere" She whispered with a grimace. She slowly opened her beautiful red eyes. For the rest of my life, I will cherish those eyes and the life that it represents. She moved her right hand and touched my face. "Thanks for coming so fast." She whispered with a smile

"Thanks for not leaving me. Can you move your legs?" I asked to see if she had any neck injuries.

She shifted her legs but grimaced at the pain. "I think my left arm is broken and maybe my ribs. I am a little dizzy but I think I'm okay. Please Corin; Aimee and Leah are hurt too." She stuttered from the pain.

"Don't worry Mark, Tristan, and Justin are here too." I assured her.

I looked up and saw Justin running up from one of the aisle. "Is she okay?" he asked breathless.

"Yeah, where are Leah and Aimee?" I asked.

"They're both pretty shook up but alive. Let me go tell them about Gena." He informed as he ran back.

"Corin" She whispered.

"Gena, don't try to talk. Just lay still." I advised.

"Corin, I just met my first hunter and I pressed the button." She jibed.

"Yes you did, baby." I chuckled. She was unbelievable. Nearly killed minutes ago, here she jokes about it. Definitely head injury I thought to myself. I reached over and disarmed her bracelet. Four minutes and 34 seconds it took to get to her. Those numbers will be ingrained in my memory for life.

"Corin, I need you to find the Audi key." She said slowly.

"Don't worry baby, I have another key." I said to pacify her.

"No, Corin. I want you to find the other Audi keys. It should be at the end of Aisle 5." She insisted.

"Gena, I don't need the other key, now stop talking. You're aggravating your ribs by talking." I instructed.

I watched as she closed her eyes and blinked back tears. "Please Corin, I want you to find the Audi keys." She said tearfully.

"Okay, baby. Don't cry. It will really hurt if you start to cry. I'll look for it right now. Please don't cry." I begged as I kissed her face and lips.

I got up reluctantly. I didn't want to leave her side but if I didn't appease her, she would start to cry and the motion would cause her more pain. I didn't understand why she had to have this key. But I didn't want to see her upset either. By the time I reached the end of Aisle 5, I was about to turn around and tell her I could not find it but something caught my eyes.

It was an eye that caught my eyes.

The eye was stabbed by a pair of Audi keys. I walked over and picked it up. I slowly slid the eye apart from the keys.

"Happy Birthday, Corin." Aimee said. Tristan was standing behind me, with Aimee in his arms.

Startled, I turned and looked at her. "What is this?"

"Talk to Gena." She yelled back at me as Tristan carried her away.

I looked at the keys; they were not from my Audi. I wiped the flesh and blood from the key and brought them back to Gena, who was now sitting up.

"Gena, I told you not to move. You could have spinal injuries." I warned.

"Did you find it?" she asked avoiding my precautions.

"Yes. Now lay back down." I instructed.

"Corin, I just used every bit of energy to sit up. I am not going to lie back down. I obviously don't have any spinal injuries. Now give me the key." She scolded. I smiled because I realized beside from a broken arm and maybe some ribs, she was perfectly fine. I handed her the key.

"Happy now" I said.

"Corin, Happy Birthday" She said handing me the keys back. She smiled warmly at me.

"What is this?" I asked

"Your birthday present" She said quietly

"You brought me a car?" I asked surprisingly.

"I bought you a new Audi R8; of course you're just going to have to wait to see it since we are busy at this moment but it is parked in Blaine's garage."

"Do you always present gifts this way?" I teased.

"I try to make it as memorable as possible. I bet you can't top this." She bragged

"Though this is pretty memorable, but I bet you I can and I will." I vowed

Alain and Rolfe immediately rushed through the broken door. I stepped aside so that Alain can assess Gena. When he was done, she was placed on a gurney and loaded into an ambulance. Leah and Aimee were already on their way to the hospital via other ambulances. Edwin Daniels declared North's a crime scene so that no one can go in or out until we cleaned up some of the damages. Rolfe and Blaine assessed the hunter's body.

"Corin, we'll see you later. Don't worry we'll take care of this. Go with Gena." Blaine instructed.

When we got to the hospital, the girls bypassed the Emergency Room and went straight to the XRAY department. They were all covered in scrapes and bruises. Aimee sported a huge bruise to the left side of her face. Leah and Gena both had rings of dark bruises around their neck. It was really hard to look at them without feeling some rage but there was no one left to take it out on. Besides the obvious, Alain had to make sure there were no internal injuries or bleeding. Mark, Tristan, and I waited patiently in the waiting area for the girls to undergo their diagnostic tests.

"Corin, did Gena say anything about the hunter? Is this the one she dreamt about?" Tristan asked

"No, I haven't had the chance to ask her." I replied.

"Leah said it was Cron." Mark replied taking in a deep breath.

"The one who attacked her years ago" Tristan asked stunned.

"She said she was coming out of the bathroom when he cornered her. He told her that he followed her here from Prudhoe Bay. But he didn't know that she was the same girl who escaped him until he over heard us at the beach. He has been watching her, waiting for an opportunity to get to her. If Gena and Aimee weren't there I am pretty sure he would have killed her. Corin, I want a tracking bracelet to link me to Leah like yours." Mark shared.

"How did he know she was in Prudhoe Bay?" I asked curiously.

"He is one of those hunters that attacked the Quebec clan. I guess they spread out looking for the survivors. Cron made his way to Prudhoe Bay. She said he told her he followed us back here to find this clan. When he found out she was the same girl years ago, he went after her again. I am so sorry guys; we led them right into Inuvik. I feel sick that Gena and Aimee got hurt too." He said remorsefully.

"Was he alone?" I asked coldly. Right now, there could be another hunter nearby.

"She didn't mention him talking about anyone else." He answered.

"Don't they usually hunt in twos?" Tristan asked to confirm.

"It depends. They will hunt in pairs if they mean to attack. If they were scouting, they will send one. Tristan do you have your cell phone?" I informed.

Without asking he handed me his phone. I called Bradley and Carl. I wanted them to scent the dead body and do a complete sweep of the area. I also called Trey and told him the same. When I was done, I handed Tristan his phone.

"What happened to your phone?" he asked.

"Mark destroyed it. You owe me a phone." I said dryly. He nodded.

Leah had a dislocated shoulder and a couple of fractured ribs. Aimee had a fractured skull. My Gena, who can not heal as fast as Leah and Aimee, broke her left arm in two different places and had two hair line fractures on her 3rd and 4th ribs. She also had a fractured skull in the back of her head.

For once, I was proud of the clout our clan had over this town. Edwin Daniels made sure there was no information leaked to the humans. Rolfe and Blaine made sure Alain had no red tape in providing complete private care for the girls. Alain kept the girls in the hospital for observation. He isolated them in the ICU allowing only clan members in. No one questioned what Alain did because of the huge amounts of money donated into this tiny hospital by Burren Oil Industries and Alain's position. The clan mothers took turn doing nursing duties. Mark, Tristan, and I stayed with them the entire time.

I stood by and watched as Alain cast Gena's arm. She was such a good sport. She did not complain or cry when he repositioned her arm. She complained more about the months she would have to wear the cast.

"Are you sure you don't want anything colorful?" Alain jibed.

"Alain, if I can get this in nude color, I would. The last thing I want to show off is my crude attempt at fighting off a hunter. I don't think I want to do that again." She smarted back.

"Gena, you survived. Not very many people can sit here and say that." he pointed out.

"I had Corin." She boasted.

"Gena, even with Corin's speed and strength, you could have been killed in seconds. How did you last that long?" He questioned.

"Well, we were pretty lucky. He was strangling Leah, when Aimee attacked him with cans. Then when he knocked Aimee out, he went after me. He would have choked me to death if it wasn't for Leah. When he knocked Leah out, he went after me again. When I was about to pass out from being choked, I managed to take his eye out with Corin's Audi key. But that really made him mad. Last thing I remember he was bashing my head into the floor." she recalled unafraid.

"Gena, you attacked him with a key?" Alain asked doubtingly.

"Yeah, she did. I found it with the eyeball still attached." I vouched.

"That is disgusting." She complained.

"I am very proud of you for thinking on the spot like that. It bought you some time. You are probably here because you were able to thwart enough time until help arrived." Alain declared.

"I am abusing this tracking device." She jested.

"I would love to implant this inside you permanently if I could. Is that possible Alain?" I teased.

"Anything is possible when it comes to Gena. I am waiting for her to put on a cape and leap over buildings." He laughed.

"Super Gena!" she laughed then grimaced in pain.

"The cast will help with the broken arm, but the ribs will have to just heal with time. It is going to hurt every time you move, laugh, or cough. So try to brace yourself when that happens. I didn't see any head injuries so just be careful with the fracture. I want to keep you here for a couple of days than if things are still okay, we can send you home. Don't worry; I am keeping Leah and Aimee here for two days too. You guys can work on your story. There is pain medication if you need it. Call me if something new comes up. Get some rest." He advised.

Get some rest was a joke. Every member of the clan came through and visited. For once, I was glad Justin liked to talk. He filled in the story over and over. Cory and Michael went with Bradley and Carl to scent the body. They came back and reported that they did not pick up any scent from another hunter. Bradley and Carl were still spanning the search 50 miles out. Justin described the fight scene like it was something out of a WWF match. I personally can't remember what I did and not do. The mothers brought in food for everyone. I can see where we got the pot-luck thing from. Lauren, Dana and Rachel brought in some clothes for the girls. It was a little after ten by the time we were finally alone. I picked her up and carried her back to her room.

"What can I do for you right now?" I offered.

"I really want a hot shower." She requested.

I helped her undress, taking in all the cuts and bruises. The bruises on her face and arms were more prominent against the fluorescent lighting in the bathroom. She did bruise easily but worse her fair skin made the bruising look even worse. The reddish purple rings around her neck were a frightening reminder of how close she came to being killed. How many times did I vow not to let anything or anyone hurt her? I have failed her twice now. The only thing I've managed to do is rid her of her attacker. I have to find a way to prevent the attacks, how many times can she escape death?

I held her cast arm while she showered with one arm. Whenever she needed help, I gently assisted. When she was done, I dressed her and tucked her in bed. The hospital bed was not big enough for the both of us, and I wanted her to be as comfortable as possible so I slept in the recliner. Many times I woke up in the night to make sure she was comfortable. Truthfully, I was assuring myself that she was safe and alive.

I woke up on the day of my birth thankful that all my wishes had come true. Looking at her now, is proof of that.

I remember our first meeting when she accidentally caressed her lips on my face. My first taste of the scent from her hair, the beginning of my life with our first kiss, and the first time she said my name. It seemed like all my wishes came true all at once. Eternity with her was not enough. *I will love you forever, Gena Reynolds.*

When she started to stir, I closed the blind so the sun wouldn't bother her eyes. "Hey, you. How did you sleep?" I whispered.

"What time is it?" she murmured under the blanket.

"It is almost eleven." I answered.

I watched as she slowly woke. “I don’t like waking up in this bed or this room. I hate the smell of hospitals.” She grimaced.

“I’ll go get you something for pain.” I said.

“No, I’m sore but I’m not in pain. How did you sleep?” she asked.

“I miss you.” I replied honestly.

“I do too. Oh, Corin. Happy Birthday.” She wished me.

“Thank you baby. Now do you want some breakfast?” I offered.

“That sounds great. Will you eat with me?” She teased.

“Of course” I said. I gave her a light kiss and left the room. I went out to the guest lounge and found Tristan and Mark gathering food on a plate.

“Hey birthday boy” Mark greeted me.

“Happy Birthday Corin.” Tristan acknowledged.

“Thanks how are Aimee and Leah?” I asked while I fixed a plate.

“They want to go home. How’s Gena?” Mark answered.

“She is probably sore today, but at least she is alive.” I replied dryly.

“I heard about your birthday present. When do you get to see it?” Tristan expressed eagerly.

Laughing at my thoughts I responded “Later.”

“What is so funny?” Mark asked.

“Tristan you know that eye I found at North’s with the key. That was the key to my new car.” I chuckled.

“Gena attacked him with the key to your new car?” Mark said astonished.

“You should’ve kept the eyeball as a souvenir. Hang it on you rearview mirror. Maybe make a key chain out of it.” Tristan teased.

“You’re disgusting.” I said walking away from his mocking. I could hear them laughing at the thought of her attacking with car key.

When I got back to her room, she was not in bed. I heard her in the bathroom. "Gena, are you alright?"

"Yeah, I'll be out in a minute." She replied.

She came out of the bathroom fully dressed as if she was leaving to go somewhere.

"Where are you going?" I asked.

"Corin, I want to go home. I feel fine. This cast is really going to mess up my clothes." She asserted.

"Gena, Alain said two days. You're not going home. Now please sit down." I pleaded.

"I've already talked to Alain. Evidently, I am not the only one who wants to go home. He is coming by to check on us." She stated factually.

"Gena, if Alain recommends you stay another night, are you going to comply?" I asked.

"Probably not. Listen Corin, I don't have good memories of hospitals. Plus, I miss sleeping next to you." She declared.

"I can't argue with that but please be reasonable." I begged. I watched her scurrying about in the room looking for different things. She moved stiffly but carefully but she wasn't grimacing.

"Where are my shoes?" she asked.

"Gena, you're moving around better. Are you not sore?" I asked curiously.

"I am sore but it's not painful." She claimed.

"I want to check your heart rate, come here." I instructed.

"Why?" she asked suspiciously.

"Yesterday, you were thrown around like a rag doll. You have fractures in two of your ribs, you also have a broken arm, yet you are moving around like this happened two weeks ago. Now come here." I directed. She reluctantly moved closer to me. I placed my ear to her chest and listened to her heart beat. It was definitely faster than mine but it was much slower than before.

"What?" she asked nervously.

"I think you heart rate is slower. Not as slow as mine but definitely slower. Do you feel nauseated or hot?" I pressed.

"No, why are my eyes red?" she questioned frustrated.

"No, but that is my point. Gena, I think you are healing." I exclaimed with excitement.

"What does that mean?" She asked again.

"Well, we will ask Alain when he gets here, but normally you shouldn't feel this great. You should be painfully sore. Rib injuries are very painful." I explained.

"Does this mean I can take this cast off?" she said eagerly.

"Don't be ridiculous, even I have to wear it for at least one week. Come eat your breakfast. Afterwards I want to look at your body." I said excited.

"Really?" she smirked.

"I mean your bruised body. I want to see if I am right." I clarified.

"Oh." She said

"Don't give me too much credit. I will still have dirty thoughts when I am looking at your body." I flirted.

"I'm glad my scrapes and bruises don't disgust you." She said.

"Are you kidding? You can be covered in dirt and I still want you." I admitted freely.

She ate quickly. As soon as she was done, I had her stand in front of me. The bruises on her face and neck were faint with a yellow hue. I lifted her shirt and looked for the bruises that covered her rib cage but they were also faint. The scrapes were all gone. "You healed very fast. I think even faster than what is normal for our kind." I remarked with astonishment.

"Is that good or bad?" she questioned with uncertainty.

"Good of course. I want to try something. Hold you breathe." I instructed.

"What?" she asked doubtfully.

"I want you to hold your breath as long as you can." I repeated.

"Okay." She said slowly looking at me strangely. She took in a gulp of air and held her breath. I timed her against the clock on the wall.

After 38 seconds she had to exhale. "Well you're not completely transformed. That is still very humanly." I jested.

'Sorry, maybe it only works on one system at a time. My skin is my first line of defense so my transformation has to start there." She explained.

"That sounds like a good explanation. We will run this by Alain when he gets here." I suggested.

"You know yesterday, when I was in the manager's office, checking on the catering list, my aura went off spontaneously. This is even before I knew what happened." She confessed.

"It warned you before the attack?" I reiterated

"I thought something was malfunctioning but I think it was warning me of impending danger." She shared.

"So you can do this without having nightmares? You haven't had one in a few days." I pointed out.

"Seven days to be exact." She corrected me.

"Catering list for what?" I looked up at her. I caught her by surprise. She didn't realize that I caught the details of her being in the manager's office.

"Corin, I have been planning a surprise birthday party for you, which was suppose to be today. I was supposed to bake your Red Velvet Cake. I was going to place the Audi keys on top of the cake, but that would be so gross right now. This hunter really ruined everything."

"He obviously didn't know you had plans. That was so rude of him." I mocked her.

"Very funny, you know what I mean." She was incensed with my sarcasm.

"Thank you for all you're planning. I will pretend to be surprised. I am excited to see this car you bought me. Now, that was really surprising. Now what should I do with my old car.?" I teased as I pulled her into my arms and took in a deep breath of her scent.

"You can give it to me. I would take care of it." She suggested as she relaxed in my arms.

"That was the plan all along. You were in love with that car from day one." I nuzzled her neck.

"I was in love with the guy in that car first than the car." She said as she placed her lips over mine. I angled my head to take in more of her soft lips. My tongue explored her mouth until I heard her moan. Without thinking, I eased my hand inside her shirt and caressed her breast. She fumbled with the buttons on my shirt but with only one hand she could not undo it. Frustrated she yanked at the shirt. I laughed at her impatience. "We are in the hospital. Your uncle will be coming in any minute now. Do you want to explain to him what we are doing?" I teased.

"Then stop messing with me." She said breathlessly.

"Your arousal is easier to hide than mine." I said as I adjusted myself.

"That is what you say." She said as she straightened her clothes.

"Maybe we should get you home today." I tempted.

By the time Alain arrived, Gena, Leah and Aimee had already made up their minds that it was time to go. Alain had no chance. Alain was surprised over Gena's quick recover. He did not allow her to convince him to remove the cast but he did agree to re-x-ray the arm in one week. His theory was that every time her aura kicked in, she would be closer to completely transforming. The fact that her aura warned her of the terror coming was a good indication that she would eventually be able to control and use her aura at will.

Rolfe came by to rehearse the incident with the girls. The version that was released to the humans was that North's was being robbed by a madman. Leah was in the wrong place at the wrong time, and was attacked. Aimee and Gena tried to help but the man was insane and had to be shot to death in order to stop him. Since the same person who examined the body was Alain, there was no question of how he died. *Two gun shot wounds to the chest.*

Even though Bradley confirmed there were no traces of another hunter; I still felt uneasy and guarded. Gena's description of the hunter in her dreams was an older man with long black hair and scars. Cron had all of those features but it just seemed too easy. What about this Nhan that Robyn talked about? Everyone was convinced that the terror predicted in Gena's dreams were over. The fact that she had not had another dream further confirmed their case against me. I personally wanted to keep the security parameters in place for another month, but I got a lot of backlash from everyone. The clan finally appeased me by allowing the security parameters to continue until the end of the month. It all depended on Gena's dreams. It didn't matter that much to me; I was going to have Gena wear the tracking device until it became a part of her arm.

Leah and Mark did not go directly home, they went over to Alain's house to see Kyle. He was a little more responsive now but still healing.

Michael mentioned that he called out Gena's name many times that first night after she healed him. That irritated me more that I cared to admit.

"Corin, I was in his head for some time. We don't know why he is calling my name. Maybe, he wants to apologize." She explained.

"I don't want him thinking about you. He could be dreaming about what he wanted. I think I am being very reasonable here in asking that you do not see him unless I am present and he is completely lucid." I firmly requested.

"I will not see him without you. But you can not control what people are thinking." She pointed out.

"I may not be able to control what he's thinking but maybe if I am standing next to you he wouldn't dare act on those thoughts. I will put him back to sleep if he tries anything." I said sternly.

"Let's not talk about him anymore. It is your birthday. I had all these plans but since those things have changed what do you want to do?" she asked.

"I want to spend my birthday alone with you." I confessed. As we pulled up the driveway, parked in the driveway was my new car with a huge red bow placed on top. I looked over at Gena and she smiled back at me. "Do you like it?" she said proudly.

"Wow, it is gorgeous. You spoil me." I responded joyfully.

"Now, give me the keys to this car. It is mine now." She demanded playfully.

We got out and I handed her my old keys. She knew exactly what I liked. It was Ice silver with Apollo silver side blades. The wheels were 19" 5 arm polished alloys that made the tires looked gifted.

"Are you going to get in or just stand there?" She teased. I pulled out the new keys from my pocket and automatically opened it. We both got in and sat there quietly as I took in all the amenities that she added to this already perfect car. The black Alcantar leather sport seats were comfortable and sleek. She made sure every option from the Bang and Olufsen Audio system, to the Concert Radio with Sirius satellite, blue tooth, and MP3 technology, to the Audi Navigation system and the CD system were included.

"Thank you, this is a dream car. I don't know what to say." I said graciously.

"Say you love it and give me a kiss." She said adoringly.

"I love it; I love you and thank you very much." I replied lovingly. I kissed her softly on the lips.

"Take me for a ride." She whispered.

I smiled. "Let me show you what 420 Hp feels like." We sped away but this time I enjoyed the ride. She giggled at the excitement. We ended up at Tuk beach parking lot.

"That was really nice driving. Now I know how you got to me so fast." She complimented kissing my fingers.

"I don't need a car to get to you." I corrected as I pulled her face close to mine.

She shifted herself, straddling over my lap. Her arm cast bumped into things clumsily. "Only you could fit into a space so small." I whispered as I moved the seat back further so she could be more comfortable.

"I feel so clumsy with this thing." She complained at her cast.

"Don't worry it will be off soon." I said silently looking directly at her.

"Happy Birthday, Corin Randall." She declared before she started kissing my face and neck.

"Happy indeed" I agreed. I relaxed as she continued to kiss me. "I don't think I have ever made out in a car before."

"I don't think there is enough room for us to do much. I should have gotten you a minivan." She chuckled.

"Let's get home and finish this." I said impatiently. I lifted her and placed her back in the passenger seat.

When we pulled up, we noticed the cars crowding our driveway. I turned and looked at her. "Surprise party, remember?" she admitted.

"Bad timing" I complained.

"It is your birthday, the timing is perfect." She declared.

We walked in to find the house readied for a birthday party, surprised or not.

"Happy Birthday!" they yelled.

My mother ended up making my Red Velvet Cake. The food was a culmination of everyone's efforts since North's was temporarily closed. I spent a lot of time outside showing off my car.

With all the laughter and joy, it was hard to believe that just 24 hours ago, three lives were almost lost. Morbidly I let my thoughts wandered to the horror of a funeral today instead of a birthday party.

"Thank you" I thought to whoever was controlling my destiny.

Chapter Twenty-Nine

I was disgusted with this tracking device. I am a walking technology magnet. Not only did I have a tracking bracelet but now I have a new cell phone that acts like a tracking device also. My old phone was small and simple this new one had so many buttons; I rarely used it because I didn't want to spend all day trying to make a call. Corin's over-protectiveness bordered on irrational and possessiveness. I totally understood the need for him to be protective right after the attack but after two months of no nightmares, no red eyes, and no nausea, it was hard to justify wearing the thing. Since the tracking bracelet only had a radius of 100 miles, he gave me the phone to cover the rest of the world. It could track via satellite. At least Leah and Mark had to same phone so I didn't protest.

For weeks I have been able to hide the bracelet by wearing long sleeve shirts. The weather in December was unbelievably cold and bitter. I finally experienced the sunless days. It was eerie but after awhile you just get use to it. The cold however was unforgivable. There were days, I did not want to get out of the house because it was so cold. It was so cold that most mornings the cars had to be jump started because the batteries died. Of course, the cold did not bother anyone except for me. Corin was pretty good at trying to make things more comfortable for me. Every morning he would warm the car up for at least 30 minutes before I had to get in it.

I spent majority of my first winter running from car to house or school building. Anything that required long exposure outside, I avoided.

The only place that I continued to go to was the lab. Corin always made sure to escort me since Kyle was still staying at Alain's house. Two weeks after I healed him, he was able to talk lucidly. His first request was to see Leah. They spent a lot of time healing their differences. His band covered up his absentness with a rehab story. The press was searching for him in Los Angeles or Beverly Hills. It turned out he did not have a drug or alcohol problem. He claimed it was the first and last time. He wasn't to clear on what he did to me, but Leah and Mark filled him in. When he requested to see me, there were more efforts made to assure Corin than myself of Kyle's genuine intentions. After Leah prepped Kyle for our visit, she let Corin and I talk to Kyle privately. Corin kept his arm wrapped possessively around my waist. His face was cold and unforgiving. Kyle was nervously sitting on the side of the bed facing the door. When he looked up; he stared at me for some time before he closed his eyes and grimaced like he was in pain.

"Are you too ashamed to even look at her?" Corin hissed angrily.

"Corin, please." I pleaded with my eyes. He rolled his eyes and turned away.

"Gena, I am so very sorry for hurting you. Please believe me." He said sadly.

"I believe you, Kyle." I replied warmly. I started to move towards him, but Corin tightened his grip around my waist.

"Are we done now?" Corin gritted. I glared at him.

"Kyle, who is Gabriella?" I asked curiously. Corin glared at me. He wanted us to be in and out quickly, and I just opened up a long conversation.

"How do you know about Gabriella?" He asked attentively.

"I saw her when I healed you." I answered quickly.

"Oh, thank you for that. I don't deserve that, mostly from you." He admitted shamefully. When he looked up again, he was staring at me again. This made Corin angry and I could tell he was about to said something crude and mean. So I abruptly asked "Was she you're soul mate?"

"She was a girl I met when I was 18 years old. She lived in Minnesota. She was killed when a hunter attacked her clan. I witnessed her death and could not save her." He spoke with agony.

"The memory is very painful for you, was she your soul mate?" I repeated. It wasn't a question but more like a confirmation.

"I don't really know. I don't believe in that stuff. All I know is that I saw her killed and that memory has never left me." He confessed.

"It's just that I felt a very strong painful lost when I saw her in your memories."

"You saw her?" he asked stunned by my revelation.

"Well, I know she has long brown hair. I could not see her clearly. Am I right?"

He stared at me again and then lowered his eyes to his hands. He looked like he was lost in his thoughts. I looked up at Corin and he shrugged his shoulder.

"Is this painful for you?" I asked kindly.

"No, I was just thinking about what you just said about her brown hair." He explained.

"Why? Because I have brown hair" I asked annoyed by his hesitation.

"No, because you could be her twin" He declared as he looked up to stare at me. I was too stunned by his comment to reply.

"Is that why you attacked her? Because you thought she was your soul mate." Corin hollered. I had to stand in his way to prevent him from moving toward Kyle. His loud voice caused Leah and Mark to come barging in.

"When I saw her, I thought it was Gabriella coming back to haunt me for not protecting her. I was confused and scared. Gena, I am sorry. Corin I know you can never forgive me and I don't blame you but I swear I would never hurt her again." He cried.

"I know you won't." He assured with a firm tone. Mark was holding him now. Leah moved to her brother. I stood there too stunned to continue. *He said she could be my twin.* Twins ran in my family. What if she was my twin? No one really knew what happened to me after my mother was killed, could I have been a twin? Maybe somehow we were both saved but than separated.

"Corin, I have to talk to Rolfe." I said dazed. He looked down at me confused by my sudden change of course.

"Gena, are you alright?" he asked.

"Did you hear what he said? He said she could've been my twin. What if I was a twin?" I explained. He understood immediately.

"What?" Mark asked confused.

"Kyle said Gabriella looked like Gena's twin." Corin asserted. Mark turned to confirmed this with Leah.

"Mark, I didn't know her. I just knew of her." She confessed.

We left Mark and Leah to question Kyle further. On the way over to Uncle Rolfe's house, I wondered the possibility of the new revelation. If I was a twin, why were we separated? If we weren't separated, she would still be alive today.

"Gena, I don't want to upset you but you are aware that she was killed 5 years ago." He reminded me calmly.

"I know Corin, but I just want to know if it was possible." I replied flatly.

"Okay, but just don't be sad over things you have no control over. You've been through enough." He advised. I nodded.

When we arrived at Uncle Rolfe's house, Justin greeted us at the door.

"Hey, this is different? Come on in." he announced cheerfully.

"Hey, Justin is Rolfe in?" Corin asked briskly.

"Yeah, he is in his office. Is everything alright?" he asked curiously.

"Yeah, we just need to ask him about Alexandria's pregnancy." Corin explained as we made our way to Uncle Rolfe's office.

He heard us before we got to the door and invited us in. Blaine and Alain were sitting on the sofa next to the hearth enjoying a drink.

"Hi, Corin, Gena. Corin do you like your new car?" Blaine asked proudly.

"Yes, thank you Blaine. You did a great job." Corin said gratefully.

"What's going on? Is everything okay?" Uncle Rolfe asked.

"Well, we were just over at your house talking to Kyle. Do you remember when I asked about Gabriella?" I asked Alain.

"Yeah, you said he was Kyle's soul mate." Alain remembered.

"Well, he denies it but he told me that I looked just like her, that I could be her twin? Could my mother have been carrying twins? Could I have been a twin?" I asked breathlessly.

"Gena, Your mother was not carrying twins. We only felt one aura during her pregnancy." Uncle Rolfe explained.

"What if I had an aura but she didn't? Wouldn't that explained why you could only feel one aura? Twins run in this family." I said exasperated.

"Gena, what is this about? Didn't Leah say she was killed five years ago?" Alain asked.

"I just want to know if it possible that I was a twin. Maybe if we find out how she got to Minnesota, we can find out who saved me 18 years ago." I continued restlessly.

"Rolfe, she is right. We can send Bradley to get a DNA sample from her burial plot. It certainly could not hurt." Blaine sided.

"Gena, is this alright with you?" Uncle Rolfe asked.

"Yes, thank you. How long will this take?" I asked impatiently.

"You sound just like your mother just now. Impatient and stubborn" Uncle Rolfe remembered.

"Well, Bradley has to find the burial plot than, have it dug up. The DNA testing takes about 2 weeks so maybe one month. There is no rush. Be patient." Alain informed.

"Thank you so much." I said graciously. I knew that they would do anything to indulge me.

When we left, Justin chimed in with all the questions. Corin tried to pacify him with as much information as possible but somehow he invited himself and Rachel to dinner at our house. Corin gave up on dissuading him from coming over.

Life in Inuvik went back to normal by the end of October which is when the security parameters were lifted. Of course Corin opposed, reminding everyone that there were other dangerous hunters around but everyone ignored him and eventually he did not pursue the issue.

Luckily everyone was too busy helping with Rachel's wedding, even Christmas had to wait. Because there hadn't been a wedding in Inuvik for almost 20 years, everyone was involved in the planning and prepping. Rachel chose Elizabeth (her sister) to be her maid of honor. Justin's best man was Preston. Rachel's bridesmaids were Lauren, Aimee, Leah and I. Her brother Mitch and sister Elizabeth arrived with their parents two weeks before the wedding. Because the weather was so bitterly cold, I was glad when Rachel had all the fittings at my house. I met her sister Elizabeth, who was a carbon copy of her. I didn't have a chance to meet her parents or her brother, Mitch. Corin thought he was cool. With the multiple fittings, our house was a haven for the girls. This however made Corin restless and grouchy. Our house was always filled with people. We had no privacy. People was always stopping by or staying for dinner or just hanging out. Nights became our most valuable time together.

By the middle of November, I became restless and impatient because I had not heard from Uncle Rolfe regarding Gabriella. Bradley was having a hard time finding the bury plot. I became discouraged but Corin kept my trust in Bradley's skills. By December, the weather became too harsh for him to continue with the ground search of the burial plots because of the snow and ice. The search had to be temporarily called off until the ground could be tracked again. Instead of being a nuisance and pestering Bradley I tried my hands at being patience. Even though Christmas was pretty much on the back burner this year, I made a conscious effort to decorate my house with the usual Christmas motif. My tree and wreaths were up. There were no presents under our tree. We decided to adopt an Inuvik family of seven for Christmas. It was easier to by gifts for a family who actually needed something than to buy for ourselves. We were happy and content. We did not need or want anything. When the clan found out what we did, it set off a new trend. By Christmas everyone had a family to buy gifts for.

"Corin, I am the only one still wearing this bracelet. For today, can I please take it off?" I pleaded with him coming out of the dressing room.

When Rachel asked me to be one of her bridesmaid, I was thrilled but now looking at the dress she chose, I cringed. There was no way I could keep warm in this dress unless I was wrapped in layers of down. The dress was absolutely beautiful but it was not meant to be worn in weathers of -30 degrees. It was a very light pink, strapless, princess-like dress with a band of bugle beads bordering the A-line top and the waist. Thank God, it was a full-length gown made of heavy European satin. Rachel wanted all of us to wear our hair up but since so much of my neck, shoulder and arms were exposed, she allowed me to wear my hair down to keep warm. The only thing that adorned my neck was my Mobius strip necklace, which does nothing to keep me warm. The only other piece of jewelry was my stupid black tracking bracelet.

"We've had this argument many times the answer is no." He responded stubbornly from the bathroom.

"Corin, I think I have been very good about this but it has been two months, I haven't had any nightmares. My aura has practically been asleep. Corin, please be reasonable. It sticks out like an eye sore. " I pointed out.

He came out of the bathroom and stood at the doorway. "No one is going to even notice it because you look absolutely stunning in that dress. I thought you weren't supposed to out shine the bride on her wedding day?" he complimented.

"Don't even try that with me. I know what you're doing. Compliments are not going to work. Please Corin, I can't cover this with anything." I continued to plead, turning around so he could help me with the rolls of delicate buttons on the back.

"Okay. On one condition, you must promise not to wonder off anywhere without me. I want to be able to see you at all times." He agreed as he fastened the buttons. "The compliments were not a ploy, they were genuine."

"I promise." I vowed elated, raising my wrist up so he could disarm and remove it. When he was done, he gently kissed the inside of my wrist.

"Do you want your Christmas present now?" he murmured against my wrist.

"What? Corin, I thought we agreed no Christmas presents." I said annoyed.

"I could not help myself. This is our first Christmas. Come on. Let me spoil you." He convinced.

"I didn't get you anything." I said sadly.

"I have everything. Let me spoil you this year and you can spoil me next year." He pleaded holding my face close to his.

"You'll cheat. Next year you'll come up with some other plan. I should have known." I pouted.

"Scouts honor." He vowed with a hand gesture over his heart.

"You're not a boy scout." I pointed out. He chuckled, than his beautiful smile magically appeared. I was defeated instantly. "Okay, let me have it."

"Close you eyes." He instructed. I close my eyes and waited. I felt him taking my hand and for a brief moment I thought he was going to propose but than I realize it was my right hand that he was holding. I felt him closing a metal object over where my tracking bracelet used to be. "Okay open your eyes."

I stared at my wrist to find a beautiful thick band adorned with single diamonds all the way around. "This is so beautiful."

"It's an eternity bangle." He whispered.

"It sure beats the tracking bracelet. Wait, did you hide a tracking device in here?" I teased.

"I wish I could, but I don't think Tiffany's is in to that stuff." He jibed.

"Thank you, Corin. It really is beautiful. I love it. I love you." I replied.

"You look absolutely breath-taking." He adulated pulling my body closer to his.

"Thank you, I have to look this good since I am standing next to the most gorgeous man in the world." I countered adoringly as I tied his bow. When I was done, he playfully ran his hands through my hair, lifting it up and inhaling my scent.

"I love the way you smell." He whispered caressing the side of my neck.

"Corin, don't start. I had to work really to get my hair to set in these curls." I warned holding him at bay.

"Well, what part of you can I touch without ruining something?" he teased.

"You can help me with my heels." I played along.

"Come on, Cinderella." He teased pulling me to sit on the bed. Kneeling in front of me, he eased my skirt up and exposed my knees. He gently caressed the right calf with his hands and lips as he slipped the stiletto on. He repeated the same on the left leg.

"I will never be able to put on stilettos normally again." I said gasping.

"That was the point." He tempted with a crooked smile.

"Hey, are you going to be alright with Kyle being there?" I asked changing the subject. Rachel invited Kyle to her wedding to get him to mingle with the clan. The only person he socialized with was Leah, Cory, and Derek. He wanted get back to his band. Rachel played on his guilt and got him to promise to attend. She was trying to buy Leah some time with her brother.

"I told you; as long as he behaves I will behave." He repeated.

"Okay, just remember it is Rachel's day. Be nice." I advised.

"I don't know why she has to have him there?" he complained.

"It is for Leah's sake."

"This wedding has gotten out of control. Do you know there will be more than 200 people there?" he complained.

"Darn, I was thinking about inviting 500 people to our wedding." I teased

"We will elope to Vegas; I don't think I can stand the long procession line." He played along.

"I wouldn't mind that."

"I was just kidding. I would not want you to miss one beautiful thing in your life. Plus my mother would totally hate me." He revealed.

"I think I would be okay with not having a grandiose wedding."

"Let's survive the next two than we can make our own plans." He acknowledged.

Aunt Madeline brought in every limousine within a 100 miles radius of Inuvik. We shared our limousine with Mark and Leah. When it arrived, Corin met the driver outside and gave him a thorough interrogation. The poor guy never saw it coming.

"Nice replacement bracelet. What happened to the tracking bracelet?" Mark teased coming from the stairs.

"He is rational today." I said sarcastically as I watched Corin come back in.

"Gena, do you have your phone?" he asked undaunted by his irrational thinking.

"Yes, Corin it is in my purse, which I will carry next to my body at all times." I replied annoyed. I could see Mark hiding his amusement.

"Mark, where is Leah?" he asked impatiently. We weren't late but Corin hated waiting.

"She is going to need another 30 minutes." Mark said walking back upstairs.

"You're annoyed with me." He said quietly. I did not respond. "Gena, don't be angry at me."

"How can I be good for you? You're so busy worrying about me; you're missing all the good things happening around you. We are going to a wedding and you're busy checking out the limousine driver. You know what, just forget it. I don't want to be mad at you today." I turned away and headed toward the kitchen.

He reached out and gently pulled me back to face him. "Gena, you are good for me. Don't doubt that. I know I have been difficult and over bearing but I am not blind. I see every thing. I see you."

"Your obsession with losing me clouds your personality and spirit. I don't see you enjoying yourself. This is not how we are supposed to love each other. You worry about losing me and I am worry about what that is doing to you." I said frustrated.

"Gena, part of my personality is to protect the ones I love. I can not change that. But, my spirit is you. I am this alive and happy because of you. My heart only wants you." He confessed tenderly taking my hand and placing it over his heart.

"I just want you to enjoy life *with* me. I feel so guilty doing this to you. You're life had to have been easier before me." I expressed sadly.

"It was easier but not happier. It may not look like it to you but I am immensely happy. I will not trade this for an easy and boring life. I don't want you to worry about me." He said kissing the inside of my wrist.

"I just want you to relax and stop the worrying." I requested.

"The bracelet is gone. The cell phone is just the latest thing out there. Leah has one." He explained wittingly.

"Yes, every girl gets a phone with a satellite tracking device built in." I responded with sarcasm.

"Okay, but that was really Mark's fault. He broke my last phone. Since he was getting me a new phone, I just wanted us to match." He added smiling at me.

"What were you doing with the driver just now?"

"Okay, I'll stop that. What else do you want me to do?" he said defeated.

"I don't want you to do anything."

"I will try. Okay?" he offered with a smile, the same one that always melts my heart and wins our battles. I nodded to our fragile truce. "I want to kiss you." He whispered.

"What is stopping you?" I dared. With that, he crushed his lips over mine. Hastily, he buried his hands inside the curls of my hair forcing our lips closer. He angled his lips to take in more of my mouth leaving me gasping for air.

"Ahem, we are ready to go whenever you guys get through with what you're doing." Mark interrupted.

Breathless, I broke away and buried my face in his neck. "We'll meet you in the car." Corin answered.

"When are they moving out again?" I whispered. Corin chuckled and gave me a quick kiss.

"My bad hospitality is rubbing off on you and I think I messed up your hair."

"Well it wouldn't have stayed like that for long anyway." I said as I started pulling out the pins that kept my hair neat and together. I liked my hair down naturally anyway. Corin helped pull out the rest of the pins. "Let's go." I said before I shook and tossed my hair back into its normal wavy mess.

"I like your hair like that." he complimented adoringly. He held out Lauren's fur coat for me. After tucking me in securely, we meet Mark and Leah outside.

The ride to North Chateau took longer than usual because everyone was in a limousine. It was an hour before our limousine made it to the entrance, but Aunt Madeline's careful planning made sure we had enough time to get in place. Aunt Madeline and the other mothers did a wonderful job of turning North Chateau into a beautiful wedding fantasy. Rachel's colors were light pink and crème. Every tree in the front lawn was heavily decorated in pink and crème Christmas Ornaments. The lighting started from the end of the driveway all the way up to the door entrance. When we got to the entrance, we quickly made our way into the Grand Lobby. Aunt Madeline rushed us into one of the dressing rooms.

"I am so excited, you have to seen Rachel?" Lauren greeted us.

"Do we have time to go see her now?" Leah asked

"I think so, follow me this way." Aimee ushered. Leah and I followed Aimee through a hallway and into Rachel's dressing room. Elizabeth was helping Rachel with some final details. Rachel's gown was made of heavy silk and antique lace. The neckline was squared with an empire waist line. Her beautiful red hair was braided into French twist than pleat underneath to secure the veil.

"Rachel you look absolutely gorgeous." I complimented.

"God, I am so nervous. I just hope I don't trip." She admitted.

"Don't worry, we will catch you." Leah offered.

"Do you have everything you need?" Aimee asked.

"Yeah, I think we got everything covered." Elizabeth answered.

"Ladies, Aunt Madeline wants you all to get in your places." Aunt Idelle announced from the doorway.

"We will see you out there." Aimee assured.

"Breath Rachel" Elizabeth advised.

We met the guys in the foyer. Corin came over and immediately ushered me to our place in line. Before we got in line we were interrupted by a gigantic handsome man with red hair and blue eyes.

"Corin is this Gena?" he bellowed.

"Gena, I want you to meet Rachel's brother Mitch. Mitch this is my Gena." He introduced proudly.

"Hi, Mitch. It is really nice to meet you." He could easily be seven feet tall.

"They said you were beautiful, but you are absolutely stunning." He complimented kissing the back of my hand.

"Corin you're very lucky. I can't believe this little thing rides a Ducati. If there is anyone listening up there, I want a woman like this." He prayed. "The women here are absolutely stunning. I may have to move here." He announced.

"Sorry, Mitch. Most of them are spoken for." Mark added.

"Well, please introduce me to the ones that are not and we can start from there. Gena, if you ever get tire of looking at Corin, you know where to find me." He teased looking back at Corin.

"Thanks for the offer Mitch but I don't think that would ever happen." I answered back smiling at Corin.

"Ouch, you break my heart. At least let me have the first dance." He flirted.

"Sorry Mitch, all first and last dances belongs to me." Corin declared.

"You can't hog her all night, I'll find a way." He challenged.

"You obviously don't know Corin." Tristan chuckled.

The procession started with Aimee escorted by Tristan, than Leah and Mark, than Corin and I followed by Lauren and Mitch and finally Elizabeth with Preston. We proceeded from the foyer into the Grand Room where the congregation was seated. Aunt Madeline wanted us to proceed until we reached the end of the dual ascending stairs; the girls would walk up from the left side of the stairs while the guys proceeded to the right side of the stairs, finally meeting at the top atrium. The entire Grand Room was heavily decorated in beautiful pink and crème satin. Pink roses and petals covered the entire room.

As the bride entered, I watched as Justin's face lit up and his eyes welled up. Preston discreetly passed him a tissue while Mark elbowed him. I looked to Corin and he was staring right back at me. The whole building could have caught on fire and I wouldn't have known. His eyes trapped me in this timeless place that no dream could conjure up. When they were reciting there vows, Corin and I were lost in our own ceremony.

After the ceremony, everyone retreated to the Grand Ballroom for the reception. Most of the people invited were from Justin's side due to his family's business and family size. I lost count of how many people were invited but there were at least 35 tables of six. Corin introduced me to so many people; I could not keep up with there names or where they were from. I just politely smile and nod.

When we finally made it back to our table, Leah and Michelle were talking about Kyle. Mark and Corin left to go have drinks with Justin and Preston.

"I think Kyle likes Natalie." Michelle said.

"What's going on?" I chimed in.

"Michelle thinks Kyle and Natalie have something going on." Leah explained.

"Natalie and Kyle have not stopped talking since they were introduced by Derek and this is their fourth dance together." Michelle defended.

"Why don't you go over there and talk to him?" I instructed Leah.

"What do I say to him—*Hey Kyle is this your soul mate*?" He would literally laugh at me. You know how he feels about that." Leah replied.

"I could eavesdrop for you." Michelle plotted.

"And who are you eavesdropping on?" Mark asked startling her from behind.

"None of your business Mark. I'll tell you later." She promised Leah.

We watched as she made her way back to her table. I could tell Leah was hopeful for her brother. It would be nice to see him find a soul mate amidst all his doubts.

Mitch finally got his dance with me when he cut in on Michael. He was so tall; my neck ached from straining to look up at him. He was very charming and funny. He asked me questions about every girl in the room and who I thought would be best suited for him. For some weird reason, I pointed out Trisha, even though I did not know her well. After the dance, I walked him over to her table and introduced them. *The rest was up to them, I thought.*

On my way back to my table, Corin came up from behind me and wrapped his arms around my waist. "You owe me a dance, Ms.Reynolds." he flirted.

"I was just looking to settle that debt." I played along

He pulled me along to the dance floor. With one arm wrapped around my waist and the other cupping my face, he leaned in until our noses touched. "I miss you while you were out matchmaking."

"Well, I didn't want to pull you away from your drinking buddies." I whispered inhaling the alcohol from his breath.

"I only had two drinks."

"Be careful I may take advantage of you if you become too inebriated?" I teased.

"I would let you take advantage of me anytime." He chuckled. He leaned in and brushed his lips over mine. "Is this where we left off earlier?"

"No, I think we were much further along." I flirted. I felt his grip tightened around my head and hair as he lowered his lips over mine. His arm crushed me up against his body. As our kiss intensified, the room and everyone around us disappeared.

"I would say get a room but I know that would be a waste of money." Justin laughed bumping his dance partner up against me.

"People are staring." Aimee whispered into my ear.

"I didn't get a kiss when we were dancing." Mitch complained loudly.

"Corin, she will need to come up for air soon." Max teased in Corin's ear.

I could tell Corin was laughing but he did not break away. We just continued to until the music was over. When we left the floor and returned to our seats, we got a round of applauds from everyone.

"That was interesting." Rachel jibed.

"Glad to entertain you Rachel." Corin responded.

"Babe, it's our turn. We can't have them out do us at our own wedding." Justin bellowed towards Rachel. It was time for the bride and groom's traditional dance.

The night ended with Trisha catching the bouquet and Lawrence catching the garter belt. I went home with the prize.

Chapter Thirty

"They killed Cron. Are you just going to sit there and wait for them to grow bigger and stronger?"

"Nhan, Cron's death is your fault! We did not sanction the attack. If we attack now they will be prepared. We lost too many brothers and sisters during the Quebec attack. You have disappointed me with your stubbornness and irrational behavior."

"Brother Bron I am merely asking revenge for my brother."

"Nhan, why were you and Cron in Inuvik?"

"Lucos, we followed the scent from the survivors to Prudhoe Bay then we follow them back to Inuvik."

"You did this on your own. I told you to stop. Cron's death is your fault."

"How dare you blame me for Cron's death? I came back here to seek help from my brothers and sisters to rid us of this clan that seeks to destroy us. They now have a healer. Nothing will stop them from growing stronger. We have to kill her while we can."

"I don't believe you. I was there when she was killed."

"Nhan, you will say anything to get this clan to bend at your will. I am the leader of this clan. You will not use us as pawns to seek your revenge. You brought on Cron's death when you disobey me and went on your own."

"If you are the leader than you should lead like one? Your coward actions disgust me. Maybe there should be another leader."

"Nhan are you challenging me for the right to lead this clan."

"No, I don't want to be apart of this clan anymore. You've grown lazy and fat. You no longer care about the reason why our ancestors came here. I will not stand by and watch as you change the course of our people. Those who want to join me are welcome."

"Those who leave with Nhan will never be welcome back. Follow him and you will surely die."

"I see that this clan is made up of cowards. Your lives are worthless if you don't continue the cause."

"Nhan, we listened to you and attacked the Quebec clan. We lost many, you don't care about us. Your hatred rules your heart. We don't trust you!"

"Bron, you have always been a coward and a stupid dog. Why don't you ask your wife why the healer fetus survived?"

"My wife said she killed the fetus. I believe her!"

"Why is the healer child alive?"

"Leave Nhan. You are no longer apart of this clan!"

It is suppose to be spring but all I see is snow and ice or more like slush. Why do they even bother calling it spring here? No flowers or anything alive growing out from the grown. At least the weather has gotten warmer. I can actually leave the house now. This winter was harsh but somehow it went by fast, I can't believe it is already March. So much has happened since the wedding. Ella and Trey ran off and got married. Now she is pregnant. Trisha and Robyn left with Mitch for Colorado. Corin was really proud of my instinctive match. Kyle went back on tour with his band. I guess we were wrong about him and Natalie.

"Gena quit daydreaming and help me with these boxes." Leah interrupted.

"Oh, sorry. I was just looking at the yard. I can't believe this is supposed to be spring. There are no flowers or birds chirping or any of those things." I complained.

"Birds are not stupid. They know it is too early to return. Here take this." She handed me a box she just got finished marking. Corin and I volunteered to help Mark and Leah move into their new house. Lately, it seemed like all we do was help people move. We helped Justin and Rachel into their new home last weekend and here we are moving Leah and Mark.

"We are back for more boxes!" Mark exclaimed.

"Here, these are the only ones left." Leah pointed out. "I think we are officially moved. Thanks so much Gena, Corin."

"I am going to miss having you around. I have to learn to cook again." I teased.

"Well, you can always come over and eat with us. Thanks for taking us in. Listen, I will meet you over at Rachel's house tonight. Thanks again Corin. I have to go before he breaks something." She rushed giving Corin a quick hug before leaving.

"Quick lock the door before someone else wants to move in here." Corin teased.

"Stop, you know you're going to miss them not being here."

"I miss being alone with you." He said seductively as he moved toward me.

"I miss it too." I confessed pulling at his shirt leading him up the stairs.

"I love it when you look at me like that." He said in a lustful trance. He followed me into our bedroom. When he closed the door behind him, he pulled me to him. With one quick motion he swung me up into his arms and carried me to the bed. He gently lowered me into the bed, pausing only to pull off his shirt. I gazed up at him, marveling at his beautiful body. With my fingertips, I traced the corded muscles on his arms, feeling the heat of his skin. He took hold of my wandering hand and lifted it to his mouth, kissing each finger then kissing the inside of my wrist, slowly working his way up my arm. He worked his way teasing tender kisses along the length of my collarbone

"God, I love the way you smell." He murmured.

"You like smelling my hair?" I asked

"I like the smell of your body." He whispered against my shoulder. His fingers caressed up and down my arm causing goose bumps to form. "Are you cold?"

"No, your fingers caused my body to do that." I explained. I was disrupted when the phone rang.

"I'll get it." He moaned as he reached over and grabbed the phone. I got up and went to the bathroom. I deliberately waited to get into the shower until I heard him hang up the phone. I stood and let the hot water wash my body. I heard when he entered the bathroom.

"That was Rachel. She wanted to remind us about tonight." He yelled from behind the shower curtain.

"Do you think we would ever get tired of this?" I asked from behind the curtain.

"I could never get tired of you. I could spend an eternity kissing to you and still want more." He expressed lovingly.

"You're pretty addictive too." I responded finishing my shower.

"I like that. You're getting better at one-upping me." He boasted.

"I learned from the master." He handed me my robe.

"How can I be the master when you own me?" he pointed out as I covered myself with a robe and started leaving.

"I don't own you yet." I yelled back at him pointing at my third left finger.

He chased behind me and swung me up in his arms. "You've owned me from the first time I saw you." He declared before he covered my mouth with his.

Rachel's house was built with all her designs in consideration. She loved Colorado and since they went to the Swiss Alps for their honeymoon, her house was a luxurious ski chalet. The exterior was built from gray stones and Western Red cedar with a black metal roof. A Contemporary Savoyard Chalet with three floors connected by a spiraling staircase, and over 5000 square feet. The floors were finished in acid washed and stained concrete. The interiors were adorned with cedar and glass. The split lower level was Justin's man cave. It included a Theatre Room (equipped with a 72' Flat screen TV, Professional Bar, Luxury recliners), a game room (with a 26' TV and all the latest games and game systems), and two guest bedrooms with private bathrooms. The Main level included the Great Room, designer kitchen, formal dining room, 2 bedrooms with individual bathrooms, and indoor/outdoor pools. The Great Room had floor to ceiling windows walls like my house and a spectacular centre fireplace. The Master level was entirely dedicated to the Master bedroom and bathroom. There was a balcony on the Master and main level that wrapped around the entire house. My favorite place of course was the kitchen. She had all Viking Stainless Steel appliances with a custom built Subzero refrigerator/freezer and her pantry was as big as her kitchen housing the panic room in the back. At night the lighting made this house stand out from all the other homes. It was incredible to see against the white snow banks.

Tonight was the first official dinner party at her house. All the guys immediately went to the Theatre Room while the girls hung out on the Main level. We were looking through her honeymoon pictures and wedding pictures. Leah was getting advice about wedding details since hers was a month away.

"Diane is pretty much doing everything, I'm so glad to have her. I don't know if I could have done this without her." Leah confessed.

"They all live for this stuff. My mother is fussing over when she gets to start on mine." Aimee admitted.

"I know, after Justin's wedding my mother has already worked out the details for Preston and mine. I told her that I wanted to wait so she wouldn't have to work so hard but she is in her own world right now." Lauren shared.

"I told her I didn't want anything big." Tina stated.

"You know she don't know what that means." Dana laughed.

"How many weddings are we talking about here? I'm getting confused." I asked stupidly.

"Well mine is in April." Leah added.

"I'm tempted to do what Ella and Trey did." I jibed.

"Don't you dare elope? Diane would probably never forgive you. I am pretty sure after ours she will be hounding you and Corin." Leah declared.

"I still can't believe they did that. Isn't that bold?" Dana whispered.

"It doesn't matter they were going to eventually do it. I think she just didn't want to go through all that stuff again." Aimee suggested.

"I think it is because she is pregnant. How far along is she now?" Lauren asked.

"Well she said five months. She doesn't even look pregnant. I have to start planning her baby shower soon." Aimee answered.

"God, I hope I look that good when I am pregnant." Lauren wished.

"Does she know if it is a boy or a girl?" Leah asked.

"She and Trey doesn't want to know." Aimee answered.

"I hate it when people do that. It is hard to buy a gift for an *it baby.*" Lauren complained.

"Come on, Lauren there are plenty of things to buy babies besides pink or blue things." I assured her.

"I want all girls." She chimed in.

"I want three boys with their daddy's good looks." Leah said proudly.

"I want one of each than a surprise one for the third." Rachel planned.

"I can't believe we get to play with a baby in a few months." Tina said excitedly.

"Don't you get started on that? If you and Preston aren't careful you would probably have to elope too." Lauren warned Tina.

"I don't care. I want to start a family with Preston as soon as possible. What am I waiting for?" She said proudly.

"I am not asking you guys to wait. I just don't want to move into Grandfather's house right now." Lauren complained.

"Why are you guys waiting?" Dana asked.

"Dad's got some sort of thing about moving into Grandfather's house." Lauren admitted.

"You don't like grandfather's house?" I asked.

"No, I love his house but I have a lot of things. If I move now, than when Max and I get marry in the summer, I would have to move again. That is just too much moving." Lauren explained.

"Your stuff alone could break a man's back. Why doesn't Preston just build a new house and let you have that house?" Aimee suggested.

"I don't know, Tina why don't you ask him?" Lauren plotted.

"Well, did you hear? Michelle moved in with Brent right after Trisha and Robyn left with Mitch." Dana announced.

"Poor John and Diane, all their children moved out all at once." Rachel pointed out.

"It's not like we moved out of the country." Leah teased.

"It's still kind of sad." Tina voiced quietly.

"Hey why don't we go check on the guys?" Rachel announced.

I was glad for the change in conversation because we were beginning to gossip and I didn't like that. We found the guys paying poker. I went over and stood behind Corin. He wrapped his arm around my waist.

"Hey, keep your hands on the table, Corin. No cheating." Justin jibed.

"You're the only one cheating. Look how much you've racked up over there?" Corin retorted.

"It's newlywed luck." Justin teased.

"You are practically an old married couple now, so you must be cheating." Mark pointed out.

"You Randalls have a hard time losing to us Burrens." He teased

"I guess that makes us totally losers at the pot." Tristan added elbowing Max.

"Justin if you win again, I'm quitting." Max declared.

'Well, read them and weep boys." Justin boasted as he spread his cards showing two pairs.

"Wait there brother, look at these." Preston showed triple fives.

"Alright I quit. Justin and Preston cheated." Max announced.

"Can't handle the lost, huh Redman?" Justin jibed.

"I've had enough too." Derek chimed in.

"Hey let's try out the pool." Lauren suggested.

"That sounds great. Come on guys." Dana agreed.

"Did you guys bring bath suits? I am a married man now so I can't be around naked women." Justin teased.

"You're such a pervert. I am going to go get mine. Gena, do you want to go get yours?" Lauren asked

"Lauren, I haven't gone swimming since I moved here." I pointed out. Was she crazy? When is it appropriate to swim here? The weather could never be warm enough for me.

"I'll let you have one of mine." She quickly offered.

"Oh, that's ok. I don't think I want to swim tonight." I dissuaded her.

"I don't care. You are going to swim whether you want to or not." She dismissed me.

"I have never seen you in a bathing suit." Corin whispered in my ear.

"There isn't much you haven't seen." I murmured back.

Lauren and Dana left to go get bathing suits. Aimee and Leah borrowed what Rachel had. Justin offered the guys what he had. When Lauren handed me her bikini I was a bit surprised at how tiny it was.

"Lauren, where is the rest?" I teased.

"Ha, ha. That is going to look good on you. Trust me, have I been wrong before?" She assured.

"It doesn't cover much?" I pointed out.

"Don't worry it covers enough." She said.

I quickly changed into the white string bikini with matching string triangle bra. I think some of my lingerie covered more than this bikini. Lauren helped me tie the string around my neck.

"You look great. I am so good, I shock myself." She boasted.

"I think this would shock Corin." I said

"I've got to get a picture of his reaction." She exclaimed as she rummaged through her purse.

"I think you like messing with him." I noted.

"I've grown up with Corin all my life. I have never seen him behave the way he has since you've been here. It's priceless."

"Okay, let's go before I chicken out." I sighed.

"You look great. I may have to keep my eyes on Max." she jested.

I shook my head in disbelief and followed her out to the Main level and to the indoor pool. The room was kept nice and warm compared to what the temperature was outside. When we walked in everyone had already got into the pool. Justin and Max started whistling. I rolled my eyes. Justin elbowed Corin to get his attention.

"Who is that?" he announced loudly to embarrass me.

"She is mine." Corin boasted getting out of the pool. He rushed toward me and swung me up in his arms. "You look too good to be real." He whispered before he kissed me. Before we could protest Lauren was snapping pictures of us.

"I told you he would like it." She bragged.

"You had doubts?" he asked with a crooked smile.

"It's a little small." I whispered embarrassed.

"It's perfect on you." He said before he jumped into the pool. Even though they said the water was warm, it was colder than I expected. He kept me close to his body to keep me warm. After some time Justin, Mark and Tristan went to the outdoor pool. Max and Lauren disappeared into one of the rooms. Derek and Dana had other plans with Michelle and Brent. Leah, Rachel, and Aimee went to reheat more food since the guys got hungry after swimming. Corin and I stayed in the indoor pool after everyone left.

"Are you cold?" he asked as he pulled my back against his body. His hands rubbed my arms under the water.

"No, I am getting used to the water. I think getting out is going to be bad." I thought.

"I can stay in here with you to keep you warm." He tempted kissing my shoulder.

"I think Rachel and Justin may want us to leave sometime."

"You look so good in this thing." He murmured in my neck. His hands roamed over my navel.

"It doesn't cover much. I think some of my lingerie covers more than this." I pointed out aroused by where is hand was.

"I like that." He said. I leaned back against him. With his other arm he circled my waist and hugged it tight against his body.

"Do you want to go home?" He said breathing heavily in my ear.

I nodded as my lips quivered. He instantly noticed.

"Okay, go change. I will tell them that you got really cold and had to go home. Meet me at the door okay?" he instructed. I could not nor did not want to move away from him. "Do you want to stay?" he said impatiently.

"No, I'll meet you at the door." I said hating it when he pulled away. He lifted me out of the pool and carried me to the changing room.

"Gena, bring the bikini home." He whispered as he left to go change. I quickly changed and wrung out the wet bikini. I rubbed my hair and went to wait by the door. Within minutes he was back with my parka. We rushed to the car and left before anyone could pick up on our intentions. My hair froze against the cold temperature but I was too excited to even think about that. When we got home, he carried me upstairs and to our bedroom.

"I want you to change back into the bikini. We will have our own pool party in the hot tub." He said as he ran into the bathroom and started the water.

Without any protest, I quickly changed back into the bikini. He was already in the tub when I joined him. He was sitting back, so I eased myself down between his legs and laid back against him body. The water was warmer but not as hot as usual hot baths.

"You don't know how sexy you look in that bikini." He groaned against my shoulder.

"You've seen me naked, how can this be sexier."

"It is the temptation of what its covering that makes it sexy." He admitted.

Frustrated with the confinements of the hot tub, he abruptly got up and lifted me out of the water and carried me to the bed. "Sorry baby, but it was getting too hot for me." He explained as he placed me on the bed

"That was unbearable." He labored stroking my wet hair away from my face.

"I will have to agree." I said breathlessly.

I felt him tracing the string on my bikini with his finger.

"So this is what bikinis do to you?" I teased.

"This is what you do to me. I forgot about the bikini long time ago." He corrected.

"I am so hungry. Are you hungry?"

"I am ravenous. I'll go get us something to eat if you would change the sheets. Our pool party ended up getting the bed wet." He noted as he got up and changed into his pajama pants. Before he left he asked "Any request?"

"No just don't take too long." I answered.

"We've got all night, baby." He teased as he left.

I quickly got up and put on a camisole and boxer short. I stripped the bed and replaced it with clean sheets. Since I had some time, I blew dry my hair.

"Babe, come let's eat." He bellowed from the room. I went to join him.

"Grilled cheese sandwiches and tomato soup, perfect." I praised.

"Hope you don't mind, soup is from a can. But the sandwiches were hand made." He teased.

"What happened with the hot tub? It wasn't that hot." I asked.

"It was hot for me, plus there wasn't enough room to do anything. Would you like for me to build you a pool?"

"Why do you want a pool?" I questioned.

"It doesn't matter to me, I just thought since everyone around you has brand new homes maybe you may want something."

"Corin, I don't want a new home. I happen to love this house. I am not competing with anyone here."

"Well, it just that I haven't given you anything." He said as he fed me.

"What you've given me far outweighs any material thing in this world." I declared.

"You are so different than any woman I've ever met. You have all the money in the world but you don't flaunt it on yourself. You are content with everything." He described.

"Is that good or bad?"

"It's admirable." He praised as he caressed my face with his finger.

"You think too highly of me."

"You're wrong. I admire your strength and courage to sustain all the tragedies in your life to be here today. Not many people can pick their lives up and continue without being angry and resentful." He marveled.

"Well then we are a perfect match. I think your strength and courage to protect me and this clan is very commendable. Most men your age can't handle those kinds of responsibilities."

"It wasn't like I had much of a choice." He explained.

"You could've rebelled, but instead you marveled it."

"I took on the job because I knew it would lead me to different places, and I hoped that those different places would eventually lead me to you." He confessed.

'Too bad you never came to Crew, Indiana. We would have met earlier."

"I'm just glad you are here. My life would have been pretty desolate if you weren't in it."

"And all it took was one drop of blood." I smiled.

Chapter Thirty-One

I can tell Mark was nervous again. We have been at this for over three hours now. The jeweler was an impatience man anyway but Mark's indecisiveness was annoying him. Mark was looking for a setting for Leah's solitaire. I had already put in my order, now I was just helping Mark. At first, I was intimidated by this man's enormous displays but luckily I had already decided what I wanted for Gena. It came to me when I was helping her rearrange her parents' portrait. Her mother had a beautiful sapphire and diamond wedding ring that I wanted to match. After speaking with Idelle, I found out it was not sapphire but a blue diamond, which was quite rare. When I told her of my intentions to get Gena one similar to Alexandria's ring, she suggested a rare gem specialist Mr. Merchan Supps. She also setup a meeting at her house for us guys to get some help. Mr. Supps worked directly with importers who only dealt in rare color diamonds. It cost $10,000 just to retain his services and have him come to Inuvik. So while he was here several of the guys decided to look into what he had to offer. Max ordered a 3-carat radiant cut pink diamond for Lauren. Tristan and Preston stayed with the traditional white diamond but ordered color diamond settings for their solitaires. When it came to me, I knew specifically what I wanted. For my Gena, I ordered a three-carat oval cut blue diamond sitting on a diamond paves setting.

The matching bands were of the same pave design. I wanted to get her a bigger diamond but Idelle said her hand was so small that anything bigger would look ostentatious. Getting the ring was not so bad but, now I had to plan the magical proposal. That posed harder than I anticipated.

"Sir, that setting will not compliment her solitaire. To be quite honest it would look very gaudy if she wears it together." He suggested with a great deal of arrogance.

"Mark, her solitaire is quite big. Just get her some earrings." I suggested.

"I wouldn't have this problem if you guys didn't go and get all *rare diamond and special design* on me. I think she would really like these red diamonds. What do you think?" he asked.

"We can find some smaller round red diamonds and have her solitaire sit in the middle like this." Mr. Supps drew out on a piece of paper.

"Yeah, that would look really nice." Mark agreed.

"The only problem is I will need her solitaire to make this ring." Mr. Supps pointed out.

"She is wearing it. I can't just take it back." Mark exclaimed.

"It is up to you sir." Mr. Supps sighed annoyed with another setback.

"Mark, why don't you get her a separate ring, with these red diamonds and give it to her as a bridal gift." Tristan suggested.

"That is a great idea. Why don't you give her an eternity ring with red diamonds? That is pretty unique." I chimed in.

"Okay, that sounds good. That's what I want." He readily agreed.

The jeweler rolled his eyes with relief and quickly filled out the paperwork. He closed his case to prevent Mark from pondering through anymore displays. He promised to have Mark's expedited since his wedding was less than three weeks. The larger rarer stones would take some time. He would call and let us know when they were ready. I told him as long as I get it before June 28th. That's was when I planned to propose to Gena, on her birthday.

"Hey if we're done, let's get back to my place. Leah has prepared a really nice dinner." Mark announced.

"Sorry guys, I have to meet Tina and the contractors to go over plans for our house. I need them to get started as soon as possible. Maybe next time" Preston declined.

We all knew what he meant. Last week, Tina found out she was pregnant and Preston had to put everything on full gear. Rolfe finally made the decision to move into William Burren's house. Somehow Tina persuaded Preston to build her a new house and leave Rolfe's house to Lauren. This clan was expanding practically over night. Even I found it hard to not relax and enjoy all the changes.

Max, Mark, Tristan and I met the girls back at Mark's place. Rachel and Justin were visiting with her parents in Colorado. Gena and Lauren were making cupcakes for Madeline's Easter party for the Inuvik children. Leah and Aimee were making grilled steaks with new potatoes.

"Hey, guys. How was the game?" Lauren asked.

"Full of surprises and last minute changes." Max jibed.

"Who won?" Gena asked.

"It was a tie. Everyone walked away with something." I said slyly giving Tristan and Mark a quick nod.

"I hate soccer. How can a game be tie?" Lauren said annoyed.

"You just don't understand it, babe." Max pointed out.

"Can I have a cupcake?" Mark asked.

"No, these are for the children." Lauren exclaimed.

"All of them?" He complained.

"If you have a problem, talk to Aunt Madeline." She warned. When the phone rang, I went to answer it.

"Hello."

"Corin, just the man I wanted to talk to." Justin exclaimed.

"Justin, how is Colorado?"

"It is beautiful right now but I am calling to let everyone know that Rachel is pregnant. I had to wait to tell you guys because we wanted to tell our parents first. Could you pass this along?"

"Wow, congratulations. I am really happy for you guys. I'll tell everyone. How far along is she?" I asked.

"Well we are not too sure until we see Alain but she thinks 3 weeks." He guessed.

"I am happy for you two. I'll tell everyone."

"Thanks Corin, I have to go. Bye now."

I didn't have to say anything because everyone in the room was eavesdropping on the conversation when I said *congratulations*. Lauren was ecstatic with the news of being an aunt to two babies. The topic of babies consumed the dinner conversation. It was hard not to be excited with all the changes happening.

Gena and I didn't have any problems getting accepted at Aurora College, so school was not an issue with us. According to Max, Natalie would have to graduate in the summer since she was not doing so well in two of her classes. It didn't make things better when she repeatedly skipped school. Dana spent a lot of time talking to her but she was not showing any concern about failing. This wasn't unusual for her, she had never planned on going to college but everyone knew something was amiss. She was distant and cold, even towards Dana. I overheard Lauren and Dana telling Gena that it was because she was jealous because she did not have a soul mate. Thanks to that bit of information I wasted a whole Sunday reassuring Gena that it was not her fault and no one was blaming her for Natalie's sudden cold shoulders. She even tried to talk to Natalie but after several attempts she realized Natalie's problem was not her but something else.

Gena has not had another nightmare since October. We were finally able to live the kind of life we dreamt about. Even with Kyle coming for Leah's wedding, it did not bother me as much. I still didn't like him but I could tolerate him in Inuvik. Something was going on with him because he came to visit Leah more often than when she lived in Prudhoe Bay.

At the end of March, Bradley and Carl left to head back to Minnesota to investigate the body of Gabriella. It was hard on Gena to wait this long for some bit of information but the weather was finally warm enough to melt away the ice and snow that covered that area. After two weeks, they were able to get enough tissue to send out for testing. We now had to wait on the lab. They warned that since the tissue was so poorly preserved over the past 5 years, this could take at least 2 months.

School was coming to a close soon. Seniors could take their finals in April and exempt the last two weeks of schools if they had passing grades. Thanks to Trevor and Gena, I was on track in Calculus and Physics. Ironically, Trevor and I became good friends. He was still goofy but he was smart and genuinely good. He was getting ready to go to MIT in Boston. He was given a full scholarship there. We promised to visit him whenever we could. Mark's wedding was April 30th, so it landed right into Finals week. The only finals I had to take this time were the English Literature exam. Gena and Trevor exempted all their exams again. Thomas Redman did not make it mandatory for us to attend graduation since so many things were planned around that time.

On Wednesday April 27th, Gena and I went to see Trevor off to Boston. Part of his scholarship required him to be a part of some elite team of engineering competition team. I convinced Thomas to grant him a reprieve to leave school early to join his team in Boston over the summer. Our gift to him was the use of the luxury jet to go to Boston. We wished we could go with him but we had so much to do with Mark's wedding. I was actually sad to see him go. He promised to be back for our wedding whenever we plan the exact date.

After I took the English Literature final on Thursday, I was able to relax and help out with the details of Mark's wedding. Gena was Leah's Maid of Honor and I was Mark's Best man. We were busy trying to keep everything in order. My mother planned everything down to fine details. The morning of the wedding Gena spent most of the day at Mark's house helping Leah with her last minute details. I was a little nervous since Kyle was there but Leah assured me that Lauren and Aimee would also be there. I had to help Michael, Derek, and Cory set up the band equipment since Kyle's band was due to arrive any minute. By 4pm, I finally broke away and went to Mark's house to pick up Gena, so we could get ready for the wedding. Kyle greeted me at the door.

"Kyle." I greeted blandly and pushed pass him into the foyer.

"Hi, Corin." He answered briskly. I could tell he still felt uneasy around me, not from fear but from the guilt of what he did. I was not as forgiving as Gena.

When I walked in, I noticed the living room was full of unfamiliar people. They were obviously members of his band but they weren't dressed for a wedding. They looked tired and hung over. There were also a group of women that looked like groupies spread out on my brother's couch. I noticed some of them smoking and using my brother's coffee table as an ash tray. I gave them a look of disgust and turned to Kyle. I walked over and picked up the cigarette butt on the table.

"Whose is this?" I asked staring each one of them down.

"Relax, man. I couldn't fine an ash tray." I heard coming from a skinny spiky blonde male stand at the corner of the room.

I walked up to him and glared at him. "That is because Mark and Leah do not allow smoking in their house. Do you think it is appropriate for you to damage their coffee table?" I questioned angrily.

"Look man, relax. I can buy him a new one." He laughed.

"Corin, we are sorry. I'll pay for the damages. We don't want any trouble." Kyle interrupted.

"Is this your band?" he asked repulsed.

"Yeah, they just got here. There isn't a hotel here for me to put them in." he answered

"Are they going to the wedding looking like this?" I said irritated.

"Man, who do you think you are? Do you know who we are?" yelled one guy sitting on the couch with two of the groupies displayed over him. He was a skinny Asian with long black hair.

I towered over him with loathing disgust. "I don't care who you are or what you are. If you don't get cleaned up and dressed for this wedding, I will make sure you will spend a couple of months rehabbing here. Now, I want all these women out of this house. I don't care where you put them. They were not invited." I averred.

"Hey they go where we go." I heard from another band member behind me. I turned to face a pale guy with spiky green hair. He looked drugged up.

"Are they part of the band?" I asked daring them to lie.

"We keep them around for our personal needs." The green haired guy laughed.

"Kyle, I am going to take Gena home. When I come back here, your band better be cleaned up and presentable. These groupies can sit in the limousine all night long, I don't care. But if they are your *dates*, they better put some decent clothes on." I warned before I walked off and headed upstairs.

When I got to the master bedroom, I knocked gently. Dana came to the door.

"Hey Corin!" she greeted. "Come on in."

"Hey Dana. How is everything going?" I responded as I walked into the room. Gena was standing next to Leah helping Lauren do Leah's hair. She looked up and smiled at me, making a weird smirk with her lips. She was mocking herself because we both know she hates doing hair and make-up.

"Corin, did you meet Kyle's band?" Lauren asked disgusted.

"Yes, and I reminded them of the proper dress code for the wedding." I replied sarcastically.

"See Leah, I told you he would take care of it." Lauren assured.

"Thanks Corin. I can't believe they came looking like that. When Kyle wanted to serenade our song, I was afraid of this but I just wanted him to be a part of my wedding." Leah worried.

"Leah, stop worrying. You are messing with your make-up and hairdo. Everything will be fine. Corin is practically the sheriff here." Aimee advised.

"Gena, are you ready to go?" I asked her.

"Leah, I will get dress and meet you in the dressing room at the Chateau." She confirmed.

I escorted Gena downstairs making sure to shield her from the disgusting presence in the living room. “Corin, I need to get the bouquets in the refrigerator.” She said.

“Why don’t you go to the car, I’ll get the bouquets.” I directed handing her the keys. She nodded and left for the car.

I walked passed the living room and into the kitchen. I picked up the box that had all the bouquets. While exiting I noticed two of the band members (the spiky blonde and the Asian) hovering over the passengers side of my car.

“Hey, baby. What is your name?”

“Why don’t you open the window? We just want to introduce ourselves.”

I noticed Gena sitting inside the car trying to ignore them by turning the other way. I could feel the anger and rage rising in me. I have had enough of these clowns.

“Get away from the car.” I warned as I came up behind them. They stumbled away laughing.

“Gena are you alright?” She nodded from inside.

I got in the car. “Idiots” I said.

“Just ignore them Corin. We are too busy to deal with idiots today.” She assured.

When we got home, we showered and I put on my tuxedo. She changed into a lavender full length empire waist chiffon gown. As usual, I helped her into her heels. When we were ready we took our limousine over to the Chateau. I left her with Leah, Lauren and Aimee in the dressing room. I had to go check on Mark in his dressing room.

“Mark, are you ready for this?” I announced when I walked in.

“Corin, did you see some of those people with Kyle? Mom is going to have a cow.” he exclaimed.

"Mark, what do you want me to do?" I replied.

"Leah does not want any groupies at the wedding. Could you take care of it for me?" he pleaded.

"Can I use force?" I jibed.

"I don't care." He responded.

I left Mark's dressing room and headed over to the Grand Ballroom. I saw Derek and Mitch on the way over and asked them to join me. When we got to the stage, I waved Kyle down.

"Leah does not want any of these groupies to be seen at her wedding. So get rid of them." I said flatly.

"Where am I going to put them? There aren't any hotels around here." He expressed.

"Kyle, you should have thought of that before you brought them here. This is your sister's wedding, it is not a concert. Get rid of them or I will." I glared.

"Hey, I'll share my girl with you if you give me the brunette." The Asian yelled out from behind the drum set.

Mitch had to hold me back.

"Kobi, shut up!" Kyle warned him. "Okay I'll get rid of them."

Before we left Mitch climbed on the stage and picked Kobi up from his collar and yanked him from behind the drums. "I will stuff these drums up you ass if you ever speak so crudely of Gena again. She is a lady and I will not tolerate your disgusting filth spoiling the air around her. Worse, next time I will not stop him from beating the shit out of you." He threatened before he tossed him down the floor.

"Nice and subtle" I complimented him.

"What assholes? I am going to go home and shred their CDs." Derek said.

When we got back to the dressing room, Mark handed me the wedding rings. I gave him a quick hug and left to go get Gena. The wedding started on time even though things were chaotic. I could not believe how much Mark cried during his wedding. It was irony slapping him in the face. Gena stood across from me smiling; I could tell she was daydreaming. I knew exactly what she was daydreaming about, because I couldn't wait for the day when we said our vows too.

Kyle did live up to his promise. I don't know where he put the groupies but they were nowhere to be seen. The only good thing that came out of Kyle's band was his serenade to the bride and groom. I could not believe what beautiful music he could produce when he really wanted to. I stayed by Gena the entire time. I kept me eyes on Kobi most of the night. He did stay away from her as he was told. The only person that hung around the band was Natalie. They ended leaving early because Rolfe would not allow them to smoke inside the Chateau. We later heard that they left Inuvik. Kyle stayed behind for his sister's sake.

All and all everything went beautifully.

Sunday, Gena and I spent the day sleeping in. This week was exhausting and busy for both of us. After we had breakfast, we went into the living room and relaxed on the couch. We were watching the Food TV network when my cell phone vibrated. I answered quickly.

"Hello."

"Hello, Mr. Randall, this is Merchan Supps."

"Oh yes, hold on." I got up and moved into the kitchen.

"Sorry, how are you?" I replied.

"I am fine. I just wanted to let you know that your ring is ready. The only problem is that I will not be able to bring it to you." He informed.

"Can you ship it to me?" I asked.

"Mr. Randall, this is a very rare item. I would rather not do that. I know a trusted jeweler in Dawson City. With your permission I will entrust it with her, you just have to travel to Dawson City to pick it up. Would that be alright?" he asked.

"When"

"I am meeting her today in Edmonton. She assures me that you can pick it up tomorrow."

"That is fine. Where can I pick it up?"

"Her jewelry store is *Diamond Expo* on Labin Street in downtown Dawson City. Do you know where that is?"

"Yes, I've been there before. I'll be there by 2pm to pick it up. Is that too early?" I asked.

"No, that will be perfect. Thank you." He ended

I was excited to see the ring that I ordered for Gena. How ironic that it was the same jewelry store where I brought her necklace? I walked into the living room and stood watching her carefully. I don't know if I could wait to propose in June.

"For once, I would like to go to a wedding without being in the wedding party." She complained.

"Well that is going to be pretty hard because Aimee, Tina, and Lauren are next. I bet you will be asked to be in their weddings." I declared as I went to sit next to her.

"I am going to have a closet full of bridesmaid gowns by the time this summer is over."

"Yeah, my tuxedo is pretty worn. I may have to get another one. I think I will go to Dawson City tomorrow and order another tuxedo. Do you want to go with me?" I plotted.

"I would love to but I have to help Aimee with Ella's baby shower." She said disappointed.

"Oh yeah, I forgot. Well you will just have to miss me while I'm gone." I teased.

"Or you can go another day?" she suggested.

"No, I'll just be gone the same time you're at the baby shower. You won't even notice me gone." I persuaded.

"Okay, but I expect you to be home by the time I get home." She teased.

"I don't plan on being away too long. I would miss you too much." I said playfully nibbling at her ear.

I left around 1pm Monday for Dawson City. Gena had already left for Aimee's house. I wanted to get there and be back by 4pm, just in time for Gena to get back from the baby shower. The drive to Dawson City would normally take only one hour but with the spring weather, the roads were pretty slushy. When I got to the jewelry store, I was greeted by the same salesperson that helped me with Gena's necklace.

"Hello. How may I help you?" she greeted.

"Hi, I am Corin Randall. I am here to pick up something from Merchan Supps." I replied.

"Yes. Let me get Mrs. Deason." She said before she disappeared in the back room.

After some time, she returned and ushered me through the backroom and upstairs to an office. The office was beautifully adorned with pictures of many different types of colored diamonds. The massive desk in the room was covered with paper and jewelry cases. She asked me to sit and wait. I waited patiently until a beautiful middle age woman walked in and greeted me.

"Mr. Randall, my name is Lisa Deason. It is a pleasure to meet you." She greeted shaking my hand.

"Please call me Corin." I responded.

"This ring you commissioned, it is very interesting. May I ask what was you're inspiration?" she asked as she sat down.

"My girlfriend's mother had the same design."

"That is very interesting. May I ask who your girlfriend's mother is?" she inquired.

"Alexandria Burren, is there a problem?" I asked thinking that I had violated some sort of copyright law by duplicating the ring.

"No, there is no problem. I would like to show you something." She said as she stood up and opened the vault behind her. She produced a black leather box from the vault and handed it to me.

I took the box and opened it. Inside was the ring I ordered for Gena. It was beautiful. I would have to thank Mr. Supps for doing a great job. "Wow, Merchan did a great job. I can't believe how beautiful it is." I awed.

"Corin, that is not the ring you ordered, this one is." She corrected as she handed me another box.

Surprised, I opened the second box to find the same exact ring. "I don't understand. Did he make two rings?" I questioned confused.

"No, Corin. I have had that ring for 18 years now waiting for someone to come and claim it." She shared.

"Wait, what did you say?" I was startled.

"Many years ago, a young woman was brought into my late husband's hospital in the middle of the night with very bad injuries. The woman who brought her in threatened my husband to perform a C-section on the injured mother. My husband performed the surgery because the injured mother was rapidly dying; he wanted to save the babies. After the surgery the woman took the babies and left. My husband was threatened not to tell anyone about the babies. Disturbingly, that same night someone broke into the morgue and stole the mother's body and a dead fetus. My husband took this ring off the finger of the dead mother before someone stole her body; you see he was also the coroner for Dawson. All I have to remember that night was this ring. I have been holding on to this ring hoping to find out what happened that night. You see soon after that night, my husband was killed while at work and I have always suspected that it had something to do with what happened. I believe that ring belongs to Alexandria Burren, look at the inscription inside the ring." She instructed.

"Did you say babies?" I asked.

"Yes, my husband delivered twins. One was strong and the other one was very fragile and small. When they disappeared he feared for the small one." She declared.

I was too stunned by what she had just told me to ask any questions. I looked at the first ring and inside the band was the letters *DR and AB forever* inscribed. "DR is Daniel Roese her husband" I whispered.

"That means that your girlfriend was one of the twins taken that night. I have always wondered what happened to those babies. After my husband's death I tried to talk to the police but by that time there were no bodies or evidence that any of that ever happened. I kept this ring because I did not want it to be sitting in a police station only to be stolen one day. It is a very rare stone. When Merchan showed me your ring, I was shocked at the resemblance." She continued.

"Did your husband ever tell you what the other woman looked like?" I asked.

"The only thing I can remember him saying was that she was big and strong with long black hair." She recalled.

So Gena was a twin. This other woman sounded to be a hunter mother. She must have taken the babies and separated them. Somehow Alexandria appealed to this Hunter mother and got her to save the babies. This would give Gena some relief to know what happened to her mother.

"Mrs. Deason, thank you for you help. I would like to buy this ring from you." I offered.

"I don't want any money for it. You should give the other twin this ring. One of them should wear their mother's ring." She exclaimed.

"Thank you. I will make sure one of the twins wears this ring." I vowed. I didn't bother telling her that the other twin was no longer alive.

As I made my way out of town, my phone vibrated. I answered on the third ring.

"Corin! Where are you?" Justin yelled.

"I'm in Dawson, what's wrong?" I asked frantic. His tone scared me.

"Corin, you need to get back here as soon as you can. We think Gena is in the panic room." He cried.

"What! She knows not to go in there. What do you mean you think she is in there? What happened?" I yelled.

"Corin, she was attacked by a hunter disguised as a laundry worker." He screamed tearfully. My heart went completely cold and heavy.

"Where is he now? Does he have her?" I yelled.

"We killed him already, when we got here he was still in the house. We killed him but we can't find Gena. We can't find her. We think she is in the panic room. The blood trails end at the panic room in the pantry." He cried frantically.

My whole body trembled when I heard him say *blood trails*. I could not swallow, my throat would not function. My mind was numb. I forced the car at a speed that worked every piece of metal to exhaustion. Everything outside of the car was white and blurry. I blinked away the tears and every time her face came to me. The ache in my chest was crushing me. The pain was unbearable, I screamed out to stop the pain.

"Justin, how long has she been in there?" I yelled at him.

"We don't know. Aimee said she left the baby shower around 2pm and that was the last time anyone saw her." He explained tearfully.

It was now 4:00 pm. If she has been in there for 2 hours she would not be able to survive. "Justin, get her out of there. She can't survive in there. Is my dad there? Let me talk to him." I waited as he handed my dad the phone. "Dad, please, please dad get her out of there. She can not survive. Please I am on my way. Get her out of there." I screamed tearfully.

"Corin, we are doing everything we can. Our last resort is the Robotic Nano cutter." He explained

"Dad that will take forever to get her out. Can't you do anything else?" I pleaded tearfully.

"Corin, we have tried everything. The only family member that has not scanned is her grandmother and she is too far away to get here in time. I am sorry Corin." He explained sadly.

"Dad, Justin said there was blood trails, did you use that blood?" I bellowed. I cringed at the thought of him using her spilled blood that way but she did not deserve to die in there.

"We've already tried that. The blood must be mixed with his blood. He is dead too." He responded painfully bearing the worse news that could ever come out of his mouth.

Tearfully I murmured "Dad please, she is all I've got, I can't lose her." I wasn't sure if he could understand me because the pain in my heart was choking me, my throat could not form whole words.

"Corin, I swear to you we are doing everything we can." He assured but his tone was clear. There was no hope. Those who use the panic room are supposed to be able to get themselves out from the inside. If she was injured, she could be dying inside a heavy metal tomb and not conscious enough to get herself out. Worse, with every passing second she was not getting air. She was suffocating.

I could not talk anymore. I knew they were doing everything they could to get her out. There was no guarantee that getting her out now would even save her. If she was still alive, she would have scanned herself out. The thought of her dead crushed me. Tears ran down my face blinding me. The pain was choking me. My brain told me she was dead, logically she would not survive without air for this length of time but every cell in my body was willing her—

Gena please don't die. Gena please don't leave me here. I can't live with out you. I don't want to live without you.

Chapter Thirty-Two

I made it a point to wake up early to watch him sleep. It's funny how my day begins and ends with him every day. He was everything a woman could ever want and need but he was also more. He often says he dreamt of me but I am pretty sure I have fantasized of him too. Ever girl in her lifetime dreams of meeting someone who would love them unconditionally. Corin did not just love me, he valued everything about me. He yielded his heart to me without hesitation or doubt.

I watched his eased relaxed features. He was beautifully put together. His skin was flawless but not soft. His nose was sharp and high but not large. His lips were perfect in that the lower lip was full enough to compliment the top lip. I pictured his eyes when they were opened. He had a pair of perfect blue eyes that even the ocean could not compare.

Looking further down to his hands, they were large masculine hands representing strength but I have always known them to be gentle. His upper body was tight with hard muscles. He didn't have softness to his physique but I know when he touches me I felt no pain.

"You like what you see?" he whispered.

"I love what I see. How long have you been watching me?" I said as I touched my lips over his abdomen.

"You forget, this is my enjoyment"

"Well, we will just have to take turns watching each other sleep. I kind of enjoy looking at you sleep." I was trying my hand at seducing him by kissing the trail of hair running down his navel stopping just at his pants.

"Do you really have to be at that baby shower today?" he murmured.

I chuckled. "Yes, this is the first of many baby showers to come."

"I hate the thought of being away from you today." He complained.

"It is only for 3 hours. Just keep this in mind and you should be okay." I assured.

"If I think about this all day, I wouldn't make it out of the driveway." He was playing with my hair, inhaling its scent.

"What time are you leaving?" I asked.

"I was thinking about around one." He replied.

"Well, I have to be at Aimee's house by noon. When will you be back?"

"Well since they already have my size and measurements it shouldn't take too long. I should be back by 4pm." He responded.

"Good, the shower should be over by that time. I will be here waiting for you."

"Well if you put it like that, I don't want to go." He teased.

"Too late, you have to go. This would be good for us. Let's see how much time you can endure with out me." I dared.

"I never want to take that challenge." He declared caressing my face.

"I don't mean permanently, I am too selfish to let you go too far." I explained.

"I like your selfishness. What would you like for breakfast?" he asked.

"I already had my breakfast." I teased.

"I mean food silly." He laughed.

"Whatever you're having is fine with me. I have to shower and strip this bed, so get up. Today is laundry day." I declared.

"Want to join me in the shower?" Now he was seducing me, the temptation was too great but I had things to do today.

"No, because then we would end up back in bed." I scolded.

"Okay, but you don't know what you're missing? He teased as he made his way to the bathroom.

I smiled. He was incredibly adorable. How I wished I didn't volunteer to help Aimee with the baby shower. It would have been nice to just lounge around in bed with him all day. I have to remember that before I volunteer for something the next time. I stripped the bed and gathered the rest of the laundry and placed it outside. I quickly showered and joined him in the kitchen.

After breakfast, he helped me with Ella's baby shower gift. I ordered a Moses basket and filled it with many different baby items. Corin and I also got a saving bond of $1000 for her baby.

"Everything is so tiny." He said admiring the tees.

"I know, it's so cute. I love the little booties."

"Is she having a boy or girl?"

"They don't want to know." I replied as I wrapped the basket in yellow cellophane.

"What do you want?" he smiled.

"I want my girls to look like me and my boys to look like their daddy." I said adoringly.

"The girls would be absolutely stunning."

"And the boys would be unbelievable handsome." I remarked with a wink.

"Actually I was referring to how many girls or boys do you want?" he asked.

"I don't have a preference. Leah said she would like all boys so we may have to counter with three girls." I teased

"I don't mind having three girls. I would be the most prized father here. Every guy would come knocking on my door hoping to win a hand. That would be interesting." He laughed.

"You know, most human fathers fear having three girls." I pointed out.

"Well it is not the same for our kind. I know whoever is destined to be with my daughter is the only person for her. Trust me if I was a human father I would be much different." He declared.

"You don't have to tell me, I see the way you are with men around me."

"It isn't because I don't trust you, it's because I don't trust other men. You have a little bit of jealous streak in you too." He corrected.

"I know what women want. Natalie made it pretty clear that she wanted you. Even Dana admitted that she liked you at one time. This is a small town. Three women competing for one man, that's pretty competitive." I said.

"There is no competition. I never liked Natalie or Dana. They were the only two girls; I know of, that didn't believe in finding their soul mates but look at Dana now. She can't stand to be away from Derek. I just hope Natalie finds her soul mate one day. Everyone deserves this." He said as he kissed my hand.

"I bet if this was Indiana, you would have never met me. I wasn't outgoing or social. I knew more about the racetracks than girls stuff. I like motorcycles while other girls liked Barbie dolls and make-up." I admitted.

"Are you kidding? You're every guy's dream girlfriend. Mark still can't believe that you can be ready in 20 minutes. He said it takes Leah one hour to decide what to wear. Max wishes Lauren could ride a motorcycle.

Tristan and Justin would love it if their mates cook like you. And if you weren't related to Cory and Michael, I think I would have a serious issue about the way they pine over you." He confessed.

"That is your view. Mark likes Leah getting all dressed up like that. Max only lust after what Lauren would look like in leather straddling over a bike. Tristan and Justin thinks with there stomachs. And Cory and Michael would pine after any woman." I corrected.

"I have lived with these people all my life. I think I would know them better than you." He smiled.

"You are biased. Your opinion has been greatly swayed maybe blinded."

"I am not biased. I am just thankful that I have what every man wants." He said as he lightly kissed my neck.

"Don't start what you can't finish." I dared.

"Oh, I can finish." He chuckled.

"I have to get going, so stop it!" I playfully darted away.

"We will pick this up tonight." He warned. I laughed as I walked away.

I left for Aimee's house around 10:30 to help her decorate the family room with baby shower décor. Lawrence came in to help but he spent more time talking about my Ducati. I have been driving Corin's Audi so much that I had pretty much neglected my Ducati. I told him if his parents allowed him to have a motorcycle, I would be glad to share it with him. He could ride it in the winter time when it was too cold for me, but I would like to enjoy it in the summer time. He was so happy with our agreement that he abruptly left without saying thanks. Aimee just rolled her eyes at him.

After we decorated the room, we started on the hors d'oeuvres. We made little sandwiches filled with crème cheese and cucumber, some with pimento, and some with chicken salad. The shrimp cocktail we got from North's the day before. I made mini quiches while she started on the seafood stuffed mushrooms. We both worked on getting the chocolate covered strawberries ready. Corin was obviously biased because Aimee was great in the kitchen. She could rival me any day.

Baby shower gifts usually consist of onesis, booties and baby blankets, but since Lauren was among the guests Ella got a mink baby blanket with matching booties. Dana gave her an antique baby carriage. The mothers pitched in and decorated her baby room with all the furniture and appliances. Rachel and Leah pitched in and had Justin install a state of the art baby monitoring system. Rachel warned me that Justin and Tristan would be by today to get some tools to install the monitoring system.

We had a good time picking out baby names and guessing the baby's sex and birth weight. She wanted to name the baby Randolph for a boy and Cynthia for a girl, in honor of Trey's parents. Her due date was in the middle of July. This baby would be the first baby born into the new generation of this clan. Rachel and Tina were due in December. Aunt Madeline was in a rush to get Tina and Preston married. Preston was in a rush to get their house built. Tina however was in a blissful calm love filled nirvana. She said that coming close to death made her appreciate everything about life, everything was beautiful. She worshipped Preston and this baby was the culmination of their love. It was nice to hear her blissful thoughts. I am sure we all have them but we kept them reserved to ourselves. It was nice to talk with women my own age about a future filled with the same concerns and desires. It was like having a large group of sisters all within the same age.

I was daydreaming when my cell phone went off. Before I looked, I was guessing it was Corin. *He was missing me already.* Surprisingly, it was not Corin's number but Natalie's. I excused myself to go answer the phone.

"Hi, Natalie."

"Gena, I know this is a bad time but can I see you?" she asked.

"Um, sure? When do you want to meet?" I asked curious by the sudden request.

"Can I come over your place now?" she demanded.

"Well, I'm at Ella's baby shower right now, why don't you join us? Everyone would really love to have you here."

"Please Gena, the last thing I want to talk to people about is babies. I really need to talk to you, alone." She sounded distressed.

"Okay, how about later this evening?" I offered. Corin would really hate this.

"Gena, it is really important. It's about Kyle. I really need to talk to you now." She requested frantically.

"Is everything alright? Did Kyle do something to you?" I feared.

"That is the problem Gena, he doesn't do anything with me. He told me something happened between you two. I want to know what is going on." She demanded.

I had a bad feeling I knew what this was about but how can I refuse her. For weeks I have been trying to talk to her but she was always so distant and cold. She has been so sad lately that maybe if I spend some time with her she would open up about what was bothering her.

"Look Natalie, do you like Kyle?" I asked sternly.

"Gena, I love him, and I think he loves me but every time we start to get close he leaves. He is leaving tomorrow. He mentioned something about you but he wouldn't tell me about it. I don't want him to go." She cried tearfully.

"Natalie is he the one?" I asked quietly.

"Yes, we both felt it the first time we met at Rachel's wedding. But he keeps denying it and he keeps distancing himself, but every time he comes back here it is undeniable. Please help me. If you're hiding something from Corin, I will not tell him. Please I just want to know what's going on." She pleaded tearfully.

"Natalie if he is your soul mate, nothing else matters. You tell him that." I advised. I didn't want to tell her what really happened. It would probably scare her away from him. I honestly believe he was good and that he really did not mean to hurt me.

"Gena, did you cheat on Corin with Kyle?" she accused.

"Let me make this very clear to you. I love Corin very much. Corin and I do not have secrets. I would never hurt him in anyway. I do not want anyone else. You are angry and upset with Kyle, do not make this about Corin and I." I warned. I was angry at her accusation but I understood why she would come up with such absurdities.

"Than please tell me what happened?" she was crying harder now.

"Okay, just let me leave here. I'll meet you at my house in 30 minutes okay?"

"Okay, I'll see you in 30 minutes."

I went back to the party. Dana pulled me aside.

"Was that Natalie?" she asked nosily.

"Yes."

"Is everything alright?" she asked trying to fish information from me.

"I am not too sure. Do you know about Kyle?" I asked her.

"I was the one who pointed out that he was her soul mate. Those two are so stupid. I tried to tell her about me and Derek but she just kept denying it. It kills her every time he leaves. I am beginning to hate him." She hissed.

"Who else knows?"

"Well just us right now. I am surprised she told you." She whispered.

"I think it is because Leah is not here." I lied.

"I have been trying to help her through this since Rachel's wedding. They felt it instantly but something is wrong with him. Do you think he is doing drugs again?" she pondered.

"I really don't know him that well. I don't think he is doing drugs again. Leah said he doesn't believe in soul mates." I said. I was careful with my words.

"A lot of people don't believe in it until it happens to them. I didn't believe it. Natalie didn't either. Now every time he leaves she spirals into despair." She revealed.

"Well, I don't know how I can help. Maybe I'll have Corin talk to him." I lied. Corin would never talk to him. I knew what I had to do but I really did not want to tell anyone about what happened. I didn't trust that Natalie would keep quiet about it. I didn't want to betray Leah or cause her any embarrassment.

I decided I would feel Natalie out. If she genuinely loved Kyle, than I would tell her. But if this was one of her conquest, I would not be so kind. If she loved him she would understand and forgive him. He would also have to forgive himself. That is one thing I can not help him with.

After a few minutes I pretended to have an errand to do for Corin and left the party. I could tell Dana was suspicious but I did not waver. Rachel reminded me that Justin and Tristan would come by and pick up some tools to install the baby monitoring system. When I got home, I noticed the laundry had not been picked up. That was rather usual but I had Natalie to worry about right now. I knew what she was going to ask me and I didn't know if I was comfortable talking about what happened with her.

I was tempted to call Corin to ask his opinion about what to do but than I would have to admit to being the first one to miss him. It was only after two so it was too early for him to call me, I'll wait. I went upstairs to change into a pair of jeans and a long sleeve t-shirt. I have to at least look comfortable when I talk to Natalie. I went downstairs to wait for her.

When the door bell rang, I stood up quickly to answer it. The sudden movement made me dizzy and nauseous. *Wow, what was that about? Was I that nervous?* As I got closer to the door, I felt a wave of nausea and sweat hit me so hard I had to grasp onto the banister for support. I knew instantly my aura was triggered. I looked at the mirror in the foyer and saw that my eyes were blood red.

The door bell rang again. I was scared to go near it. Who was behind the door that would want to hurt me? I have had no nightmares to warn me any hunters. I thought about calling Corin but than I heard Natalie's voice.

"Gena, it's Natalie." She yelled from behind the door.

Why would my aura go off with Natalie? Was she here to hurt me?

The door bell rang again.

"Natalie, I'm coming." I stuttered. My hands were shaking with fear. *Would she come here to hurt me? Did she hate me that much for taking Corin from her?* That was absurd. She would not hurt me? She wasn't that type of person. I quickly pulled myself together and answered the door. With my hands still shaky, I opened the door. She was about to ring the door bell again.

"Gena, what took you so long?" She asked. She appeared distraught like she had been crying. Her eyes were swollen from crying and lack of sleeping.

"I'm sorry but I was in the kitchen." I said keeping my eyes down so she could not see my eyes.

"Are you alright? Is something wrong?" she asked as she walked thru the door making no eye contact with me.

Suddenly a great force slammed her into me knocking us both to the floor. Before I realized what happened, I was picked up and thrown across the living room, slamming my body against the glass wall. I heard the wall crack as I fell sharply to the floor. The impact knocked the air out of my lungs. I tried to fill my lungs again but everything hurt too much.

"So you are the healer who killed my brother?" he snarled walking towards me.

Still disoriented by the attack, I looked up to stare at a large evil figure with long black hair. After months of not having any nightmares about him, he was now standing in front of me as real as the pain from my body. His eyes were yellow, his face was heavily scarred and he was wearing a uniform that was too tight to be for him. He had blood on his hands. Standing over me, he grabbed me by my hair and slammed me into the glass wall again, this time shattering the glass. The glasses cut into my head and shoulders. I screamed out in pain when I felt the gashes over my shoulder and back. He took one of the long pieces of broken glass and rammed it into my left thigh. I screamed out in pain again. The pain was blinding. I had never experienced such great pain as when he pulled it out. I felt every bit of the slicing from the glass pulling out of my flesh. I almost fainted from the pain.

He quickly turned when he heard Natalie moving. He raced to her and grabbed her by her hair. He slammed the front door shut and dragged Natalie by her hair over towards me. He threw her forcefully into me; grinding my body back into the glass shards again. I felt her kicking at him.

He lifted her up in the air and slammed her down into the coffee table, crushing the table underneath her body. She tried to get up but he took a piece of the table and repeatedly beat her with it.

When he was done with her, he picked me up from my neck and raised me up over his head. I kicked and struggled against him until he abruptly dropped me down on the glass shards. I felt many pieces cutting into my skin. I picked up a long piece of glass as I scrambled as fast as I could through the kitchen trying to get to the panic room. I watched him following me with his evil eyes.

"It is fate that brought me here today to kill you. You are an abomination. I will take my time to make sure you are dead this time. You should be thankful that I will not kill you right away. I will wait for your boyfriend to come home. I want him to see you dying in front of him, just like your father watched your mother die." He said with great hate as he crouched over me. My hand curled around the glass shard just before I sent it across his face cutting both his face and my hand. He stood up touching the cut across his face. His roared out in anger, as he kicked me in my stomach, knocking the air out of me. I laid there curled up in pain waiting for his next attack. Then he heard Natalie moving around again.

When I heard Natalie's screaming, I realized that I could not go into the panic room alone. I had to try to help her. I heard him throwing her around like he did me. She screamed for me to help her. I pulled myself up on the kitchen counter and grabbed a large kitchen knife. I staggered to the living room but before I could move two steps, I saw Natalie's body hurled at me. Her body slammed us both back to the far end of the kitchen near the pantry entrance. I felt a sharp pain to my right side. Looking down I saw the kitchen knife protruding from my body. Natalie was unconsciously draped over me. I saw him coming towards us. He grabbed a hold of the kitchen knife and pulled it out. The sudden ejection left me withering in pain underneath Natalie's weight.

"I will enjoy killing you slowly." He hissed as he plunged the knife into Natalie's chest causing her to jerk and gurgle for air. He turned and left the kitchen. I looked at Natalie, she was choking and gurgling from the blood in her mouth. I could not move her off me. I heard him coming again. I closed my eyes and grabbed a hold of the kitchen knife and pulled it out of Natalie. She jerked forward and rolled over. I closed my eyes.

"Don't pretend to be dead; I can still feel your aura." He snarled.

I opened my eyes to see his face inches away from mine. With all the strength I had left, I drove the knife into the right side of his neck; he suddenly jerked away causing the knife to slice forward cutting him deeper into his airway. I saw him grabbing his neck and stumbling back. He was not dead; he was still struggling with the knife. I pulled myself up, and with everything I had, I dragged Natalie's lifeless body into the pantry. Every pull was excruciating and I could feel the blood gushing out of my body every time I strained. I thought about giving up but I could hear him still moving around in the kitchen. I dragged her up and against my body, leaning against the panic room door. As I passed my bloody hand over the scanner, I saw him coming towards us. The door forcefully opened and we fell into the room. The door slammed shut immediately. I faintly heard his screaming. He pounded the door shaking the whole frame.

I pulled myself up against the wall and sat there cradling Natalie's broken body. My vision was completely red. The pool of blood that surrounded us was a combination of our injuries. I was too tired and weak to attempt at holding any pressure to my stab wounds. He pounded at the door again. Luckily I could not hear him but the shaking of the structure proved that I made the right decision in trapping us in here. I would rather die in here than let him torture me to death.

I knew I could not survive being in here for too long but I least I would try to heal Natalie. If anything, one of us would make it out of this coffin. The warmth and nausea was excruciating. I felt like I could not get in any air. I prayed that it would be quick but I knew that suffocation took a long time and the agony would be torture. Bleeding to death wasn't any easier or faster. Slowly I felt my conscious slipping away. My body became numb to the pain. My breathing took in less and less air. I choked and vomited copious amount of blood over Natalie's face. I made a feeble attempt at wiping it off her but I watched my vision blurred. I started to cry thinking about Corin. I would never see him again. I didn't want him to suffer with my death. I closed my eyes to envision him. I tried to think of him as my body slowly begins to fail. I could feel my heart struggling with every beat. My lungs did not expand enough for me to get any air. I blinked away the tears that were blinding me. I closed my eyes so that I could see him. If anything, I wanted my last thoughts to be about him. I remember the first time my eyes saw him. His smile warmed me. I slowly moved my hand over my chest to feel for the Mobius Strip. When I felt it I held it up and kissed it. *I love you Corin.*

Chapter Thirty-Three

I raced through the town and as I near Alain's house; I remember her blood in the lab. I crashed up their driveway and invaded their home. When I got to the lab refrigerator, I grabbed the rackwith blood tubes in them. I raced back to my car. When I got to my house, everyone was standing in and around my house. I got out and raced for the door. The carnage from the attack was still displayed throughout the house. Glass and broken debris was everywhere. I saw puddles of blood from the living room and thru the kitchen. When I got to the pantry, my dad and Rolfe was still working on the door.

"I have her blood." I cried. They instantly got up to allow me room to get in. My hands shaking and trembling, I fumbled with the tubes. Alain grabbed the tube marked ***GR*** and went into the pantry. I followed behind him. The panic room door was badly dented and covered in blood. The site of the door sickened me. Tears came down my face at the thought of what she had to endure to lock herself inside knowing that she would die in there. When he smeared some blood into the scanner, I heard the locks disengage and the door snapping back but since the door was badly dented it could not open all the way. From in front of me I could see Natalie's body and Gena's underneath her. There was a thick pool of blood around them.

"Oh my God, Natalie's in here too. Someone get Thomas." I heard Rolfe yell out.

I tried to squeeze through the opening but I could not. "Gena! Please Gena." I screamed. Anger swept over me. I wanted to get to her. I pulled with all my strength until I felt the door give way. When I had enough room to get in, I lifted Natalie's body off and handed her to Alain. I turned and looked down at Gena's lifeless body. I fell to my knees down onto the bloody floor and gathered her in my arms. There I sat crying and rocking her. Her small frail body had no chance against the same force that dented the door. I kissed her bloody face and lips. My heart was gone. The hole left behind was so deep nothing could fill it. *"I'm so sorry, baby. I am so sorry."* My body shook with grief. I could no longer control the rush of aching pain that consumed me. Tears washed over my face. As I wailed in grief, Alain and Rolfe pulled the door further back and stepped inside, slipping against the bloody floor.

"Corin, I am so sorry." Alain said tearfully. Rolfe could not speak. His face was riddled with grief and anguish.

Justin came to the doorway and braced himself against the site of the horror. "Oh, God. Gena!" he cried out. He stood at the door crying. Rolfe came to his side and pulled him away. Alain left when Thomas Redman asked him to come outside.

I wanted desperately for the door to slam shut and seal us both in here forever. I wanted only to be with her even if it were only in death. My life would be like death to go on without her. I grabbed her hand and kissed it. Her right hand was closed tightly around her necklace chain. I pried her hand open to find the Mobius strip pendant. Even as she lay dying she remembered me. I kissed her palm with the Mobius strip pendant.

Alain appeared thru the doorway. "Corin, bring her out here. I need to examine her." He ordered.

"No, please leave us alone." I pleaded tearfully. I would rather wither and die in here with her than have her buried alone in the cold ground. I did not want anyone to touch her.

"Corin, please." He said softly.

"No! Get out. Everyone get out!" I yelled madly.

"Corin, I need to check if she still has a pulse." He explained.

"What are you talking about? Look at her!" I screamed insanely at the top of my voice.

"Corin, I don't want to give you any false hope but Natalie is awake. Just let me check her." He explained as he started to reach for her.

"No, let me do it!" I yelled.

"Okay Corin." He said cautiously.

I cautiously leaned down to her chest and held my breath praying that I would be granted one last miracle. I listened intently but could not hear anything. I glared back at Alain angry that he would even thought to give me this tiny hope.

"You have to listen longer." He said with some doubt.

I pressed my ear against her chest. I muted all my other senses to tune into the one noise I wanted so desperately to hear. The entire room was zoned out. I had complete silence. ***Ta dum***. Then I heard it. Did I hear it? I looked up at Alain. ***Ta dum***. There it is again. I scrambled slipping against the floor.

"Alain, I heard it!" I screamed. He quickly took her from me and rushed her out. I scrambled to my feet, continuingly slipping against the slick floor.

I followed behind him as he carried her to the kitchen floor. "Get the stretcher in here!" he yelled.

I came to her side. "Alain what can I do?" I begged.

I watched as he placed his stethoscope over her chest and listened for her heartbeat. Then I watched as he started blowing air into her mouth. I sat there helpless.

"I can't get any air in her. Try to clear her mouth." He directed frantically. "Get me my bag." He yelled at Cory.

I pried her mouth open and stuck my finger inside to check for anything blocking her throat. I felt around and pulled out thick clots of blood. When I thought I got it all, I took in a deep breath and blew it into her mouth. Her chest did not rise.

"Air is not getting in. She must have more deep down her throat." He explained. He turned and directed Cory to get him a respiratory air bag.

When Cory appeared with the bag, I watched as Alain pulled out a surgical blade and quickly cut into the base of her throat. Bubbling blood came oozing out and her chest choked. He pushed a clear plastic tube down and placed the respiratory air bag and forced air into her lungs. We watched intently as her chest rose.

"Here, keep doing this. Slowly" He instructed me as he checked her for a heart beat again. "She has a heartbeat. It is very weak but its there. I have to get her to a ventilator. She is not breathing on her own."

Alain and Cory lifted her onto the gurney and we rushed out to the waiting ambulance. Cory threw the ambulance driver out of the van and took over driving to the hospital. Alain got on the phone and ordered the hospital staff to put together an emergency ventilator setup in one of the ICU beds. While in the ambulance, I watched as Alain placed two IV lines into her arm and forced fluids as fast as he could into her body. I continued to push air into her body with the respiratory bag.

When we got to the hospital, we rushed her through the front lobby to an awaiting elevator. When we got to the ICU, there were only two nurses there to help Alain. They looked at me and were frightened by my appearance. One grabbed the bag from me and continued pumping air into her. The other assisted Alain on hooking Gena up to the ventilator. Cory pulled me out of their way as they worked on her. When they placed the heart monitor on her and the number 20 came up the nurses looked at each other.

"Dr. Burren, she has a heart rate of 22." One nurse whispered sadly.

"Just keep ambuing her. Are you done with the vent settings?" He asked the other nurse. When she confirmed the vent settings, he attached her neck tube to the ventilator hose and let the machine take over.

"Dr. Burren, do you want to give her anything for her heart? It is only in the twenties."

"No, not right now. Thank you for coming in. If you don't mind I'll take over from here." He directed them.

Cory and I watched as they left. We could hear them whispering. "He must be insane she can't survive too long with a heart rate of 20". The other nurse whispered back "It's his niece. I think he just feels like he has to do something." They got into the elevator and left.

"Alain, please give me something to do." I whispered. I really wanted to ask him about her condition but I wasn't sure if the news would be what I wanted to hear.

"Cory, could you go check on where they placed Natalie?" He ordered.

"Corin, I want you to remove all her clothing and wash away as much of this as possible. I need to know if she is still bleeding anywhere. I will check on Natalie. I'll be back." He instructed.

"Alain" I choked.

"Corin, I don't know but right now she has a heart beat and she is getting air. She has lost a lot of blood and we are not really sure how long she went without air. We will have to wait and see." He said sadly before he left.

I slowly remove her shirt and picked out some glass shards that were embedded into her skin. I lightly washed her body and found one large puncture wound to her abdomen. The cut was clean and I did not see any blood coming out. I found multiple cuts to her shoulder and back. I removed so much glass from her back that it pained me to know what happened to her. When I removed her jeans, I found a large jagged puncture to her left thigh. It too was not bleeding anymore. I washed her body then washed away all the old dried blood on her face. I came close to her ear and whispered "If you can hear me, baby. I am here. Please don't leave me. I love you. Gena, I love you."

When I was done washing her, I found a hospital gown and covered her with it. When I went to snap the gown on the back of her neck, I noticed her body felt hot. I looked up and saw the perspiration on the bridge of her nose and over her upper lip. I remember seeing this same thing when she was healing Kyle. I cautiously lifted her eyelid up and saw that her eye color was red. *Her aura is healing her.* I didn't know if it confirmed anything and I wasn't a doctor but I was so happy to see her eyes red that I burst out into tears.

"Corin, what happened?" Alain asked as he came rushing into the room.

"Her eyes are red." I declared.

"I figured as such. When Natalie was brought out and she was healed I had a feeling that Gena's aura kicked in. I also hope that since it was healing Natalie, it would heal her too. If she was dead she would not have been able to heal Natalie. That is why I wanted to check her." He explained.

"I am so sorry."

"Corin, if this was my child or my wife, I don't know if I could be sane enough to even talk. You have witnessed more heartaches than any one person can endure. Now, did you see anything bleeding?" He asked.

"She has got two large puncture wounds to her thigh and abdomen, but neither one is bleeding. She also has a bunch of lacerations all over her back and arms. She has this big gash on her head here." I pointed out to him.

I watched as he thoroughly assessed each wound. "Wow she heals fast. These cuts were pretty deep but somehow it is not bleeding." He wondered. He picked out more glass shards from her thigh wound. I showed him the bowl filled with the glasses I had already picked out. "I guess glass walls aren't so great anymore."

"How is Natalie?" I asked.

"She has a stab wound to her chest and a lot of bruises and cuts but she will be alright. I heard Tristan and Michael had to pull Kyle out of the room when he found out Natalie was injured."

"Why?" I asked stupidly.

"Guess?"

"Are you kidding? He is her soul mate?" I said in disbelief.

"Everyone has one." He acknowledged.

"I guess so." I replied.

"Well, this is all I can do for her right now. We will have to wait and see how her aura heals her. The only concern I have right now, since she can not breathe on her own, is brain damage." He explained.

"What do you mean brain damage? Wouldn't her aura heal that too?" I questioned.

"Well, it depends. If her aura kicked in before or after she ran out of air. If she ran out of air before her aura could protect her than she may have some brain damage, that maybe why she is not breathing on her on." He informed.

"What about her heart rate. I heard the nurse say she could not live long with that heart rate."

"Corin, her heart is stable." He assured.

"So when will she wake up?" I asked.

"I don't know." He replied honestly.

"What can I do?" I pleaded.

"You are doing everything you can. Talk to her, she can hear you." He comforted.

"Thank you, Alain." I said gratefully.

I continued to wash her sweaty face. I remember her describing it to be uncomfortable and hot. I kissed her face and lips. "Gena, if you can hear me. I am here. I love you." I whispered close to her ear.

After awhile, I heard Justin at the door. He stood at the doorway with tears running down his face.

"Alain said she was stable. Can I come in?" he asked sadly. I nodded.

"God, Corin. I can't believe she is still alive." He said tearfully.

"She is pretty tough." I commented.

"I don't know how she fought him off. He was huge. He was at least three times her size." He expressed with awe.

"How did you guys know she needed help?"

"We didn't. Tristan and I stopped by to get some tools to set-up Ella's baby monitoring system. When we got to the door, we heard pounding noises from inside. The front door was unlock so we walked in and found all the mess. Then he appeared from out of the kitchen. He had a knife stuck in his neck but he still fought vigorously. It took everything we had to kill him. When he was dead we looked for Gena but we could not find her. We knew something happened to her because there was all this blood. Tristan followed the blood trails and we assumed she was in the panic room. We called your dad first than you." He recalled.

"Where is the body now?"

"Bradley and Carl took it to the morgue. Rolfe and Alain are going over the body right now."

"Thanks for being there."

"Corin, I wished I could have done more. We all felt so helpless. Your dad was insane. He felt so bad that he could not get her out. We tried everything. We had every family member scanned. Then we smeared blood from all the different puddles. I didn't think about the lab. I am so sorry, Corin."

"No, I want to thank you guys for getting to her. If you guys didn't stop by when you did, she and Natalie would have been in there longer." I pointed out.

"What was Natalie doing there?"

"I think it has something to do with Kyle."

"What does this has to do with Kyle?"

"Alain just told me that Kyle is Natalie soul mate."

"Are you kidding me?" he said surprised.

"No, they said he went ballistic when he found out Natalie was almost killed."

"That doesn't explain why she was at your house?"

"Well if Natalie and Kyle is an item, maybe he told her what happened with Gena."

"Well that would explain why she has been crazy lately. Anyone who has to deal with that jerk has got to be crazy."

"There's a soul mate for everyone." I noted.

"Hey, the girls want to see her. Do you want me to tell them to wait?" he asked.

"Maybe tomorrow." I replied. He nodded and left.

I spent the rest of the night cleaning the rest of the old dried blood off her body. I washed her hair and got most of the thick dried clots out. I kept myself busy by doting on her. Around 3am, I watched a hospital program on how to care for a loved one in the hospital, so I spent most of the night learning how to massage her arms and legs. Alain walked in and thought I was losing it until I explained to him where I got the idea.

Sometime during the night I fell asleep sitting on the side of her bed. I woke up when Alain came in to check on her. I went to her ear and whispered "Good morning, baby. It's Corin. I am here. I love you."

I watched Alain change some of the settings on the ventilator. He also took her vital signs. He showed me how to wash and change the dressing on her wounds.

"Is everything alright?" I asked.

"Well, she isn't breathing completely on her own yet but she is trying. I've just lowered the setting. The machine will do half and she will do the rest. Her body temperature is 116, which means her aura is working in full gear. She would probably be more comfortable if you wash her with cold water. She is sweating a lot. Her heart rate is still stable between 20's and 30's. We'll just have to wait to see how she comes out." He informed.

"Thanks Alain."

"Corin, you need to get some rest." He advised.

"No, I want to be here when she wakes up." I declined.

"Well, there is a bunch of people out there that wants to see her. Is it okay if they come in?" he asked nicely.

"Yeah, sure" I said quietly.

"I'll send them in." he said as he left.

The first people that came in were my parents and Rolfe and Madeline. They offered to stay with her if I wanted to leave to go change but I declined. My dad had the panic room removed until a new one could be built. Rolfe and Blaine had some people in to clean up the house. I was thankful for that. I didn't know if I could ever clean up Gena's blood. When they left other members of the clan came and visited her, bringing food and flowers. Justin and Rachel stayed with me the whole day. Justin brought me some clean clothes. Rachel and Lauren washed Gena's hair and styled it. Tristan and Aimee brought in a more comfortable recliner for me. Aimee read somewhere that reading to the patient would help them recover faster. So they each took turns reading food recipes to her. We kept the TV on the Food TV network channel. Around dinner time, they brought in dinner and ate with me. When Alain came in to check up on her, I asked him about how long she could go without food.

"Well after three days if she is not responsive, then I will put in a feeding tube." He informed.

"Alain when will she wake up?" Lauren asked.

"Well, Lauren I don't know. Time is the always worst for those who are waiting." He lectured.

When they all left, we watched TV together and I read some Gourmet magazine articles to her. After her nightly massage, I sat there quietly and washed her face. I spent most of the night talking to her. I took Aimee's advice and talked to her to keep her updated.

"When you wake up, I have a surprise for you. You won't believe what I found out when I went to Dawson City. I am not going to tell you until you wake up."

"Justin and Tristan took care of Nhan. He is not going to hurt you anymore."

"Natalie is doing really well. You saved her life. Thomas and Amanda Redman are really grateful."

"You don't have to worry about the house being in a mess. Rolfe had someone in to clean it up. I think the glass walls have got to go. I loved it just as much as you but I think drywalls would be better to crash into. My dad had the panic room removed. I think we will have to make a decision on a different model. I don't think I like this kind."

"Don't get mad but Justin called Leah and Mark. They are on their way back. Lauren and Rachel fixed your hair. I had nothing to do with that."

"Guess what, Kyle is Natalie's soul mate. Will you believe that? Did you know already? I bet you did. You're so smart about those things."

"Alain said that if you don't wake up and eat he is going to put a feeding tube in you. I don't know what that is but I bet it don't feel good. I wonder what foods you could get through a feeding tube. It doesn't sound good."

"Rachel made lasagna tonight. It doesn't taste as good as yours. You may have to help her."

I continued to talk to her about nonsensical things to keep myself sane. I finally fell asleep holding her hand. When Alain came in the next morning, I noticed him resetting the ventilator again. I lend over her ear and whispered "Good morning baby, I love you."

"How is she doing today?" I asked him.

"Well I just changed the ventilator setting. It will only kick in if she fails to breathe in less than 12 breathe per minute. If she does okay with this, I will take her off the ventilator tomorrow." He informed.

"So she would be breathing on her own now?" I asked nervously.

"Yes, now let's look at her wounds." He said as he removed her dressings. "Wow, she heals fast. This was opened yesterday, now it's closed. I bet tomorrow it would scar over. She heals two times faster than us. Her aura is phenomenal." He praised.

"How come we don't have information about the healer aura? All we have are a bunch of stories from people's experiences." I questioned.

"Good question. When she wakes up you should talk to her about documenting her experiences so that future generations would have something to look to." He suggested.

When he left Dana, Derek, Trey and Ella came by to see Gena.

"Corin is there anything you need." Ella offered

"No, I have everything I need right here."

"Natalie told us that Gena saved her. She can't remember much but she said that he barged through the door. She remembers him attacking Gena and then he attacked her. She said she passed out when he threw her into the kitchen. Gena must have pulled her into the panic room because she doesn't remember getting in." Dana recalled.

"What was she doing there?" I asked.

"Well she wanted to ask Gena about something that happened between her and Kyle. I guessed Kyle must have told her yesterday because she was so mad she threw him out and banned him from the room. I don't get them. First she wants to be with him but he doesn't want to be with her, now he wants to be with her but she doesn't want him near her. Do you know what's going on?" Dana asked curiously.

"Maybe you should ask Natalie." Ella pointed out.

When they left Lauren, Max, Aimee, and Tristan came in. Justin and Rachel went to pick up Mark and Leah from the airport. They brought me a fresh change of clothes and some food. When I went to shower, Lauren and Aimee bathed Gena and fixed her hair. They ate with me while we waited for Mark and Leah. Aimee continued to read to Gena while Lauren painted her nails. When they arrived Justin started on the retelling of the story.

"I can't believe she stabbed him with a kitchen knife." Mark awed

"Well she didn't have her regular weapon of choice, Corin had the keys." Tristan jibed, we all laughed for the first time since the attack.

"She is a tough cookie; you should have seen this hunter. He was huge. He was bigger than Cron." Justin exaggerated.

"This is the one that Robyn warned us about. He was supposed to be sadistic and really vicious." Aimee noted.

"What were you doing in Dawson City?" Mark asked.

"I was picking up her engagement ring." I said sadly.

"Oh, Corin. Were you going to propose that day?" Leah asked.

"No, I was going to wait until her birthday but now after this I don't want to wait." I planned.

"That is so sweet. Max you should be paying attention to what Corin is doing." Lauren complained.

"I am working on it. Thanks Corin." Max replied dryly.

"When I was there I met someone that was there that night when Alexandria died." I declared.

"What? Are you talking about the woman who saved Gena?" Justin asked.

"No. Justin do you remember the jewelry store on Labin Street."

"The Diamond Expo, right?"

"Yeah, well the jeweler had in her safe a ring that matched what I ordered for Gena. When she saw the ring I ordered for Gena she told me about a story that happened eighteen years ago. Her late husband was the town doctor and coroner. He was forced to do a C-section on a dying mother. The dying mother was Alexandria."

"How do you know it was Alexandria?"

"Well the ring she showed me is the same ring I saw on her portrait and the engravings inside were *DR and AB forever.* I have the ring in my car."

"How did she get the ring?" Justin questioned.

"Well, the doctor delivered twins babies." I informed

"Twins?" they all voiced

"So does this mean that Gabriella is Gena's twin?" Leah asked

"Who is Gabriella?" Aimee asked.

"Well let me finish. The woman, who brought Alexandria in, took the babies and separated them. By the description, she must be a hunter mother. She gave Gena to a human couple and Gabriella to the clan in Minnesota."

"Is this the clan that was killed when you were taken?" Aimee asked. Leah nodded to confirm.

"Wait, Alexandria and Daniel's bodies were found in the woods."

"Well according to the jeweler, that same night someone took Alexandria's body and a dead fetus. I think the same woman who saved Gena did this to protect the babies' existence."

"Why did she separate them?' Tristan asked.

"Well I can't be too sure but if you were a hunter, wouldn't you want the healer aura to be away from her clan. See Gabriella did not have an aura. This hunter mother did not want to kill the babies but she also did not want to weaken her specie either." I explained.

"So this jeweler took Alexandria's ring?" Lauren question confused.

"No, her husband removed the ring before the body was stolen. When her husband was killed, she tried to go to the police but since there was no body they didn't take her seriously. She kept the ring because it was the only thing left from that night. Someone killed her husband over what happened." I continued.

"Unbelievable. Every time I leave I come back to hear more things about Gena." Mark nodded.

"So what are you going to do with two rings?" Justin asked.

"Well I'll let Gena make that decision. I am just waiting for her to wake up so I can propose."

"What did Alain say about that?" Mark hesitated.

"Well, she is breathing on her own right now. If she does okay like this then he will remove the ventilator tomorrow. Her wounds are pretty much healed."

"Wow, she heals fast." Tristan boasted.

"Yeah, that is what Alain said."

"Well then why isn't she waking up than?" Lauren asked.

"I don't know. Alain doesn't either. We just have to wait." I replied.

It was after 9pm when they left. I gave Justin my car keys so he could get the rings from the car. I continued with our nightly routine. Looking at her, I missed her voice.

"Gena, you have to wake up baby. I am losing my sanity." I mumbled tearfully.

"Please I don't want Alain to put that feeding tube in you. It might hurt and you know how you feel about pain. Just give us a sign that you're coming around."

"Lauren is threatening to put makeup on your face tomorrow. You should see what she's done to your nails."

"Mark and Leah are here to see you."

"Rolfe said you will need a new kitchen. I really don't know what you want. You're going to have to help me pick out some appliances. You know I don't know all the good stuff. You don't want me to pick some crappy name brand stuff. I will you know."

I continued to babble on throughout the night to keep myself sane. I woke up the next morning when Alain came through the door. I bent down and whispered in her ear "Good morning baby, I love you."

I watched as Alain detached the ventilator tubing from her neck tube. He carefully checked her wounds and removed the dressing. We were both surprised to see the wounds completely sealed. After he was done with the wounds, he took some measurements and vital signs.

"I am going to hold off on the feeding tube today. Her weight is stable. She doesn't show any failure to thrive. Her vital signs are stable and she is now breathing on her own. The rest is up to her." He concluded.

I thanked him. I didn't want to ask him the same questions over and over. I am pretty sure he has been getting the same questions from everyone else.

Around 10am, Max brought Natalie to see Gena. She was in a wheelchair. She recanted the story to us and blamed herself for Gena being home that day. According to Thomas, Nhan killed the regular laundry guy and stole his uniform. His body was found at Tuk beach. He had been dead for one week. That means that Nhan had been watching and studying our habits for a few days. He found the perfect opportunity when I left for Dawson City. I tried to explain to Natalie that she was not to blame. I also found myself defending Kyle. *My sanity must be gone.*

Max didn't understand what the issue with Kyle was but Natalie knew what I was referring to. When they left, Lauren, Aimee, and Leah came by to help with Gena's bed bath. Justin and Tristan went to see Rolfe regarding the story about what happened in Dawson City. Mark brought me some clothes to change into. I went over what Natalie told me about what happened that day.

"Kyle left his band." Leah admitted.

"Really? Is he going to live here?" Aimee said excitedly.

"I think he wants to talk to Natalie about that." She replied.

"Well Natalie has to speak to him first." Mark added.

"Why can't things just be simple?" Aimee said exacerbated.

When Justin and Tristan showed up, they handed me both rings. Lauren and Aimee fawned over the rings. I spent the day going over plans on how to rebuild the kitchen and living room. Rolfe wanted to do away with all the glass walls and replace them with drywalls. We settle on just removing the glass walls in the living room and kitchen. Rachel helped pick out all the appliances for the new kitchen because I knew Gena liked her kitchen. Madeline took over redecorating the living room with new furniture. The only thing that did not need to be changed was my birthday present, the TV. Everything else was either broken or had blood on it. I requested the kitchen made bigger because I knew how much she liked to cook. I even had them put a TV in the kitchen for her to learn while cooking. After they left for the night, I started on my nightly routine with her. *God, I miss her.* I thought as I stared as her sleeping form.

"Gena, you're going to have to wake up because Natalie and Kyle needs help to get together. Aimee can't do it by herself."

"Rolfe wants to destroy our house and build one like his. Do you want Greek statues or columns?"

"Leah made chicken parmesan tonight. I think since you're not around she is slipping. It just didn't taste right. I didn't want to tell her. You're going to have to straighten her out. She is probably slacking off because you're not around."

"Lauren painted your nails hot pink."

Again, I babbled throughout the night until I fell asleep next to her. I was startled awake when my phone fell out of my pocket and landed on the hard floor. I went to pick it up and noticed the time was 4am. I laid there staring at her. *Please wake up. I miss you so much.*

"Gena, I was going to wait until your birthday but you give me no choice. I am on my knees. I am begging you to wake up and accept my proposal."

"Gena, I will love you forever. With you there will be no other. Will you marry me?" I asked as I slipped the ring over her third finger. Tears came down my face.

Chapter Thirty-Four

My aura must be triggered. It is so hot in here. My whole body is sticky and sweaty. The nausea is unbearable. My mouth is so dry. Where am I? I need to open my eyes. Everything is so heavy. I felt like I have been asleep for days. Even my eyelids are heavy. I could hear something falling and hitting the floor but my eyes and body would not move. The noise was so sharp and clear. I could almost identify the object just by hearing it hit the floor. My body felt so tired. How could I be so exhausted if I have been sleeping? I felt my hand being touched. My skin was alive as soon as it felt his skin. I heard his voice. This was my angel's voice, the same voice that I was so keen in hearing. His voice was magical and bewitching. My ears enjoyed the tone.

"Gena, I was going to wait until your birthday but you give me no choice. I am on my knees. I am begging you to wake up and accept my proposal."

"Gena, I will love you forever. With you there will be no other. Will you marry me?"

I tried to answer but I could not make a sound. I felt a cold metal sliding onto my finger. *Yes! Yes!* I thought, but nothing came out. Where is my voice? I lost my voice. I tried to open my eyes again but it would not move. I laid there unable to move. My body was hot and sweaty. What is happening to me? Am I in a coma? No, I can't be in a coma. I wouldn't have thoughts if I was in a coma. What is wrong with my body? Was I paralyzed? No I can't be paralyzed I can feel him touching me. I can feel the heat and sweat. The wave of nausea was coming again. I need something to drink. My throat is so dry and uncomfortable.

I laid there forcing my eyelids to open. I can feel my eyeballs darting around under my eyelids. *Come Gena, open your eyes. Just open them.* It felt like I was using every ounce of energy and muscle just to open my eyelids. I can't imagine having to move my arms or legs. When my eyelids slowly eased up, I had to focus my vision. The room was dark but there were blurry lights blinking. I couldn't make out where I was. This is definitely not heaven or hell so I must be still on Earth. When my vision focused, it was clear and sharp. I could see the fine details in the ceiling and curtains. I moved my eyes to my right and noticed Corin's head on the side of my bed. He was sleeping. I could feel his breath on my hand. The sensation tickled my skin. I moved my eyes over and saw my left hand lying over my stomach. I could see the ring on my finger. I felt its weight on my finger. I want to see it close up. *God, how I hated to have to work on moving my hand.*

I stared at my hand willing it to move. I was sweating buckets now. The nausea was excruciating. I could feel the pounding in my head from the straining. When I felt my thumb twitched I knew this was going to be a long night. Throughout the night I worked at moving my fingers than when that was done, I slowly moved my hand inching it towards my face. When the sunlight broke through the window, I recognized the room. Oddly I could smell the sunlight. It was a weird warm smell. I looked around. I was back in the ICU room. I was alive. The hunter did not kill me. I didn't suffocate in the panic room. I was able to move my hand to my face now. I could see my ring. I felt tears run down the side of my face. It was beautiful. He did make my proposal magical. I would remember this for the rest of my life. I slowly moved my heavy dead hand over to touch his head. His hair was so soft, *has it always been this soft?* He moved his head but was still asleep. I stretched my right fingers underneath his face. His head moved again but this time he looked down at my hand. He jerked himself up and turned to look at me. There were those beautiful blue eyes I love. My heart skipped a beat. He was definitely worth coming back for.

"Gena?" His face was a mixture of surprise and fear. Tears ran down his face. He grabbed my face and kissed me all over. I inhaled his scent. His smell was so much stronger and definitely intoxicating. I missed his scent. "Oh, God. Thank you so much. Thank you so much for waking up. I love you so much. Thank you for not leaving me. Baby thank you." He was crying forcefully, his tears wet my face. I moved my lead arms and grabbed at his hair. He touched our noses and whispered "I love you." I smiled back at him. I tried to speak but no voice came out. My mouth kept moving but I could not hear my own voice. He looked down at me curiously trying to read my lips.

"Wait let me go get Alain." He rushed out of the room. I moved my heavy hand over my throat and felt something plastic there. I felt around it to try to figure out what it was.

"Gena, that's an airway tube. Don't pull it out." Alain warned coming into the room. "I have to plug it before you can talk."

I watched as he worked over my neck. Corin was standing on the right side of my bed.

"Now, try to speak." He directed. "It's going to sound funny but that is because you have a hole in your neck."

I hesitatingly moved my mouth. The voice that came out was unfamiliar to me. It was raspy and dry.

"What? What did you say?" Corin moved his face closer to my mouth.

My second attempt at talking was much easier. I was able to say "Yes."

"Yes what?" Alain asked. He was also leaning into my face.

"Yes, I will marry you." I uttered in my new raspy dry voice.

They both smiled. Corin's face lit up. "I think she is talking to you." Alain teased.

Corin kissed me and then whispered "I love you."

Alain spent most of the morning assessing me. After some time, I was able to move around easier but my limbs were still heavy and clumsy. He removed my airway tube and covered the hole with padded gauzes. That helped with my voice but it still sounded weird. My voice was not the only thing that was weird. My whole body felt strangely alien to me. My senses were keener. My body was alive with new sensations.

"You have got to be the luckiest girl in the world. You have survived two attacks with very minimal damage. You had us pretty scared for awhile there." Alain was nodding his head in disbelief.

"I would like to redefine luck as not being attacked to begin with. It seems like I am always around when these hunters want someone to pound on." I tried to be humorous over the situation.

"I guess this is coming from a girl everyone thought died 18 years ago."

"It's just not my time."

"Time has nothing on you." Alain teased.

"Can I eat or drink anything?" My throat was so dry and hot.

"Certainly, just take it slowly and sit straight up when you're eating or drinking." Alain said as he finished working on me. Before he left the room he turned and said "Gena, I am so happy that you are here with us."

Corin helped me sit straight up and handed me some water. "Take it slowly babe."

The water never tasted so good. I wonder if this is what it is like when someone died and came back. Everything tastes better, smells better, and looks clearer and beautiful. Was this the gratitude of life?

"When did you wake up?"

"I woke up when I heard you propose."

"If I knew that was all it took I would have done it earlier. Why did it take you so long to answer?"

"My brain was awake but my body did not move. When I finally got my hand to move you were asleep. How long was I asleep? How is Natalie?"

"Well its Friday so four days. She is doing really well. You saved her life too."

"Well, she was in the wrong place at the wrong time."

Without any warning he buried his face on my lap and cried. I could not stop or comfort him. I pulled him up to me and we held each other, while he continued to cry he kept repeating "I am never going to leave you again. Everywhere I go, you have to go. I can not go through that again. I can never lose you. Every time I close my eyes I see you in the panic room. As long as I live, I will never forget that. I love you. I love you. I love you."

"I guess as much trouble as I am; I am going to need you around."

"Thank you for being a survivor. I love your aura. I love you. You are the strongest person I know." He was kissing my hand and face.

"I have a very good reason to live. We have a very good reason to live. I plan to be with you forever."

"Forever sounds good to me." He leaned in and kissed me more passionately. I missed that.

"Thank you for a very magical proposal. You really made it memorable."

"I didn't have a choice you wouldn't wake up." He smiled.

"It looks just like hers." I said admiring my ring. It was a little big but I could have it resized.

"It is hers." He sprung on me.

"What? How is that?"

"Well, first I want to show you the ring I actually got for you." He said as he produced a black leather box. I quickly opened it and found an exact replica.

"It is identical." I lifted the ring out and exchanged it on my finger. This one fit perfectly. I smiled. He bought me the perfect ring.

"The jeweler had your mother's ring in her safe." He kissed the ring on my finger.

"How did she get her ring?"

"Gena, her husband helped delivered you and Gabriella the night your mother died. A hunter mother brought your mother in and had him deliver you guys by C-section. She then planted Alexandria's body with a dead fetus and took you guys to safety."

"Why did she separate us?" Thinking about what life would have been if Gabriella and I lived together in Minnesota or Indiana.

"I am not too sure but it is probably because your aura would strengthen our specie and weakens theirs. She didn't have the heart to kill you but she was still loyal to her kind."

"So who gave the jeweler this ring?" I held it up for a closer inspection taking note of the inscriptions.

"Her husband was also the coroner. He removed it before someone took her body. She kept it all this time until she saw the ring I had made for you."

"So you went to Dawson City to get my ring. What about the tuxedo story?" I looked at him.

"Just a story" He said sadly.

"I think we should not do that anymore. It tends to get us in trouble. No more surprises." I watched as he smiled at me. I reached up and wiped away his tears.

"I don't mind if you chose to wear her ring." He said quietly.

"I want to wear your ring. This is perfect in so many ways. I will pass this one on to our children. And thank you again for the most memorable proposal." I reached up and pulled his face to mine. "I love you, Corin Randall."

As soon as people heard that I woke up, we had no time to ourselves. Mark and Leah were the first ones to come by. Since our house needed some repair, we would stay with them for now.

"We moved some of your things over to our place. Whenever you get to go home we've got you all setup. And don't worry about Kyle. He will stay with Rolfe and Madeline until him and Natalie straightens things out. They're a mess right now." Leah declared.

"Thanks so much. I am so sorry you guys had to come back from your honeymoon." I apologized.

"It is not like you got yourself beat up to get attention." Mark teased.

"Don't worry about it. Mark didn't like Greenland anyway."

"Why was the food not good enough?" Corin asked.

"Everything was mutton. Mutton this, mutton that. Hell if they could make mutton pie they would." Mark complained. We all laughed at him.

"Hey there's my hunter magnet!" Justin announced as he walked in with Aimee, Rachel and Tristan.

"I am so glad to see your beautiful face. The last time we saw you, it was literally a bloody mess. Damn look at those beautiful red eyes." Tristan exclaimed sincerely. I was a little self conscious about my eyes. I started to look away but Corin kissed my forehead and whispered "They are the most beautiful eyes."

Aimee could not say anything she just grabbed me and hugged my tightly. "You just could not leave those hunters alone, could you?" she teased tearfully.

"Yeah, you know me, always looking for cheap thrills." I said dryly.

"I would advise that you fine your cheap thrills with Corin. Leave those hunters alone." Justin laughed.

"Justin! Gena, thank God you're alive. I don't know if I could handle losing you." Rachel added.

"How are you feeling?" Tristan asked.

"My throat feels funny but other than the heat, sweat and nausea, I am good. I'm alive."

"So how long will this last." Rachel asked referring to my aura.

"I think as long as I still need healing." I said as Corin handed me a cool wet cloth to cool my face.

"Man, your aura is awesome. When we saw all that blood in the living room and kitchen we thought you were dead somewhere." Justin recanted.

"Where are Lauren and Max?" Corin asked abruptly changing the subject. I could tell he wasn't comfortable talking about what happened.

"They're coming. Lauren is making lunch for us. So I ate already." Justin jibed. Rachel glared at him.

"I'm so hungry I can eat anything right now." I mentioned.

"I can get you something right now." Corin quickly offered.

"No, I want to eat with you guys. I miss our get together."

"Well if you can tolerate Lauren's cooking, we can count that as possible brain damage." Justin teased.

"Justin you complain but you're the first to fill your plate." Tristan confessed.

"Well you can't waste food even if it is no good. There are children starving in Africa, you know." He expressed sarcastically.

"Did I hear complaints about my cooking?" Lauren whined coming around the corner.

"You know Tristan, always complaining." Justin playfully accused.

"Whatever Justin. Maybe you should go down to the cafeteria." She threatened. "Gena I brought you some clam chowder. This is my mother's recipe." She came over and hugged me.

"Thanks Lauren. It smells great."

"If she made it right, it should be heavenly." Justin commented.

"So Gena, I don't understand how come your aura did not alert you this time?" Aimee asked.

"Well, it did. When Natalie came to the door, my aura went off at the same time. I thought for sure it was wrong. I opened the door and he barged in from behind her. It all happened so fast. One minute I was greeting Natalie, next thing I know I was thrown into the glass wall. Not once but twice." I recanted. I watched Corin's face the entire time. His face was sad and tortured.

"How did you get away from him?" Justin fished.

"When he was attacking Natalie, I crawled into the kitchen and got a kitchen knife. But I ended up stabbing myself with the knife when he threw Natalie on top of me. He has this sadistic thing about stabbing and pulling out the weapon to cause more pain." I continued.

"So you had to pull the knife out and use it against him?" Justin asked dramatically.

"No, he pulled it out and stabbed Natalie with it. I had to take it from Natalie to defend us. When he came close enough I stabbed him in the neck. As he was busy with his injury, I managed to get us into the panic room." I spoke quickly trying not to elaborate. I did not want to cause Corin any more grief and guilt.

"God, I don't know if I could think to defend myself the way you did. I would have just let him kill me." Lauren admitted.

"He did not want to kill me right away. He wanted to torture me until Corin was able to witness my death. He admitted killing my parents the same way. He said my father witnessed my mother's death. Since I am not into torture, I decided the panic room was better off." I said trying to lighten the mood since Corin looked like he was getting sick.

"He obviously doesn't know Corin. You would have ripped him to shreds." Tristan boasted.

"I think Gena did a great job on her own." Corin finally chimed in.

"You have to be careful around Gena; she will use anything as a weapon. She's like a weapon specialist. She can turn a cucumber into a weapon of mass destruction if she wanted to." Tristan teased making everyone laugh. This lightened the mood tremendously.

"What was it like being in the panic room?" Justin asked morbidly.

"It was pretty uncomfortable. It needs a females touch." I teased

"You're crazy, Gena. It is not meant to be lived in." Mark jibed.

"I think she is right. It should at least have a bed or cushion seat or something." Lauren added.

"Are you planning on staying in there for awhile?" Max asked.

"No but you've heard of people staying in there for hours. Imagine sitting on the hard floor for hours." She defended.

"I don't plan on getting in a panic room. I would fight." Justin boasted.

"What if you were outnumbered?" Rachel dared.

"Hey given my situation, the panic room was paradise." I summed up.

We gathered around and ate Lauren's clam chowder. The nausea did not allow me to eat too much. I ended up eating more bread and crackers than soup. Corin had to explain to Lauren about why I wasn't eating her chowder. Every once in awhile I would look up and notice someone looking at my eyes. Max was especially keen at his stares. I knew the others where trying to be polite but it was quite distracting.

"Max, is there something you want to ask me about my eyes?" I finally called him out because he was unusually quiet and when he wasn't staring he was looking downward.

"Gena, it's not your eyes I am staring at, it's you." He admitted.

"Max, you know I am standing right here?" Corin dared.

"Relax Corin, I don't mean it like that. Anyway Lauren would do more damage to me than you would." He replied.

"If my eyes aren't bothering you than why the awkward stares?" I rephrased.

"You have been beaten, stabbed, suffocated and nearly bleed to death yet here you are, four days later, eating clam chowder. So many of us here lived in fear of the danger you have already experience. I don't see how you are still sane. Wouldn't you place this under some sort of miracle?" he opened up.

"Max, she is a miracle." Corin answered as he came to my side.

"So the eyes don't bother you?" I reiterated.

"No, I kind of think it's sexy. Corin you can't deny that they're not a turn on. I thought you on a motorcycle was hot, the eyes are really hot." He chuckled shamefully.

"I'm sorry Gena but I would have to agree." Tristan added.

"Okay, stop looking at my fiancée with lustful thoughts. And I've been seduced by her, the red eyes are not the only thing that draws you in." Corin boasted playfully.

"You guys are dogs. Gena, please ignore them." Lauren rolled her eyes.

"Come on babe, it is really a compliment." Max defended himself.

"Did I hear you say fiancée?" Aimee picked up.

"Oh, we forgot to mention that, sorry." Corin smiled at me.

"When did you propose? Tell me everything." Aimee asked nosily.

"Was she alert? It doesn't count if she was unconscious or disoriented." Justin teased.

"Well when I proposed she was still unconscious." Corin admitted.

"Actually I was conscious when you proposed. I was just too weak to wake up. I heard your proposal but I could not answer because of this hole in my neck. Throughout the night I willed myself to move. By morning I was able to open my eyes and move my hands. You were at my bedside asleep. I could not speak because of this hole. So when I finally got your attention you went and got Alain to take this thing out." I explained.

"Her first words were *yes I will marry you.*" He declared proudly as he lean in and kissed me.

"See, Max that is a proposal." Lauren pointed out.

"Lauren, I am working on it." Max pleaded.

"So, have you guys decided on the date?" Leah asked.

"No, she hasn't been conscious long enough." Corin teased. We were laughing when we heard Dana coming.

"Oh my God, Gena! You are a blessing to see." Dana expressed as she and Derek came through the open door.

"Hey you guys." Derek greeted and handed me a bouquet of pink roses. When I reached up to take the flowers, I noticed my nails were painted hot pink. I gave Lauren a questionable look. She smiled.

"Thanks. Corin will you hand me a mirror." I asked. If my nails were hot pink, I was curious to see what she did with my hair and face.

"Gena, I was told to take care of you so I did what I thought was best given the circumstances." Lauren confessed.

"I told her not to do it." Aimee deserted her.

I looked at the mirror that Rachel handed me. My eyebrows were waxed. I had some light plum eye shadow on. My lashes were curled and mascara was used. *No wonder I had a hard time opening my eyes.* I was wearing makeup. There was a hint of blush. The only thing I didn't have on was lipstick. My hair's natural wave was replaced with tight wavy curls. "You dressed me up?"

"We didn't have anything to do waiting for you to wake up." Lauren defended.

"Ah, so it really wasn't the eyes. It was all that make-up." Justin teased.

"Gena, how are you doing?" Dana asked.

"Good thanks. I hope Alain comes by and take these IVs out. I'm tired of looking at them." I complained.

"I don't think Uncle Alain is coming by tonight." Dana revealed.

"Why? Is everything okay?" Justin asked.

"Sorry to tell you guys this but Kyle is meeting with all the elders at Rolfe's house. He is going to tell them what happened that night." She admitted looking directly at me.

"Did Natalie tell you?" I asked.

"Yes but only because Kyle told her he was going to tell everyone. He is asking them to accept him as part of the clan. He wants to stay here and work on his relationship with Natalie."

"Did you know about this?" Corin asked Leah.

"I had a feeling he was going to do this but I didn't know he was going to do it tonight."

"Could someone fill us in on what's happening?" Lauren pointed out.

"The day before Thanksgiving, Kyle came to Inuvik drunk and attacked Gena." Justin said nonchalantly.

"Did he hurt you?" Tristan distressed.

"Let's just say Corin hurt him more." Justin commented slyly.

"So he wasn't beat up in a bar?" Aimee asked confused.

"Its okay guys, just tell them what happened. Kyle is telling them everything right now, so you don't have to hide anything because of me." Leah declared.

"Kyle came to Gena's house drunk and drugged up. He mistook her for a groupie and assaulted her. Luckily Gena was able to alert Corin with her bracelet and he came just in time before something unforgivable happened. Gena and Corin has talked to Kyle. Gena has forgiven Kyle. Kyle now has to forgive himself. The thing with Natalie will be solely between them." Rachel summed up.

"He tried to rape you?" Lauren asked upset.

"That is not important. What is important is that he explained himself. I have forgiven him. Right now he is confused and trying to find his way to the only thing that would probably heal him of his woes. We should all help him and not judge him." I declared. I watched Corin's reaction to my defense of Kyle. I thought he looked proud of me.

"Corin, you did a number on his face." Max jibed. Justin nodded.

"You're so insensitive." Aimee glared at him pointing out that Leah was present.

"So, what's going to happen now?" I asked.

"Well, it's kind of up to Rolfe. If he feels that Kyle warrants another chance he would allow him to stay with the clan. If not Kyle would have to go elsewhere. Natalie will have to make a decision on whether to go with him or stay with the clan." Corin explained to me.

"That doesn't seem too fair, one person making the decision to forgive someone or not. Kyle must feel very strongly about Natalie for him to put away his pride and admit to being wrong and willing to suffer the consequences. Corin I want you to talk to Rolfe on Kyle's behalf." I requested.

"Gena, I have already accepted him being here. Please, it is hard enough to know that he was staying next door. Sorry Leah, no offense." Corin justified.

"Babe, it just doesn't seem fair. If not for Kyle than do it for Natalie. I think she deserves to be happy too." I clarified.

"Corin, I agree. I can go with you if you like." Justin is probably the only one besides Corin that can sway Rolfe.

"Okay Gena, but I am doing this for you, not Natalie. Right now, I would do anything for you." He said tenderly.

"Shut up Corin, she had you eating out of her hands from day one." Mark teased.

Leah and Aimee stayed with me while everyone else left. Corin and Justin went over to Rolfe's house. Aimee helped me remove all the make-up and brush my hair out. By 6pm, Corin came back and relieved Aimee and Leah. He brought dinner provided by Aunt Madeline. We ate and spent most of the night watching TV and talking about what happened at Uncle Rolfe's. Rolfe wanted to talk things over with Thomas because Kyle would affect his daughter the most. Natalie still refused to talk to Kyle.

"Do you think everything will be alright?"

"Gena, I don't want you worrying about anyone else. You're the one in the hospital. We have done all we can. Now, I have some good news."

"What news?"

"Alain said we can remove your IVs."

"Great!" I watched as he carefully removed all the tape and pulled the catheter out of my arm. When he removed the second IV, I moved my arms around freely. "I feel liberated."

"Now do you want to shower?"

"How did you know?" I teased.

"Because you have been sweating all day and I know you would not feel clean until you have had a shower." He knew me.

He helped me to the shower. He wanted to carry me but I insisted on using my wobbly legs. He stood outside, while I showered. My skin was so sensitive to the hot water that I had to shower in cooler water. The cool water felt so nice against my hot sticky skin. Corin helped wash my back

"What does it look like back there?" I asked cautiously remembering what it felt like when my body was repeatedly grinded against the glass shards.

"It looks beautiful." He said kindly.

"I mean my scars." I redirected.

"You scar beautifully."

"Corin, will you be serious. No one scars beautifully."

"Well you do. I can barely see them now."

"Really?"

"Yes. Are you not cold?" he questioned.

"No, the cold water feels nice. I have been hot and sweaty all day."

After my shower, I dressed in my own clothes and ate dinner with Corin. Aunt Madeline made a nice chicken noodle soup. It wasn't as heavy as Lauren's chowder so I could tolerate it better.

"Have you been sleeping in that recliner?"

"Sometimes" He replied.

"Will you lay with me tonight?" I missed him.

"I don't think there is enough room."

"Please, just until I am asleep."

"Well, since you used your magic words, how can I refuse?" he smiled.

After dinner, he got into bed with me. He lay on his side and pulling me close to his body.

"So, when do you want to officially be my wife?" he asked.

"As soon as possible" I liked hearing him call me his wife.

"How about this summer?" he offered.

"What about Lauren and Aimee's plans? We are also competing with Tina and Preston's wedding coming up. I think the mothers are pretty occupied." I pointed out.

"Well, we can't stop Preston's wedding because it is set to go for May. Madeline wants this done as quick as possible before Tina starts to show. Lauren will probably have to wait to give Madeline a break and I think Aimee will give the Daniels' a chance to enjoy their grandchild before she starts demanding any attention for her wedding. Idelle will probably like to have Stella's input in this wedding since Ella didn't allow her mother to enjoy planning hers to Trey. We can get marry in June around your birthday if you like." He proposed.

"That would be a very nice birthday present."

"For me" He said lovingly.

Chapter Thirty-Five

By Sunday, I was restless. I wanted to go home but I knew home would be with Mark and Leah.

I didn't care, as long as it was not in the hospital. Physically, I was great. My body was strongereveryday. Corin can barely see the scars on my back and shoulders. My scars on my abdomen and left thigh were tender but healed. I was moving around without assistance. The hole in my neck was closing so my voice was back to normal. But most importantly, my eyes were brown again. When Alain came to assess me, I was ready to make my case to be discharged.

I watched patiently as he took my vital signs and checked my wounds. After he looked at he neck wound, he checked my heart rate again.

"Alain, is everything okay?" Corin worried.

"Well, it is better than okay. Gena, do you remember what time your eyes changed back to brown?" he asked.

"I noticed it when she opened her eyes this morning." Corin responded.

"Well it's been 5 hours since your aura relaxed yet your heart rate is between 20-30. Do you feel any changes?" he questioned.

"What do you mean changes?" I asked confused. Of course I felt changes, I don't hurt anymore, I am breathing and I am not dead.

"Think about your senses. Tell me if you think their different." He hinted.

"Well, everything feels so raw and sensitive. I am not sure if its change or maybe I just appreciate everything more." I described.

"Gena, try holding your breathe like last time, remember?" Corin suggested.

I took in a deep breath and held it. I waited for my body to tense up like it usually does. I waited for the uncomfortable ache from my chest. I waited for the anxiety and fear to kick in. But as time elapse, I could not feel the tension, or the uncomfortable ache. The anxiety and fear never came. It was weird to feel so easy not breathing. I didn't realize, until I focused in on what was happening, that the gulp of air I originally took in was not inside me anymore. *I was standing there not taking in any air and I was not panicking or fighting. The innate fear of having no air was gone. No panic. No fight and flight response. I was inhuman.* I looked at both Corin and Alain. They were both staring at me waiting for me to do something.

"How long has it been?" I said without taking in any air.

"Well it is way pass human possibility. Did you have to breathe just now?" Corin asked.

"No, I didn't have to breathe but I was curious about the time. It's weird I don't feel uncomfortable or fear." I was astounded by my revelation.

"Alain, what are you thinking. Has she transformed?" Corin asked.

"I believe she has. Her heart rate is very slow. She's able to withstand little to no oxygenation. Her healing is phenomenal. I bet if she focuses on her senses she could tell you the differences." He declared.

"But how is that possible? It has only been nine months. You said it could take up to three years. How do we know for sure?" Corin questioned.

"Well, it would take that long if her aura was allowed to run its course normally. These attacks on her have forced her aura to work harder and more intense. This would explain why it took less time to transform. How else can you explain the heart rate and breathing?" he defended.

"Should we monitor this longer just in case her aura goes back to dormant again?" Corin questioned.

"It doesn't hurt to be for sure." He answered.

"Does this mean I can go home?" I asked nicely.

"Well, I don't have any reasons to keep you here. Anyway by the way you're acting I think I would have a battle on my hand if I didn't discharge you today. Am I right? Do you want to go home?" he asked absurdly. I was so excited I didn't even bother to answer him.

"Thanks Alain. I'll take care of everything from here." Corin said apologetically for me since I was already in the bathroom getting dressed to leave.

On the way over to Mark's house, Corin told me that Kyle was allowed to stay with the clan. I was relieved. He was staying with Uncle Rolfe's in Grandfather's house with Aunt Madeline. He was spending time repairing his relationship with Natalie. Justin noted that he had changed his appearance with a different hair cut and different clothing. I could tell Corin was still guarded and suspicious. He didn't care for the cosmetic changes.

Mark and Leah's house was an English Tudor home made of gray stone. It was a little over 4000 sq ft with 5 bedrooms and 4 baths. Like Rachel's house, one floor was dedicated entirely to the master bedroom. We were setup in one of the guestrooms downstairs on the same floor as Mark's *Mancave*. The main floor had a grand room with a gigantic fireplace, a family room with a separate parlor room, a huge kitchen, formal dining room and a guest room. It was confusing at first because when you walk into their home, you are overwhelmed with the high ceilings and grand decors.

"Wow, Leah this is really overwhelming. You did a great job with everything. Your house makes mine look like a toy house." I teased.

"A lot of this is actually Mark. He likes thing big and grand. I set you guys up down here so you could have more privacy." She directed us downstairs. The entertainment room was a haven for Mark and the guys. It was an exact copy of Justin's entertainment room. She ushered us further down the hall into one of the three guestrooms. The guestroom was large with its own bathroom. When I saw the bed, I smiled at Corin. Mark adorned every room with a custom sized bed. "I tried to match the colors of your bedroom so you would feel more at home."

"Leah, this is perfect. Thank you so much for being so thoughtful." I said.

"Okay, well I'll leave you guys to get situated. Let me know if I can get you anything." She instructed. We watched her leave.

"Wow, this room is huge."

"Well Mark likes things big and grand." Corin replied.

"That bed is so big; I may need a tracking device to find you." I jibed.

"I don't plan on letting you stray too far away from me." He whispered against my hair.

"I miss you."

"I missed you too." He nuzzled my neck. His arms gently moved around my waist. I flinched when his arms came across my abdominal wound. He immediately jerked back. "I am sorry, did I hurt you?"

"No, but it is a little tender. I think I'm just a little guarded that's all."

"Well than I promise to keep my hands to myself until you are completely healed." He vowed.

"No, don't you dare say that. I want you to touch me just not here and here." I protested pointing to my abdomen and left thigh.

"That, I can do." He said as he lowered his lips to mine. I started to reach up to pull his head to me but the stretch caused a sharp pain. He did not miss my reaction. "Let me come to you." He murmured. As he kissed me I pulled him toward the huge bed. When I bumped up against it, I felt his arms supporting me as we both ease down. He was cautious not to bump into my abdomen or left leg.

"God, I miss you." I whispered breathlessly. My hand started to unbutton his shirt.

"Gena, let's just wait. I don't want to hurt you." He said in a cautious tone.

"You won't hurt me. I am just a little tender." I pleaded.

"Gena, you have stab wounds to your right abdomen and left thigh. Any kind of abrupt movement you make is going to hurt. It has only been 6 days. Unless you can promise that you would stay completely still, I will not cause you more pain." He said adamantly.

"Staying still would be really hard. How long do we have to wait?" I reasoned.

"Until you can do jumping jacks without pain" He answered.

"What? I didn't do jumping jacks before my injury. Hell, I may even injure myself trying to do jumping jacks." I complained.

"Well, I will help you. We will do stretches first than work our way to the jumping jacks." He teased.

"Well what are we going to do while we wait?"

"I don't know about you but I have a wedding to plan." He jibed.

"When are you going to tell your parents?"

"Mark already did. My mother will be hounding you soon. First thing she is going to want to know is the exact date. Have you decided?"

"Well the closest date to my birthday is June 25th. Would that be alright?" I answered. I watched him reach over and grabbed a pen and paper from the night stand. He wrote down the date like he was taking a restaurant order.

"That's perfect. Now what colors do you like?" he continued to ask.

"Aren't you going to have any input?"

"This is already the happiest day of my life. I don't care if we get marry in a barn with sheep and cows as our witnesses. As long as in the end you say *I do.*" He admitted freely.

"Well why do I have to make all the decisions? I would rather elope. I already have the ring. All I need is to drag you to the altar." I said sarcastically. If he was going to be blasé about the whole thing, than so can I.

"Okay, I am sorry. I will choose one color and you choose the other." He compromised.

"I want sage green."

"I want crème." He smiled as he wrote the colors down.

"That's going to look beautiful together."

"We will look good together." He corrected with a light kiss.

"Okay so the next thing is what flowers do you like? I am very partial to hydrangeas."

"White hydrangeas with crème blossoms, that is beautiful. I would have never thought about that. You're better at this than I am." I complimented.

"I got straight A's in Home Economics remember?" he teased with my beautiful smile. He wrote down the flowers. "Okay, how about how many people do you want at this wedding?"

"Well, I have so many people that would fly to Inuvik from Indiana." I kid.

"Oh, right. Sorry. Well, then it will mainly be all your family here. This is where my family will be very crazy about. My father will invite hundreds of his friends and business partners. I know most of them but I don't consider them close friends but it is part of his networking." He commented.

When he spoke of family, my mind went straight to Gabriella. Her body was buried in a lonely grave. Even in death she was not near me or our parents. "Corin, can we change the subject for just one minute?" I said sadly.

"Are you tired? Are you in pain?" he quickly checked.

"No, I was just thinking about Gabriella. I want to move her body to the graveyard here in Inuvik. I want her buried next to my parents. She deserves to be near her real family."

"Gena, I have already talked to Rolfe about that. They will move her body at the end of the frost season which is probably soon. There is already a plot ready for her. Madeline will arrange for a memorial for her." He said. My heart was overwhelmed by his thoughtfulness. This was true love. His heart and mind always thought of me.

"Thank you. You are too good to me." I said as tears came down my face. He reached up and wiped them away.

"Everything I do, I do because I want you to be happy. You have given me so much happiness in my life; I will have to spend the rest of my life making up for that. Now, let's get back to our wedding plans."

"Okay. What about dresses and tuxedos?"

"Well, that is one thing she will leave entirely up to you and me. She will take care of everything else. How many bridesmaids do you want?"

"Is two enough?"

"You are going to upset some people." he warned.

"Alright how about four, is that okay?"

"Who are you choosing?"

"Well, Lauren and Aimee definitely. Dana too. Rachel would be too pregnant. And Leah"

"Leah maybe pregnant by that time too."

"What?" I thought he was hiding something from me.

"Well she is twenty years old. I know Mark wants to get started right away." He said confidently.

"Is she pregnant now?"

"Mark said they didn't have much to do in Greenland." He teased.

"Oh, I'm sorry. How about Michelle?" I said. I realized he was steering me to make the decision to include his sister on my own.

"She would be so happy. Thank you."

"Why didn't you just say something? You know I don't mind."

"I didn't want to push the decision on you. This has to be your choice."

"It would be easier if you just come out and tell me. Remember I could have some brain damages." I joked.

"I seriously doubt that. You could out wit me anytime. Okay the last thing is where you want to go for our honeymoon?" he finished.

"How about Hawaii?"

"It would be hot as hell there."

"Oh, I forgot. Maybe you should just surprise me."

"I know the perfect place. Do you want to know?"

"Is it in the United States?"

"No."

"Is it in Europe?"

"Yes."

"Okay, where?"

"Charmonix, Mont Blanc, France. It is a beautiful village nestled between Italy and France. My family vacationed there to see the Winter Olympics. I have always wanted to go back. You would love it. One of my dad's clients has a chalet there. I am sure he would let us use it." He explained enthusiastically.

"I don't know how to ski or speak French."

"Don't worry we will be too busy for skiing." He hinted.

"That's exciting. You know I've never been to Europe."

"We can see both Italy and France."

"Okay so is everything settled?" I asked

"I think so." He said as he got on the phone and read off the list to his mother. When he was done, he came back to bed and lay beside me. "Gena, I want to talk to you about what Alain said this morning."

"About my transformation?" I knew this was coming. We have been patiently waiting for this day to come. Suddenly I was nervous at the prospect of making love to him. I wasn't sure what I was nervous about. I wanted him and I know he wanted me. It was just the unknown.

"I want to wait." He said quietly. He waited for me to respond but I was too shock by what he said. "I love you. I cherish you more than anything in this world. I want to give you the greatest pleasure a man can give a woman. I want our first time together to be as husband and wife."

My heart soared with more love for him now than ever. I was suddenly inundated with so much feeling and adoration for him, I felt tears running down my face. The sudden jerking of my chest from crying sent sharp pain from my wounds but I could no longer control my emotions.

"Please don't be upset. It isn't because I don't want you. I want you in everyway." He comforted me. He pulled me close to him and held me. "You might not think about it now, but one day you are going to thank me for waiting."

"I love you. Thank you for waiting. I am not upset. I am just so happy that you are so respectful and considerate of me. This is important to me too." I held onto his arms. We lay there silently until we heard Mark knocking on the door.

"Hey, guys. Leah sent me down to call you to dinner. If you are busy, we'll just save you something." He yelled from behind the door.

"We'll be up in a minute." Corin answered. "Do you want to freshen up?"

"Yes, I will meet you up there."

When I emerged from downstairs, I was greeted by Lauren and Aimee. They were both excited and jubilant.

"Gena, look!" Lauren and Aimee both shoved their hand in front of my face. I immediately noticed their engagement rings. Lauren's was a pink diamond solitaire and Aimee had a white diamond but the side diamonds were pink.

"Wow, those are gorgeous. When did you guys get them?" I was thrilled for them.

"Max proposed to me today. It turned out he had ordered the ring weeks ago but was just waiting for it to come in. He was on his knees." She oozed giddiness. I smiled at her silliness.

"Of course he has to be on his knees. You probably would have fainted and he was prepared to catch you." I teased.

"Tristan wrote me a kindergarten love letter. When I checked the *yes* box, he handed me a box that had the words **YES** on it. Isn't that adorable?" Aimee admired.

"Wow, those guys really did a romantic job. Well congratulations ladies. Welcome to the newly engaged crowd. Now I am going to need bridesmaids. Are you guys busy?" I announced.

"Oh, really. Gena this is so great. How many are you having?" Lauren asked.

"Well, I need four so I was also going to ask Dana and Michelle."

"I am so glad you're asking Dana. She felt left out with the Rachel's and Leah's wedding." Aimee added.

"Are you going to have a maid of honor?" Lauren asked.

"No, you all mean so much to me. I am not going to single anyone out."

"That's smart thinking. I don't think I would have a maid of honor either." Aimee said.

"Well I just want a lot of bridesmaids. I don't need a maid of honor either." Lauren concluded.

"I am going to need a lot of help with the dresses and my dress." I pointed out.

"That is what we are here for." Lauren said excitedly.

Over dinner everyone was busy discussing future plans and weddings. As of right now, Preston's wedding was coming up. Corin announced that he had already put in plans our wedding for June 25th. Lauren wanted the month of July which was good because Aimee could get her wedding in August.

"Back to back weddings, we are going to be exhausted. I can't believe a year ago we were just thinking about mine and Aimee's now we are the last to get married." Lauren noted.

"Sorry, I didn't mean to jump in line." I teased.

"Please Gena, I am so happy that Corin has found someone. I don't mind waiting." Aimee commented.

"Was I that bad Aimee?" Corin asked.

"Corin, you deserve good things in life. You have always made sacrifices for this clan and never got back anything in return. For example: you should have graduated last year but you were so busy doing things for Uncle Rolfe that you had to but school aside. I always felt bad for that." Aimee pointed out.

"Everything works out for a reason. I'm glad I was a senior this year." He responded looking back at me.

"Yeah, if you had graduated last year what would you do when Gena was in classes?" Max laughed.

"He would probably stalk the school grounds. That's what I did last year. Your dad had to threaten me." Tristan added.

"That's what you get for being so smart." Aimee said adoringly.

"Gena have you decided on your wedding stuff? Because what Diane does is she has a list of questions and you have to fill out the blanks than she takes care of everything else. You and Corin just has to take care of your dresses and tuxedos. I have a copy of that list if you need it." Leah asked.

"I think we did that already." I smiled looking at Corin. He knew his mother's techniques. Those questions earlier were probably from her list. He made things so easy for me.

"Yeah, I was on the phone with my mom just before we came up." Corin validated.

"So what are your colors?" Lauren asked.

"We decided on sage and crème." I answered.

"We?" Mark questioned.

"Yes, *we* decided. This is our wedding. I am not going to make all the decisions by myself." I reiterated.

"See? Max. If Corin can help Gena, than you can help me too!" Luren complained.

"Thanks Corin." Max dryly.

"I am helping Aimee too. If I don't she has threatened to put me in a powder blue tuxedo." Tristan confessed.

Justin and Mark laughed. They were obviously relieved that theirs were over with. Throughout the night the girls continued to talk about wedding and babies. Rachel's pregnancy has been very easy and smooth. Lauren revealed that Tina has been afflicted with morning sickness. Tina's wedding would be much smaller than the other weddings. She only asked Lauren to be her bridesmaid. I called Tina and spoke to her about when her fittings were done so I could arrange to meet with the same designer to get my dress done. Lauren and Aimee called Dana and spoke to her about being my bridesmaid. Dana and Derek were with Michelle and Brent chaperoning Natalie and Kyle. That was the agreement Thomas Redman made with Kyle and Rolfe. Before the night was over Lauren and Dana would take care of the bridesmaids dresses and all I had to do was take care of my dress. *I like having female cousins.*

It was strange to actually have to wear my own dress to a wedding. The last two weddings my dress was picked out by the bride. Preston and Tina's shotgun wedding was really well put together even though Aunt Madeline had less than two months to put it together and so soon after Justin's wedding. For the past month, I was inundated with fittings and fabric. If I wasn't helping myself, I was helping Tina. It really was a bad idea to have my fittings with her because she was so indecisive. She finally settled on an Empire waist silk and chiffon wedding dress. The design left room for her to grow if necessary.

Lauren and Aimee were really helpful in helping me with my wedding dress. My dress was a mutual agreement between Lauren and me. I wanted something simple but she would not allow it. We finally settled midway on a designer gown made of French taffeta. It was a strapless gown with an A-line pleated empire bodice. The midriff and bustled side skirt was adorned with beaded lace. It had an attached train made of tulle. After a couple of fittings, the designer told me I could not lose one pound or else I had to go back to be refitted. Once my wedding gown was done, I was able to relax and enjoy Tina's wedding.

For tonight's wedding, I wore a dark blue halter top silk knee-length dress. The dress really highlighted my engagement ring. Lately I have been wearing a lot of blues and I think it is because I wanted to highlight my beautiful engagement ring. Sometimes I find myself just gazing at it. I still can't believe that in one month I would be married. I wasn't nervous or scared. *I was ready.*

"You are daydreaming again." Corin whispered in my ear. I was standing in the bathroom lost in my thoughts.

"I have been in a dream since the day I met you."

"Good comeback. Are you ready? I have your heels." He said holding up my blue stilettos. I really didn't need help putting them on but I enjoy the way he plays with my legs while he does it.

"Keep this up and I will have to relearn to tie my shoes." I teased.

"You look absolutely stunning in blue." He admired pulling me to the bed.

"You said that about the crème dress, the lavender dress and the pink dress. I am beginning to think you just use the same lines over and over." I jibed.

“I can go get the thesaurus and find different words to use but it means the same thing.” He pointed out as he slid the heels over my feet. I watched as his hands roamed over my calves and thighs. When he fastened the straps he kissed the inside of my ankles. “You smell good.” He said as he inhaled the scent from my calf.

“Don’t start messing with me. This dress is silk. It will wrinkle horribly.” I warned.

“You can always change into something else.” He murmured against the skin on the opposing ankle.

“Or you can wait until we move back home tomorrow.” I suggested.

“Home sounds nice.” He murmured. He slowly got up pulling me along. He wrapped him arms around me and started nuzzling at my neck.

“I know. I am thankful for Leah and Mark but nothing is like home.” I let him nuzzle my neck while inhaling the scent from my wavy hair. I loved hearing him sniff at my skin and hair.

“Corin, we have to get going.” I reminded.

“I know, just one more minute.”

“You always say that. You don’t even have your tie on. Where is your tie?” I asked pulling him back.

“It’s upstairs. Let me find my cufflinks and I’ll meet you upstairs. You can put my tie on for me.” He directed.

“Is Leah and Mark already gone?”

“Yeah, they left 30 minutes ago. They had to see Alain first.”

“Really? Do you think she is pregnant?”

“I hope so they have been working pretty hard, don’t you think?” he hinted. We learned that living with Mark and Leah was quite interesting. They spent a lot of time in their bedroom. Sometimes we only saw them during meals.

I left him and made my way upstairs. I was looking around the grand room for his tie when I looked up; Kyle was standing in front of the fireplace. I have not seen him since I healed him. He definitely did not look like the same man. His messy blonde hair was cut short and clean. He was healthier. He was actually very good-looking once he was cleaned up. Natalie had a good affect on him.

"Hi, Gena." He said politely.

"Hi. Kyle. Are you looking for Leah?"

"No, actually I wanted to talk to you." He said awkwardly.

"What do you want to talk to me about?" I asked I looked downstairs to see if Corin was coming. I knew he would be very unhappy to see Kyle and I in the same room alone.

"I went to visit Gabriella's grave today." He said cautiously. "I need to tell you what happened to her."

"Kyle, you were very young when this happened. I don't blame you for being scared. You probably would have been killed if you tried to help her." I assured him.

I watched him struggle with himself. He rubbed at his hands. His face was wrought with anguish. I walked over to him and placed my hand on his shoulder. "Look Kyle, that was in the past. You have a wonderful future now. You have to let it go or else it would eat you alive."

"Gena, I lured her away from her family that day. I wanted her. I thought that she was my soul mate. When she was attacked, I could not move. I froze. I ran back to the clan. I led the hunters to the clan. Everyone was killed because of me. I have been living with this guilt for 6 years now. It has destroyed me. I can not ask for her forgiveness but since you are her twin, I thought that if I tell you and beg for your forgiveness I can get some peace." He said tearfully. He fell to his knees.

He was so distraught he grabbed my hands and cried into them. I tried to pull my hands back but he held onto them and placed them to his face.

"Kyle, I am going to give you one second to get away from her before I kill you." Corin declared angrily as he staunched towards us.

"Corin, wait!" I yelled pulling my hand away and moving to block Corin. Kyle stood up quickly.

"I told you never to touch her again." Corin bellowed.

"Babe, it is not what you think. He was apologizing." I tried to explain as I put myself it his path.

"What are you apologizing for now? What did you do to her?" he asked accusingly.

"I was telling Gena what happened with Gabriella." He quickly explained.

"Then why were you kissing her hand." Corin gritted between his teeth.

"Corin, he was really apologizing. He blames himself for Gabriella's death." I coaxed trying to redirect Corin's anger.

"You can apologize without touching her. I am not going to warn you again. I don't care what you are doing. Do not touch her." He bellowed angrily.

"Corin, I am sorry. I promise I won't do that again. Gena will you forgive me for what happened?" he pleaded.

"Kyle, I forgive you. Now, can you forgive yourself?" I stated. I watched as he stared at me. He started to say something but than he stopped. We watched him leave thru the front door. I turned to Corin and pulled his face close to mine. "You have got to calm down. Please baby, he was just apologizing."

"People can apologize without kissing someone's hands." He said stubbornly.

"Corin, he has been living with this incredible guilt over her death. He told me that he thought she was his *concero flamma.* He lured her away from the clan. When they were attacked he panicked and ran back to the clan. The hunters followed and killed everyone. That would explain why he didn't believe in the soul mate thing. I think finding Natalie has changed him. Please be understanding." I pleaded as I worked the tie around his collar.

"I would understand if he just keeps his hands of you. God, he is so messed up. I don't want you around him alone. I hate the way he stares at you. He could snap and do something stupid." He warned.

"He stares at me because I remind him of her. It isn't what you think."

"You don't know that?"

"His soul mate is Natalie. You once told me that you could never want anyone else because I am your soul mate. The same would be true for him."

"Evidently he doesn't really know what a soul mate is. He was wrong before." He argued

"I don't think he is wrong this time. Look how he has changed."

"Were you looking at him?" he questioned.

"Corin, I am merely pointing out that he has changed. You have nothing to be jealous about. I love you. I could never be with anyone but you. No man can ever touch my heart, you own it." I assured him as I pulled his face close to mind forcing him to focus only on me. "You have my heart. You have my soul. There's only you."

I watched his face relax and a smile come across his face.

Chapter Thirty-Six

This was the first morning in over 11 months that I did not wake up with her at my side. I knew she was safe at home but a part of me wanted to break with tradition and go to her. I woke up in my old bedroom this morning. After the house party at Max and Lauren's house, I drove her home to our house and stayed with her as long as I could. She kicked me out before midnight. I didn't mean to wake up so late today but I stayed up last night talking to her on the phone until she fell asleep. I left the phone on purposely so I could hear her sleeping, too bad she didn't snore. Every once and awhile I would hear her move or bump into the phone. Finally sometime during the night she accidently knocked the phone off the bed and it turned off.

It would be 8 hours before I could see her. After that she would be Mrs. Gena Randell. I loved the way that sounds.

I got up and took a quick shower. When I got out, I quickly looked over my tuxedo and her wedding rings. I don't want anything to be out of place today.

Max would be here soon. I wanted to give him the rings and go over the flight plans with him. He and Lauren were dropping us off at the airport for our honeymoon to France. He was also going to pick up Trevor today at 2pm. Brent and Tristan were in charge of getting the limousines to the right house. Our wedding guest list ballooned to 300 by the time we finalized everything. My family went a little too far with the wedding list. Gena was such a good sport, she did not say no to anything my mom asked of her.

Unable to contain myself, I found myself calling her.

"Hi, Mr. Randall." she answered.

"Good morning, Ms.Reynolds." I played along.

"What can I do for you today?" she tempted.

"How about we get together for a date?"

"Sure, why don't you meet me at the North Chateau at 6pm?"

"Sounds like a date. How would I know who you are?"

"I will be the girl wearing a big white gown walking towards you." She laughed.

I laughed along with her. "I miss you. Last night you fell asleep on me."

"Well that's what people usually do when they go to bed. They sleep. I don't think I have ever talked to anyone on the phone that long before. What time did you get to bed?" She asserted.

"I think around 3am." I yawned.

"You better not use that excuse to be late. I will come get you."

"I can guarantee you I will not be late for this party." I assured her.

"Sorry baby, but Lauren wants me off the phone. Guess what? I am wearing make-up today. Lip gloss too. It must be a very special occasion."

"Tell her not to put too much on. I may not be able to recognize you." I expressed. I could hear the phone exchanging hands.

"Corin, we are busy right now. Talk to her during the wedding if you have to but right now we are busy. Now, say goodbye." Lauren scolded before she handed the phone back to Gena.

"Sorry, Corin. I have to go. I love you!" she said quickly before she hung up.

"You are so pathetic. It was only one night and you act like it has been months." Max teased coming into my bedroom.

"Shut-up Max. You are lucky that you have always been around Lauren." I defended.

"I still wouldn't act like a lovesick dog."

"I don't believe it. I know you flunk out last year just so you could be a senior with her."

"You promised not to tell anyone."

"Then quit teasing me. Today is my wedding day. I can act anyway I want." I handed him the rings and the flight itinerary.

"I still don't know where to take Lauren for our honeymoon."

"Take her to Edmonton Mall and leave her there for two weeks. She would be in heaven." I teased.

"Be serious man, do you think she would like where you guys are going?"

"No, there are no stores there." I replied seriously.

"Edmonton sounds good right now."

"Just take her to Edmonton, stay at the Grand Fairmont. She would absolutely love that. You can't go wrong with that place. Treat her like a princess for a few weeks." I suggested.

"That actually sounds good. Thanks man."

"Call me Mr. Romantic."

"You don't act like a nervous groom."

"I am not nervous. I have been waiting for this day ever since I saw her. I am having a harder time trying to get by the next six hours."

"Your mom wants all of us over there to make sure everything is in place. She is a monster with details." He complained.

"Hey don't forget to pick-up Trevor today." I reminded him.

"Railroad mouth Trevor." He mocked.

"Hey, don't call him that. He is actually a good guy. Anyway his braces are off."

"Oh, I forgot, he's your best friend now." He jibed.

"I have to get my tuxedo over to the dressing room. Oh, hey look what I have for Gena's bridal gift." I showed, handing him a big blue velvet box. I had a diamond necklace made with the infinity signs linked together.

"Wow, this is nice. When are you going to give it to her?" He asked.

"Well, I was going to sneak it into her dressing room. It will be a nice surprise, don't you think?" I planned.

"That's cool. I like that. Anything else today"

"No, I think everything else is done."

"Alright, I'll see you later." When he left, I went back to my desk. I decided last night that I was going to honor her with a speech during the toasting. I knew what I wanted to say but I had a hard time getting the words right. After some time, I decided I was just going to say whatever I felt at that time, even if I was to just repeat *I love you Gena*, over and over. She would love it anyway.

I got over to the Chateau around 4pm. My mother made sure I knew which doors to go into to avoid seeing Gena before the ceremony. *Two more hours.* As I made my way through the Chateau, I took in all of my mother's hard work. My mother had every hydrangeas on this continent brought in. The little petals were everywhere. Every fabric in the building was changed to crème and sage satin. Instead of having a flower girl, the aisle was adorned with the hydrangeas petals. The altar was a hand-made arch with thousands of white hydrangeas with green stems, satin sage fabric wind around the arch. As I made my way across the Grand Ballroom, I appreciated the 50 tables adorned with crème and sage satin chairs. The centerpiece on the table was made from white hydrangeas with satin sage fabric wrapped around them. The curtains that adorned the ceiling to floor windows were changed to crème and silk sage fabric. I passed by the Grand Ballroom and went into my dressing room. On my vanity was a note, it was from Gena.

My heart belongs to you.
My soul will never part from yours.
My brain can never decide against you.
My body will only want yours.
I am yours forever.
I love you.
Gena

I kissed the note and tucked it in my shirt pocket. I will always remember those words for the rest of my existence. I sneaked pass the Grand Foyer and across to her dressing room. I knocked on the door. Dana came to the door.

"Corin! you are not to be over here. Do you want to have bad luck today?" she scolded.

"I just need you to give this to Gena." I said handing her the blue velvet box.

"Okay, now go back over there." She warned closing the door. I went back over to my dressing room. When I got back, Tristan was standing outside the door.

"You are not supposed to be on this side of the foyer. Do I have to get physical with you?" he teased.

"I needed to give Gena something."

"I am so sure. You couldn't give it to her last night?"

"It is a surprise bridal gift. I didn't even get to see her."

"Don't make me bar this door. Get back inside this room."

He ushered me back into my dressing room. When I heard my cell phone ring, I knew it was Gena.

"Hello, this is Corin Randall. I am busy at this moment. I am about to marry the most beautiful girl in the world. Please leave a message at the end of the beep." I smiled with my cleverness.

"Corin, it is so beautiful. Thank you. Did you get my note?"

"Yes, I am going to have those words tattooed on my arms so when I get old and can't remember, I can read it off my body." I declared

"I love you. See you at the altar." She ended.

Tristan and Max shook their heads in disbelief.

"Lovesick dog" Max jibed.

"He would be a dead dog if he tries to go over there again. I will tell your mom." He threatened.

"Are you not nervous?" Brent asked.

"Nope" I answered confidently. I started to change into my tuxedo. Tristan helped me with my bow tie.

"He is probably going to crack at the altar. They always do. Max make sure you have a rope when he tries to run." Brent asserted.

"He isn't going to run away from her. He would probably grow impatient while she is walking up the aisle. Next thing you know, he'll grab her and drag her to the altar." Tristan teased.

They continued to poke fun of me until my dad came and escorted me to the altar. Max, Tristan, Brent and Derek meet the bridesmaids in the foyer. I stood at the altar trying my best not to fidget or look impatient. Every chance I got, I looked down the aisle to see if I could catch a glimpse of her. I waited patiently as people started filling the chairs.

When the music started, I held my breath. It took forever for Michelle and Brent to walk up the aisle. By the time the last couple walked up, I could have sworn Max and Lauren was deliberately going slowly just to rile me. When then finally took their place, the music changed and the audience stood. I was a bit irritated because this blocked my view of the aisle. My eyes focused intently, until I finally saw her slowly walking up the aisle with Rolfe escorting her. She wore a beautiful white gown that hugged her upper body but then opened up into a full ball gown. Her beautiful neck and shoulders were exposed. She never looked more beautiful. The infinity necklace hugged her neck gracefully. Her hair was left down, with natural wavy curls worked into it. She wore makeup but it wasn't enough to change her natural beauty. She wore a thin veil over her face but I could still see her eyes. When our eyes locked, she smiled at me. I was paralyzed and numb.

When she came to stand by my side, Rolfe took our hands and placed them together. My eyes never left her. I lifted her veil and touched her face. Max bumped me to bring me out of my trance. During our vows, I placed the ring on her finger and pulled her hand up to my lips and kissed it. Max bumped me again. I was clearly violating some sort of traditional wedding etiquette. I listened intently as she recited her vows to me. She spoke them beautifully. As she slid the ring on my finger, she lowered her head and brushed her lips over my hand. It melted my heart. My eyes welled up. I had to blink to clear the tears from my eyes. Tristan slipped a tissue in my hand. When it finally came to the kiss, I no longer cared about etiquette. I grabbed her and crushed her lips to mine. If she wore lipstick, I took it all off. I finally broke the kiss when the audience clapped their hands.

"Nice and subtle, Corin" Tristan whispered.

"I liked it." She whispered.

After the photographer got all the pictures he wanted, we entered the Grand Ballroom announced as *Mr. and Mrs. Corin Randall.* Our face lit up and we join everyone in the celebration. The next four hours went by like a dream. I could not take my eyes off her. She kept her hands glued to mine. I can't remember what I ate or what the cake looked like. I can't remember whether I danced with anyone else. All I know is that my eyes were always on her, my hands kept her near me and my body could not tolerate her being away for one second. When it came to make my toast to her, I pulled her to the middle of the dance floor. With a microphone in one hand, I turned to look straight into her eyes and recited from my heart my message to her.

"Many people spend their lives searching for their soulmate, their one true love. Some people are lucky to find the person they can truly call their *concero flamma*, while others spend the rest of their lives searching and never finding. I am happy to count myself among the lucky ones, because I found you. From the very moment I saw you, I knew you were the one for me, the one that I know I have to spend the rest of my life with. I love you, Gena. I know that you are the only one for me, my one true love. And now that I have found you, I shall never let you go. I promise you, Gena that I shall love, honor, and cherish you. I give you my heart and my soul. I will love you in this life and the next. I will love you forever."

I saw tears come down her face. I handed my microphone to someone and pulled her close to me for our traditional dance. I kissed her face while

I moved her around the dance floor. The whole room disappeared and we were alone.

"That was so beautiful. I love you." She said tearfully. She buried her face into my chest.

I whispered the words she wrote to me into her ears. I will cherish those words for the rest of my life. She was finally mine to cherish and love forever.

By midnight, everyone gathered around to bid us farewell. I shielded her from the shower of rice and ushered her into the limousine. When we were safely inside, I watched as she released her hair from all the pins. I ran my hands through her hair to help her.

"I love your hair like that." I whispered to her.

"I know." She smiled. I brushed my fingers over her lips than slowly lowered my lips to hers. I pulled her over my lap and took in more of her lips exploring her mouth with my tongue. My hands roamed all over her trying to find any part of her skin I could touch. There was so much fabric and material I was starting to get impatient.

"Careful baby, this is not a $30 t-shirt. I plan to pass this on to my daughters." She said breathlessly in my ears. I had to forgo the thought of ripping her clothes off her and settled my hands to her neck and shoulder.

"I'm sorry, I want you so bad. Your scent is driving me insane." I murmured against her neck. She roamed her hands over my shirt. I pulled off my jacket. "Please tell me all these buttons are just props"

"Patience baby. We are almost home." She said softly kissing my neck.

When the limousine finally stopped, I impatiently got out of the car pulling her alongside of me. As soon as she was out of the car, I swung her up in my arms and race for the door.

As soon as we got into our bedroom, I kicked the door shut and placed her down.

"Nice crossing over the threshold."

"Turn around, let me help you with these damn buttons." I directed. The gown had a long row of buttons that ran down her spine. I was so tempted to tear them off and promise to repair them later.

"You don't have to undo all of them just half way down; I can slip the dress off. Don't you want me to wear the fifth package from Secret Lingerie?"

"I don't want you to wear anything right now. You can wear that when we are officially on our honeymoon." I whispered in her hair as my shaky hands worked on the rows of buttons. When I was finally towards the middle, I unzipped the gown and pushed it down and over her hips. I impatiently lifted her out of the gown and carried her to the bed. I gently placed her down, as I removed my shirt. When we were completely naked, she pulled me down over her. Her body was so warm and soft against mine. My hands roamed all over her, not satisfied with any one area. My lips hungered for her skin. I kissed her until she was breathless. Holding her face close to mine I whispered "I have waited all my life for you."

"And here I am."

"Yes, here you are."

As the sun entered the room and bore against my closed lids, I turned toward the scent of her. When the alarm went off, I gently shifted over to turn it off. My beautiful bride was still asleep. I slowly ran my fingers up and down her spine, tickling her awake. I watched as she stirred but refused to wake.

"Wake-up baby. We have a plane to catch."

"I rather stay here. This is my honeymoon." She murmured against my chest. I chuckled at her laziness.

"Come on. I put a lot of planning into this day. I want to celebrate you birthday on our honeymoon. Max and Lauren will be here soon." I pleaded.

"Okay but only if you shower with me."

"We don't have time for that either."

"See? It is already starting." She mumbled.

"What is starting?" I asked confused with her comment.

"The beginning of the end"

"What? Are you awake?"

"You know the saying *after a woman gets married she lets herself go*. Well in this case, you're making excuses to avoid sex." She explained.

"You are absolutely absurd. I want us to get on that plane. When we get to France, I will thoroughly ravage you with so much sex, you're going to regret saying what you just said." I declared.

"Is that a promise?" she teased.

"That is a promise, guarantee, vow, scout's honor, whatever you want to call it." I vowed.

She smiled back at me and quickly got up and head for the bathroom. While she was in the shower, I made the bed. I picked up her gown off the floor and straighten it over the bed. I went to shower in another bathroom. When I was done, I met her downstairs. She was waiting for me in the kitchen. After a quick breakfast, Max and Lauren arrived on time to pick us up. When we got to the airport, we made our way over to the awaiting plane. Margaret was the first to greet and congratulate us.

"Congratulatons Corin, Gena. Who would have ever thought? Just a few months ago you two were on the same plane, and now you're married."

"Thank you Margaret."

"Margaret is Jack our pilot today?" I asked.

"Yes, he is in the tower waiting for instructions."

"Gena, why don't you go ahead? I have to go over the itinerary with Jack."

"Come on Gena, let's get you settled." Margaret ushered Gena up the ramp and into the plane. I walked across the tarmac to the tower. I reviewed our destination and dates of travel with Jack. We walked back to the plane. As I entered the plane, as flash of déjà vu came to me, when I looked over the plane and saw her sitting in the same recliner as she did 11 months ago. Margaret was standing over her talking. I smiled to myself. My life has definitely changed. I glided over to her. I sat in the same seat that I was in the last time. When Margaret left I turned to her and smiled.

"Hello, I'm Corin Randall." She quickly caught on to what I was doing and played along.

"Hello, it is very nice to meet you Mr. Randall. My name is Gena Randall."

Epilogue

Five Years Later November 8th

"Corin, I can't take it anymore. Please I am so tired."

"Gena, I know you're tired but just one more time. Come on baby, you can do it."

My body was in excruciating pain. I was sweating buckets. We have been at this for 4 hours now. Whoever said that third babies were much easier were liars. I have been in labor for two days now. When I was finally allowed to push, it made the contractions more painful. Not only was I in pain, I was physically exhausted. They said one more. That is all I am going to do. *Just one more*. I gathered what ever energy I had left, sucked in a gulp of air and lifted my upper body forward and pushed as hard as I could. Corin held my back as I pushed through the blinding pain. When I felt a gush of release, I collapsed back against Corin's arms.

"Good job! Gena. Congratulations you guys have a beautiful baby girl." Alain declared.

"Did you hear that baby? You finally got your girl." I heard Corin say. I was utterly exhausted but when I heard her cry, my heart jumped up and startled me.

"Where is she?" I muttered.

"They're cleaning her up."

"I want to hold her."

"Okay, I'll bring her to you."

After sometime, Corin came back and placed a beautiful baby girl next to me. I was too weak and exhausted to hold her but I cuddled next to her face. "She is so beautiful." I whispered.

"She looks just like you."

I put on a weak smile and closed my eyes. When I finally woke up, I saw Corin sitting on the recliner holding our baby girl. He was busy talking to her

"Oh, look mommy is awake." He said softly as he brought her over to me.

"Hi, you" I cooed. She was perfect. Brown eyes, brown hair with pink rosy lips. "Mary Francine Randall."

"That is lovely honey. Gabe and Alex want to come in and see her. Poor Mark he has been trying to keep those boys busy in the lobby."

"Let them in."

When Corin came back in carrying Alex and holding Gabe's hand, I smiled beautifully at my lovely boys. Jonathan Gabriel "Gabe" was my oldest son. He is 4 years old. We conceived him during our honeymoon. My second little angel is Alexander Daniel who just turned two this past June. "Hi, sweetheart. Come say hello to Mary Francine."

"Mommy she is so little. Is she special like us?" Gabe asked.

"Yes, sweetheart. She has the healer aura like you and Alex."

"You too mommy" He corrected.

"Yes, mommy has the healer aura too."